INTIMATE DANGER

Faith and Jo—
two women at crossroads in their lives,
where only one path leads to love.

Cort and Cam
are the men who meet them there,
offering their hearts....

But when danger becomes an intimate companion
to love, is there hope for a happily-ever-after?

Relive the passion and intrigue...
Two complete novels
by two of your favorite

Susan Mallery is the bestselling author of over forty novels for Harlequin and Silhouette Books. In addition to appearing on the Walden's bestseller list and the *USA TODAY* bestseller list, Susan's stories have been nominated for several awards, including the prestigious RITA®. Susan makes her home in the Pacific Northwest, where she lives with her handsome prince of a husband and her two adorable-but-not-bright cats.

Award-winning, bestselling novelist Ruth Glick, who writes as **Rebecca York,** is the author of close to eighty books, including her popular 43 LIGHT STREET series for Harlequin Intrigue. Originally, Rebecca York was the pseudonym for the writing team of Ruth Glick and Eileen Buckholtz, from 1986 to 1997. When they split up to pursue their own interests, Ruth continued writing under the pseudonym.

Ruth says she has the best job in the world. Not only does she get paid for telling stories, she's also the author of twelve cookbooks. Ruth and her husband, Norman, travel frequently, researching locales for her novels and searching out new dishes for her cookbooks.

INTIMATE DANGER

Susan Mallery
Rebecca York

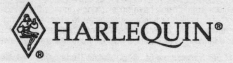

TORONTO • NEW YORK • LONDON
AMSTERDAM • PARIS • SYDNEY • HAMBURG
STOCKHOLM • ATHENS • TOKYO • MILAN • MADRID
PRAGUE • WARSAW • BUDAPEST • AUCKLAND

HARLEQUIN BOOKS

by Request—INTIMATE DANGER

Copyright © 2002 by Harlequin Books S.A.

ISBN 0-373-21734-X

The publisher acknowledges the copyright holders of the individual works as follows:

TEMPTING FAITH
Copyright © 1994 by Susan W. Macias
SHATTERED VOWS
Copyright © 1990 by Ruth Glick and Eileen Buckholtz

This edition published by arrangement with Harlequin Books S.A.

Visit us at www.eHarlequin.com

Printed in U.S.A.

CONTENTS

TEMPTING FAITH
Susan Mallery

Chapter 1

"You need the extra security."

Faith Newlin shook her head and smiled. "Are you trying to convince me or yourself?"

"Maybe both."

"I'm already convinced. If you think I need the protection—" She shrugged. "I'm hardly going to argue. After all, you're the expert. What did that last promotion make you? Head spy?"

Jeff Markum, the chief of a division in an agency whose name Faith had never been told, grinned. "That's *Mr.* Head Spy to you."

"Give a man a promotion and it goes straight to his—" she paused for effect "—head."

"Watch it, Faith." He pointed at the badge hanging from a chain around her neck. "I could have your security clearance pulled in a second. Then where would you be?"

"Back home where I belong." She laughed. "Don't try threatening me, Jeff. You're the one who arranged for me to be here today. I'm pleased to know your agency trusts me, but if you want me to go back home, I'd be happy to." She grabbed the ID badge and started to release the chain.

"Don't leave yet." He pushed off the wall of the small observation room. "Let me go explain the situation to him."

Faith raised one hand and touched the two-way glass that allowed her to see into a hospital room, but didn't allow the patient to see her. "He doesn't know?"

Jeff shook his head. "Even though you need the extra protection, I was afraid you would fight me on this." He held up his hand to stop her interruption. "I know you think I'm overreacting. Maybe you're right. But there's this knot in my gut. I have a bad feeling about the whole thing. I want to keep you safe."

She looked up at the man towering over her. He had the easy good looks of a California surfer, but behind his deep blue eyes lurked the mind of a computer and the temper of an injured panther. Faith knew she should be intimidated by Jeff, but she'd known him too long. She trusted him— *and* the knot in his gut.

"It's your call," she said.

She turned back to the two-way mirror. This was no ordinary hospital. No mothers-to-be came here to give birth, no child had broken bones set. This secret facility, concealed behind high fences and guards with dogs that attacked on command, catered to those without identities. Shadowy figures who lived in the dark, who disappeared at will and carried out elaborate operations in places with names she couldn't pronounce.

"He's not like one of those wounded strays you take in, Faith. He's the best I've got, but he's damned dangerous, too. Be careful."

Faith glanced at her companion. "Because he knows fifty ways to kill me with his bare hands? Give me a break, Jeff.

Use the scare tactics on your green recruits. They'll impress easier.''

"You think you're so tough." His good humor faded into regret. "I wish we had time for dinner."

"I'll take a rain check. Next time I'll pack something nice to wear and you can take me to an expensive restaurant."

"You're on." He squeezed her arm and left the room.

Faith stared after him. He'd already forgotten her, except as she related to his operative. She smiled to herself. *Operative.* She was starting to talk like them. She fingered the tag at the end of the chain. Jeff saw her for what she was: a nice person, competent at her job. She sighed. At one time she'd hoped for something more than friendship, but it wasn't going to happen. No great surprise. Her luck with men had never been the best. But there were compensations, she told herself. She had a fine life, a career she loved. She didn't need anything else to feel fulfilled. Yeah, right, she thought. Now who was trying to convince whom?

She turned her attention back to the two-way mirror and the man on the other side, in the hospital room. He stood next to his window, the one that looked out over the grounds. Instead of a hospital gown, he wore a T-shirt and jeans cut off on one leg to accommodate the thick bandage around his calf. There was something tense and watchful in his pose. Ever alert, he scanned the open area. Perhaps it was the set of his head, or the way he kept glancing over his shoulder toward the mirror, as if he sensed someone watched from the other side, but he intrigued her. He reminded her of Sparky. She smiled, wondering if he would care for the comparison to her favorite cat.

His lips moved, but the two-way glass didn't allow her to hear his words. With a quick twisting motion, he picked up the crutches that rested next to the window and slipped them under his arms. Despite the bandage on his leg, and the crutches, he shifted his weight with graceful ease and began to pace the room. From end to end he moved, swinging his useless leg along, mumbling phrases she couldn't make out.

On his third pass, he paused, then turned toward the mirror. He looked directly at her. She knew he couldn't see her, but she backed up instinctively, as if he'd threatened her.

Light hit him full in the face, sharpening already gaunt features. Was the thinness the result of his injuries or the mission he'd been on? The cut on his chin looked raw. Tiny stitches held the skin together. Fading bruises darkened his left cheek. Tawny hair, more gold than blond, fell over his forehead. But it was his eyes that captured her attention and held her immobile.

Dark brown irises glittered with suppressed rage. A trapped animal. The predator had been captured and wounded. Jeff was right: this man *was* dangerous. Without thinking, she rubbed her right hand against her upper arm. It wasn't until her fingers felt the ridges of the four long scars there that she realized what she was doing. Marks left by another predator, the four-legged kind.

The man blinked and turned away. She followed the movement and saw that the door to his room had opened. Jeff appeared and spoke to the man. Faith stared at their mouths, trying to lip-read, but it wasn't any use. From their angry gestures, she knew they were arguing. The injured man stood eye to eye with Jeff, and neither gave an inch. Jeff wore a suit, but he still looked muscular and dangerous. Two lions fighting for their pride. If the stranger weren't injured, it would have been an even match.

For the second time, he glanced at the two-way glass. Faith felt a flash of guilt. Eavesdropping, even without sound, wasn't her style. She turned and walked out of the observation room. It was almost eleven in the morning. She had a six-hour drive ahead of her, plus supplies to pick up. She was leaving within the hour, with or without Jeff's wounded man.

"I need to know, dammit." Cort Hollenbeck grabbed the crutches and leaned on them. "And you're going to tell me."

His boss sat on a corner of the hospital bed. "The doctor said—"

"The doctor can shove his advice." Cort swung around on the crutches and glared. "There are things I can't remember. I spent three weeks in South America on a mission. I don't know what happened there." Sweat popped out on his back. His leg throbbed from the surgery two days before and his head pounded. "For all I know, I went on a killing spree and shot up an entire town. So you're going to tell me what the hell happened down there!" He raised his voice until he shouted the last few words.

Jeff didn't look the least bit intimidated. He crossed his arms over his chest. "No."

Cort tightened his hands on the crutches. He wanted to force Jeff to answer. Not a chance of that. Between his bum leg and his aching head, he would barely get off the first punch before Jeff nailed him. He swung the crutches forward and eased himself into the plastic chair in front of the window.

"The doctor said you would remember on your own." Jeff leaned forward. "I understand what you're going through."

"Like hell you do."

Jeff ignored him. "And I sympathize."

"I liked you better before your promotion," Cort snarled.

"I didn't think you admitted to liking anyone," Jeff said calmly. "Professionals don't get involved. Aren't you the one always preaching that?"

Cort didn't bother answering. He dropped the crutches onto the ground and leaned his head back in the chair. As hard as he tried, he couldn't remember. There were bits and pieces of conversation. A word or two in Spanish and Portuguese. The flash of a face, then nothing. Three weeks of his life gone. He remembered leaving the States on a private plane. He remembered waking up in the same craft, only with the mission over, and he didn't have a clue what had happened. He fingered the cut on his chin. Bullet to the leg and a slight concussion. So much for bringing back souvenirs.

"You'll remember in time," Jeff said. "Don't push it."

"That's easy for you to say. You're not the one—" Cort bit back the words. God, he had to know. "Is he dead?"

Jeff didn't answer.

Cort sprang to his feet and almost fell when his bad leg gave out. Instantly Jeff was at his side, supporting him. Cort grabbed the other man's suit jacket. "Is he?"

Jeff stared at him. His mouth tightened. "I'm not going to fight you."

Cort released his grip on the jacket and slumped back in the seat. "Only because you know I'd beat the crap out of you."

"I'm shaking with fear." Jeff stared down at him. "So you remember that much?"

"Dan, you mean?"

Jeff nodded.

"Yeah. I remember I was meeting Dan. I don't know why, or if I did."

"And you think he might be dead?"

Cort closed his eyes and rubbed his thumb and forefinger over the bridge of his nose. No, he thought. I think *I* killed him. But he couldn't say that. No matter how much he thought it, he couldn't say those words.

"Is he?" he asked.

"Yes."

Cort snapped his head up. "You're sure?"

"We have a witness."

The pain in Cort's leg intensified. He thought of the dead man. They'd met in training, almost fifteen years ago. They'd worked together countless times. Had he killed his friend? Jeff was right, it wasn't supposed to matter. But, dammit, it did. It mattered a lot.

"Don't push it," Jeff told him. "It'll come to you." He returned to the hospital bed and perched on the corner. The morning sun flooded the small room, highlighting the institutional furniture and scarred green linoleum. "And while you're getting your memory back, I have an assignment."

Cort raised his injured leg. "Aren't I on medical leave?"

"Yes."

"Then I'm going home."

Jeff stood up and shoved his hands in his pockets. "I need you to do something for me."

"But you said—"

"Unofficially." Jeff walked over to the window and stared out. "I can't assign anybody through regular channels. I don't have specifics, just a gut feeling."

"Which is?"

"There's going to be trouble." Jeff looked at him. "I need you to look after a friend of mine. Provide a little security. Nothing high tech. She's located—"

"She?"

"Her name is Faith. She lives up in the mountains. Runs a way station. I left a package in her care. The men we took it from might want it back. I want you to be there to stop them. If there's any trouble, I'll have the proof I need to officially provide backup. I know it's asking a lot. I wouldn't, if I had another option. You up to it?"

Cort thought about his small one-bedroom apartment in D.C. It was late spring. The tourists would be flocking into the city, and the temperature would be rising. Last time he'd stayed at the apartment, the air-conditioning had given out twice in three days. He thought about the time he and Jeff had spent in Iraq. On more than one occasion, the other man had been there to save his skin. This favor sounded like a way to even the score.

Cort grabbed the crutches and used them to help him stand. "I'm up to it."

"Thanks, Cort." Jeff collected the duffel bag from the locker against the far wall. "The place isn't fancy, but I think you'll like it. Plan on staying a few weeks. Two months at the outside."

"Who's this woman? Agency?"

"Private. A friend. You can trust her."

Cort was doubtful. Trust wasn't something that came easily to him. "She know what I'm there for?"

"She understands that there might be some problems and is willing to take precautions." He pointed at the bandage around Cort's calf. "She's great with wounds."

"Sounds like you speak from personal experience."

Jeff's blue eyes grew stark. "She took care of me after Lebanon."

Cort moved into the small rest room and collected his belongings. He worked slowly, giving Jeff time to put the past in its place. His boss had almost died in Lebanon, but that wasn't what caused his expression to grow bleak. He'd also lost his wife and young son to terrorists.

Cort zipped the shaving kit and hobbled over to the bed. He dropped the case into the open duffel bag. "Seems like I'll be gone long enough to get back to a hundred percent. You didn't happen to plan that, did you, boss?"

Jeff shrugged. "It works for both of us."

"What about South America? What if I don't remember?"

Jeff pulled the duffel bag shut and slung it over one

shoulder. "If you don't remember by the time you're healed, you can read the file, and to hell with what the doctor says. You have my word."

Cort nodded. It was something to hang on to. But he knew the price of Jeff's offer. If he hadn't recovered his memory, he wouldn't be coming back. The agency didn't have a place for someone who couldn't remember whether or not he'd killed a fellow operative.

"Thanks," he said. He shrugged into a dark blue jacket, then slipped the crutches in place. "If I have a choice, I won't be taking you up on your offer. I'll be at work instead."

"Good." Jeff walked to the door and held it open. "I want you back. You're my best man."

"You always say that," Cort grumbled. "I heard you were telling John the same thing. We can't both be the best."

Jeff grinned but didn't answer.

Cort followed his boss into the hall of the hospital. Several medical personnel nodded as he passed them. They wore ID tags with photos and numbers, but no names. At the end of the corridor, Jeff turned left. Cort hobbled along behind. He scanned the smooth floor, the walls, the doorways they passed, instinctively looking for escape routes. It wasn't necessary; he was safe here. Old habits, he thought grimly. In his current condition he would get about ten yards before being taken down. He needed time to heal...and to remember.

A woman stood in the waiting room. As Jeff entered, she smiled her greeting. They spoke softly, but her eyes strayed past her companion. Cort paused in the doorway and met her gaze.

Blue eyes, he catalogued, taking in the flicker of guilt that told him she'd watched him through the two-way glass in his hospital room. Hair: brown, nondescript, long. Medium height for a woman. Work shirt, jeans, boots. Instinctively, he calculated an approximate weight, made a mental note of her straight posture, evidence of physical confidence, and guessed she was in reasonably good shape. Ordinary.

No danger, unless she came armed. His gaze moved back to her face. Mid- to late twenties, he thought, then dismissed the idea that she and Jeff were lovers. They stood close together, as if they'd known each other a long time, but there wasn't anything between them. The throbbing in his leg picked up a notch, and he shifted his weight to relieve some of the pressure.

"Faith, this is Cort Hollenbeck," Jeff said, placing his hand on the small of her back and urging her forward. "Cort, Faith Newlin."

"Nice to meet you." She extended her hand.

It took him a moment to untangle himself from the crutches. Most people would have been uncomfortable and dropped their arm, mumbling something about it not mattering. She stood there patiently, waiting as if she had all the time in the world.

Her grip surprised him. Not so much the strength of her grasp—given her wardrobe, she wasn't a socialite. No, it was the rough skin he felt on her palm, the calluses. This woman did physical labor on a daily basis.

Their eyes met. Not unattractive, he thought. He studied the straight short nose and full lips that curved up slightly. As he'd decided before—ordinary. Little temptation there. Just as well. He didn't need the complication.

"Ms. Newlin." He nodded.

"Faith." Again her lips curved up slightly, as she withdrew her hand.

"I'm ready, if you are."

"Fine." She glanced at Jeff. "What about medication?"

"Something for pain, some antibiotics in case of infection. I'll get them.'' He looked at Cort. ''You'll want to be armed. A Beretta?''

Cort raised his eyebrows. ''Works for me.''

''Faith?'' Jeff asked.

She shrugged. ''I have rifles, but only one handgun. A small revolver.'' She looked at Cort. ''You'd probably be embarrassed to be seen with it.''

Interesting. A woman who knew about guns. He hadn't had a chance to think about this new assignment, but so far it wasn't too bad. Close quarters with Faith Newlin. She wasn't a fashion model, but all cats were gray in the dark. Maybe the thought of bullets flying would scare her. Just enough, he thought, trying to remember how long it had been since he'd eased himself between a woman's welcoming thighs.

''I'll get the medication and the gun and meet you at the truck,'' Jeff said, handing her the duffel bag and leaving.

Faith hung back, but Cort shook his head. ''I'll go behind you,'' he said.

''Suit yourself.'' Her long hair, pulled back at the front, but otherwise left free, hung over her shoulders. With a quick flick of her wrist, she sent the strands flying out of her way. ''I'm parked in the rear lot. Do you want a wheelchair?''

The look he tossed her had often caused armed criminals to flinch. She simply blinked twice and waited patiently for his response.

''No,'' he said at last.

''It's your neck.''

''Actually it's my leg.''

She smiled quickly, and he had the thought that it made her look pretty.

''Humor,'' she said. ''A good sign.''

As she walked past him, he inhaled the scent of her perfume. French. The name of the brand escaped him. Expensive. Out of place. The information joined the rest of his mental file on her. Shifting his weight, he swung the crutches in front of him and started down the hall.

They'd covered about twenty feet when she started to turn right down another corridor. Suddenly she gasped and jumped back, blocking his path. He couldn't see what had startled her. He heard a loud crash.

Instinctively he dropped the crutches. With one arm, he grabbed Faith around the waist and threw her to the ground. He dropped to the floor, rolled to cushion his fall, biting back a grunt of pain as his weight settled on his injured leg. He came to a stop beside her. With a smooth, practiced motion, he reached for the gun in his waistband.

Nothing. No holster, no weapon. He looked up. Two terrified orderlies stood beside the pile of fallen trays. They started forward to help, took one look at the expression on his face and turned in the opposite direction.

Faith raised herself up on one elbow and studied him. Her blue eyes radiated nothing more than concern. "Did you hurt yourself, Mr. Hollenbeck?"

"Cort," he grunted, between waves of pain. "I'm fine. What about you?"

She pushed herself into a sitting position. "Nothing broken. Do you need help up?"

"No."

She scrambled to her feet. After retrieving the crutches, she stood patiently while he maneuvered himself upright. She handed him the crutches.

"I'm not crazy," he said, knowing exactly how it all looked. Had they told her he'd lost part of his memory?

"That thought never crossed my mind." She turned and continued walking down the hall.

He could feel blood oozing out of the stitches in his leg. Damn. It had finally begun to heal. Maybe he should get somebody to look at it before—

No. It would stop soon enough. Now that he was close to leaving the hospital, he realized how much he'd hated the confinement. He'd been pretty out of it the first week, but the last few days had crawled by. He'd slowly been going crazy trying to force himself to remember.

Faith stopped at the rear entrance and stepped on the automatic door pad. Smiling at the guard on duty, she spoke her name, then Cort's. The older man punched a few keys in his computer keyboard, then nodded.

Freedom. Cort inhaled the dry desert air and held back a sigh. Sweet and clean. Enough to go around.

Suddenly the ground shifted and his vision blurred. Instead of the guard and the woman, he saw the dusky interior of a South American warehouse. Dank smells indicated he was near water. The ocean? Was the scent salty?

Danger! The thought exploded in his mind. Get out. Yet as he turned to run, the picture dissolved. His crutch caught on the lip of the door pad. As the flashback receded, he felt himself slipping. Faith leapt to his side and grabbed the shaky crutch. One strong arm gripped his waist and held him steady.

She had curves under that baggy work shirt, he thought as her right breast flattened against his side. The intellectual information battled with a sudden rush of sexual interest. That, more than the fall, returned him completely to the present.

"You all right?" she asked, looking up at him.

She was wary, but not afraid. She should be. Hadn't Jeff told her what he was capable of? His head began to throb. He'd remembered. Not a lot, but something new. Sweat coated his body. He just wanted to get out of here.

He jerked himself free. "I'm fine. Where's your car?"

She pointed toward a battered four-wheel-drive pickup. He angled himself in that general direction and began to lurch toward it.

Jeff met them at the truck. "This should keep you comfortable." He held a bag of medicine in one hand and a gun in the other.

Cort thought about telling him he'd remembered something, but he held back. He'd know soon enough—when the whole memory returned. Jeff opened the car door and tossed the medication on the dashboard. Cort hopped until the seat pressed against the back of his thighs. After sliding on the cracked vinyl, he lifted his bum leg into the cab and handed Jeff his crutches. Jeff settled them in the back and gave him the pistol.

"Here's a spare magazine and a hundred rounds." He set a small paper bag on the floor of the cab. "Try not to shoot yourself in the foot."

"I'll do my best."

Faith dropped his duffel bag in the back of the truck, then gave Jeff a hug. "Don't forget about my rain check," she said.

"I won't." He held her for a minute.

Cort watched the expressions chase across his boss's face. He knew the flash of pain came from remembering his wife. Cort looked away. Caring turned a man inside out. Exposed him. That's why he would never get involved.

Faith slid in next to him and fastened her seat belt. She stared at him until he did the same. Then she smiled. Again, he thought it made her look pretty.

"You going to hold that in your hand the whole way?" She pointed at the gun.

He stared at the weapon, then thought about how he'd reacted to the crashing sound in the hospital. He was tired, and the surgery two days ago had used up the little reserves he'd had. What he needed was twelve hours of sleep. Until then, he wasn't going to be much good at protecting anyone.

"Here." He handed her the gun. "You keep it until tomorrow."

She studied his face. "Fine with me." She checked the safety, then pressed the button to release the magazine. After pocketing it, she jerked back the slide and looked in the chamber to make sure it didn't contain a round.

He raised his eyebrows. "I'm impressed."

"Then you impress easy." The gun went in the glove box. "And you're exhausted. We've got over a six-hour drive. Why don't you get some sleep? I need to make one stop. I'll wake you there and you can eat something."

"Sounds great." He leaned his head back and closed his eyes. She wasn't the sort of woman he normally picked, he thought as she started the truck and backed out of the parking space. He couldn't remember a single one of his lady friends ever owning a gun, let alone knowing how to handle one. And although she'd been friends with Jeff for years, his boss had never mentioned her.

"Here."

She thrust something soft into his hands. He cracked open one eye. A sweater.

"Use it for a pillow. Lock your door first. I don't want you falling out if I hit a bump."

"Thanks," he muttered as he bunched the sweater and pushed it up against the glass. He pressed down the lock and inhaled deeply. Her scent surrounded him, the elusive essence of that damned French perfume. What was it? He fell asleep still trying to remember the name.

She saw the first evidence of blood after they'd been on the road an hour. Keeping her attention on the sparsely traveled highway, she occasionally glanced at her sleeping passenger. He rested deeply, barely moving except for the rise and fall of his chest. Her gaze swept over him as she noted his size and strength and wondered at the cause of his injuries. At first she'd thought the dark stain on his white bandage was a shadow.

"Damn," she muttered softly. Over the next hour, the stain spread until it was the size of a half dollar. It showed no signs of letting up. He must have torn open his stitches when he'd dropped to the floor in the hospital.

She picked up a cassette and pushed it into the player. The radio was the only thing new in the cab. The vehicle itself had almost a hundred and fifty thousand miles on the odometer, but the engine had been replaced in the last six months and the tires were only two weeks old. She didn't care how the truck looked on the outside; she spent the money necessary to keep it running well. Without her truck available to pick up food, the cats would starve in a matter of days.

Two hours later she saw the sign for her turnoff. She moved to the right of the four-lane freeway then exited onto the two-lane highway that would take her north and home. Her passenger continued to sleep. She turned off at the tiny town of Bowmund and headed for the grain and feed.

At least one thing had gone right today, Faith thought as she signed for the supplies. Everything was ready. As soon as the boxes were loaded, she could head up the mountain. After picking up a quart of orange juice and a plastic wrapped sandwich from the grocery store, she walked back to her truck. Cort slept where she'd left him, resting his head against her sweater and the passenger window.

She eased open her door and slid into the seat. Where was that bag of medicine? She saw the white paper in the far corner of the dashboard. As she grabbed it, she glanced down. The blood on his bandage had widened to a circle the size of a grapefruit.

"If that doesn't stop, we're both in trouble," she said, not bothering to keep her voice down.

He didn't stir. She counted out the antibiotic dosage, confirmed that the instructions said to take the medication with food and touched his arm.

"Cort, wake up. You've got to take a couple of pills."

Nothing.

She pressed harder against his biceps, noting the thickness of the muscle. "Cort, wake up!"

It was like teasing a tiger. Without warning, he jerked upright, then spun and grabbed her. Before she could catch her breath, he'd pulled her head against his shoulder, holding her tight with one arm across her throat and pressing the other arm against her midsection.

"One more move," he growled into her ear, "and I'll kill you."

Chapter 2

Faith didn't move. She didn't even breathe. She held herself still, stifling the overwhelming urge to fight him. She wouldn't win. He had the strength and the skill to snap her neck with one swift jerk.

Her lungs burned for air. Panic threatened. Don't, she commanded herself. She'd been in worse situations. The trick was to keep her head. He would figure out she wasn't the enemy.

The steely arm around her throat loosened slightly. She drew in a deep breath. Her gasp sounded loud in the still cab.

Cort swore and released her completely. She fell forward and supported herself by pressing her hands against the seat. She inhaled deeply and coughed. Thank God. The cab darkened for a second, then came into focus.

After she caught her breath, she gingerly touched her neck, knowing that she would bear bruises for several days. She should have known better than to startle him, she thought, shaking her head in disgust. The same thing would have happened if she'd walked into a cage while a wounded animal was sleeping.

She located the pills she'd dropped when he grabbed her, and she turned slowly to face Cort. He leaned against the door of the cab and stared at her. She couldn't read the expression in his dark eyes. Something flickered there, something black and ugly, but she didn't know what it meant. Was he berating himself, or her? Silence stretched between them, broken only by the sound of their breathing.

"It could have been worse," she said at last, her voice a little raspy from the pressure on her neck.

He raised his eyebrows.

"You could have had the gun."

He didn't answer. Apparently he had no intention of apologizing.

She held out the pills and the container of orange juice. He took them, tossed back the medication and gulped the liquid without taking his eyes from her face. She wanted to look away but sensed he was challenging her. She forced herself to meet his gaze.

"How long since you've been in the field?" she asked.

"Two weeks."

"That explains—"

"Did Jeff tell you I was having flashbacks?" he asked, cutting her off.

"No." She swallowed. *Great.* "Should he have?"

"You tell me."

He held out the empty juice bottle. She took the plastic container and set it between them. Still his gaze locked on hers. He was making her nervous, but she refused to let him see her squirm. She allowed herself to study the straight line of his nose and the stubble darkening the hollows of his cheeks. He was handsome, she thought with some surprise. Perhaps even beautiful, with the wild unholiness of natural predators.

She shifted in her seat and reached for the sandwich she'd placed on the dashboard. "You're probably hungry," she said. "The instructions said to take the medication with food. I have to hook up the trailer and then we'll leave."

He didn't answer. She set the sandwich on his lap and turned toward the door. Before she could touch the handle, he spoke. "I tried to kill you."

"I know. You're also trying to intimidate me."

"What the hell are you still doing in this truck?"

"I don't scare so easy."

"Lady, there's something wrong with you."

She detected a note of grudging respect in his voice. "You're not the first person to notice," she said, looking at him over her shoulder. The early afternoon light caught the gold flecks in his brown eyes. Cat eyes. "How long has your leg been bleeding?"

He glanced down at the stained bandage. "Since I fell on it at the hospital."

"When was the surgery?"

"Two days ago. I think I ripped out some stitches."

"Terrific." She opened the door, then paused. "At the way station, we're over forty minutes from town and an hour and a half from real medical care. Do you need to see a doctor?"

"No."

She pointed to his leg. "If it gets infected, I'll probably just cut it off."

He rewarded her with a slight smile. It didn't make him look any less dangerous. "Deal."

She waited, hoping he would say something more. He didn't. "I've got to see to the supplies," she said. "I'll be right back." She slipped out of the truck and closed the door behind her.

Cort watched as several men finished loading supplies from the feed store into the back of Faith's truck. Carelessly, he picked at the food she'd handed him. His head ached, his leg throbbed and the pain in his gut came from a lot more than medication.

He'd almost killed her. If he'd had a knife or, in that split second when he'd lost track of what was real, his gun, she would be dead. For no good reason. She wasn't the enemy. Just an innocent bystander. He'd never lost control before, and it scared the hell out of him. How was he going to get it back?

He glanced in the side-view mirror and saw Faith talking to a man with a clipboard. She went down the list and pointed at the boxes they were loading into a separate trailer. The man started to argue. Before he'd said more than ten words, Faith planted her hands on her hips and started in on him. In about five seconds, he was nodding and backing up toward the building.

Who the hell was she? He tossed the half-eaten sandwich on the seat and clenched his hands into fists. He'd almost killed her, and she acted like nothing had happened. Jeff had said she needed protection. Cort shook his head. She seemed capable enough to him. He stared at the mirror. Faith stood by the back of the truck, counting the crates being loaded. She moved quickly and easily, as if she'd performed this task a hundred times before. Cool and competent—she turned and he saw the curve of her rear—and very much a woman.

He shifted his leg and felt a spurt of blood, then the warm dampness as it oozed against his skin. He closed his eyes. With a new bandage and a good night's sleep, physically he'd be fine. A couple of days and he would be a hundred percent. But what about the rest of it? What about his memory?

He went over what he'd remembered right before they

left the hospital. Salt air. The ocean. He licked his lips as
if the taste still lingered. Darkness. He remembered that.
And danger. But from what? He strained to see into the
gray mist of his mind. Had Dan been there with him? Had
he died there?

Nothing. The past refused to focus. He groaned in frustration. What if he never remembered? Had he killed him?
Had he killed Dan?

Cort propped his elbow on the door and rubbed his forehead. What was his mission? Dan was a fellow agent. Deep
inside his memory, something clicked into place. Had his
friend gone bad? Had Cort been sent to kill him? If he'd
gotten the job done, he should forget it. Had he, though?
Thoughts circled around and around, until even what he
could remember blurred with the fog.

"Stop it," he commanded himself. He would get nowhere like this. Dan was dead. He knew that for sure. The
rest of it would come to him. It had to.

He'd gone too far with the last mission, he realized. He'd
felt the warning signs of burnout and had ignored them. He
should have turned down the assignment and taken a break.
He'd been fighting the war for too long. He hadn't wanted
to be cautious, and now he was paying the price.

Faith opened the door and slid onto the seat. He ignored
her. He heard the click as she buckled her seat belt. He
needed a plan. Whatever security he had to provide
wouldn't take up too much of his time. He needed to get
back in shape physically, and his memory would follow.
First— A bump against his shoulder broke into his musings.

"Sorry," Faith said as she rested her arm on the top of
the seat and began backing up the truck. "I hate this part."

He glanced out the rear window. "What are you doing?"

"See that big trailer there? It's supposed to be attached
to this truck. That's what we haul up the mountain."

The trailer looked to be about as wide as the truck, maybe

ten feet long and eight feet high. The painted sides didn't bear a logo.

"What's inside?"

"Food." She adjusted the steering wheel slightly and eased up on the accelerator. "Damn. Why do they have to watch? It makes me crazy."

He followed the direction of her gaze and saw a group of old men standing on the porch in front of the feed store. The building itself looked like it had been built during the forties. "What are they waiting for?"

"Me to mess up. They can't believe that a mere woman can handle a truck, let alone a trailer. They do this every time I come in for supplies."

"You ever mess up?"

A strand of her long hair fell over her shoulder. She flicked it back with a quick jerk of her hand and grinned. "Nope."

He found himself smiling in return. She made a final adjustment of the steering wheel, eased up on the accelerator and waited for the truck to roll to a halt.

"Did it!" she said and faced front. After rotating her shoulders to release the tension, she bounded out of the cab. "I just have to hook us up and then we're out of here. You want something more to eat?"

"No," he said. Then added a belated "Thanks."

As promised, she made quick work of the hitch. In less than ten minutes, the tiny town had been left behind and they began to drive up a steep mountain road.

Cort shifted in his seat, trying to ease the pain in his leg. Faith handled the truck easily, as if she were used to the winding roads. He studied her strong but small hands as they worked the gearshift. Who was she, and why wasn't she frightened of him? He'd almost killed her. She didn't look or act stupid, so what was her story?

He watched the road ahead. Tall trees, a few of them

redwoods, came down to the edge of the highway. Recent spring rains left a carpet of lush new grass.

"I'm sorry," he said, staring straight ahead. "For what happened before. I could have hurt you."

"But you didn't. Apology accepted."

"That's it?" He glanced at her. She seemed intent on her driving.

"What more do you want?"

Something. He could have done a whole lot more than hurt her. "I almost killed you."

"I'm as much to blame. I shouldn't have startled you. I know better."

"How? Jeff said you were a civilian."

She gave him a quick smile. "Don't worry. I am. But I'm used to working with dangerous animals."

"It won't happen again," he promised.

"I know."

"How?"

"It won't happen again, because I won't startle you a second time. I'm a quick study."

He shifted in the seat until he faced her. He propped his injured leg on the hump in the floor that divided the cab in half. She rested both her hands on the steering wheel. Short nails, he thought. No polish. Sensible work clothes. He inhaled. But she wore French perfume.

"How do you know Jeff?" he asked.

"We met about six years ago. He was friends with the lady I worked for. When Jeff was hurt in Lebanon—" She glanced at him.

"I know about that," he said.

She nodded. "He came to stay with us for a few months. I helped patch him up. Kept him company. That sort of thing. We became friends."

"So you're a nurse?"

"Not exactly." She flashed him a smile, then sobered.

"I guess when you go through what he did, you remember the people who got you through it."

Cort thought about those days. Jeff's injuries had been life-threatening, but it was the loss of his wife and child that had almost killed him. Four years ago. Before Jeff had been promoted. They'd worked together several times. Been gone enough for Jeff's marriage to falter and Jeff to start worrying about it. The worry distracted him and ultimately almost got him killed. He'd made the decision to do whatever it took to save his marriage, then boom. Jeanne and his son were dead.

Cort shook his head. It wasn't worth it. Relationships weighed a man down. Caring about anyone got in the way of getting the job done.

"Tell me about the way station," he said.

"We're about fifteen miles from our nearest neighbors," she said. "I have three college kids coming in part-time to help. We personally own about two hundred acres and have another thousand of leased forest land. There's a fence around most of the compound and a main gate at the entrance. We're pretty isolated."

"What's the way station for?"

She looked at him. Surprise widened her blue eyes. "I keep cats."

"Cats?" He rubbed his pounding temple.

"Jeff didn't explain?"

"No." He cursed under his breath. Cats? What had his boss gotten him into? He glanced at Faith. In her jeans and shirt, with her sensible work boots and unmade-up face, she didn't look like his idea of a person who kept bunches of cats, but then when had he ever met one? "So you keep, what, twenty of them in the house?"

She chuckled. Her smile could only be described as impish. "No cats in the house, I promise. And no more than forty or so at a time. I don't have the room."

"Forty?" He swallowed. Maybe he should have taken his chances with his D.C. apartment and the tourists.

"They aren't a bother."

"I bet."

"Oh, but Sparky does sort of have the run of the place."

"Sparky? Does *he* sleep in the house?"

"No, he sleeps in the office. He's our mascot."

"Great." He pictured some flea-bitten alley cat cowering in the corner.

"He was Edwina's favorite. Edwina is the lady who used to run the way station."

"So there really are forty cats?"

"And Sparky."

Oh, Christ. Cort leaned his head back and closed his eyes. Why was Jeff doing this to him? His boss was normally a pretty fair guy. Had the last assignment been messed up that badly?

He allowed himself to get lost in the pain, controlling his breathing and counting out his heartbeats. It wasn't until the truck slowed that he looked around.

She'd stopped to make a left-hand turn onto a dirt road. A small sign stated that they were entering the Edwina Daniels Feline Way Station.

She stared at the entrance. "The gate's open. I wonder why?" She shrugged. "Maybe the kids knew I'd be coming back."

"What's normal procedure?" he asked.

She pointed to the small black box attached to the sun visor on the passenger's side of the cab. "It's remote controlled."

He picked up the transmitter. "Looks like it's for a garage-door opener."

"It is. We modified it."

Which meant the electronic device on the gate could be defeated by a ten-year-old.

After shifting into neutral, she pulled on the lever that switched the truck from two- to four-wheel drive. "Hold on."

He gripped the window frame with one hand and the back of the seat with the other. His fingers rested inches from her shoulder. The truck turned onto the dirt road and immediately hit a huge bump.

"The gullies got worse with the spring rains," she said.

"I'll bet."

They lurched over a rock as, behind them, the trailer hit the first bump. The combined action loosened his grip and jarred his injured leg.

He swore.

"Sorry." Faith gave him a quick glance. "I'll try to go slower."

"Not on my account," he ground out as fresh blood seeped from the wound. He resumed his hold on the window frame and the back of the seat. This time, a few strands of her hair became trapped under his hand. The soft silkiness distracted him from his pain and he wondered what a woman like her was doing out here, alone except for some college kids and a few dozen cats.

Before he could formulate an answer, they took a sharp turn to the left and rolled onto a paved road.

"What the—" He glanced behind at the dirt torture session, then ahead at what looked like a good mile of asphalt. "You care to explain that?"

"It's to discourage visitors. We keep the bumps and rocks because they'll scare off anyone in a car."

"Probably lose the whole chassis."

"That's the idea."

"And the paved road?"

She shrugged, then moved the lever from four- back to two-wheel drive. "It's convenient. We have another two miles to go."

"You *don't* want anyone near your cats, do you?"

"Only invited guests. The foundation is privately funded. There are about two hundred donors. The bulk of the money comes from Edwina's estate. We have the donors out a couple of times a year for fund-raisers, but we put planks over the ruts so their limos don't lose their transmissions."

"Smart move."

She rolled down her window and inhaled. "Almost home. I can smell it."

He rolled down his window and took a tentative sniff, half expecting to smell eau de Kitty Litter. Instead the scent of leaves and earth filled him. The road was plenty wide enough for the truck. Tall trees and thick underbrush lined both sides of the pavement. Birds and rustling leaves filled the quiet of the warm June afternoon. He inhaled again, noticing the sweet scent of flowers. Peaceful. Exactly what he needed.

Faith chattered about the weather and the house. Cort shifted his position and didn't listen. He craved a good twelve hours of sleep. Then he would regroup.

"We're here," she said, breaking into his thoughts. They rounded the last corner. He was nearly jerked from his seat when she unexpectedly slammed on the brakes.

Less than three hundred feet up the road stood a large open area. Trees had been cleared to create a natural parking lot. The pavement circled around in front of a long, one-story building. High bushes and trees concealed everything behind the structure.

In the middle of the parking area, looking very bright and very out of place, stood a shiny van. The colorful logo of a Los Angeles television station gleamed in the late afternoon sun.

"I told him no." Faith shook her head and looked at Cort. "Reporters. One of them called from an L.A. station and asked for an interview. He'd heard rumors about the kittens. I told him I wouldn't talk to him."

Cort stared at her. Did she say kittens? Before he could ask, she'd pulled the truck up next to the van.

Faith set the brake. Five people glanced up at her. Two looked incredibly guilty, three vaguely surprised.

"This is private property," she told the newspeople as she got out of the truck. "You don't have permission to be here. You're trespassing. I want you out of here, now!"

It wasn't hard for Faith to pick out the reporter. Aside from being indecently handsome, he wore a coat and tie over his jeans. The other two men with him, one holding a camera, the other operating a mike, smiled winningly and began clicking on switches.

"Hey, I'm James Wilson, from Los Angeles. K-NEWS," the reporter said, moving next to her and offering his hand. "We spoke on the phone yesterday. What a great story. I've got all I need from your assistants, but maybe we could talk for a few minutes. It would really add some depth to the piece."

Faith ignored the outstretched hand. "You're right, Mr. Wilson. We did speak on the phone. I told you not to come up here. The kittens aren't to be taped or photographed. This is private property. You are trespassing. Please leave."

His perfect smile faded slightly. "I don't understand."

"It's simple," she said. "You don't have permission to be here, or to write a story. You're trespassing."

"Hey, this was on the wire service. Don't blame me. Besides, the freedom of the press—"

"Does not include trespassing. Leave now."

"Lady, I don't know what your problem is."

She turned away without speaking. She heard the slamming of the truck's passenger door. Cort was about to get an interesting introduction to the way station. It couldn't be helped.

Beth and Rob, two of her college employees, were inching toward the main office building. The low one-story structure stood across the front of the compound.

"Freeze," she ordered.

They froze.

Faith walked into the building, past the offices, to the supply room. She pulled a bunch of keys out of her jeans pocket and opened a metal locker. Choosing a rifle from the assortment of weapons, she picked it up and held it in her left hand. The barrel had been modified to shoot darts instead of bullets. She put a couple of tranquilizers in her pocket and left the building.

"This is private property," she said as she walked back into the sunlight. "I'm only going to say this one more time. You are trespassing. Leave, now." She loaded one of the darts. "Or you'll be sleeping for the next twenty-four hours." The barrel snapped closed with an audible click.

Behind her, Beth and Rob chuckled.

The reporter's handsome face froze. "Listen, lady, there's no reason to get violent. Mac, Vern, tell her."

But his two friends had already abandoned him and were tossing their equipment into the van.

"Wait for me," Wilson called. He spun on his heel and jogged to the van, then ducked into the passenger seat.

Within seconds, the engine roared to life and the newspeople made a tight U-turn, then headed down the drive. Cort stood next to Faith's truck, leaning his weight on the fender and watching the proceedings with interest. She ignored him, popped the dart out of the rifle and lowered the butt to the ground.

"Where's Ken?" she asked, turning back toward the kids.

Beth, a petite brunette with gold-rimmed glasses, stared at her feet. "Putting the kittens back in their cages."

Faith held on to her temper. "Why did you let in the reporters?"

"We left the gate open for you," Rob answered. "They just kind of showed up."

"You didn't ask them to leave?"

Rob shook his head. "Ken said—"

Faith held up her hand. "I'll deal with Ken in a minute. Why didn't *you* ask them to leave? Either of you?"

Guilt was written all over their young faces. Faith hired college students because they had enthusiasm and dedication, plus she preferred part-time help. The only problem was sometimes they weren't as mature as she would have liked.

Beth stared at her shoes. "He was so nice, and it seemed so exciting that I didn't think about how you said you didn't want any publicity about the kittens until it was too late."

"You just thought he was totally cool," Rob said, rolling his eyes in disgust. "Some good-looking older man says a few nice words and you melt like butter."

"That's not true." Beth flushed with anger. She stood a good eight inches shorter than Rob's six feet, but that didn't intimidate her. "I didn't see *you* ordering him off the property. In fact, you were real interested in the sound equipment and asked the guy a lot of questions."

"That's better than swooning. You won't see me on the six o'clock news."

"Stop!" Faith held up one hand. "You know the rules."

Beth nodded. "You're right, Faith. I apologize. I should have thought about what would happen. I know the kittens are important to you and the facility. I wouldn't purposely do something to hurt either."

"Me, too," Rob mumbled, nudging Beth on the arm when she turned and glared at him.

Faith fought back a smile. Eloquent to the last, that boy, she thought. These kids were basically well-meaning.

They'd been caught up in the excitement of the moment. She didn't like it, but she understood how it happened.

"I accept your apologies," she said. She heard footsteps behind her, but didn't turn around.

"What's going on? Beth, why are they leaving so soon? I wanted to show them— Oh God, Faith. You're back."

"I'm sure there's an explanation, Ken," she said coldly, still not turning around. "Make it a good one."

"Gee, Faith. I'm sorry. This isn't what it looks like."

Her grip on the rifle tightened. She tapped her booted toe against the asphalt. A couple of deep breaths didn't help, either. "What the hell were you thinking?" she said as she spun to face the young man. Her voice rose in volume. "Reporters? Reporters?"

Rob and Beth slunk away, leaving Ken alone. The young man stood over six feet tall. With broad shoulders, long brown hair and a scraggely beard that hadn't completely filled in, he looked more like a teenager than a college senior. At her words, his bravado faded. He slumped visibly and stuffed his hands in his pockets.

"It wasn't like that," he mumbled.

"It wasn't like that?" she said loudly, then forced herself to lower her voice. "We have a few rules here. They are for your safety and for that of the cats. Rule number one is no reporters without my say-so. Ken, you know where those kittens came from. The last thing we need is word getting around about their whereabouts."

"I'm sorry." Brown eyes pleaded for understanding.

She gripped the unloaded rifle in both hands and tossed it at him. He caught it. "'Sorry' doesn't cut it," she said, pacing in front of him on the asphalt. "I should bust your butt back to the dorm and never let you on this mountain again."

"It was an accident." He shuffled his feet.

"How do you figure? The reporter said the wire service

had the story and…'' Realization dawned, and she was grateful she wasn't holding the rifle anymore. "It's that girl! You let her take pictures."

For weeks Ken had talked about nothing but Nancy. Nancy the beautiful. Nancy the brave. Nancy the journalism major. He'd asked Faith if she could come and take pictures of the cats for an assignment for one of her classes. Maybe do a story to drum up publicity. Faith had refused.

"Just a few," Ken admitted. He looked up at her. Regret pulled his mouth straight. "She took them to the local paper, and they got picked up by the wire service. That's what brought the reporter out. I'm sorry," he repeated. "Am I fired?" He sounded like a ten-year-old.

She jammed her hands in her pockets. "I don't know," she said at last. "You've worked here two years, and you've done a good job. But in the last few months you've come in late, you've skipped work without calling, now this." She pinned him with her best glare. "You're thinking with the wrong part of your anatomy. All the trouble you're having is because of that girl. Get that under control and you can work here. If not, you're out. Consider this a final warning. One more screwup and you're fired."

"Faith, I'm sorry."

"Put the rifle away, then get out of here. I don't want to see you for the rest of the week."

"I understand."

"Did you at least remember to feed the cats?"

"Yeah. An hour ago."

"Fine." Faith waved her hand in the direction of the supply building. "Get going."

The young man walked off, his body slumped forward, his steps slow and shuffling. He was the picture of misery. Part of her regretted the harshness of their conversation. Still, the lecture had been necessary, and he deserved it.

"Don't you think you were a little hard on him?" Cort

straightened from where he'd been leaning against the truck. Using his crutches to support his bad leg, he stepped toward her.

"No." She flushed, realizing she must have sounded like a fishwife. "I have rules—"

"They're just kids."

"They work for me. I expect them to do their job."

He stared down at her, his brown eyes gleaming with amusement. Obviously she'd really impressed *him*, she thought, her temper starting to get the best of her.

"What I don't understand," Cort said, "is what that reporter wanted. All the way up here from L.A. to get pictures of a few kittens." He shook his head. "Slow news day."

If he didn't know about the cats, he sure didn't know about the kittens. Part of her wanted to slap him upside the head until his ears rang. The other part of her wanted him to find out the truth for himself.

"I like the way you handled the reporter, though," he said, looking around the compound. "He won't be back. Still, you have some major security problems. I'll have a look around and see what I can do."

"Good, because we're going to be on the six o'clock news tonight."

He took a step toward the building. "So? What's the worst that will happen? There'll be a cat show here this weekend? At least you've got the parking for it." He jerked his head at the space behind her truck.

His condescending attitude was the final straw. Her hold on her temper snapped. "You think you're so hot, Mr. Spy? I'm just some crazy cat lady, right? A friend of Jeff's, so you're going to humor me? Fine." She pointed to the main building. "Go right through there. Pet any kitty you like."

Cort stared at her. She was so ticked off, he could practically see steam coming out of her ears. She sure was hung up on this cat thing. He'd better give her a chance to cool off.

Awkwardly moving forward, he went through the open door of the building. Once in the dark hallway, he could smell something musty. He inhaled sharply. An animal scent. Not unpleasant. Not Kitty Litter either. He heard odd snuffling noises and a low cough. He walked out the other side of the building onto smooth dirt. The sounds increased. There were a few grunts followed by a muffled roar. A muffled *roar?* He started to get the feeling things weren't as they seemed. His crutches sank slightly into the ground. He adjusted his weight and turned to his left.

And came face-to-face with a tiger!

Chapter 3

The black-and-gold-striped cat stared at him. Cort took a step back. He forgot about the crutches, tried to spin away, and promptly tripped and sat down hard on the ground. The tiger sniffed the air and grunted.

A pair of boots appeared next to him. He looked up past her jeans-clad legs, past her trim waist and worn blue work shirt, to the smile curving the corners of Faith's mouth. It was, he thought with disgust, a very self-satisfied smile.

"Cats?" he said, shifting so the pain in his leg didn't get worse.

She nodded. "Big cats."

"Well, I'll be damned." He held out his hand.

She braced herself and hauled him to his feet. He balanced on one leg while she collected his crutches. When he'd tucked the supports under his arms, he looked around the compound.

Seven large habitats, bigger than he'd seen at any zoo, stretched out from the right of the main building. To the left, a narrow road led into the forest. Past the road, more enclosures formed a curved line. In the center of the open area were a group of telephone poles, a huge wading pool and a stack of bowling balls. The dirt had been freshly raked. All the enclosures were clean. Most had grass and trees, a few had swimming pools. In the far corner, a small cat—smaller than a tiger, he thought, but bigger than a collie—stuck its head under a man-made waterfall and drank.

"You want to explain this?" he said.

Faith tucked her hands into her back pockets. "I told you. I keep cats."

"Uh-huh. You left out one detail."

"No. You assumed." Her eyes sparkled. She rocked forward onto the balls on her feet, then back on her heels.

"I could have been lunch." He used one crutch to point at the tiger's cage.

"Hardly." She pulled her left hand free of her pocket and glanced at her watch. "It's after four. You could have been a snack."

"Nobody gets the better of you, do they?"

She shook her head. "Not without trying hard." She looked at his leg. "How does it feel? You want to relax first and have the tour tomorrow?"

He glanced around again. He'd never been this close to a tiger before. Most of the animals had come to the front of their enclosures to watch him. Gold eyes stared. He stared back. So this is what it feels like to look into the face of a predator. The tiger he'd seen first made a coughing noise.

"He's saying hello," Faith told him.

"More likely he's figuring out how many mouthfuls I'd make." His leg hurt, but not badly. Rest could wait. "Give me the nickel tour," he said. "Enough for me to get a feel for the place. I'll see the rest of it tomorrow."

"Okay." Faith pointed to the enclosure in front of them.

It was forty feet by sixty. The tiger had stretched out on the grass in front of his pool and rested his massive head on his paws. The afternoon sun caught the colors in his coat, turning the gold a deep orange and making the black stripes seem brown.

"This is Tigger." She shrugged. "I had nothing to do with the name. It came along with him. He's a Bengal tiger. Partially tamed."

"Partially?" Cort raised his eyebrows. "So he'll eat you but feel guilty?"

She laughed. The sound of her amusement, so carefree and open, made him want to hear it again. It had been too long since he'd been around people who laughed. For him, everything was life and death. It was the price he paid for fighting the good fight. Funny, he'd never thought about that particular sacrifice before.

"Most of our cats are partially tamed, which means you can go into their cages, but someone needs to be watching. A few are wild, and they have to be locked in their dens when we come in to clean." She pointed at the compound. "In the back, there. That rock structure."

"What? No carpeting?"

"Hardly. We try to keep the habitats as natural as possible. The water in the swimming pools and ponds is filtered. There's a sprinkler system. Inside the den, the walls are about eight inches thick, to keep the temperature even. We've also got low-light video cameras in there so we can monitor the animals if they seem sick or are giving birth."

He gave a low whistle. "This is some setup." He looked around at the other habitats. "Are they all like this?"

"Yes. The enclosures are different sizes, for different types of cats. Cats that swim out in the wild, like Tigger here, get pools. We don't have habitats for all of them." Her smile faded. "They cost over a hundred thousand dollars each. We're building them one at a time, using both trust money and private donations. In the back are a few cats that live in cages. We're working on getting them their own enclosures." She moved close to the bars. "You can pet Tigger if you'd like. He's really gentle."

Cort shook his head. "No, thanks."

She called the cat's name. Tigger glanced up at her and yawned, showing rows of very large, very sharp teeth, then slowly rose to his feet. Muscles bunched and released with each step. His feet were the size of dinner plates. He padded over to the front of the cage and leaned heavily against it.

"Tigger used to work in the movies, didn't you, honey?"

Faith scratched the cat's forehead and rubbed his ears. The cat made a noise that wasn't a purr, more like a grunting groan, but definitely sounded contented. Cort inched closer, but stayed safely out of paw's reach.

"What happened?" he asked.

"He's a little stubborn and wouldn't take direction."

"Ah, a temperamental artist."

"Something like that." She looked at him over her shoulder. "You sure you don't want to pet him?"

"Positive."

From where he was standing, he had a view of the cat, and of Faith's rear, as she bent to pet the animal. Her jeans pulled tight around her curves. It had been months since he'd spent time with a woman, he thought, then looked around. If he tried anything, she would probably have him treed by a mountain lion.

"Bengal tigers are coming back from extinction. Tigger is doing a lot of breeding with females from zoos around the country, and even with a few in Europe."

Cort stared at the three-hundred-pound male cat. The animal sat leaning against the bars with his eyes half-closed in ecstasy. Faith continued to scratch his ears.

"What a life," Cort said.

"He seems to like it." She straightened. "Over here we

have a couple of mountain lions. We're trying to breed them, as well.''

"Tigers, mountain lions. What do you need me for?" he asked. "If an intruder shows up, just open one of the cages. You'll solve the problem and cut down on the feeding bill.''

"I don't want any of the animals hurt."

"Nice to know I'm expendable."

"It *is* your job."

He looked at the tiger. "Maybe we could work out a swap."

They walked around the right side of the compound. Faith pointed out the various cats. She called each animal by name and explained how they came to be at the way station.

"He was dumped here," she said, pointing at a bobcat. "Someone probably found him as a kitten and raised him, thinking he'd be a fun pet. Then he got big enough to be a problem."

The pointy-eared cat jumped to the front of his enclosure and hunched down like he wanted to play. His short tail quivered.

"Not today, Samson," Faith told the cat. He continued to stare at her hopefully. "As I mentioned, all the cats over here are pretty tame. Samson is declawed. Still, don't go in any cage by yourself."

"I hadn't planned on going in their cages at all," he said, staring at the bobcat. The playful animal made a purring noise, then turned away and slunk to the back of the enclosure.

"On the other side, we have the wilder cats." She turned and pointed across the compound. "We try to have as little contact with them as possible. Sometimes we get an injured animal that we treat, then release back into the wild."

She started across the open area, keeping her stride slow

enough that he could keep up. He felt the cats watching him and knew *they* knew he was injured.

"Lunch," he muttered under his breath. They passed the wading pool and stack of bowling balls. "What is all this for?"

"Recreation. When the weather's good, we let the friendly cats out to play."

"They bowl?"

She laughed. Again the sound caught him off guard. Sweet and happy. Innocent of the evil in the world. "The balls are donated by the bowling alley in town. They play with them."

"Play?"

She looked up at him. "They bat them around, jump on them, throw them in the air."

"Bowling balls?"

"The big cats can weigh several hundred pounds."

He shook his head. Who would have thought? He inhaled deeply. The musty smell didn't seem so intense. In another day or so, he wouldn't even be able to notice it. But he could smell Faith's perfume. The sultry French essence teased at him as he still tried to remember the name. He studied the woman walking beside him. Work boots, straight hair, big cats and French perfume. An intriguing combination.

When they reached the other side of the compound, he saw waist-high poles had been set in the ground, about two feet in front of the enclosures. A chain ran from pole to pole.

"This fence is to remind us not to get too close," she said, pointing at the barrier. "These cats will lash out and scratch you."

A powerful spotted cat with huge shoulders and a wide face paced menacingly at the front of the cage. The animal didn't look directly at them, but Cort sensed it knew exactly where they were standing.

"These jaguars," she said, pointing at the two cages on the far end, "are only here for another few weeks. They're a breeding pair."

He stared at the separate cages. "Wouldn't it work better if they were in the same enclosure. I don't know that much about cats, but—"

"I know." She reached up and brushed a loose strand of hair out of her face. "We tried that. They nearly killed each other. You need to know about these cages." She pointed to the corners. There was a gated opening in the front and the back of the steel-enforced cage. "The hinges by the gates are wide. We'd planned to house two Siberian tigers here. They get to be seven hundred pounds. They aren't here yet, and when the mating couple took an instant dislike to each other, we had to separate them. Unfortunately, the jaguars can stick their paws out at the front and back hinges. Just don't try walking between the cages." She smiled up at him. "They'd probably just scratch you up a bit, but if one stood at the front of its cage and the other stood at the back of the other one, you'd be trapped between them."

He eyed the pacing animal. Rage radiated with each step. "I'm not planning to walk between any cages, but thanks for the warning."

He heard footsteps behind them and turned to see one of Faith's employees approaching. The young woman stared from him to her boss and back.

"Faith, the food's all unloaded. We're leaving."

"I'll see you tomorrow. Don't forget to lock the gate behind you."

"I won't." The young woman looked Cort up and down, glanced at Faith questioningly, then blushed suddenly. She spun on her heel and jogged to the main building.

"Damn," Faith muttered.

He glanced at her and saw matching spots of color staining her cheeks.

"I should have introduced you," she said. "I forgot to tell them about the extra security. They don't know who you are." She sighed. "I'll explain tomorrow."

The same woman who patted live tigers and didn't bat an eye when a stranger practically strangled her in her own truck got embarrassed because one of her employees thought she'd brought a man to spend the night? There had to be a piece missing. He suddenly realized what it was.

"You married?" he asked.

She looked shocked. "No, why?"

He shrugged, as well as he could, supported by the crutches. "You seemed upset. I thought maybe you were afraid your husband or significant other would get the wrong idea."

"No husband," she said shortly. "I live here alone. We'd better get your leg bandaged."

"Good idea." The mention of his wound made it ache more.

He followed her toward the main building. They passed the narrow road. "What's down there?" he asked.

"The Big House." She reached the glass door and held it open. "I don't live there anymore. There's an apartment in this building, at the end of the hall. It's easier to stay here. I use the Big House for fund-raising parties and that sort of thing." She closed the glass door behind them.

He turned and looked at it. "No lock?"

"Just on the side facing the parking lot. The scent of the cats keep four-legged intruders away. I need to be able to get out of here quickly, in case something happens."

He swung the crutches forward and moved to the front door. Cheap lock. He shook the door. It rattled. He shook it again. "Some security. Anyone over a hundred and forty pounds could break through this just by running up and hitting it with his shoulder." He glanced around at the foyer. A couple of chairs and a vinyl sofa stood on either side of the front door. Long hallways stretched out toward both ends of the building. He looked at the low ceiling, then at the wide windows on either side of the front door. "Alarm? Video?"

She shook her head.

"But you have special cameras to watch the cats?"

"They get priority."

"Not anymore. I'm going to call Jeff with a supply list. You need new locks and a decent gate. Some kind of security system. How often you get up in the night?"

"Depends. Why?"

"Motion detectors."

"Wouldn't work. Sparky usually has the run of the place. Come on, that bandage needs changing."

He followed her down the left hall. The linoleum had seen better days, and the walls needed painting, but everything was clean. Prints of big cats hung on both walls. Sparky?

"Who did you say named him?"

"Edwina. He was her favorite."

He should ask exactly what kind of cat—or lion or tiger—Sparky was, but he didn't want to know. Faith led him into an examining room. From the placement of the metal table and the size of the cage in the corner, he knew she treated her cats here.

"Have a seat," she said, patting the metal table.

He set the crutches against the wall and swung himself up. "You know what you're doing?"

She opened a metal cupboard door and rummaged around inside. "Does it matter? I'm the only one here."

"I could change it myself."

She glanced at him over her shoulder. "I know enough not to kill you."

"Great."

He shifted his weight and scooted back on the table until he rested against the wall. The throbbing in his leg increased. "I assume the 'package' Jeff wants me to protect is really a three-hundred-pound feline."

"Nope. Closer to twenty pounds. I'll introduce you to them in the morning."

"Them?"

She looked amused. "Twins."

Twins? Cort fought back a sigh. Jeff was going to owe him big-time for this one, he thought, then turned his attention back to Faith.

She placed scissors beside him, along with clean bandages, antiseptic and a damp cloth. Her long light brown hair fell over her shoulders. She reached in her front jeans pocket and pulled out a rubber band, then drew her hair back and secured it. After washing her hands, she looked at the bandage.

"This may hurt. You want a stick to bite on?"

He looked at her. "A stick?"

"You're a spy. That's what they always do in the movies. I thought it might make you feel better." Her lips remained straight, but humor danced in her eyes.

"You're not digging out a bullet."

"Just thought I'd ask."

She picked up the scissors and cut through the bandage. It fell away revealing his blood-covered leg. Cort told himself it looked worse than it was. Faith didn't even blink. She picked up the damp cloth and began cleaning his skin.

"Here," she said, pointing at but not touching the incision. "You pulled two stitches. I've never sewed up a person before. Would you mind if I used a butterfly bandage instead?"

"Not at all."

She worked quickly. After wiping away the dried blood,

she doused the wound with antiseptic and then taped it closed. She wrapped gauze around his calf and secured it firmly.

"That must hurt a lot," she said sympathetically. "There should be pain medication with the other pills Jeff gave me. I'll grab them from the truck. Be right back."

He was too busy staring at her to answer. Faith Newlin knew about guns and big cats and did a great field dressing. None of this made any sense.

She returned with his duffel bag and the containers of medication.

"Just as I thought," she said, tossing him a bottle.

"Great," he said, as he caught it. "First thing in the morning, I'll get on the horn to Jeff and get your security under control."

He slid to the edge of the examining table and stuffed the medicine in his pocket. She handed him his crutches and led the way into the hall. Two doors down she entered a small room. There were rows of file cabinets, a bare wooden desk and a cot against the far wall.

"It's not much," she said. "I didn't have a chance to get a bedroom ready for you up at the Big House. Plus, I want to keep an eye on you tonight."

He lowered himself onto the cot. The blankets were soft, the pillow down-filled. "I'll be fine."

"There's a bathroom across the hall. It has a shower built in. Do you want to try it or wait?"

He shifted his injured leg, and pain shot up to his thigh. His head still throbbed. "I can wait. Thanks."

She set his duffel bag on the desk and opened the top side drawer. After clicking on the desk lamp, she pulled out his shaving kit and began putting his clothing in the drawer.

"I can do that," he said.

"You're dead on your feet. I don't mind. Are you hungry?"

"No." He leaned back and let the exhaustion flow through him.

When she finished unpacking, she folded the duffel bag on top of the desk and left. She was back almost immediately, carrying a glass of water.

"For your pills," she said.

He raised himself up on one elbow, dug the pills out of his pocket and took one out. As he reached for the glass of water, the light from the lamp caught the side of her face and her neck. Dark bruises stained her honey-tanned skin. He drank from the glass, then set it down on the floor without taking his eyes from those marks. Time and his job had changed him, he knew. But when had he crossed the line and become a brute?

She sat next to him on the cot. "What's wrong?"

"I hurt you." He raised his hand and gently touched the side of her throat. She stiffened slightly, but didn't pull away. Her warmth contrasted with his cool skin as he brushed one finger down the smooth length.

"I told you I understood what happened," she said. "It was my fault. I shouldn't have startled you."

"A high price to pay for a mistake." He dropped his hand back to the cot.

"I'm not afraid. I won't startle you again, so you won't have reason to hurt me."

"A hell of a way to live."

"For you or for me?" she asked.

Blue eyes searched his, looking for something he knew didn't exist. Humanity, the connection, the bonding of two souls. It was beyond him, always had been. He held her gaze, let her search, knowing she would seek in vain.

When he didn't answer the question, she leaned forward. "You don't believe me. That it doesn't matter, I mean."

"No."

She thought for a moment, as if trying to find a way to

change his mind. "We had a mountain lion here once. I was pretty new at the time, still idealistic." She sat up straighter on the cot. "He'd been a pet, then abused and abandoned when he got bigger. By the time he was brought to the way station, he was skinny, bleeding and mean. We patched him up and fed him. It wasn't enough. His leg got infected and required surgery. After the operation, he was pretty out of it. I went in the cage to change his bandage and give him water."

She moved down a little on the cot, so that she was sitting by his thighs instead of by his waist. She began unbuttoning her blouse. He ignored his surprise and forced himself to hold her gaze and not follow the movements of her fingers. But in the periphery of his sight he saw the blouse fall open. She held it together just above her breasts.

"I hadn't bothered to check to see if he was still sleeping. I crouched down to pick up his water bowl."

She turned away from him and shrugged out of the shirt. He wasn't sure what to expect. Her blouse slipped off her left shoulder. Cort stared. From just below the nape of her neck, across the top of her back, along her shoulder blade and ending on the back of her arm, four scars traced the route taken by the lion's claws. The parallel lines puckered in some places, as if the depth of the slashing hadn't been uniform.

"He was awake and he attacked me." She pulled up her blouse and turned to face him. "I was lucky. I got out before he *really* hurt me."

Though she held the front together, he could see the paleness of her chest and swelling curve of her breasts. Her choice in lingerie matched the rest of her wardrobe. Sensible cotton trimmed in a thin ribbon of lace. A female who dismissed the need to entice a man with satin, though her choice in perfume was anything but pedestrian.

"Do you see why I'm not afraid of you?" she asked.

No. He and the mountain lion had little in common. The creature of God killed for food or to protect itself. Cort killed because it was asked of him.

She touched his arm briefly. "Sleep now," she said. "I'll be right down the hall. If you need anything, call me." She rose and walked to the door.

She stood there watching him. Although her hands clutched her blouse together, he could still see the top of one breast. The unexpected view of that female curve hit him low in the gut, spreading need throughout his body. All cats are gray in the dark, he reminded himself, then closed his eyes. Maybe. But something told him Faith Newlin was a special brand of cat...and one he should leave alone.

He could hear the tide lapping against the pilings that supported the dock. And he could smell salt air.

The warehouse.

Cort shook his head to clear it. Was he meeting someone, or picking something up? Why couldn't he remember?

Something was wrong. Danger! He heard it, felt it. A voice called to him. Dan? He had to get out, to run. The explosion! There wasn't time. He spun to leave, but something blocked his way. Danger! Run!

"Hush, Cort. You're safe now." Gentle hands pressed against his shoulders.

He forced his eyes open. Instead of a damp South American warehouse, or even the fires of hell, he stared into wide blue eyes and inhaled the scent of French perfume.

"Je t'aime." he murmured.

"A lovely thought," the woman said, then smiled. "But you've just met me."

"Your perfume."

"Ah. Yes. That's it."

He blinked several times to clear his vision and his head.

Everything came back to him. The time in the hospital, the cats, the woman. "Faith."

"Good morning. How do you feel?"

He sat up. Sometime in the night, he'd woken up enough to strip off his clothes. The sheet pooled around his waist. He raised his arms above his head and stretched. "Like a new man. What time is it?"

"Almost nine."

He'd been out almost fourteen hours. "Guess I was tired."

"Guess so. You want some breakfast?"

His stomach rumbled.

She chuckled and rose to her feet. She looked fresh and clean. Her long brown hair had been pulled back into a braid. Jeans and boots covered her lower half, but the plaid work shirt had been replaced by a pink T-shirt. She handed him the crutches.

"I put your shaving kit in the bathroom," she said.

He took the crutches and pulled himself to his feet. As he rose, he realized he was wearing nothing but his briefs. A quick glance at Faith told him she didn't even bother to look. Yeah, he'd impressed the hell out of her.

He took an experimental step. The leg felt stronger and his head didn't hurt anymore. He rubbed one hand over his face. Stubble rasped against his palm.

"I need a shave," he said.

"When you're done, I'll have breakfast ready." She ducked ahead of him in the hall and tossed a pair of jeans and a shirt into the bathroom. "The towels are clean. I put a plastic bag out, so you can shower without getting the bandage wet."

Before he could thank her, she was heading down the hall. Her braid swayed with each step, as did her curvy hips. He stared after her until she turned the corner.

By the time he'd made himself presentable, he could

smell food cooking. He followed the delicious odors past two more offices, through a door marked Private and into a small living room.

"Faith?" he called.

"In here."

He maneuvered the crutches around the maple coffee table and rocking chair into a cheery yellow kitchen. A Formica table stood in front of a bay window that looked out into the forest. The stove appeared to be older than he was and the refrigerator older still by ten years. But everything gleamed in the morning light. He sniffed, smelling mint along with the cooking.

Faith looked up from the stove. "I hope scrambled is all right." She motioned to the table. "Have a seat."

She'd set a place for him and lined up all his medications in a row. A glass of orange juice sat next to a cup of coffee. He looked at the setting, then at her. "Very nice. Thanks."

He pulled out a chair, sat down and sipped the coffee. She served his breakfast, then poured herself a cup and took the seat opposite him. A stack of papers rested in front of her. As she studied them, she nibbled on the corner of her mouth. Was it worry or simply a habit? Who was this woman who took in stray lions and spies? He buttered the toast she'd made, then sorted through the jars of jelly.

"What are you looking for?" she asked.

"Mint. I can smell it. Can't you?"

She looked down. "Yes." He could have sworn her shoulders were shaking.

"What's so funny?"

She looked up, her face expressionless. The innocence didn't fool him. "Nothing," she said.

"Sure." He cautiously took a bite of the eggs. "This is great. I was half-afraid you'd feed me cat food."

"Eggs are cheaper."

He heard a rumble, like a low-flying plane. The sound

continued for several minutes as he ate, then it stopped. He chewed a mouthful of food and swallowed. "What *do* the cats eat?"

"Anything I can get my hands on. Chicken mostly. The bones keep their teeth clean and exercised. Sometimes hunters leave me extra venison."

"Must get expensive."

She nodded. "The biggest cats eat up to fifteen pounds a day."

The rumble started again, broke, became an almost coughing sound, like someone sawing wood, then resumed. "What the hell is that?"

"What?"

"That rumble. Can't you hear it?"

She chuckled. "I'm so used to it, I only notice when it's not there." She glanced at his plate. "Are you done?"

"I guess."

"It's never a good idea to have food around when you meet Sparky," she said.

"Sparky?" He remembered his vision of the mean black alley cat. That was when he'd assumed Faith's cats had been the ten-pound, domestic kind. "Sparky isn't what I think, is he?"

"Probably not." She pursed her lips together and whistled softly, first a high, then a low tone. "Sparky," she called. "Come."

From a room beyond the kitchen, the rumble stopped for a moment. Cort heard the scratchy coughing noise again, then the sound of a thick chain being dragged across the linoleum floor. What he thought was a shadow cast by the overhead lights quickly became a very large, very black, leopard.

"Holy—"

The animal approached slowly. Yellow eyes, more almond-shaped than round, flickered around the room, then settled on him. As the cat walked over to Faith, the smell of mint grew. Cort realized it came from the animal. "Sparky," she said, patting its head. "This is Cort."

The black leopard continued to hold his gaze. The rumbling went on. The cat's massive head rested on Faith's thighs. Powerful muscles rippled as the animal sat down. A faint pattern of spots was barely visible in the dark coat. Its long tail moved back and forth in a slow but menacing rhythm.

"Is this your idea of a pet?" Cort asked, wondering what Jeff had been thinking of when he'd sent him here.

"No. Edwina is the one who took him in. He was less than four weeks old when his mother died. He was hand-raised after that. Edwina couldn't bear to put him in a cage, so here he is." She rubbed the animal's forehead, then scratched behind its ears.

Like a huge house cat, the leopard arched toward the stroking and butted his head against her leg, asking for more. This gentle butt, however, nearly knocked her out of her chair.

"Easy," she admonished, giving the animal a slight slap on its shoulder.

Sparky was properly cowed and broke his gaze with Cort to glance up at Faith and yawn.

A perfect domestic scene, if he ignored the glistening teeth designed to rip and tear flesh and bite through bone.

"Why does he smell of mint?" he asked.

"Leopards conceal their own scent. In the wild he'd use certain herbs or animal dung."

"I can see why you'd want to discourage the latter."

"You bet. There's a mint patch for him out back."

"Where does he sleep?"

"In the office." Faith continued to stroke the leopard. "Or with me. Give me your hand."

He offered his left.

Faith grinned as she took it. "You're right-handed, aren't you?"

"I don't take chances."

"Sparky won't hurt you without provocation. He's just a friendly little kitty, aren't you, boy?" She found a particularly sensitive spot behind its jaw, rubbed vigorously, and the purring deepened.

Faith laced their fingers together. "Sparky," she said. "This is Cort. He's going to be staying here awhile." Her soft voice, slightly higher pitched than her normal speaking tone, soothed both him and the cat.

The leopard remained indifferent to the stranger's hand being drawn closer and closer to his head. Faith continued to stroke the cat. She moved her free hand lower onto the animal's shoulder and placed their joined hands on its head.

Cort resisted the impulse to pull back. The short black fur felt coarse under his fingers. Thick, not at all like a domestic cat. But everything else seemed familiar, just on a larger scale. Ears moved back and forth as if following the conversation. The rumbling purr continued, unbroken, except when Sparky shifted to lean more heavily on Faith.

Power, Cort thought, looking at the long legs and thick ropes of muscle visible under the fur. A perfect killing machine. Elegant. Beautiful. A creature without a conscience. Is that what Jeff saw when he looked at him?

"He likes most people," she said, patting Sparky with his hand, then slipping her fingers away.

He hesitated. Their eyes met, and he continued stroking the cat. "Most? When do I find out if I'm one of the lucky ones?"

"He wouldn't have come in here if he didn't like your scent."

Sparky straightened, as if he'd just realized Faith wasn't the one touching him. He rose to his feet and walked the two steps over to Cort. Even though the kitchen chair was relatively high off the ground, Sparky practically stared him in the eye. The cat sniffed at his hand, then his arm. Cort wanted to get the hell away, but he held his position. He knew that much.

Predator to predator. He recognized Sparky's need to understand the intruder. If this was her chaperon, it was no wonder Faith wasn't married.

Sparky made the coughing sound again, then turned away and walked next to the refrigerator. The one-inch-thick chain trailed behind him. The rumbling purr became a humph as he laid down, then resumed.

Faith began to clear the table. When she went to put the butter away, she nudged Sparky out of the way so that she could open the door. Cort wasn't sure if he should respect Faith or have her committed.

"Do you want to drive around the compound?" she asked. "I've cleared my morning so that I could show you anything you would like to see."

Before he could respond, a loud shriek pierced the morning. Even Sparky stopped purring.

"Damn," Faith muttered, apparently more annoyed than concerned as she walked out of the room. "What are you two up to now?"

Cort grabbed his crutches and followed her. The shrieks came again, this time followed by plaintive mewing.

"You can't be hungry," Faith said, moving down the hall toward a dim light in a room on the right. "I just fed you."

The mewing got louder. Cort continued to hobble behind her. When they entered the room, he saw a big cage that filled most of the floor space. Inside, blankets formed a soft nest. Newspapers lined a far corner of the cage. The striped bundle in the middle of the blankets moved as they walked closer. Two white tiger cubs looked up and mewed piteously.

"Here they are," Faith said as she crouched down beside the babies. "Jeff sent them along to me last week."

"This is what the reporter was after?"

"Yes. They were confiscated at the border. Something about being added to the collection of some big-time crook." She looked up and smiled. "Think you can keep them safe?"

William Thomas paced the small motel room. He needed a drink, but he couldn't afford to miss his phone call. What would happen to him now? he wondered for the hundredth time. What would they do to him? Second chances didn't exist in his organization. But it hadn't been his fault. They had set the rules. No killing, they'd insisted. If he'd iced the border control officer none of this mess would have happened.

He swallowed thickly and again wished for that drink. Maybe he could run to the liquor store across the street. It wouldn't take long and—

The ringing of the telephone cut into his thoughts. He picked it up immediately.

"Yes?" he said curtly.

"I'm very disappointed, Mr. Thomas."

"I know. It was an accident. The rules I had to work under were too restrictive."

"I don't care about accidents. I want the job done."

"Of course." William forced himself to speak calmly. The fact that they hadn't killed him yet meant he might be given the chance to redeem himself.

"Our mutual employer is still out of the country," his caller said, the voice low and cold. "You have exactly twenty-one days until his return. If the cubs are recovered by then, he would be very forgiving of your little accident."

"I can get them back. As soon as I find out where they are—"

The man on the phone cut him off again. "They were on the news last evening."

"What? The cubs?"

"Yes. A reporter, a James Wilson, filed a story. Locate him and you'll locate the cubs."

"Consider it done."

"Mr. Thomas, I shouldn't have to remind you that you can't afford to make another mistake."

William wished he could ignore the implied threat, but doing so would cost him his life. "I need to be able to do whatever is necessary," he said. "You can't tie my hands and then complain that the job isn't done."

"Recover them. *At any cost.*"

William nodded. He'd just been given permission to get rid of anyone who stood in his way. Better. Now he could finish the job. "You can count on me."

"Twenty-one days, Mr. Thomas. Our mutual employer spent a lot of money on the cubs. They are the centerpiece of his collection. If you don't succeed, we will be forced to discontinue our association. Do you understand?"

Who wouldn't understand a .45 slug between the eyes? "I understand."

There was a click, and the line went dead.

Chapter 4

"Hush, babies," Faith said as she crouched down and opened the cage. "Come on. We're here." The larger of the two tiger cubs tumbled toward her, mewing loudly. "You're lonely, aren't you?" When the kitten reached her, she picked it up and cradled it in her arms. "All this fuss over twenty pounds of trouble."

Cort looked stunned. He reached out to pat the cub. The white-striped cat made a garbled sound that was supposed to be a growling hiss and hunched back against her.

"Hold your hand out," she instructed. "Let it sniff you."

"It?" His gold-flecked eyes met hers. He shifted his weight and leaned on the crutches, offering his fingers to the cub.

"One's a boy, the other's a girl, but I still have trouble telling them apart."

"How old are they?" he asked.

"Around three months. We can't be sure. They can see what's going on around them, and that doesn't happen until about two months. You want to hold it?"

She looked at Cort. The scar on his chin looked less raw this morning, and the shadows under his eyes had faded. Except for the crutches and the gaunt hollows in his cheeks, she wouldn't know he'd ever been injured.

"Sure," he said, shifting his weight so he leaned against the wall. He set the crutches next to him, securing them near the cage.

"Here, baby," Faith said, moving close to him and petting the cub. "They thrive on attention. In the wild, they're totally dependent on their mother. They won't even stray from her side until they're more than a year old. They want to be cuddled, don't you?" She softened her voice and nuzzled the kitten's soft ears. "You're a sweet baby. Hold your arms out, Cort, and cradle it while I'm still holding on."

She moved until she was inches from him, then felt his hands slip between her and the cub. His knuckles brushed against her belly. A shiver raced through her, and she had to fight not to jump. What on earth...?

"You got it?" she asked.

"I think so. God, he's so soft. Come here, monster," Cort said, keeping his tone low and calm. "Get a load of those feet."

She gave the cub one last pat and stepped back. "They'll both grow to be several hundred pounds."

"That's a lot of kitty." Cort held the kitten in his arms. The animal looked from her to Cort, then mewed and snuggled close to his chest.

"It likes you." Something sharp nibbled on her ankle. "You want attention, too, don't you?" She leaned down and picked up the smaller cub. Icy blue eyes stared back at her. The small triangular nose quivered as it inhaled her scent. "The changes have been hard on them. I don't know how many people have handled and fed them, but it's pretty obvious they haven't had a stable life."

"So now you're doing cat therapy?"

"Cort!"

He grinned. "How rare are white tigers?"

"It depends," she said. "Some people are breeding white tigers, but they aren't true mutants. You can tell by the eye color. A true white tiger has blue eyes. Just like yours, huh?" She scratched the cub's head. The baby arched back against her hand and wiggled to get closer. "They have brown stripes on white fur, and the nose and lips are pinkish gray."

"I never thought of tigers as having lips."

He held the cub securely, but without too much pressure. The lonely cat sniffed at his neck and face, making throaty noises and generally looking pleased.

"Not quite the same as fighting warlords and terrorists, is it?" she asked.

Their eyes met. She felt that same shiver again, but this time he wasn't even touching her. Her heartbeat clicked up a notch, pounding harder and faster in her chest. Her palms suddenly felt damp, and she fought the urge to moisten her lips. What was happening to her?

"So who takes care of them?" he asked. "You?"

"I've been sharing the duties with the kids, when they're here, but it would be better to have just one person. After all the cubs have been through, they need some stability."

Cort shifted suddenly and disentangled the cub's claws from his shoulders. "I'm not a scratching post," he told the animal. "They're feisty little buggers, aren't they?"

"Yeah, and hungry. They get fed every few hours. They have to be rubbed down and massaged to keep their circulation and bowels going. They need attention and affection and a lot of other things I don't have time for."

"You want a volunteer?" he asked.

"I wasn't hinting."

"Yes, you were."

"Okay, maybe I was. But it's a lot of work and time."

He glanced around the small room. "Once I get the security system installed, maintenance shouldn't take much of my day. If they don't object to a gimpy role model, I'll give it a try."

She told herself the sensation of nerves in her stomach came from relief and nothing else. Certainly not from being near Cort. He was here to protect her and the cubs. She knew better than to risk being attracted to any man.

"Are you sure?" she asked. "I really didn't mean to make you think you had to help. Keeping the cubs safe is my main priority."

"Mine, too." He gave her a slow smile. It caused lines to crinkle by the corners of his eyes. She felt her own lips tug in response. "I'm here because of them, Faith. If I help you with feeding and whatever else you do, I'm also looking out for them."

It seemed easiest to accept gracefully. After all, she really didn't have time to take care of the cubs along with all her other duties. "Thanks." She placed the baby she was holding back in the cage and reached for the other one. "Let me show you the feeding schedule. Then we can tour the compound. By the time we're done, it'll be time to feed them and you can get your lesson in Tiger Mothering 101."

She secured the cage. Cort collected his crutches. The cubs stared up at him and began to mew. He looked at her. "How do you resist them?"

She shrugged. "Practice, and the knowledge that if they had their way, someone would be with them twenty-four hours a day." She shook her head. "That's the worst of it. People smuggle in rare animals because they want to own something unique, but they don't bother to consider the animal itself. They don't think about the special diet and attention, the needs of babies this tiny." She crouched down and patted the smaller of the two through the wire cage.

"Poor sweeties. We need to find you a good home, and fast." She rose and started out of the room.

"How long will that take?" Cort asked, hobbling behind her.

"It depends. It's not that easy to hand them over to a zoo or a breeding center. Tigers are expensive to keep and cubs are demanding. Most facilities don't have the room, the personnel or the funds. Jeff wants to make sure he gets it right the first time. That's why they're with me. I can hold them longer than most places."

They entered her office. Photos of big cats lined the walls. Her scarred, thrift-store desk took up a good portion of the space. File cabinets and a couple of chairs filled the rest. Faith waved him into the seat in front of her desk. Cort settled into the chair and placed the crutches on the floor.

"How's the leg?" she asked as she pulled open a file cabinet drawer and withdrew several forms.

"Not bad. I should be walking without help in a day or so."

"Good." She turned around and looked at him.

In his jeans and long-sleeved cotton shirt, he looked like any local. Most of the men living on the mountain did physical work for a living, so his broad shoulders and defined muscles wouldn't set him apart. It had to be something else that made her heart flutter foolishly. Maybe it was the shape of him—lean and graceful with a concealed power. Even with the bandaged leg and crutches, he reminded her of her cats, moving carefully, deliberately, the wary instincts of a predator never far below the surface.

"These are the forms I use to keep track of the cubs' care." She handed him several papers. "I don't think you'll have any trouble with them."

He glanced at the sheets and nodded. "Looks simple enough."

"When we feed them, I'll go over the amounts of formula each needs.'' She closed the file cabinet and sat in the old rickety wooden chair behind her desk. ''They usually just scarf down whatever we give them. These are not picky eaters.''

''Good.'' He read on. ''Playtime?''

She nodded. ''They need a certain amount of social interaction. You'll probably want to wear gloves.''

The flecks in his eyes seemed to glint with amusement. He smiled. ''Gloves?''

''You've seen their claws.''

''Felt them, too.'' He rubbed his shoulder. ''Could be worse, I suppose. You could be asking me to wrestle Sparky.''

She smiled. ''Not until you're feeling better.''

''Great.'' He leaned forward and placed the papers on her desk. He bumped several other sheets, and they fluttered to the ground. ''Got 'em,'' he said, reaching down and grabbing them.

''Thanks.'' She took the offered forms and grimaced. ''Government paperwork.''

''Aren't you used to it?''

''No. We're privately funded. I'm helping Jeff with the cubs as a favor, but for the most part, I don't work with government agencies.'' She stared at the papers stacked on her desk. ''Most of these files are for a new project I'm thinking of starting. I counted. There are one hundred and eighty-seven forms there. Who knows how many agencies and bureaucrats for me to deal with.''

''What for?''

She tossed the sheets on the desk and leaned forward, lacing her hands together. ''I want to breed snow leopards.''

She half expected him to laugh. She'd mentioned the project to one of the way station's contributors, and he'd patted her on the head and told her not to bite off more than she could chew.

"Why?" Cort asked.

"They're almost extinct. I bought some land a few years ago in North Dakota. It's away from everything. The climate is good for the leopards. If I could get a few breeding pairs and mate them in captivity, in a couple of generations there would be enough to release several back into the wild. They would help not only with the numbers, but by increasing the gene pool. That's the problem when a species becomes endangered. There aren't enough genes to create a healthy population." She stopped suddenly, aware of how she was going on.

But Cort seemed interested. He adjusted his injured leg, then rested his hands on the arms of the chair. "What's all the paperwork for?"

"I have to get permission from federal, state and local governments. I have to have the approval of all the neighbors. There are zoning permits, financial qualifications. I've seen an attorney, and she gave me some direction, but I'm a little overwhelmed by the whole issue."

"Why? You run *this* place."

"It's not the same. The way station was already established when I arrived. Edwina was a little eccentric, but she had a head for business as well as cats. My changes around here have been minor." Faith fiddled with a pencil, fighting the familiar feelings of inadequacy. "I have a two-year degree in animal husbandry, but no formal business training, which presented a problem. Before her death, Edwina had asked me to take charge, but several of the board members tried to get it away from me."

One gold-blond eyebrow raised slightly. "Why? You're damn good at your job."

"How would you know?"

He pointed at his leg. "You did a terrific field dressing."

"Why, thank you. I'll explain that to the IRS and my attorney when I set up the nonprofit foundation."

She was smiling, but Cort saw the faint worry lines puckering between her brows. He was intrigued by what Faith was telling him, yet knew better than to get involved. Until the cubs had been moved somewhere else, she and this facility were his responsibility. When the danger was over, he would be long gone. It was one of the advantages of his job.

"You ready for the real tour?" she asked, obviously trying to change the subject.

"Sure." He collected his crutches and stood. "But first I'd like my gun back."

She studied him for a second, then pulled open her desk drawer and drew out the Beretta and its magazine. He took them from her, loaded the gun, chambered a round and checked to make sure the safety was on. Then he slipped the gun into the waistband at the small of his back and turned toward the door.

"So if we're invaded by a small third-world country, you're prepared," she said.

"Always."

"Good to know." She led the way into the hall.

As they walked past the room containing the cubs, the kittens cried out. They were so small, he thought, remembering holding one of them. Hard to believe something like that would grow into a five-hundred-pound killer.

They walked to the foyer and out the front door to the parking lot where Faith had scared off the newspeople. This morning the circular area stood empty. She waited while he maneuvered his way down the single step.

"Beth will be here in a couple of hours," Faith said, leading him to the left. "She has morning classes. The two guys have different schedules on different days, but someone comes here every day. Most days there are two of them."

"I'll need to look at their personnel files," he said. "Run a few things through the computer."

She paused and looked at him. In the bright morning light, her skin glowed. The faint color on her cheeks owed its presence to her temper rather than makeup. Clear blue eyes framed by dark lashes bored into his.

"I trust my kids."

"This is routine," he said, leaning on the crutches. "Maybe something happened to one of them in the last month or so. I'm not accusing anyone, but it's better to know."

She folded her arms over her chest. "What does your spy computer say about me?"

"Jeff didn't tell me."

"But I've been investigated." She wasn't asking a question.

"You wouldn't have been allowed in the hospital yesterday if you hadn't been cleared."

She stared at him for several seconds. "I don't envy you your world, Cort," she said, dropping her arms to her sides. "Come on. The Jeep is this way."

A three-car garage jutted out on one side of the main building. She lifted the single door and stepped into the shadows. Ten seconds later he heard an engine start up. She backed an open, black-and-white-striped Jeep out in front of him. He stared at the vehicle. It looked like something from an animal park—a zebra on wheels.

She stepped out and lowered the garage door. "Don't ask," she muttered. "I had nothing to do with it. The vehicle was a donation. We were all humiliated when it was delivered."

He tossed his crutches in the back and climbed in. His bum leg bumped the side once and he fought back a curse. When the pain eased, he turned to her. "Why zebra stripes?"

"I have no idea." She slid in beside him. "I guess they thought the cats would think they were back on the Serengeti." She rested her hands on the steering wheel. "What do you want to see first?"

He thought for a minute. "How much of the perimeter is fenced?"

She smiled. "Perimeter? Should we be wearing fatigues and a little beret?"

Her humor surprised him. He knew Faith wasn't happy about him investigating her employees. He understood her reluctance and admired her loyalty, however misplaced. He thought about the casual way she'd handled the Beretta yesterday and reminded himself she wasn't like any of the women he'd known. He would do well to remember that.

"We'll save the camouflage for night maneuvers," he said. "How much of the compound is fenced?"

She shifted into gear and started down the driveway toward the main road. "Not enough of it. We count on the forest to keep most people away. There are a few places where it would be pretty easy to hike into the facility. Most people just want to get a look at the cats, so the gate and the road discourage them."

As they drove down the paved driveway, she pointed to where the fencing started and ended. When the asphalt gave way to dirt ruts, she slowed down and eased forward in second gear. About twenty yards from the gate, she pulled a remote-control device from her jeans pocket and pushed the button. The gate swung open.

"Let's start here," he said. He climbed out and hobbled over to the gate. "Worn hinges. You could cut through this with a nail file." He leaned on the frame. It groaned and gave slightly. "Item one, a new gate."

Two hours later, they stopped at the top of a sloping rise. Most of the trees had been logged in the last twenty years, and the new growth didn't yet block out the terrain or the sun. Cort squinted and peered down in the direction of the way station.

"Can't do much about fencing up here," he said. "It's a roundabout route, but fairly impassable, especially at night."

"Good." Faith leaned against the Jeep. "You're really taking this seriously, aren't you?"

He glanced at her. A couple of strands of hair had escaped from her braid. They floated around her ears and temples. He thought about smoothing them back in place, then dismissed the idea as foolish. He didn't want to start something he had no intention of finishing.

"It's my job."

"I know. I guess I didn't want to think the cubs were really in danger."

"Would that have affected your willingness to take them in?"

She thought for a moment, then shook her head. "No. They had nowhere else to go. I would have spent the last couple of days being nervous, though."

He scanned the quiet hilltop. A faint earthy smell mingled with the sweetness of spring flowers and Faith's French perfume. Birds chirped from nearby branches and small creatures rustled in the underbrush.

"Nothing's going to happen," he said.

"I have every confidence in you."

"Thanks."

"You want to talk about it?" she asked softly.

"What?"

"The dream."

He swung around to face her. She leaned against the vehicle. With her elbows propped up on the closed driver's door, her chest thrust forward, enticing him with her feminine shape. He ignored the faint stirrings inside and concentrated on her statement.

"What dream?" he asked, even though he knew.

"From this morning. I heard you calling out." Her face was as open and readable as a child's. She wasn't judging.

"No." He spoke sharply. The word cut through the late morning like a gunshot. She tried to control her reaction, but his skilled eyes saw the slight stiffening of her muscles and the way she forced herself to relax.

"Just asking," she said. "You ready to head back?"

He hobbled over to the Jeep without speaking. She didn't look up at him. Nothing in her manner indicated anything had happened, but he felt like a jerk. He was here to do a job. Whatever personal problems he brought with him had no business spilling out into the assignment, or involving Faith.

"How much did Jeff tell you?" he asked, settling his crutches in the back of the vehicle.

She opened her door and got inside. "Only that you'd been injured on your last assignment, and that you were having trouble remembering everything that happened."

"That about sums it up," he said curtly, sliding in beside her. Faith started the engine and made a tight turn in the small clearing.

Cort's feeling of helplessness returned. He couldn't force himself to remember. He couldn't do a damn thing except wait for his past to catch up with him. In the meantime, he could wonder if he'd killed his friend.

That was the problem. In his line of work, he wasn't supposed to have friends. If he'd remembered his own rule, none of this would matter. Dan's death would simply be another casualty of war. Nothing personal about that. It was the price paid for fighting the good fight. But it *was* personal, and it was too late to change that fact.

"I've been thinking about painting the hallway of the

main building," Faith said as she drove down the narrow path. "It really looks shabby. Maybe a light cream or even white."

He stared at her. What the hell was she talking about? She spoke about remodeling, moving from paint to flooring, then about replacing the vinyl couch. A shaft of sunlight filtered through the trees overhead and highlighted her right side. He stared at the snug-fitting jeans hugging her slender thighs and the way her breasts bounced with each bump in the road. Inside, heat coiled, the awakening desire defusing his temper. He moved his gaze to the muscles in her arms and up to the wisp of brown hair floating beside her ear.

His stomach clenched. There. Where the pink T-shirt met her neck. The faint shadowing in the shape of a man's hand, his hand, wouldn't let him forget what he'd done. He started to curse himself, but her quiet voice kept getting in the way. She soothed him, and he realized she spoke to call him away from his demons.

"Is this what mother tigers do?" he asked.

She stopped speaking in midsentence and glanced at him. "Excuse me?"

"You're talking to relax me. Is that what cat mothers do? Is this human purring?"

She smiled and returned her attention to the road. "And here I thought I was being subtle."

"You were. I'm very observant."

"I guess you'd have to be. Tigers don't purr. None of the big cats do."

"Wasn't Sparky purring? He looked like a big cat to me."

"Leopards are big cats. And yes, he makes a purring-like noise. Only leopards bred in captivity and hand-raised purr."

She drove around the compound and turned east on a narrow road. He stared at the greenery around him. The crisp smells and budding trees were so different from what he'd left in South America. There he'd seen...

He shook his head. Damn. He didn't know what he'd seen there, only that it had been different. He forced himself to concentrate, but his mind refused to open and the mist only got thicker. He balled his hands into fists and tensed his muscles. He *had* to remember. He had to. If he didn't—

"Cort?" Faith spoke his name. He looked at her. She'd stopped the vehicle and put her hand out, as if she'd considered touching him but had thought better of the idea. "Are you all right?"

"I'm fine."

She held his gaze, then slowly, deliberately, placed her hand on his curled fingers. She worked against his fist, forcing him to relax. Her skin, rough calluses at the base of her fingers, smooth everywhere else, felt warm and alive.

"You'll remember," she said. "Give yourself a break."

In her casual clothes, with her hair pulled back in a sensible braid and her face devoid of makeup, she wasn't anyone he would look at twice. But there was a gentle set to her mouth and a fearless compassion in her eyes. He knew why the cats trusted her and allowed her to help them heal. He knew why Sparky purred for her. He wanted to lean close and taste her generous mouth. Sex had always been his way of getting lost. He smiled. She would be shocked at his actions. Not because she was inexperienced—she moved with the easy grace of a woman who knows and appreciates her body—but because she didn't see him as a man.

He hadn't realized it until now, but the clues had been there all along. The way she calmly excused his attack on her by comparing it with that of a wounded panther. Her impersonal dressing of his wounds, the instinctive way she stroked him now, soothing him with the healing touch of her hand.

He thought about pulling her close and showing her he was very much a man, with a man's needs, but he dismissed the idea as soon as it appeared. Sleeping with Faith would simply complicate their situation.

He pulled his hand away from hers and reached up to gently touch her cheek. She started at the slight contact. Her eyes widened with surprise, as if one of her cats had spoken her name. Then he opened the door and stepped out.

"What's this?" he asked, pointing at the tall, two-story house in front of them. The Victorian-style manor looked completely out of place in the middle of the forest.

Faith joined him. He leaned on the front of the Jeep, testing his bad leg. It didn't hurt too much, and so far hadn't started to bleed.

"Edwina used to live here. She loved the cats but didn't want to be too close to the compound. We call it the Big House."

"Who owns it now?"

For the first time, Faith looked uncomfortable. She stuffed her hands in her pockets. "She left it to me in her will. The foundation owns the way station and all the land except for one acre and this house."

He glanced from the building to Faith and back. "You mean you've stuck me on a cot in some back office and I could be sleeping here?"

She smiled. "Yeah. It has big bathrooms and everything. You're welcome to move in. Most of the rooms are empty, but a couple of the bedrooms are furnished."

He shook his head. "It's tempting, but I've got to stay near the cubs. Why aren't you living here?"

"I never really fit in." She stared at the Big House. "It will always be Edwina's place, not mine. I did live there with her, but when she passed away, I moved into the apartment behind the office. Much more my style."

"So what's this old place for?"

"Parties."

"You don't strike me as the party type."

"I'm not." Her shoulders slumped. "It's for fund-raising. We have gala events about three or four times a year. We bring out the tamer cats, serve fancy food and collect big checks."

"Don't sound so enthused."

"It's awful." She looked up at him. Her mouth pulled into a straight line. "Black tie, caterers. It takes tons of time, but it's necessary. We need the funding. I even have to give Sparky a bath."

"He must hate that."

"It's not fun for either of us." Her eyes widened. "You're making fun of me."

"How bad could it be, Faith? You make it sound worse than getting a tooth pulled."

"Fine. See how much you like it. I hope you brought a tux."

"What?" He glared at her.

"Oh, didn't I mention it? There's a fund-raiser next week."

He thought about the faulty gate and the fence that didn't run all the way around the property and the hundreds of ways a really determined individual could break into the compound. "No, you *didn't* mention it. You can forget about it."

"Sorry," she said blithely as she climbed back into the Jeep. "The invitations have already been mailed. It's too late to call the event off."

Cort glanced at the empty bottle and scribbled the amount of formula the cubs had eaten. From inside the cage the larger of the two, the male, tumbled with a knotted towel and growled as he wrestled his imaginary prey. Every few minutes he looked up to make sure Cort was still within sight. The female cub sat near the gate and mewed piteously every few seconds.

"I'm not going to hold you," Cort said, trying to ignore her. "I've spent the entire morning with you."

She was unimpressed. Her vivid blue eyes locked onto his. With big ears and clumsy puppy feet, the cubs were growing on him. In less than four days they'd figured out he was a soft touch and spent most of their time trying to manipulate him. She meowed again. When he didn't respond, she hung her head dejectedly and trembled.

Cort swore, opened the cage door and hauled her onto his lap. Instantly the cub cuddled next to his chest and began chewing on the rolled cuff of his shirt.

"You are the worst," he told her. She just gazed up at him. Cort rubbed her fur, scratching the spot that she loved best behind her ears. He glanced at his watch. "You're making me miss lunch."

She yawned, showing small white teeth that would grow large and deadly. Before she could trick him again, he placed her back in the cage next to her brother, latched the door closed and walked into the hall. She mewed once, then snuffled a few times and settled down to sleep.

Faith wasn't in her office, so he limped toward the compound. His wound was healing and he'd stopped using the crutches the day before. As he stepped out into the bright spring sunshine, a black shadow crossed his path.

Cort stared at the leopard. Although he'd grown comfortable with the tiger cubs, the sight of Sparky roaming free through the offices and outside always brought him up short.

The big cat made a coughing noise low in his chest and moved close enough to butt his head against Cort's thigh. Cort reached down and patted the animal. Sparky looked up. Wide, almond-shaped yellow eyes held his own. Behind the facade of domestication lurked the cold determination of a killer. As he stared down at the leopard, recognition flashed. He was like this predator: a creature who killed in the night, a creature without a soul.

The cat broke away suddenly, raced across the compound to the central play area and leapt onto the telephone poles planted in the raked earth. Except for the red collar around his neck, he looked like an escaped wild animal. The first jump put him almost halfway up the pole. Using his claws, he climbed to the top of the first pole, crouched and jumped to the cross beam six feet below. He landed perfectly in the center of the beam, then ran across it and up the pole on the opposite side. Black fur gleamed in the bright light. The pattern of his spots was barely visible. Cort walked haltingly around the perimeter of the play area, watching the beautiful cat. He leaned against the safety chain, taking the weight off his healing leg.

"Cort!"

He looked at Ken jogging toward him. "Did Faith warn you about the jaguars?" the young man asked as he approached.

Cort looked over his shoulder at the two flat-faced cats pacing and snarling in their cages. "She said not to get too near them."

"Good." Ken stopped in front of him. "They can fit their paws through the sides of the gate. You could get a nasty scratch."

"Or worse," Cort muttered, not liking how they were eyeing him. "When are they going back to the zoo?"

"Another couple of weeks. Then we'll be getting the tigers."

Cort studied Ken. The college student had been suspended from work until today. Cort remembered how he'd thought Faith had overreacted to the newspeople taking pictures of the cubs. Of course, four days ago he'd thought the "kittens" were the domesticated kind.

"Faith says you're in charge of security," Ken said.

"That's right."

"I saw the new gate and the fencing. So you work for the government? The CIA?"

"Not exactly." He started back toward the office building.

Ken fell into step beside him, matching his gait to Cort's slower limp. "You think there's going to be trouble?"

"You planning to cause any more?"

The kid flushed. With his big frame, beard and long hair he should have looked tough. Instead, he looked like a boy being reprimanded for stealing candy from a local store.

"I didn't mean for that to happen," he said glumly. "I'm really sorry. I would never deliberately put the cubs in danger."

"Then follow the rules and keep me informed of anything unusual you see. Strangers coming by, people asking questions, anything out of the ordinary."

"Okay. Anything happens, you'll be the first to know." Ken stopped and looked at him. "Thanks for letting me help." He offered Cort a quick smile. "I've got to finish cleaning the cages." He trotted off.

Cort watched him leave, then turned back toward the building. Had he ever been that young and enthusiastic? It had been so long, he couldn't remember. Ken was impressed by the new gate and a little fencing. Hell of a lot of good that would do against someone determined. They were all sitting ducks out here. In the past he wouldn't have doubted his ability to keep Faith and the cubs safe, but now— He shook his head. He wasn't so sure. In four days he hadn't remembered a damn thing about his last mission. What if he never remembered?

He walked a little faster, putting more weight on his healing leg. He tried lengthening his stride, but his calf muscle cramped and he almost went down. He stopped to rest for a second, then continued moving.

From the corner of his eye, he caught a flash of black flying through the air. Before he could prepare himself, something plowed into him, and he hit the ground. Instantly he was transported back in time.

The explosion nearly deafened him. Below him, the wooden floor of the warehouse shook with the impact. Dust billowed around, filling his lungs. He tried to cough, but he couldn't seem to draw in air. A burst of light split the night, illuminating the stacks of boxes. Where there should have been a wall, he could see through a gaping hole to the sea beyond.

He inhaled again and tasted the salty air. And something else—smoke. He tried to raise his head, but couldn't. Still he could feel the heat of the flames, hear the snapping as the fire began to consume the wood building. In the distance, men screamed out in agony. His head. He reached up to touch the bump on his forehead and felt instead a warm, wet tongue.

As quickly as it had begun, the flashback receded. Cort dug his fingers into the dirt of the compound as if he could hold on to the past, but it slipped through his fingers like sand. He gritted his teeth. He *had* been in an explosion. He'd been unable to move. Someone must have pulled him to safety. But who? And what the hell had happened to Dan?

Chapter 5

Faith was standing by Samson's cage when she saw Sparky leap up and Cort hit the ground face first. She dropped the buckets she'd been carrying and took off at a run. By the time she reached Cort's side, Sparky was licking his face and grunting nervously. She pushed the leopard out of the way.

"Cort?" she said, dropping down beside him. "Are you okay? Can you hear me?"

He groaned and shook his head. "What the hell…?"

"Sparky jumped you. I think it's because you're still limping. He probably thought you were playing."

"Great." He pushed as if to sit up.

"Don't move," she said, touching his arms and then his back. "Anything hurt?"

"I just got tackled by a three-hundred-pound leopard. Everything hurts."

"Don't try to get up."

"I'm not going to lay here and eat dirt."

She sat back on her heels. "You must be feeling all right if you can complain."

He rolled onto his back. Dust coated the front of his shirt and jeans. His hair hung over his forehead. "Thanks for the expert medical assessment."

She bit back a smile.

He raised himself up on one elbow and glared at her. "That cat is a menace."

"He's very sweet and he likes you."

Cort rubbed his head and shifted until he was sitting up, then brushed the grit from his hands. "I'd hate to see what he could do if he didn't like me."

She leaned forward and stared at his face. The cut on his chin had stayed closed and his eyes seemed clear. She bent over and ran her hands along his legs. She could feel his warmth through his thick jeans. As she touched him, his muscles rippled in response. She ignored the answering tightness in her stomach and concentrated on locating sudden swelling or lumps. Nothing out of the ordinary. Just long, lean legs.

"Everything seems in place," she said, not quite able to meet his gaze. "Does anything feel broken?"

He stretched out his legs and rotated his ankles. "Nope."

She glanced over her shoulder at Sparky. The leopard sat a short distance away. He looked like he expected to be punished. "You're going to have to tell him you're still friends," she said.

Cort rolled his shoulders. "Friends? Are you kidding? That cat could play pro football. As a defensive tackle. I bet a lot of teams would be interested. You could go for the big bucks."

He grinned at her. The midday sun caught the gold in his short hair. His flecked eyes glinted with amusement. Despite the dirt on his work shirt and jeans, he'd never looked more handsome. Her hands still tingled from their contact with his body. She didn't like knowing he affected her. It was easier when she thought of him as one of her patients, or simply as the guy Jeff had sent along to keep the cubs safe.

She got to her feet and held out her hand. When Cort took it in his, she braced herself and he pulled himself to his feet. She hated that she liked the feel of his fingers against hers. She hated it more that she didn't want him to let go. For a second they stood there, staring at each other. She wondered if he would pull her close and... The erotic visions that filled her head frightened her. Deliberately, she pulled free of the casual contact and stepped back.

Sparky approached her and butted her thigh. "I'm not the one you need to apologize to," she told the animal.

Cort glared down. "She's got that right, buddy."

Sparky looked at him and coughed.

Cort shook his head. "All right, Sparky. Come." He patted his leg. The black leopard stepped over to him and sniffed his arm. "I forgive you." He grabbed the collar and tugged on it until the leopard looked at him. "Just don't do it again."

Sparky twisted his head so Cort scratched his ears. Faith grinned. Cort looked up at her. She tried to smother her smile, but he saw it.

"What's so funny?" he asked, obviously annoyed at being observed making up with the cat.

"Nothing."

"I know Sparky's a wild animal. He was just reacting. I'm not a complete jerk. I wouldn't hold it against him."

"That's why I'm smiling."

Cort pushed the leopard away and started toward the main building. She walked beside him.

"I really understand," she said. "That's why I wasn't upset with you."

He stopped suddenly and stared at her. The emotion left

his face as he once again became a cool professional.
"What are you talking about?"

"The drive up here. In the truck. When you—"

"When I tried to kill you," he said bluntly, cutting her
off.

She ducked her head, sorry that she'd brought it up.
"Yes." She tossed her long hair over her shoulder and
stared up at him. "It was just like this. That's why I didn't
mind. You simply reacted."

If anything, her explanation made him grow more still
and distant. His mouth tightened into a straight line and all
the light faded from his eyes.

"There is a difference," he said slowly. "I am not one
of your cats. I am a man. I wasn't reacting; I tried to kill
you."

"Now you're trying to scare me." Unable to stare at the
emptiness in his eyes, she lowered her gaze. The right
sleeve of his shirt was torn and blood trickled down his
arm. "You're bleeding."

"I hit a rock on my way down."

She pulled open the tear. Dirt and tiny pebbles clung to
the gash. "Why didn't you say something? We've got to
get this clean and bandaged."

She hurried in front of him and held open the door to the
office building. He hesitated as if he wasn't going to accept
the change in subject or her offer of aid, then he followed
her into the examining room and sat on the metal table.

"You'll have to take off your shirt," she said as she
washed her hands. She dried them, then reached for the
antiseptic. After pulling a gauze bandage and tape from the
drawer under the counter, she turned toward the table.

He'd done as she asked and removed his shirt. She stared
at his broad, bare back. Despite his lean build, muscles rippled with each movement. The tanned skin looked warm

and inviting and she curled her fingers around her supplies to keep from reaching out to him. Her throat tightened.

It had been a long time since she'd been with a man. Even longer since she'd allowed herself to care about one. She let herself get lost in the day-to-day cycle of dealing with the cats and never thought about her owns needs. It was easier that way. She couldn't get hurt. But sometimes the loneliness overwhelmed her and she ached for all she'd given up.

Faith drew in a deep breath and walked over to the metal table. The hair on Cort's chest was slightly darker than that on his head. She forced herself to look no higher than his throat. She didn't want him to figure out what she was thinking. A man like him would never be interested in a woman like her. He was wild and untamed, like her cats. Forgetting that would be as dangerous as walking into a wounded panther's cage.

"This shouldn't sting," she said, sliding a towel under the wound and flushing it with the cleaner. "Even Sparky doesn't flinch and, at heart, he's a baby." The liquid washed away the dirt and pebbles. When the wound was clean, she reached for the antiseptic.

As she uncapped the bottle, the smell of alcohol filled her nostrils. But it wasn't enough to erase the musky scent of the man. Even without trying she could see the bare, broad expanse of his chest. As she worked, she almost brushed against him. She wanted to. Desperately. Between her thighs a hot ache came painfully to life.

"This one *will* hurt," she said, damping a wad of cotton with the antiseptic. "But it's the best I have." She held his arm in one hand and ignored the warm feel of his skin and hard muscles just below the surface. Ignored how touching him made her want to be touched. "Deep breath. Now." She pressed the treated cotton against him. He tensed once, then relaxed.

She set the cotton down and picked up the bandage. As she began to peel back the covering, Cort reached out and gripped her wrists. He pulled her until she stood between his spread knees.

"Look at me," he growled.

She licked her lower lip, then slowly did as he asked. Past the waistband of his jeans, past his flat stomach, the hair of his chest. Past his broad shoulders to the cut on his chin and the faint shadow of stubble darkening his jaw. Past his straight nose to his oddly flecked brown eyes.

Something hot flared to life there. She wanted to respond, but she was afraid. He held her forearms tightly and shook her.

"I am not one of your cats," he said.

"I know."

"I don't think you do."

"Why does it matter?" she asked desperately.

"What are you hiding from?"

Part of her noted he hadn't answered her question, so she wouldn't answer his. She knew exactly what she was hiding from. Him. Pretending he was just like one of the cats made him safe. It was dangerous to think of him as a man, because he tempted her. He made her think of family and forever, and she'd learned long ago she didn't have what it took to inspire a man to want either.

His grip on her loosened, and she jerked away. She thrust the bandage at him. "Here. Finish it yourself." Then she fled the room.

William Thomas paused outside the news reporter's dressing room. On the drive over to the TV station, he'd planned several different ways to approach the man and get the information he needed, but he had dismissed them all. It would have been easiest to simply pull out his gun and demand he tell him everything. But if he didn't waste the reporter afterward, the jerk was likely to blab the entire incident to someone, and then Thomas's advantage of surprise would be lost. No, he would have to come up with a plausible story. He adjusted his jacket to make sure his gun was concealed then knocked once on the door.

"Come in," the reporter called from inside.

Thomas took a deep breath and forced himself to smile. "James, my man. How's it going?" he said as he pushed open the door. "It's been a long time." He walked forward confidently and held out his hand.

The handsome reporter stared at him. Instinctively James Wilson took the offered hand and shook it, then frowned. "I'm sorry, I don't remember meeting you."

Of course not, you little twit, Thomas thought. We've never met.

"Harry Williams," William Thomas lied. "Work for the *Times*. We covered that big scandal downtown together."

Keep it vague enough and they'll believe, Thomas reminded himself. People are basically stupid and trusting. If you say you know them, they'll do their best to remember you. Thomas was banking on the fact that in Los Angeles "downtown" could mean anywhere from the West Side to East L.A., and that a scandal could have occurred in city politics, at one of the big universities, or in the movie business. Surely James had covered at least one story like that.

"Of course," James said suddenly, his brow clearing. "The bribery case."

"Bingo," Thomas said jovially. "Been meaning to look you up. We were supposed to grab a drink some night, but hey, you know how that is."

"Sure," James said, eyeing Thomas's cheap sports coat. "I'm afraid I'm working the four o'clock news so I can't—"

Thomas gave a hearty laugh. "That's not why I stopped by." The laughter turned genuine when he saw James's look of relief. He knew the newsman's type. The big dressing room with a long vanity and a closet full of suits didn't hide the truth. James might like expensive clothes, whiskey and women, but underneath, he was a wimp. Wouldn't last a day on the streets. "I saw that piece you did on the tiger cubs."

"What a disaster that day was." James shuddered and turned back to the mirror. "The woman in charge is crazy."

Thomas pulled a notepad out of his pocket and pretended to consult it, even though he'd had the information memorized for three days. He'd wanted to come to Los Angeles and confront the reporter as soon as he'd heard about the newscast, but James had been in Sacramento covering some hearing.

"Faith Newlin," he said.

"That's her." James looked at him in the mirror. "Are you doing a story on the way station?"

"Kicking it around. Probably for the Sunday magazine."

James shook his head. "Don't bother talking to that woman. Do you know she threatened to shoot me?"

Thomas clucked with artificial concern. To be perfectly honest, he didn't blame the woman one bit. He wouldn't mind shooting the yuppie reporter himself.

"I checked with the station's attorney." James picked up a brush and smoothed his perfect hair. "I wanted to sue her for distress, but they said that since there hadn't been any actual damage, it might not look good for the network."

"But you got a great story."

James grinned. "Pets and kids get 'em every time. I don't usually like either, but those tiger cubs were something else. Still...that woman." He shook his head. "I won't be going back there again."

"She's up north, isn't she?" he asked casually, as if he really knew but couldn't remember. He'd checked up on the foundation that supported the way station to get an address, but all they listed were a post-office box and some attorney's office in L.A.

"Outside of Bowmund." James grimaced. "Are you sure you want to do this, Harry? She's dangerous."

"I'm sure." It was find the cubs or die. Not much of a choice.

James looked through the clutter of papers on the vanity. "I've got the address here, somewhere. They're having their annual fund-raiser at the end of the week. The station was going to send me back, but I told them that woman doesn't deserve the free publicity." He pawed through a stack of invitations until he found what he was looking for. "Here it is." He read off the address, then tossed the invitation into the trash.

Thomas thanked him. James glanced at his watch. "Look, it's almost time for the broadcast. I'd love to talk some more, but—"

"No problem," Thomas said, pocketing his small notebook. "Thanks for the information. I appreciate it. I'll give you a call in a couple of weeks and we'll get that drink."

"Sure." James stood up and the two men shook hands.

Thomas left and quickly walked down the hallway. He ducked into a supply closet and closed the door behind him. The news sound stage was on the other side of the wall. He could hear the crew getting ready for the live broadcast, then the call for silence. The broadcast began. Several minutes later, he heard James's voice droning on about some bill up for passage in Sacramento. He cracked the door to make sure the hallway was empty, then walked purposefully toward James's dressing room.

The invitation lay where the reporter had tossed it, right in the white plastic trash container. Thomas pulled it out and pocketed it. Five minutes later he pulled onto Prospect Avenue and into the rush-hour traffic. He'd been worried about having to sneak in and steal the cubs in the dead of night. Luck was on his side. With a big party at the way station, he could walk in with the other guests and take the cubs without anyone being the wiser.

After feeding the cubs and settling them down for their afternoon nap, Cort wandered toward Faith's office. She'd pleaded too much work as a reason for avoiding him at lunch, but he knew it was something more than that. He flexed his arm and felt the bandage move with his skin. Something had happened when she'd tended his cut. In a flash of temper, he'd forced her to acknowledge he wasn't just one of her cats. He paused at the entrance to her office and shook his head. It came from thinking with the wrong part of his anatomy, and from living in close quarters with a woman who turned him on.

She sat at her desk, with her head bent. She wrote furiously on the papers in front of her. Afternoon sunlight filtered through the window. The overhead fluorescent glared harshly on her. Often she wore her hair in a braid, but today a headband held it away from her face. A single, shiny strand slipped over her shoulder and onto the page. She brushed it away impatiently.

The scent of Sparky's mint, the smell of furniture oil and the whispered fragrance of French perfume mingled together. In the compound, cats paced restlessly and called to one another, but here there was only quiet. Faith was a woman, he was a man, and they were alone. It was tempting to think about touching her and tasting her. Tempting to wonder what she would feel like next to him, under him.

But would she be tempted? And why did he care? He was here to get a job done. She would be a complication he didn't need, a temptation he had no time for. He was reacting to circumstances, not the woman, and he sure better not forget that.

This arrangement of theirs got to him. Their domesticity

was as foreign to him as the jungles of South America would be to her. It was different from his normal life. He allowed himself a small smile. Who was he kidding? He had no normal life.

"How's it going?" he asked.

She jumped in the chair. Her pencil went flying, and she looked up at him. "How do you *do* that?" she asked. She leaned forward and stared down. "You're wearing boots. I can't believe you snuck up on me."

"I wasn't sneaking." He moved into the room and took the chair in front of her desk.

She shuffled her papers together and tried not to look at him. He knew she was trying hard, because she kept glancing at him out of the corner of her eye and then looking disgusted with herself. He liked that he got to her.

"Are the cubs fed?" she asked.

"Both Big and Little tiger are sleeping soundly."

"Big and Little? Is that what you're calling them?"

"Yeah. What do you think?"

She grinned. "It's kind of basic, but it works. Having any trouble with the forms?"

"Nope." He motioned to the papers scattered on her desk. "What about you?"

She bent down and retrieved her pencil from the floor. "Don't even ask. It's a nightmare. Every government agency has its own rules. You have to document the documentation." She leaned back in her wooden chair and stretched her arms above her head. Her back arched and her shirt drew taut across her body.

The unobstructed view of her generous curves reminded him of his original premise that rooming with Faith Newlin wasn't going to be tough duty. The unconscious grace in her movements made him wonder what else she did gracefully and well. To distract himself, he looked around the office. Like the rest of the building, it needed a coat of paint.

"You don't spend a lot of money on decorating, do you?" he asked.

"The cats are my first priority."

"I guess." Pictures of the animals hung on all the walls. He glanced at a pair of photographs in dark wood frames. "Are those the snow leopards?"

She swiveled around until she could see them. "Yes. They're a breeding pair."

He got up and stepped over to the wall. "Looks like the pictures were taken from a long way off."

"A plane." Faith rose and stood next to him. Her arm brushed his. He pretended not to notice. "These two were illegally brought into the country. I don't know if it was for a private collection or what, but they escaped and were captured by animal-control people." She picked up the smaller of the two frames. "They brought the cats here and I looked after them." She glanced up and smiled. "They were so beautiful and wild."

He stared down at her blue eyes, at her faint dusting of freckles and the generous curve of her mouth. Not beautiful, he thought, but intelligent and warm and attractive enough that conventional beauty didn't matter. It occurred to him that he could get to like her. He didn't have many friends in his life; it was too dangerous. The weight of relationships slowed him down. But in another time and place, he wouldn't have minded getting to know her.

"How long were they here?" he asked.

"About four months. We healed them, fattened them back up. The hardest part was making sure not to domesticate them." She placed the photo back on the wall. "They were flown back to Asia and released in the wild. These pictures were taken about a year ago. They're both still alive."

He placed his hand on her shoulder. Her blue eyes widened slightly, but she didn't step away. If anything, she

seemed to sway toward him. He told himself he was fourteen different kinds of fool, but he didn't care. "You must
be very proud of yourself."

"I am. I'm glad they survived."

Her bones felt delicate. He knew she was strong and re-
silient, yet there was a fragility about her that intrigued him.
He also knew she'd probably drop-kick him if he ever said
that thought aloud. He gave her a brief squeeze and stepped
back.

"Is that why you want to start a snow-leopard breeding
program?" he asked.

She nodded slowly, as if trying to remember what they
were talking about. "There are so few of them left. Without
adding to the wild population, they're going to disappear
altogether. Just three or four breeding pairs would greatly
increase the gene pool. When I found out these two made
it, I bought some land to start my own breeding center. Now
I just have to worry about all the paperwork, getting the
foundation up and running, finding donors."

He perched on the corner of her desk and took the weight
off his healing leg. "What will happen here if you leave to
start your snow-leopard program?"

"Several zoos have approached me about buying the
place. They would use it for an isolation facility, either for
quarantined animals, or for breeding the more endangered
species."

"Sounds like you've got it all figured out."

"Maybe." She leaned over and picked up the forms.
"I'm just not sure I can pull this off. I would have to run
the new foundation and I don't have a lot of business experience. I'm not sure I could get funding. I have this picture of slowly starving to death our first winter."

"At least the snow leopards would keep you warm."

"Yeah, they are furry little creatures, aren't they? Oh

well, I'll deal with that problem later. Right now I have a benefit to plan.''

He folded his arms over his chest. ''I'm not happy about this.''

She wrinkled her nose. ''Fortunately, your being happy isn't a priority.''

''Gee, thanks.'' With him sitting on the desk, they were almost at eye level. She was one tough lady. ''Did you put a call in to Jeff?''

''Earlier today. I'm expecting him to return it shortly.'' She glanced at her watch. ''In another hour or so.''

''We're going to need extra security for the party,'' he said. ''I want to talk to him about that. I've already sent the guest list through the computer. Everyone is clean. You do realize that reporter you scared off is invited.''

''I know,'' she said. ''I don't think he'll show up. Do you?''

''Highly unlikely. Are there any changes?''

''A couple. I'm expecting more.'' She bent over and pulled open a desk drawer. She drew out a folder and handed it to him. ''Some of the invitations say 'and guest,' so we don't have all the names. They're supposed to call and let us know how many are coming, but they don't always. Also, here are the names of the caterer's employees, and the guys who'll be parking cars. But these haven't been finalized, either.''

He opened the folder and scanned the typed sheets. ''Are you trying to make my job harder, or is this a natural trait?''

''I guess you're just lucky.'' She leaned over and looked at the bandage partially visible under the T-shirt he'd changed into. ''How do you feel?''

''Sore. I haven't checked in the mirror, but I think I have paw-shaped bruises on my back.''

She chuckled. ''I'll bet. I'm heading up to the Big House. The bathrooms there have tubs. I'm going to take a bath.

You're welcome to join me.'' As soon as the words came out of her mouth, she blushed scarlet and stared at the ground. ''That's not exactly what I meant,'' she stammered.

''Too bad.'' Her invitation conjured up a vivid picture of a delightfully naked Faith Newlin soaking in a tub of water.

She risked a quick glance, then busied herself with straightening the papers on her desk blotter. ''The guest room has a Jacuzzi tub. It might help with any stiffness.''

''Thanks.''

''If you want to go get a change of clothing, I'll meet you by the garage in a couple of minutes.'' She fled the room without waiting for his agreement.

Cort rose and trailed after her. He could use a good soak to ease the tightness from his muscles. More than that, he wanted to talk to his boss. The missing pieces from his memory were gradually being filled in. Jeff might be persuaded to give him a couple more. He had to learn the truth. If he didn't, he couldn't go back. And he had to go back. Fighting in the trenches was all he knew.

Chapter 6

Faith shifted her tote bag over one shoulder and bent down to pull the roast out of the refrigerator. After collecting a few potatoes and some vegetables, she put them all in a plastic bag and dropped them in the tote.

No doubt Cort was waiting for her by the Jeep. She should go face him and get it over with. But just thinking about what she'd said was enough to send heat flaring on her cheeks.

You're welcome to join me. Oh! She wanted to scream. How could she have blurted that out? She hadn't been thinking anything remotely sexual. She sighed and made her way down the hall. She'd never been a good liar, especially to herself. She *had* been thinking about how handsome Cort was, and how he seemed to fill her office, but she certainly hadn't been thinking about having a bath with him. Still, it was an intriguing thought. She wasn't a virgin; she knew what went on between a woman and a man.

As she entered the foyer, she instinctively glanced out at

the compound. Ken and Sparky were playing tug-of-war with Sparky's favorite blanket. Sparky was winning. She pushed open the door.

"Ken?" she called.

He looked up. Sparky took advantage of the distraction, jerking his powerful head once and pulling the blanket free. Ken promptly sat down on his butt.

"That's cheating," he yelled at the victorious cat. He stood up and brushed off his pants. "Yes?"

"Cort and I are going up to the Big House. Please feed the cubs before you leave and make sure everything is locked up."

"No problem." He tossed her a grin, then started after the cat. "Come back here. I demand a rematch." Sparky sprinted up one of the telephone poles and looked down at him.

Faith closed the door and stepped out the front. Cort was leaning against the Jeep. His black T-shirt emphasized his blond good looks and her heart started making a funny thumping against her ribs.

"Thought you'd changed your mind," he said, stepping forward to take her bag.

"Just giving Ken instructions. He'll take care of the cubs' next feeding."

Cort lifted the tote from her shoulder and looked surprised when he felt the weight of the bag. "What do you have in here?"

"Dinner." She climbed into the vehicle. "I have to count glasses and plates, see what we have before I call the caterer. I thought I'd cook a roast while I was there. The oven at the Big House is better, and I can keep an eye on it while I work."

He settled in beside her and peered in the bag. "How do I know you're not feeding me tiger or leopard food?"

"You'll just have to trust me."

"Not something I do easily."

She believed him. Jeff never talked much about his work, but the few times he'd opened up to her, she'd been appalled by the horrors he'd seen. Cort would have shared those experiences. She didn't understand these warriors who risked their lives and fought ever-changing enemies.

"Lucky for you the meat is still in the store wrapper. You can read the label yourself."

"I'll risk it," he said.

When they reached the Big House, Faith parked in front. She pulled the keys from her jeans pocket and unlocked the front door.

"It's always a little musty," she said. "The cleaners come two days before the party and air the whole thing out. The caterers arrive the next day and then the guests."

He stepped into the house and gave a low whistle. "This is some place."

She glanced around at the familiar high ceilings and papered walls. "Let me get the roast going, and I'll show you around."

In the kitchen, she turned on the oven and prepared the meat. After she slid the pan in the oven, she turned to Cort. "We can cook for about a hundred with this kitchen."

He stared at the two large stoves, the extrawide triple sink and the subzero refrigerator. A butcher-block island stood in the center.

"All the party dishes are stored in there," she said, pointing to the pantry on the right. "Through here is the dining room." She led the way.

The rooms were large. Hardwood floors gleamed despite a layer of dust. The wallpaper was subdued and elegant, with a cream-and-rose print. Small couches had been pushed up against the walls and covered with sheets. Chairs stood in tall stacks in all the corners. Round tables had been pushed together in front of the big stone fireplace. Velvet drapes covered the tall windows, rich brocade trimmed the valances.

"We use the downstairs for our fund-raisers. We have conversational areas in these two parlors, then set up a buffet here in the dining room. There's a study over there." She pointed to closed double doors. "That's where we hold the petting zoo."

Cort glanced at her and raised his eyebrows. "Something tells me you don't bring in lambs and baby goats."

She shook her head. "The friendliest of the cats. Samson, that bobcat in the last habitat. He loves the attention. His being declawed is a real plus. There are a couple of panthers that like people, and of course, Sparky."

"Sparky ever take one of your guests down?" he asked.

"No. I told you, it means he likes you."

He rubbed the cut on his arms. "If anyone gets out of hand, we'll just tell him to go long and let Sparky tackle him."

Faith grinned. "I'll keep that in mind." She shifted the tote bag to her other shoulder and started up the stairs. "The house was built in the early part of the century. Edwina's grandfather made his fortune in lumber and construction."

"It's a beautiful place. I'm surprised you don't want to live here."

"It's expensive to keep the house heated. With the weather mild, it's fine, but in the winter, this place is drafty and cold." At the top of the stairs, she paused. "Edwina's suite of rooms is over there." She pointed at the closed door. "It's empty now. After she was gone it seemed easier to move to the way station and live in the apartment. We save a lot of money on utilities, and I'm closer to the cats."

He moved past her to the glass case lining part of the long dark hallway. "What's this?" he asked, pointing at the many ribbons and trophies.

She switched on the overhead light and stepped next to him. "My secret life."

He opened the cabinet and pulled out one of the statues. "You're a sharpshooter?"

"One of my many talents." She smiled.

His brown eyes flickered over her face. "Jeff didn't tell me."

"I'm not sure he knows."

He put the trophy back. "You ever shoot at anything other than targets?"

"If I have to."

He didn't return her smile. "If someone shows up to take the cubs, are you prepared to defend them?"

She bit her lower lip. He was asking if she could kill a man. She thought about the white tiger cubs, sleeping peacefully in their cage. And the snow leopards that had been illegally smuggled into the country, then mistreated.

She nodded slowly. "I would do my best."

He held her gaze. "Can't ask for more than that."

They were standing close together. She wasn't sure why she hadn't noticed before, but suddenly she was aware of his arm only inches from her breasts and the way his scent drifted to her. The empty house was a welcome sanctuary from her pressures at the compound. She knew she would never enter here again without remembering how Cort looked standing next to her.

She stepped back to break the spell. "The guest room is through here," she said, walking around him and pushing open a door. A king-size bed stood against one wall. A rich mahogany dresser and armoire matched the headboard. She pulled a towel out of her tote bag and tossed it to him. "The tub is in the bathroom, over there." She pointed to a half-open door. "I think it's big enough to swim in."

He looked around. "There's no phone."

"I know. I have one in my room, and there's another

downstairs. They're extensions of the main number at the way station, so we won't miss Jeff's call.''

He dropped the towel on the bed and looked around. "It's a great old place.''

"You're welcome to sleep here, if you want.''

"No, Faith.'' He placed his hands on his hips and stared at her. "I take my responsibilities just as seriously as you do.''

Faith leaned back in the tub and sighed. Hot water lapped around her shoulders. The scented bubbles teased her nose. Soft music from her portable radio filled the bathroom. This was her idea of heaven. The tension in her back eased, and she closed her eyes. She had a thousand details to worry about with the upcoming fund-raiser. She should be planning the menu or worrying about decorations, but she didn't care. Right now she didn't want to think about anything.

Her eyes drifted shut. The music swept over and through her, carrying her along on the sweet melody. She moved lower in the tub, until the water crept up the back of her neck. Warm, she thought. It reminded her of Cort's hand on her shoulder, and the feel of his body so close to hers. The brief contact had shaken her to her toes. She'd tried not to let him know how he affected her.

It was just because she lived out in the sticks and had limited her contact with men, she told herself. It wasn't anything to do with that man specifically. He wasn't interested in her, and she wasn't interested in him.

She hummed with the song on the radio and thought about how his bare chest had looked that morning when she'd dressed his cut. Broad and strong and tanned. She'd wanted to touch him, had thought about running her fingers along his ribs and—

She sat up suddenly, ignoring the water sloshing over the side of the tub. Cold air stung her wet torso. She had it bad for Cort. Faith drew her knees up and hugged them. There wasn't anything she could do about it, either, except pretend this—this attraction or whatever she wanted to call it—didn't exist.

She stepped out of the tub and grabbed a towel. As she dried off, she forced herself to think about the upcoming party and the tiger cubs. She walked naked into the bedroom, ignoring her reflection in the mirror over the dresser.

The entire room made her uncomfortable. From the pale cream carpeting to the lacy bedspread and frilly drapes, this was a feminine room. Edwina had decorated it for her when she'd first come to live with the older woman. It had been her welcoming present. Faith had never had the heart to tell her friend that ruffles and lace made her feel awkward and out of place.

She picked up the clean undergarments she'd brought with her and slipped into the panties. Sensible cotton. She fingered the plain white bra. No silk for her. As she fastened the front closure, she sighed. What was the point? The cats hardly cared what she wore. It didn't make sense to spend extra money on lingerie no one but her was going to see.

She glanced at the fresh clothes she'd brought, then walked over to the closet and pulled open the door. A dozen outfits hung on the rack. There was room for four times that many. On the floor sat three shoe boxes. The top shelf contained a bag of stockings.

These were her fancy clothes. The things she wore to the fund-raisers. They were part of a life that wasn't real to her. She fingered the midnight-blue velvet of a long dress. She became someone else when she wore these clothes. Rich men spoke to her, but their eyes dipped to her breasts. Wealthy matrons assumed she was one of them and whispered confidentially about the best caterers and florists. Wives squealed at the beauty of the cats and conveniently forgot about the fur coats they had waiting in the cloakroom. Husbands cornered her to find out if she was adverse to having a brief but torrid affair.

Faith shook her head and closed the door. They weren't all like that, she reminded herself. Many of the people came because they genuinely cared about the cats. But the foundation required money to keep it going, and that meant she had to play her role.

She picked up the clean jeans and knit top she'd brought with her. Sometimes she wanted to be more than she was. Not the woman in the velvet dress, not the competent genderless caretaker, but someone in between. A woman who wore pretty things from time to time. She slipped into her jeans. That wasn't true, she admitted. It wasn't about wearing pretty dresses and shoes; it was about fitting in. Just once, she wanted to be like other people who seemed so naturally to join up, two by two. She wasn't like that. She could give her love away, but it was never returned. She'd never been enough. She'd learned it was safer to give it all to the cats. At least they needed her.

She slipped the white knit top over her head, then pulled out a brush. After taking the pins out of her hair, she let it fall down her back and began brushing out the tangles. She'd just finished securing her French braid when the phone on the nightstand rang.

She picked it up. ''Hello.''

''Tell me there's no crisis,'' Jeff said.

She laughed. ''Why do you always assume the worst?''

''It's my job, Faith. How are you?''

He sounded weary, she thought, wishing he were here for her to talk to. Although what would she say? There were some things even Jeff wouldn't understand. She had a feeling that her attraction to one of his operatives fell in that category.

She quickly brought him up-to-date on the cubs and the security measures Cort had already installed.

"He wants to talk to you," she said.

"About what?"

"I'm not privy to that information," she said, then chuckled. "But he did want me to mention that the foundation is having a fund-raiser at the end of the week. We're expecting about a hundred and twenty guests. I think he wants some extra people for that."

She held the receiver away from her ear and listened to him squawk. At regular intervals she brought the mouthpiece closer and said his name. About the fourth time she did it, he got quiet.

"I absolutely forbid it," he growled.

"I didn't ask permission."

"Faith, those cubs are important. I don't want anything happening to them."

"I understand that, but you dumped them on me with no warning. I'm happy to keep them for you. However, this party has been planned for months. Unless you're prepared to offer me a half-million dollars, which is about what we'll be raising, I can't stop it now."

He didn't say anything.

"I'll go get Cort," she said.

Jeff sighed. "Fine."

She set the phone on the bed and crossed the hall to the guest room. After knocking on the door, she waited. He didn't answer, so she knocked again.

"Cort, Jeff is on the phone."

Could he have fallen asleep in the bath? She knocked a third time, then pushed the door open. As she entered the room, the bathroom door opened and Cort stepped into the bedroom.

He stood before her, naked. More beautiful than any of the wild cats in the compound. The soft lamplight made his tanned skin glow. Long, lean muscles covered his strong frame. Despite the bandage on his calf, he was the perfect specimen of a man.

He held a towel over one shoulder. A single drop of moisture dripped from his neck onto his chest and got lost in the matting of hair. Her fingers curled into her palms. She looked at his tapered waist and narrow hips, then at the wide thatch of blond hair surrounding the partially erect proof of his gender. Below that, long legs stretched down endlessly.

She thought of how incredible he would look moving through sunlight, each muscle bunching and releasing with powerful male energy. She could see the coiled strength just below his skin. Her gaze trailed up his body. So stunning. He took her breath away.

He pulled the towel down and let it hang from his hand. The movement startled her. She looked at his face. In a single heartbeat, everything changed. As she met his gaze, she knew he wasn't like the wild cats she so loved. He was a man, and she wanted him.

Sexual need snapped between them like the crack of a whip. She swallowed against the tightening of her throat. Her breasts swelled as her nipples poked against her bra. Between her legs, moisture dampened her sensible cotton panties. She watched an answering interest stir Cort's body, lengthening his maleness. She took a single step toward him.

He smiled. A very knowing, very satisfied male smile. Reality crashed in around her. She had been staring at him, practically begging him to touch and take her. Embarrassment flooded her, and with it horror that she had completely lost control.

"Jeff is on the phone," she blurted out, then turned and ran out of the room.

Cort started after her. He'd seen the humiliation in her eyes. "Faith, wait."

But she was already halfway down the stairs. He paused,

torn between duty and desire, then cursed and made his way across the hall to her room and the phone.

"What?" he barked into the receiver.

"Took you long enough," Jeff drawled. "What the hell have you been doing?"

Cort sat on the edge of the bed and ran his hand through his damp hair. It was all bad timing. But the look on her face...how was he supposed to resist that? Had any woman ever looked at him with such appreciation and raw desire?

"Cort, are you listening?"

"No. What did you say?"

"Tell me about this party."

Cort explained about the fund-raiser. He forced himself to ignore what had happened with Faith and concentrate on the business at hand. "I want you to send me a team. I've already faxed the guest list to your office. To date, everyone has been cleared."

"I'll take care of it." Cort heard the scratching of Jeff's pen, then his boss said, "How's everything else going?"

"I've got most of the security measures already installed. It's been quiet. No one's made any kind of move."

"They might use the party as a cover."

"I've already thought of that. I'm going to make sure the cubs are well guarded." He ran through the list of other precautions he'd taken. "Could you rent me a tux? This affair of Faith's is formal."

Jeff laughed. "Don't want the hired help standing out. We're about the same size. I'll send up mine."

"You own a tux?"

"Comes with the job, buddy."

Cort grimaced. "You should never have gone inside, Jeff. You gave up all the action."

His boss was silent for a minute. "I couldn't do it anymore. Not after what happened to Jeanne and my son, J.J."

"I know." Cort felt like a heel. He'd spoken without thinking.

"You could do worse," Jeff said. "The field gets old."

"Sit behind a desk?" Cort switched the receiver to his other hand. "I'd rather be shot at dawn. I want to be out there, face-to-face with the bad guys."

"Let me know when you change your mind. You're up for a promotion."

It was a familiar argument. Jeff offered him a promotion and a raise. The only problem was, Cort had to come in from the field to get it. Not him. He wanted to be where he could see the action. Great battles were never fought behind desks.

"Anything else?" Jeff asked.

Cort drew in a deep breath. He had to know and Jeff was the only one he trusted to speak the truth. "Did Dan die in the explosion?"

Silence.

"I know about the warehouse going up in flames. I remember being there, but that's all." Cort waited, but Jeff didn't answer. "Tell me, dammit. I know I went down there to be with Dan. He was my friend. I have the right to know what happened to him." He realized he was squeezing the receiver tight enough to crack the plastic, and he forced himself to relax his grip. "Did I kill him?"

"It really matters to you, doesn't it?" Jeff asked.

"Yes."

"You didn't kill him."

Cort slumped forward and rested his elbows on his knees. "Thanks."

Before he could ask anything else, he heard Jeff shuffling papers. "I'm glad you're getting better," he said. "How's Faith?"

Cort thought about the look on her face when she'd stared at his naked body. The desire there had him responding instantly. Then she'd become aware of herself, of the situation, and she'd run off.

"She's fine," he said.

"The way your memory is returning, you should be ready to come back to work as soon as the problem with the tiger cubs is taken care of."

"Looks that way," Cort answered, hoping he was right.

"Think about the promotion," Jeff said. "You would be surprised what a difference you can make from the inside."

"It's not for me."

"The offer stands. Take care of yourself and Faith, buddy. I'll be in touch." He hung up the phone.

Cort replaced the receiver. Relief overwhelmed him. He hadn't killed Dan. Thank God. He leaned back on the bed and stared up at the ceiling. How would he have handled that? He'd killed before. In his line of work, that couldn't be helped. But it had always been a simple decision. The bad guys had been the ones shooting at him. But Dan? Cort sat up and rubbed his jaw. This is why he didn't like relationships. Entanglements complicated everything.

Would he have done it? If Jeff had told him to kill Dan because he'd gone over to the other side, could Cort have iced his friend? He thought for a moment, then nodded. He was a damn good operative. He followed orders. So what the hell kind of human being did that make him?

He didn't like the question, so he rose to his feet and walked back to the guest room. No answers awaited him there. He wanted— He paced restlessly. He wanted to talk about it.

The need startled him. He'd never been the kind to share his troubles. But everything blurred together. Dan. The parts of the mission he could remember. What he couldn't remember. What the death of his friend meant. Why, given the order, he would have been able to pull the trigger.

He suddenly remembered Jeff hadn't answered the question about whether or not Dan died in the explosion.

"Tricky devil," Cort muttered. And wondered what Faith would make of the whole thing. She—

He cursed. He'd completely forgotten how she'd run out on him. He started out of the room. Realizing he was still wrapped in a towel, he pulled the ends tight around his waist and hurried down the stairs.

He found her in the pantry off the kitchen, surrounded by the caterer's menu and cupboards full of dishes and glassware. She sat on a high stool, a clipboard rested on her knees. The setting sun shone through a window, backlighting her delicate profile.

She didn't notice him. He leaned against the doorframe and studied the way her nose tilted up slightly at the end, how she moved her lips when she counted. A pulse fluttered at the base of her throat. She wore a clinging white top, tucked into the waistband of stone-washed jeans. With her hair pulled back in one of her fancy braids, there was nothing to obstruct his view of her torso. As she raised her arm to push some wineglasses aside, he saw the curve of her breast. The size and shape looked to be a perfect fit for his palm.

"Faith."

She jumped at the sound of his voice and spun on the stool to face him. Color flooded her face. She raised the clipboard in front of her chest, like a barrier. Her gaze avoided his.

"Dinner will be another hour," she said softly. "I just put the potatoes in to bake. I have to count the dishes, but you're welcome to use the TV in the study, or whatever you want."

"Faith," he said again.

She still didn't look at him. He walked forward and

placed one finger beneath her chin. Slowly, he pressed until she was looking up. Embarrassment clouded her blue eyes.

He hated seeing her like this. It was fine to make her squirm when *he* teased her. He liked the flush of color that stained her cheeks when he winked, or she accidentally said something suggestive like her invitation to join him in her bath. But not this bone-numbing humiliation. Not for her. She was strong and capable. That's how he wanted—no, needed—her to be.

"I would have looked," he said.

Instead of smiling, she jerked her chin free and turned her head away.

"You're an attractive woman. Why wouldn't I have looked?"

"Just leave me alone. I'm fine."

He didn't believe her. She would retreat inside herself, and he would miss the—he tightened his jaw, but dammit, he couldn't hide from the truth—the friend she'd become. He didn't have many friends. Only Dan and Jeff. Dan was dead and Cort didn't know why or how. He grabbed her shoulders. The clipboard clattered to the floor. She stared up at him.

"You are a stubborn woman," he said.

Her lips quivered slightly. It was almost a smile. "I know."

"Don't be embarrassed. I liked you looking at me."

Fresh color crept into her cheeks. She tried to twist away, but he held her shoulders tightly and she couldn't slip off the stool.

"Don't," he said, and bent down to kiss her.

He'd only meant to reassure her. But at the contact of her mouth against his, he realized he'd made a tactical error. She was soft, too soft, and the feel of it made him hard.

Hunger swept through him. He wanted to tell himself it was all about the amount of time that had passed since he'd last made love to a woman. Any woman would scratch the itch. But he wasn't thinking about any woman. He was thinking about Faith. He squeezed her shoulders and she sighed.

He brushed her lips once, then twice, and raised his head. Wide blue eyes stared into his. She looked as shocked and stunned as he felt. If he had a lick of sense he would back off now and make a strategic retreat. A cold shower would go a long way to stopping this before it started.

"Cort?" she whispered, and he was lost.

He moved close to her, pushing her legs apart so that he could step between them. He brought his arms around her and hauled her against his bare chest. Her breasts flattened against him. Her hands touched his back. Her tentative stroking on his skin contrasted with her normal competence at everything else, and he groaned.

Before she could withdraw or protest or change her mind, he bent down and claimed her mouth again. He told himself to go slow, to move casually and not frighten her away. But when he touched her lips, rational thought fled.

Faith caught her breath at the sweet contact. Cort angled his head so their mouths pressed more firmly together. She'd spent the last twenty minutes berating herself for standing there gawking while he was naked. Now, with that vision fresh in her mind, it was easy to give herself up to his kiss.

He smelled of soap and male skin. Her hands brushed up and down his back, then held on to his shoulders. The tip of his tongue delicately touched her bottom lip. The damp caress made her lips part instantly. She liked the feel of him, the way he held her close. She liked—

His tongue touched hers. Her mind exploded in a conflagration of sensation, as if someone had set a match to dry tinder. Fire raced along her arms and legs. Need followed, making her ache and hunger with a power that frightened her. His tongue swept inside her mouth. She responded to each stroke, surging against him, trying to pull him closer. Her fingers clutched at him, touching his damp hair, then moving rapidly up and down his spine. Her chest grew tight and her breasts throbbed with each heartbeat.

He moved to kiss her jaw, then down her neck to the top of her shirt. He nibbled at her sensitive skin and bit her earlobe. She gasped and arched her head back, needing more.

Both his hands moved to her waist, then reached up toward her aching breasts. She tried to lean back to give him room to move, but he bent down and claimed her lips again. This time she was the aggressor, pushing her tongue into his mouth. As she tasted his heat, his hands cupped her breasts.

She froze, unable to believe the glorious tingling that swept through her. Her hips surged toward his, and she felt the length of his desire press against her jeans-clad core. She rhythmically moved her hips. His matched the thrusting as his fingers swept over and around her breasts. Her nipples puckered in anticipation. Her hands gripped his waist. He shifted, and she felt his towel fall away.

As she reached down to slide her hands across his bare buttocks, his fingers brushed her hard nipples. She moaned her pleasure. He gently squeezed the sensitive points, then pressed slightly. Her head lolled back. He kissed her neck, leaving a wet trail from her jaw to her shirt collar.

It had never been like this, she thought hazily, as his hands pulled her shirt from her jeans. She'd never been so ready, so hungry for a man. There was an honesty to their mating. No words or empty promises, no false pretense. Just a man and a woman with a need too large to be ignored.

He pulled up her shirt and deftly unhooked her bra with one hand. She stroked and squeezed his firm buttocks. He surged against her. As he cupped her bare breasts and his thumbs teased her nipples, she shifted on the stool, bringing her center more firmly against him.

He breathed her name. Supporting her hips, he drew her legs around him. Fire burned in his brown eyes. The lines of his face tightened as he reached for the waistband of her jeans. She'd only had two lovers in her life. Each of the physical relationships had begun slowly, awkwardly, with fumblings and bumped noses. Neither had been as right as this primal mating.

He unfastened the first button. Faith leaned forward and kissed his bare chest, tasting his warm skin. She licked his nipples, making him squirm. Inside, the wanting grew until she knew she would perish from the need. She wiggled her hips impatiently. He grabbed the zipper and tugged it down. As he reached his hand inside her jeans, he lurched suddenly.

Faith straightened and wrapped her arms around his waist to support him. He grabbed for the counter. Their eyes met.

"Guess the leg isn't a hundred percent," he said hoarsely, glancing at his bandaged calf.

She nodded slowly. Self-awareness returned, pushing away the passion.

"We can continue this upstairs," he said.

She bit her lower lip. Could she? Mate like one of the cats, without thought or concern for anything save pleasure? She'd never known how people did that. Both her lovers had claimed possession of her heart before she'd given her body. Unfortunately, after taking the latter, they were no longer interested in the former. She looked at Cort, at his nakedness, the proof of his need thrusting toward her. She wanted him. But was that enough? He was like the snow leopards. Beautiful, wild. Something to admire from afar, but never claim.

"I can't," she whispered.

He swallowed hard, then touched her chin, forcing her to look at him. "I understand. No hard feelings."

"Thank you. Maybe we can just forget it."

One corner of his mouth lifted up in a smile. "You go ahead, Faith. I don't want to forget."

Chapter 7

"This is really great," Cort said, slicing off another bite of beef.

Faith toyed with her food, but didn't bother looking up or answering. It was the third compliment in ten minutes. So much for forgetting about the kiss.

It was all her fault. She shouldn't have kissed him back. She shouldn't have let him know how he affected her. She shouldn't have let him kiss her in the first place. She sighed. She shouldn't have stared at him when she'd seen him standing there naked.

The round oak table sat in an alcove of the kitchen. Behind her were the two professional stoves, the triple sink and expensive refrigerator. She'd wanted to run back to the compound and hide out in her office. With dinner already cooking and work she couldn't put off any longer, she'd had to stay. An hour had passed and she was still shaken.

She glanced at him. Cort was looking at *her*. The fact that he was dressed and sitting there as calmly as if nothing had happened didn't help. She wanted to turn away and hide. She wanted to stop the blush she could feel heating her cheeks. Instead she put down her fork and drew in a deep breath. They had to work together. He seemed to be handling what had happened exactly as she'd requested. Despite his claim to the contrary, he seemed to have put the entire event out of his mind.

"You must think I'm completely inept," she said at last.

He shook his head. "I don't think you're inept. I think you're very honest and you make a great pot roast."

She smiled slightly. "It's a tri-tip."

"Whatever. Do you want me to apologize?"

"Do *you* want to?"

"No. I'm not sorry." He leaned forward across the table and took her hand. "We're working in close quarters. We're both without significant relationships in our lives. I find you very attractive. It's perfectly natural."

She wasn't especially petite, but his wide palm and long fingers dwarfed hers. He said it was perfectly natural. She wished she could believe it was nothing more than hormones and circumstances.

"You're right," she said, withdrawing her hand from his and picking up her plate. She rose and walked over to the sink. "I know it didn't mean anything. Is Jeff going to get you the necessary security people?"

He set his plate next to hers on the counter. "All taken care of. He'll also run a last-minute check on any changes in the guest list, along with substitutions in the catering staff."

She ran water and rinsed the dishes. After pouring them each coffee, she returned to the table. He picked up a pad of paper and sat in the chair next to her.

Working quickly, he drew a rough floor plan of the house. "Tell me what happens at one of these parties. How are the rooms set up?"

She leaned over the drawing and pointed. "We put chairs and sofas in conversation groups."

He sketched them in. "Like this?"

"Yes. The buffet is in the dining room. The big table runs lengthwise. We have a wet bar in both parlors. The cats are brought into the study through the French doors. That's why we use that room. They don't have to walk through the crowd."

He asked her questions about the party. As they worked together, she felt some of her embarrassment ease. Every now and then their arms would brush, or his breath would stir a loose hair or two at her temple, and then her body would quiver with awareness. She watched him speak, the way his mouth moved, the flash of white teeth. She remembered the feel of that mouth on hers. Had it only been an hour or two before? It seemed longer.

"What about the guests themselves? Everybody I checked out was rich, right?" he asked.

"We invite a few members of the press. A couple of old friends of Edwina's. Otherwise, yes."

He leaned back in the kitchen chair and placed his hands behind his head. He raised one ankle to the opposite knee. "You could find yourself a wealthy husband, and all your worries about the snow leopards would be solved."

She smiled. "We don't get a lot of single men at these functions. All of them are married, most of them are elderly. Feisty executive types don't have much time for wildlife."

"You've never been tempted?"

"By one of them?" She shook her head. "Not really."

"And you've never been married?"

"No. What about you?"

He folded his arms over his chest. "Never. I travel fastest when I travel alone."

"Where exactly are you going?"

She'd meant the question to be humorous, but he took it

seriously. "Wherever they send me. It's not right to have a wife and kids in this business. Look at what happened to Jeff. Losing Jeanne almost killed him."

"But while she was alive, they had something very special."

He raised his eyebrows. "Such as?"

"A relationship. A close bond between a man and a woman. You've never been tempted?" she asked, repeating the question he'd asked her.

"Not my style. When I go out on assignment, that's all I can afford to think about."

She leaned forward and rested her arms on the table. "Why do you do it?"

"It's my job. All I've ever wanted to do. Fight the good fight."

"But it's not a war. Don't you get lonely?"

He waved his arm to take in the large kitchen and the big house behind that. "You want to compare life-styles?"

That jab hit home. She stared at her hands.

"Faith, I'm sorry." He leaned forward and deliberately bumped her elbow with his.

She looked up at him. The cut on his chin had almost healed. He would carry a scar as a reminder of that mission. Gold-blond hair tumbled across his forehead. She wanted to brush it back, but she didn't. It wasn't her place.

He bumped her again. "I have a hard time answering personal questions."

"I understand. People ask me strange things, too. They don't understand my commitment to the cats. I guess it's similar to how you feel about what you do."

"Friends?" he asked.

She nodded. "Friends."

Cort resisted the need to tease her until she smiled. It was the easy way out, and for once, he didn't want that with a woman. There was something fundamentally honest about

Faith. She didn't play games. When she made a decision to do something, she did it without reservation.

Which made her reaction to their kiss all the more interesting. He'd expected to be turned on by touching her. He hadn't expected to be consumed by white heat. Even thinking about his tongue in her mouth and her breasts in his hands was enough to get him hard again. If his bum leg hadn't given out on him, who knows what would have happened. He wasn't sure if he was grateful for the interruption, or mad as hell.

He looked around at the drinking glasses Faith had stacked on the counters. She'd already gone over the menus and approved the liquor list. Setting up the fund-raiser was an incredible amount of work. She never even batted an eye.

"I told Jeff we'd be keeping the cubs under guard during the party," he said.

"That's a good idea. Too many people would upset them. Even though most of our guests are aware of the dangers with the cats, even the domesticated ones, most can't resist wanting to pat a 'kitty.'"

He rotated his arm and looked at a healing bite. "Those tiger cubs aren't *close* to domesticated."

"They're sweet."

"They have very sharp teeth."

She smiled. He'd seen her smile dozens of times, but the way it changed her whole face—brightening her eyes and making her look pretty—never failed to surprise him.

"They're supposed to have sharp teeth. They're carnivores."

"Will they be released into the wild?"

She sipped from her coffee mug, then set it down. "They can't be. Aside from the fact they won't have the skills to feed themselves, we have taken away their very necessary fear of humans. Besides, their white coloring would put them at a disadvantage. They'll be safe in captivity."

"You don't sound very happy about it."

"Are you?"

He thought about the cubs, the way they were starting to follow him around. They recognized his voice and were always willing to play. He had to admit they didn't look right behind the bars of a cage.

"I guess not." He rose from his chair. "Come on. I'll help you count plates."

Once in the pantry, he climbed up on the stool and began handing down dishes. He told himself he was crazy, but he could swear he smelled the lingering scent of their desire in the small room. If he closed his eyes, he would be able to taste Faith's sweetness and feel her responsive body trembling next to his. He banished the memories. If he closed his eyes he would fall off the stool and break his fool neck. Then he'd be useless to Faith and Jeff.

But for once the thought of his job and what he couldn't remember didn't tie him up in knots. It was coming back to him. Slowly. And now he knew he hadn't killed Dan.

Faith took the salad plates and carried them into the kitchen. "That's a hundred," she said. "We need another fifty."

He passed her a stack of ten. She took them and set them on the counter. Her arm muscles flexed with the movement. She wasn't anyone's idea of an ornament. She'd been wild in his arms. What would she be like in bed?

"How come you never married?" he asked.

She looked up, obviously surprised by the question. "I've never been asked."

"Was there anyone serious?"

"A boy in college. I'd thought—" She took another stack of plates and set them on the counter, then counted. "Ten more, please. I'd thought we might, you know. But after graduation, he sort of disappeared.''

"What do you mean 'disappeared'?''

"Left without saying goodbye. Packed up and moved away. We had a date and he never showed. I went to call him and the phone was disconnected.'' She picked up the salad plates and walked into the kitchen.

"I'm sorry,'' he said.

His initial flash of outrage made him want to find the man and punch him out. He stepped off the stool and picked up a stack of dishes. Who was he to cast stones at the guy? He thought about his own past. Had he done any better?

He was about to ask another question, but when she came back she wouldn't meet his eyes. There was something sad about the set of her mouth, as if remembering the past was painful for her. Clumsy bastard, he told himself.

She cleared their mugs off the small table in the alcove and set them in the sink. "What about you?'' she asked. "You can't always have traveled alone.''

He should have expected the question. Normally he didn't talk about himself, but he owed her. "There was someone once,'' he said, hoping it would be enough.

Faith leaned against the counter and looked expectant.

"We broke up,'' he said, and went back for more plates.

Faith followed. "You must have loved her very much.''

Cort started pulling down dinner plates and slamming them on the counter without worrying about their breaking. Why did it always come down to loving someone? For once, he wanted to blurt out the truth. No, he hadn't loved her. She'd been convenient. He'd been young and horny and she thought the world of him. In the end, he couldn't wait to leave her. He hadn't loved her, because he hadn't loved anyone. Even then he'd known it was faster and safer to travel alone.

He opened his mouth to finally speak the truth. "I—''

Faith's blue eyes widened. In the muted light from the kitchen, her skin looked smooth and soft as satin. He already knew how it tasted. She could control a three-hundred-pound leopard and face down wild jaguars without batting an eye. But he saw the wistful expression on her face, and he knew that under the tough facade she was a romantic dreamer who still believed in love and happily-ever-afters. Her commitment to the cats proved it. He could kill if it were required, but he couldn't destroy her dreams.

"Yes," he said. "I loved her very much." The lie tasted heavy and bitter. He wanted to call it back and speak the truth, but the moment passed as she nodded.

"You've never forgotten her. I know what that's like. Not for me. If someone had loved me like that, well, he would be here with me." She sounded sad. "My father loves a woman like that. Not my mother. His second wife. When I was growing up, my father traveled on business. He was gone a lot, and we had to move with his job. My mother and I begged him to find another line of work. Something that would keep us all together." She leaned against the pantry counter and traced a circle in the center of the top dinner plate. "But he wouldn't."

She looked up at him and smiled. "He was a little like you. He wanted to go his own way. When my mother died, he put me in boarding school for a couple of years. I didn't want him to leave me there. He told me it was the only way."

Cort perched on the stool. "Then what happened?"

"He met another woman. She's different from my mother, but nice." Faith smiled faintly. "I like her. She told my father if they were going to get married, he would have to change his ways. He did. They live in Vegas. He works for a casino. They have three little girls and he's there for them every night. He goes to soccer games and school plays." She drew in a deep breath and tucked a loose strand of hair behind her ear. ''All the things he didn't have time for with me.''

''Faith, I—''

''Don't apologize,'' she said. ''I'm not angry. I guess I envy them. What my father has with my stepmother. What Jeff had with Jeanne. It must be wonderful to be so special to someone. To have that bond. I wanted to but I've never been able to find anyone who could love me back. I understand why you can't forget her, Cort. She must have been an incredible woman.''

If he'd felt awkward before, now he just felt as low as a snake's belly. He wanted to ease the hurt in Faith by telling her most relationships weren't as wonderful as she made them out to be. Love wasn't real. It was an excuse for sex. He'd never loved a woman in his life. But if he told her the truth, he would make her feel worse. He stood up and grabbed the stack of plates. Better for her to believe what she wanted. Easier for both of them.

As he passed her on his way to the kitchen, she reached up and touched his arm. ''Cort?''

''Don't, Faith. Don't say a damn word.''

She nodded once, then drew her hand away.

He could feel the hurt radiating from her. It burned in his gut and there wasn't anything he could do about it. This was why he preferred to travel single, he reminded himself. Relationships always got in the way.

''Oh, sit still,'' Faith told Sparky.

The black leopard glared at her, his yellow eyes little more than slits.

''You can bring down a good-sized deer. Why are you afraid of a little water?'' She raised the bucket up to rinse off the suds.

Sparky made a choking sound low in his throat, then flattened his ears as the water cascaded off his back.

"He doesn't look happy," Cort said as he strolled across the compound and stopped next to her.

"He isn't. He hates getting a bath. It's not being wet, but the fact that he doesn't smell of mint and dirt anymore."

Cort crouched down and patted the cat's face. "Could be worse, pal. I have to wear a tux tonight."

Sparky looked unimpressed.

Faith unhooked his chain from the telephone pole at the center of the compound. "Hold this," she said, handing the end to Cort. When he took it, she stepped back about fifteen feet.

He looked puzzled. "Why do you want me to—" Sparky rose to his feet and braced himself. Cort glared at her. "Why, you little—"

Faith started to laugh. "Too late." She yelped and turned away as Sparky started to shake. Water flew everywhere. When she looked back, Cort was drenched and Sparky was licking his front paws.

She walked over and took back the chain. "Thanks."

Water dripped from Cort's face. The front of his blue shirt clung to him. Drops formed a pattern on his jeans. The devilish light in his eyes promised retribution.

"You could have warned me," he said, wiping his face.

"And spoil the surprise?" She tugged on the chain. "Come on, Sparky. I don't want you rolling in the dirt and getting muddy." The big cat slowly followed her.

"What about me?" Cort asked, holding his arms out to his sides.

"I don't want you rolling in the dirt, either."

He jogged after her, his limp barely noticeable. When he reached her side, he placed an arm around her neck and squeezed gently, before releasing her. "I should have done you in when I had the chance."

"Try it. I'll sic my watch cat on you."

Their eyes met and they both smiled. She was glad they

could still be friends. The first day A.K.—After Kiss, as she thought of it—had been awkward, but she'd forced herself to behave normally around Cort, however funny she felt inside. She still had trouble looking at him without remembering how incredible he'd been standing naked, or the feel of his mouth on hers, but if she concentrated, she could push the memories aside. The upcoming fund-raiser had really helped. With a thousand details to take care of, it was easy to get lost in her work. In the last couple of days, she and Cort had slipped into a kind of teasing relationship that made her wonder if she was going to feel lonely when he was gone.

"When do the rest of the security people get here?" she asked. A team of four had arrived yesterday.

He checked his watch. "Within the hour. The cubs will be in the office and under guard at all times. Only you or I will be allowed in that part of the building."

"Be sure to tell the guards not to try to play with them. The cubs will be upset enough by the noise from all the cars pulling in."

Cort grinned. "I'll do better than that. I'll show them my bites. That'll keep them in line. What about you? Are you ready for tonight?"

They reached the main building. He held the door open for Faith, then stepped in after her. She walked into her office and led Sparky over to the blanket she'd stretched out on the floor. "As much as I can be. The caterers finished setting up this morning. The flowers are in place and most of the food is prepared." She grabbed a towel from the stack on the chair and knelt in front of the leopard. "Your favorite part, Sparky."

The leopard crouched down and closed his eyes in anticipation.

"Want some help?" Cort asked.

"Sure. Grab a towel. I rub him dry. It adds a nice shine to his coat and keeps him from going to roll in the mint."

Cort settled on Sparky's other side, picked up a towel and began rubbing the big cat. "You seem a little nervous," he said, glancing up at her.

"It's the party. They always make me crazy."

"Why?"

She leaned forward and took one massive paw on her lap. Wrapping the towel around his foreleg, she pressed out the moisture. "Anything can go wrong. I worry about a guest getting drunk enough to want to provoke the cats. I don't like playing hostess. I'm not great at small talk with people I don't know. It was easier when Edwina was alive." She patted Sparky's head and looked into his bright yellow eyes. "We miss her, don't we fella?" The leopard nudged her hand and made a purring noise low in his throat. She moved to Sparky's side and rubbed his shoulder. "Our donors are seriously rich." She smiled. "We don't have a lot in common."

"The cats," Cort said, brushing the towel across Sparky's flank.

"That's true. So I smile until my cheeks hurt, and answer questions about panthers and leopards. And I remind everyone how big cats are losing more and more natural habitat every day, and they write me checks." She wrinkled her nose. "The worst part of it is that I'm going to have to do even more fund-raising if I start the snow-leopard project."

He raised his eyebrows. "If?"

"The jury is still out on that one."

"You can do it."

"Thanks for the vote of confidence."

Sparky stiffened suddenly and Faith looked up. One of the security guards, a tall bald man in his late forties, stood in the doorway.

Faith wrapped the towel around Sparky's neck like a collar. His neck wasn't dry enough to put his leather one on yet. "Sparky, you remember Andy," she said, keeping her voice low and pleasant. "Andy, crouch down and hold out your arm." She didn't bother looking at the man, but kept her eyes on the leopard.

Nothing happened. Before she could repeat her request, Cort walked over to the man. "Do it," he growled. "Unless you want to be lunch."

Andy obeyed. Sparky sniffed the offered hand, then turned away in disinterest. The man rose. Faith released the leopard and Sparky began grooming.

"What do you have to report?" Cort asked.

The older man looked a little shaken. "Jesus, I don't know if I'll ever get used to that thing roaming around here loose." He grinned at Faith. "Great watchdog. You think when this is over I can get a picture of me and him to show my kids?"

"Sure thing," she said.

The man was as tall as Cort, but heavier. He pulled a walkie-talkie out of his utility belt. "This is for you, Boss. Frequency is all set. Every unit has been tested." He turned to Faith. "The planking is all in place over the dirt part of the driveway. Two guards are posted there. They've been logging in the catering people. All the extra lights are strung and working." He looked back at Cort. "So far, no surprises."

Cort took the walkie-talkie and stuck it in his pocket. "Let's keep it that way. When do your kids arrive?" he asked Faith.

The three part-time employees were working the party. They were responsible for bringing the cats up to the main house and showing them to the guests. "Any time now."

"And the guests start arriving when?"

"About seven."

"Then I guess we're all set," he said.

She followed the two men from the office and closed the door behind her. "I'm going to go up to the Big House," she said. "I have to check on the food and then get ready."

"I'll see you at the party."

She left the men and drove up to the house. People swarmed over the main floor, taking care of the last-minute touches. The house glowed from its recent cleaning. The crystal chandeliers glittered. Bright flowers lined the mantel. She spoke to the woman in charge, made sure everything was going well, then escaped upstairs to her room.

She stared at the contents of her closet, at the dressy clothes hanging there. These nights were the only ones when she became like other women. When she wore makeup and curled her hair. The expensive gowns and jumpsuits made her fit in with her guests. In the past she hadn't cared what she looked like, as long as she was presentable. But this night was different. She wanted to be special. A foolish dream, she told herself. Cort wasn't for her. He wouldn't care what she dressed in, because he saw her as little more than a co-worker. But there was nothing wrong with pretending, even for a night.

Cort adjusted the gun at the small of his back, then shifted the walkie-talkie to his left jacket pocket. The house was quiet. The catering staff had returned to the back rooms to change into their uniforms. None of the guests had arrived. As it always did at the start of any mission, a calm came over him.

A whisper of sound caught his attention. He turned and looked toward the staircase. Faith stood poised at the top. If he wore a tux, it made sense that she would be formally dressed, as well. But he wasn't prepared for the transformation.

The cream jumpsuit clung to her curves, outlined her generous breasts, narrow waist and slender hips. Sequins sparkled from the padded shoulders and angled down toward her midsection. The sleeves puffed out at her upper arms, then fitted snugly from her elbows to her wrists. Cream suede boots hugged her calves.

As she walked down the stairs, his gaze reached her face. Makeup accentuated her blue eyes and highlighted the shape of her mouth. Sparkling earrings dangled almost to her shoulders. She wore her hair swept up and away from her face. Curls tumbled down her back. She was beautiful.

When she stood on the last step, he moved close to her. She tried to smile, but trembled too much.

"I'll take your silence as a compliment," she said, twisting her hands together. "If you hate the way I look, please don't tell me. I'm nervous enough."

"You look terrific," he said, not quite believing the transformation.

"Really?" She flushed. "Thanks. I'm so nervous."

He took her hands in his. "Don't be. You'll do great."

She looked down at herself. "I think this color might be a mistake. What if I spill something? And I'm going to get cat hair all—"

He cut her off. "Faith?"

"What?" She looked worried. "What's wrong? Is it my hair? You hate—"

"Do you have more of that lipstick?"

She frowned. "Of course. But why do you—"

"Because I'm about to smear it."

He leaned forward and touched his lips to hers. Her eyes fluttered closed, and he felt the familiar heat throbbing in his body. He was about to draw her close to him when he heard the faint scuffing of shoes on the front porch. He stepped back.

Faith looked dazed. She touched her fingers to her lips.

He wiped the back of his hand across his mouth, then grinned at the lipstick he'd brushed off. Ken opened the front door and stuck his head in the door.

"They're here," he said. "Show time."

Chapter 8

William Thomas tapped his fingers impatiently on the steering wheel of his dark sedan. He was next in line. The limo in front was waved through. He eased his foot off the brake and the big car rolled up to the guard posted at the open gate.

"Good evening, sir," the armed guard said, and took his invitation. He scanned the thick, creamy paper. "And you are...?"

"Johnson," Thomas said. "Mark Johnson. From K-NEWS."

The reporter and his producer, Mark Johnson, had been invited to the event. A quick call to the station had confirmed Johnson was out of town. It was unlikely any of the guards would know who the man was. Safer to impersonate him than a well-known newscaster.

"May I see your driver's license?" the guard asked.

Thomas pulled out the forged ID. He loved Los Angeles. You could buy anything you wanted if you knew where to go. The driver's license was genuine, if stolen. The picture had been taken that morning.

The guard looked from the photo to his face, then smiled and handed back the ID. "Just follow the driveway up to the main house, sir. Enjoy your evening." He checked Mark Johnson's name off the list.

Thomas waved and pressed on the gas. The sedan with its tinted rear windows rolled along the planking, then onto smooth asphalt. As he moved up toward the main house, he glanced over his shoulder. The big collapsible cage he'd purchased was completely covered by a dark blanket. He patted the gun concealed under his jacket and allowed himself a small smile. It was almost over.

Faith greeted her guests as she circulated through the room. She resisted glancing at her watch. Last time she'd checked, only fifteen minutes had passed. The evening was crawling by. Her forced smile became genuine. Why was she surprised? These evenings were always long and awkward.

She stopped by the bar and ordered another glass of club soda. As the bartender poured, she leaned against the brass railing and glanced around the room. Quiet conversation filled the huge parlor, competing with the tinkle of glasses and cutlery. The excited buzz was already starting as it grew closer to the time when they brought in the cats. Jewelry sparkled, expensive fabrics gleamed. All in all, a beautiful scene.

The bartender handed her the drink, and she nodded her thanks. Across the room, a pair of broad shoulders caught her eye. Cort. Before tonight, she'd only seen him in casual clothing. Or nothing at all. She'd liked him best in the latter, but the tux he wore came in a close second. The black wool emphasized his strength and lean grace. He moved through the room, watching, nodding when noticed, but mostly staying in the background. She tried to catch his eye, but he was intent on his work and hadn't once looked her way. Gone was the passionate man who had kissed her until she trembled. In his place was a handsome stranger intent on doing his job. There was an air of danger about him that made women look twice and men step back to let him through. She felt safe knowing he was around.

"Faith, darling, you look fabulous." An older woman swept across the room and stopped in front of her, kissing the air next to her cheek. Her husband trailed behind.

"Margaret, Milton. How good of you to come."

Margaret was a carefully preserved woman of sixty who still looked to be in her late forties. Her purple silk dress showed off a figure that had defied gravity. Milton didn't resist aging as strongly. His white hair hung down to the collar of his expensively tailored formal wear. They could be difficult at times, but Faith had always liked the couple. They were two of Edwina's oldest friends and had always looked out for her.

"Where are those lovely cubs we've been hearing about?" Margaret asked, then sipped from her champagne.

"I'm afraid they're not on display."

Margaret made a moue of disappointment. "Oh, I did so long to see them."

"We have them under guard. They would be upset by all the people. They're still babies."

Milton nodded sagely. "Sensible. Don't want any trouble. You bringing out Sparky?" The old man had a soft heart for the leopard.

She smiled. "Of course. He should be ready. Why don't I take you in the study now, so you can spend a minute with him?"

The older couple glanced at each other. "We'd love to," Margaret said. She leaned forward and whispered. "Milton has done very well in the foreign market. There's a little extra in your check tonight, dear.''

Faith squeezed her hand. ''Thank you.''

She led them to the study and ushered them inside. Sparky sat on a blanket, trying to chew the red bow around his neck. Samson, the bobcat, quivered with excitement. An older panther lay on a sturdy metal table in the corner.

Margaret rushed over to Samson, who greeted her like a long-lost friend. Milton let Sparky smell his arm before patting the leopard he'd known since the cat was a cub. Faith backed out of the room and closed the door behind her. She looked at her watch and decided she'd slip away and check on the cubs.

The road from the way station wound around for almost a mile, but there was a narrow path that cut through the woods. It was about a ten-minute walk. Lights had been strung from the trees and all the overhanging brush had been cut back. Later, she would lead the group over to the compound to unveil the two new habitats paid for by some of the guests.

''Where are you off to in such a hurry?'' Cort asked from behind her.

Startled, she spun to face him. ''Where did you come from?''

''I saw you leave.''

''But I didn't ever see you looking at me,'' she blurted out, then wished she could call back the words.

Cort didn't seem upset. ''I'm good at my job. You're not supposed to see me watching you. Where are you going?''

''To check on the cubs. I want to tell the guards that we'll be bringing people over in about a half hour. A few will wander into the main building. I wanted to warn them to be firm but polite.''

Cort took her arm and turned her around until she was

facing the Big House. "I'll do that. You go back to your guests."

"But I—"

He squeezed her arm briefly. "You're doing fine. Everyone is having a great time and no one knows you're nervous."

"*You* know."

"It's my job to know. Go on." He waved her along the path. "I'll see you by the habitats in a half hour."

Thomas hovered at the back of the crowd. The woman in charge, Faith Newlin, was making a speech about the generosity of the family that had donated the big cage structure in front of them. He took a couple of steps to one side and slipped into the shadows. This was his chance. While everyone was busy, he would find the cubs.

A few casual questions had told him the tigers weren't part of the show. That would make his job easier. They were, according to a plump but talkative matron, under guard at the main building. He spun on his heel and stared at the low, one-story structure in front of him. Lights shone from several windows. That had to be it.

He walked along the back of the building, counting windows and trying to figure out where the cubs would be. The dense undergrowth didn't allow him to easily go around the structure, so he headed for the glass doors and pulled them open.

The shabby foyer was empty. In front of him stood another set of doors. They were sturdy and looked new. He pushed on one. It swung open to reveal the parking lot filled with expensive cars and limousines. Excitement flickered in his belly. He could move his car close to the building. That would make his job a lot easier. He would have to carry the cubs out one by one. No way he could wrestle the cage inside, take them, then carry it out without being noticed. He eased the door shut and looked down the long halls.

On his right, overhead lights shone on signs for the men's and ladies' restrooms. To his left, the hallway stretched down with closed doors on both sides. He stepped to his left.

Thomas slipped his hand into his jacket and rested his palm on the handle of his pistol. He slipped inside the first door. A metal table attached to one wall and open shelves containing bandages and medicine told him this was a medical office. He continued down, opening the doors, one after the other. On the fifth one, he walked into a small area dominated by a cage. He allowed himself a small smile. In the center of the cage, the cubs lay curled up together sleeping. Perfect, he thought. They'd be easier to handle and—

"Excuse me, sir. This room is off limits to our guests."

He turned toward the voice. Thankfully, he had the sense to drop his hand to his side. The khaki-uniformed security guard looked a little startled at seeing him, but not unduly alarmed. Thomas thought about taking out the man. The guard wasn't much over six feet. Before he could decide, another guard joined him.

"What's the problem?"

"I was explaining to the gentleman that this room is private."

"My mistake," Thomas said, figuring he couldn't take both of them without a commotion that would alert the other guards in the area. "I was looking for the restroom."

The first guard smiled and stepped back. "At the other end of the hall, sir. It's marked."

"Thank you." Thomas adjusted the jacket of his rented tuxedo and stepped past the guard and into the hall. As he walked down the corridor, he counted doors so he'd be able to find his way in from the outside.

He went through the front doors and into the parking

area. Several limo drivers clustered together talking. He circled around the cars, found his rental and slowly maneuvered it as close to the main building as he could. He climbed into the back seat and pulled the blanket off the cage.

He'd rented this car specifically because, although it was a sedan, it was the executive model with an extrawide back seat. He worked quickly and in about ten minutes had the cage up and secured. He tossed the blanket over the gleaming metal so someone walking by couldn't see it, then left the car and headed back to the building.

The cubs were in the second room from the end. He closed his eyes and thought about the layout of the room. There hadn't been any chairs. The guards weren't stationed with the cubs. Apparently they were patrolling the halls. He would have to be prepared to take one or both men out quickly, if he had to. He would come around the building, through the bushes, and break the window. The cluster of trees would hide his activity from the parking lot. That would make his job easier.

As he entered the main building, he glanced at the screens covering the windows, then patted his pockets. The tools he'd brought with him would be enough. He adjusted his tuxedo jacket and stepped through to the compound. It was just a matter of time.

Cort circled around the crowd of people by the new habitats. He kept an eye out for stragglers and anyone who looked too curious for their own good. He wished there was a way to keep people out of the main building, but Faith had pointed out her guests would need access to a restroom. He walked over to Andy.

"Send two more guards to patrol the outside of the main building," Cort said.

The older man pulled out his walkie-talkie and spoke into

it. "Done," he said a moment later. "Seems to be going well, boss."

"So far," Cort answered.

He moved away, scanning the area. One guard had been posted by the two jaguar cages to make sure no guest came to any harm. Three couples strolled by Tigger's habitat and spoke to the big cat. The situation wasn't as controllable as he would like, but it felt damn good to be working again. Every sense was on full alert. His leg felt a hundred percent. He'd been at the way station long enough to become familiar with the noises and smells. It all seemed right. He glanced at his watch. Another couple of hours and it would all be over.

He turned his back on the crowd and studied the main building. Nothing moving there. He walked toward the jaguar cages to make sure the guard was alert. As he moved through the darkness, something flashed in his mind. He froze. Not a memory. More of a picture. Of walking somewhere else. Where? The dock? He closed his eyes and tried to remember. Nothing.

Cort swore. When was it going to come back to him? Why couldn't he remember? He had to. He shook his head and continued toward the guard.

"Anything?" he asked the man.

"Nope. A couple of old guys came by, but I told 'em to move on, and they did."

"Good. I—" Cort paused. A sixth sense made him turn toward the narrow road leading from the compounds to the Big House. He thought he saw something—or someone—moving there. "I'll be back later," he said, walking toward the main building.

He broke into a jog, trying to remember the people who had been around a moment before. They weren't there now. Some had gone inside, others had joined the main group. Had one of them tried to slip around the building?

He saw a man silhouetted against the dense brush and broke into a run.

"You there," he called. "Stop."

The man froze for a second, then dove into the bushes. Cort raced after him, pulling his radio from his jacket pocket. He was about to call Andy when he stepped from the path into the underbrush. Instantly time tilted. He felt the sturdy floor of the dockside warehouse. The smell of the sea invaded him. He could taste the salt. Up ahead. There. Dan! Cort crouched low behind a stack of crates. His fellow agent opened a briefcase filled with documents. Cort strained to see what they were. The other men—there were six of them—stood with their backs to him. But he knew them. Terrorists, arms dealers, working for no country, instead selling to the highest bidder. He remembered his mission. To get proof that Dan was selling out his country. He stared in disbelief as he watched his friend take the money. Dan's betrayal tasted bitter on his tongue.

The scene shifted, grew foggy, then cleared, but it was later. The meeting was over. Cort approached the open area cautiously. He heard a noise behind him and spun. Dan!

"What the hell are you doing here?" Cort demanded.

Dan flushed, then grabbed his arm and jerked him close. "We've got to get out of here. They're going to come back."

Cort started to resist, then a cold feeling slid down his spine. He pulled free and started to run for the exit.

He was too late. The explosion caught him up in its power and tossed him aside like a doll. He struggled to get to his feet, to breathe, but he couldn't. Then strong hands tugged on him, pulling him to safety. Where there had been smoke, now he could breathe fresh, salty air. He coughed.

"Why?" he asked groggily, barely able to focus. His head. What had hit him?

A branch snapped.

The sharp noise jerked him back into the present. Cort blinked in the darkness of the forest and reached for his gun. As he pushed aside the flashback, he scanned the trees and bushes. The lights strung along the walking path didn't reach far into the gloom.

He circled to the front of the building, but couldn't find any trace of the intruder. He collected two of the guards and had them go around the building twice. They found some footprints made by dress shoes. All the guards wore boots. Cort stared at the tracks. They led from the main compound into the bushes, then disappeared into a pile of leaves. Maybe someone had gotten drunk and wandered off the main path. Perhaps a guest was simply trying to get a look at the cubs, but that didn't mean he was going to kidnap them.

The two guards posted with the cubs had mentioned that a half-dozen people had been near the restricted room. A couple had been lost, but the others were obviously hoping for a peek at the prized kittens. None of them, according to the guards, had looked dangerous.

By the time the last of the guests left, Cort knew that whoever had been stalking around the compound was long gone. If the extra guards hadn't scared him off, the big lights he had set up in the front of the main building would have. While Faith said her goodbyes, he had Rob and Ken help him move the cubs' cage to an interior room. Then he locked the door, pocketing the key as he left.

He walked into Faith's office and sat behind the desk. He didn't bother flipping on the overhead lights. Tiredness settled on him like a thick blanket, but he knew he wouldn't sleep much tonight. The cameras in the hallway had recorded twenty guests entering the main building. Fifteen of them had obviously been searching for the cubs. Aside from that, he'd seen nothing out of the ordinary. He didn't know who had been in the bushes or who he'd been chasing.

But he had remembered. Not all of it, but enough. He still didn't know how Dan had died, but he'd recalled most of the mission. Dan had been involved with dangerous characters. What had possessed his friend to cross the line? Had there been money troubles at home? He rubbed his forehead and tried to remember if Dan had a family. He didn't think so. They'd shared a common belief that traveling alone was always safest. Which made their friendship unusual for both of them.

Cort leaned back in his chair. The explosion and fire in the South American warehouse had been deliberately set. Someone had tried to get rid of Dan. *Or him.*

The thought made him sit upright. Was that it? All this time he'd assumed the bomb in the warehouse had been because of Dan's activities. Cort frowned. Had he been fingered, as well? Was someone after him? How much of the mission did Jeff really know?

He didn't bother glancing at his watch. He drew the phone close and punched out the familiar numbers.

"Markum."

"Could someone be after me?" Cort asked without bothering to introduce himself.

"Something happen with the cubs?"

"A guy was creeping around in the dark. Was it about me or the cubs?"

Jeff exhaled loudly. "As far as I know, you're clean. I wouldn't have sent you up to stay with Faith if I'd thought there would be any danger to her or the cubs."

"They killed him, didn't they? The arms dealers turned on Dan."

"So you remember."

"Not all of it." Cort leaned forward and rested his elbows on the desk. "Enough. Did the deal go bad?"

Silence.

"You can't be sure they aren't after me."

"Not a hundred percent, but—"

"Then replace me."

"You want to come out?" Jeff asked.

Cort felt something bump his leg. He looked down. Sparky sat next to him and butted his thigh. Automatically he reached down and scratched the big cat's ears.

"If there's even a possibility that I'm endangering them, then yes."

"I don't think you are. No one but me knows where you are. Your requests for assistance are being handled outside the agency."

Cort stared at the leopard. He glanced around the small office, at the photos on the wall, barely visible from the light in the hallway. He thought about Faith and the way he'd kissed her. He was starting to care about her and this place. He couldn't afford the distraction.

"I want out, anyway," he said abruptly.

"Why?"

"I'm a hundred percent, Jeff. Put me back in the field."

"You're still on medical leave and those cubs need protecting."

"There has to be someone else you can send."

"Sure." He heard Jeff flipping through papers. "Smith is available at the end of the week. Can you wait that long?"

Cort grimaced. "Smith? He's a jerk. Who else?"

"That's the best I can do."

"It's not good enough. I won't leave until I'm sure Faith and the cubs are safe."

"Then stay where you are," Jeff snapped. "You're supposed to be my best operative. Who can I send in who's better? Or is there something you're not telling me? Another reason you want to come out?"

Cort thought about how Faith had looked that night, a beautiful woman in expensive clothes and makeup. He thought about how he preferred her in jeans and boots, with her hair hanging straight down her back. He remembered how he'd lied to her about his past relationships and the pain in her eyes when she talked about her father deserting her. He thought about how easy it would be to go to her bed and share the passion lurking so close to the surface. The fire between them would probably burn hot enough to scar, but it would be worth it. He thought about how, when this was over, he would return to his world, because fighting was all he knew and believed in. Then he thought about Jeff's questions. There were a dozen reasons why he wanted to come out. He couldn't tell his boss even one of them.

"No," he said. "There's no other reason to come out."

"Then stay put and do your job." He hung up the phone.

Cort sat in the dark listening to Sparky's breathing as the black leopard slept at his feet. He knew he would pay a big price for letting himself like Faith. Caring could be deadly. Look at what had happened to Jeff's family.

But his boss had been right about one thing. Cort was the best. It was up to him to protect Faith and the cubs. No matter what, he couldn't let his feelings get in the way.

Chapter 9

Faith filled Cort's coffee cup. "You want to talk about why you didn't sleep much last night?"

Cort took a sip. "Is it that obvious?"

Only to me, she wanted to say, but didn't. "The dark circles under your eyes give you away."

"I had a lot on my mind."

It was past noon. The day after a fund-raiser was usually slow. Beth and Rob had arrived a half hour before to clean cages. Cort had already been out patrolling the compound when she'd gotten up shortly after eight.

Sparky came into the kitchen of her apartment, dragging his blanket behind him. He walked over to Cort and dropped it at his feet.

"I think he wants to play," Faith said as Sparky stared hopefully.

"Beast," Cort said, then jerked his head toward the door. "Come on, Faith. Let's make it two against one."

She followed him outside. The bright sunshine promised

a warm afternoon. After all the planning and hard work, it felt good to be out from under the party. She took hold of the blanket at the middle. Cort stepped up behind her and held on. Sparky grabbed the dangling end. He shook his head playfully and almost ripped the cloth from her fingers.

"You got it?" she asked, not turning away from the leopard.

"I'm ready," Cort said.

She could hear the smile in his voice and feel him so close behind her. The nearness made her insides feel funny, as if a jolt of electricity had passed through them.

"Go!" she called.

Sparky immediately hunched down with his rear end pointing skyward, and started to pull. She could hear his grunts as he strained against them. Faith tightened her grip, but the blanket was slowly being pulled through her hands.

"He's strong," Cort said from behind her, his voice tense with strain. "No you don't, cat. You're not going to get the best of me."

Sparky's yellow eyes glittered with excitement. He made low growling noises deep in his throat. The powerful muscles in his shoulders bunched with the effort. Faith held on tight. She felt herself starting to slide forward.

"He's pulling us," she said.

"That's not possible. Between us, we weigh more than he does."

"I don't care what you think. It's happening. Look." Sparky backed up toward the play area in the center of the compound. Faith's boots slipped in the dirt. From a habitat, one of the cats howled encouragement. She started to giggle.

"Don't you dare laugh," Cort ordered, bumping against her. "You'll lose your strength."

"I can't help it. They're rooting for him." The laughter became louder, and she felt her fingers slip. She let go of the blanket and immediately sat down hard on her behind. Cort jumped to avoid running into her. Sparky took advantage of his momentary loss of balance, jerked the cloth free and sprang victoriously onto the telephone poles. He held the blanket between his forelegs, as if it were his prey, and gnawed on one end.

Cort placed his hands on his hips. "We almost had him."

She shaded her eyes and stared up at Cort. He looked tall and strong and very handsome. He'd rolled his long-sleeved blue shirt up to his elbows. Jeans clung to his narrow hips and powerful thighs. She tried to ignore the quivering in her chest and the heat blossoming in her breasts. "We didn't almost have him, Cort. He never loses in tug-of-war. Even when he was a cub, he was strong."

Cort held out his hand. She grabbed it, and he pulled her to her feet. As she brushed off her backside, he looked around the compound. "How did you find this place? Were you always interested in big cats?"

"No." She started back to the office. He moved into step beside her. "I never had pets when I was growing up. We moved too much. Then, after my mother died, I was sent away to school. Besides, my father always hated cats."

"Is that why you work with them?"

She grinned. "I never thought of it like that, but maybe. I got a summer job here the year before I went to college. I didn't know what I wanted for a career, but after that first week, I knew this was where I belonged."

He held open the door and she ducked inside. Cort hovered in the foyer. He looked tired and out of sorts.

"Is it about last night?" she asked.

He raised his eyebrows. "Is what about last night?"

"I heard we had a possible intruder. Is that why you're so jumpy?"

He shook his head. "Whoever the guy is, he's long gone."

"Then I know just the thing to make you feel better."

She'd expected him to be curious about her announcement. Instead he took a step closer and she saw passion flare to life in his brown eyes. The cut on his chin had healed. Suddenly she wanted to touch the scar, tracing it up from his chin to the corner of his mouth. She wanted to be close to him, to inhale the scent of his body. To feel him on her, and in her, tasting her, touching her, until nothing existed except the moment of their joining.

Need swept through her. She started to sway toward him. He moved close, as if to catch her. She wanted to say yes. But she couldn't. Her self-respect had been hard won, and she wasn't about to throw it all away by giving her body without her heart. Cheap affairs had never been her style. She didn't know how not to care. And Cort had made it very clear he wasn't interested in any kind of a relationship. He preferred to travel light. At first she hadn't understood his reluctance to commit to someone, but now that she knew about the heartbreak in his past, it all made sense. Oh, but he tempted her.

She cleared her throat. "I was thinking of going shooting up in one of the canyons. Want to come along?"

The passion receded. "Shooting?" He raised his eyebrows.

"I haven't been in a while. I mostly use my rifle. Come on, it'll be fun."

He seemed to consider his options. She half hoped he would pick sex and simply pull her into his arms. Once he held her, she wasn't sure she would have the will to resist. Instead he smiled. "Okay, let me get the Beretta and I'll meet you by the truck."

She collected her weapons and ammunition and carried them outside. Cort helped her load everything. She went into the kitchen, grabbed a six-pack of sodas, then stuck her head out the back and told Beth they would return in a couple of hours.

They drove up the mountain in silence. Cort saw Faith glancing at him every couple of minutes. He wanted to tell her that he was fine, but he knew she wouldn't believe the lie.

He hadn't known how much Faith was getting to him until he'd asked Jeff to take him off the case. Since then he hadn't been able to think about anything else. It wasn't hard to figure out his concern. Jeff had said he hadn't killed Dan, but Jeff hadn't been in South America. Cort didn't have to have been the one who pulled the trigger to be responsible for what happened to Dan. Was he putting Faith in the same kind of danger?

He leaned his head back and watched the passing scenery. Lush growth spilled onto the narrow two-lane road. It was too late in spring for many of the wildflowers to still bloom, but wild berry bushes were already budding fruit. Squirrels jumped from tree to tree, and a rabbit crossed the road a hundred yards ahead of them.

Faith slowed the truck, shifted into four-wheel drive, then turned off onto a dirt path. Branches slapped against the cab as the vehicle slowly moved up the mountain. Ten minutes later, they rolled into a small clearing. A locked shed stood on one side.

She stopped the truck and smiled at him. "We're here."

He stepped out into the warm afternoon. Taking a deep breath, he smelled wild roses and the soft grass under his feet. "This is exactly what I needed."

"Good." Faith unlatched the gate on the bed of the truck and lowered it. "Let's see how you do shooting a rifle." She picked one up and tossed it to him.

He caught it easily, then collected three more. Faith lifted the heavy case of ammunition. She wore jeans and a T-shirt. As she picked up the case and set it on the ground, the muscles in her arms bunched and released. She was strong. She bent over and reached for the zippered case containing her handgun. Her jeans molded to the firm curves of her rear. She was also very much a woman. In the past he'd always been attracted to ultrafeminine types who would collapse at the first sign of trouble or physical activity that wasn't directly related to sex or their aerobic workout. Faith was different. She didn't need to pretend. Hell, she didn't have time. Working with the cats required total commitment.

She unlocked the shed and pulled out paper targets. "It's just through here," she said, pointing to a break in the trees. She handed him the targets, then picked up the box of ammunition and led the way.

The path ended in a narrow canyon. Brush had been cleared back to the trees, creating a narrow corridor perfect for shooting. Frames for targets had been set up in front of a muddy hillside. Most were stationary, but a couple were on jointed sections that moved with every breath of the wind.

For the first half hour, they shot using handguns. Faith couldn't match him on speed or accuracy, but she was better than most people he knew. The sound of the gunshots gave him a sense of something familiar, and something about his last assignment, but when the memory didn't focus, he tried to ignore the sensation. He'd finally learned the best way to remember the past was to let it come to him. Trying hard to recall things only made the fog thicker. At the end of each clip, they compared targets. He tried not to gloat, but couldn't help grinning when they took down the last one.

"You completely missed the bull's-eye," he said, slipping off his ear protection and pointing from the neat collection of bullet holes that punctured the center of his target to the scattered spray on hers.

Faith shook her head disgustedly. "I never was much good with a handgun."

He took her target and held it up in front of him. The bullet holes formed a pattern in the center of his chest. "I don't think you have to worry about an intruder."

Her blue eyes widened. She stared at her gun and then at him. "You asked me once before if I thought I could kill someone." She flipped on the safety and popped out the magazine. "I'm still not sure. I hope I never have to find out."

Cort remembered his own questions about Dan's death and understood her feelings. He admired her ability to admit she wasn't sure. So many rookie agents talked about wanting their first kill, as if it were a badge of honor to be won. There was nothing noble in taking another person's life.

"I'll do my best to keep you safe," he said.

"Just what every woman needs. Her own warrior prince." She grinned up at him.

The makeup from last night was long gone. Her hair hung straight again, pulled back in a ponytail. He could see the freckles on her nose, the faint lines by the corners of her eyes, and he could smell her French perfume. Her shirt was faded, and her jeans had seen better days. None of that mattered. A powerful need swept through him, stirring his blood and making him want to take her here on the spring grass, surrounded by the trees.

She picked up a rifle and handed it to him. "Prepare to have your butt whipped."

He took the weapon and loaded it. The desire was as controllable as any bodily function. He could feel it, but he didn't have to do anything about it.

"You sound pretty confident," he said.

"I am." She smiled smugly. "But doubt me all you want."

She set up the targets. Two of them went on the swinging

frames. A light breeze stirred the paper, rocking it from side to side. Cort stepped up to go first. He was used to following a moving target with a pistol, but not with a rifle. Every time he got it lined up in his sights, it moved.

"You have to anticipate which way it's going to go," she offered.

"Thanks," he said dryly, as he took a breath, held it and squeezed the trigger.

The target fluttered as the bullet went through it, but he could see he wasn't even close to center. He took several more shots, but didn't get any better.

Faith stepped next to him and gently pushed him out of the way. "Let me show you how the pros do it, honey," she purred. Her self-satisfied grin told him he was about to be had.

She didn't disappoint him. She put a dozen bullets into a space the size of a half-dollar. By the time she was done shooting, there wasn't anything left of the paper at the center of the target. She put a second sheet in place and kicked the frame so it wiggled wildly. Even with the additional movement, her shots all went in dead center.

Cort took the rifle from her. "I've been hustled."

She nodded modestly. "You should have looked more closely at those trophies. I told you I was a sharpshooter."

"Is this something you learned to do in your spare time?"

"No. Actually, I was forced into it." She reached for a can of soda and tossed him one. Then she popped the top of her own and sat down under a tree. She dropped her ear protection on the ground. "I learned to shoot a rifle because we use them to tranquilize the wild cats."

Cort settled next to her. They both leaned against the rough bark of the maple tree. He stretched his legs out in front of him. "Why you?"

She shrugged. "When I first came to work for Edwina,

I worked part-time, like the kids I have now. She saw I was interested and committed to the animals. When she mentioned a full-time job after I had my associate degree, I was more than willing to switch and study animal husbandry. It's difficult for people to get jobs working with animals. There aren't a lot of openings at zoos, and private places like this don't have the money to hire people. Edwina already had an older man working full-time, but he wanted to retire and go live with his daughter. I could do everything he could, except shoot.''

She took a swallow of her soda. "I remember the first time he brought me up here." She smiled. "I couldn't even keep my eyes open enough to aim at the target. I was terrified. I'd never handled a gun before in my life. Plus, tranquilizing a cat is complex. You have to know the body weight so you get the correct dosage. The dart has to land in a big muscle group. If it hits bone, you'll break it. If the dart passes through soft tissue into the animal's internal organs, you can kill the cat." She pulled her knees up to her chest. "That's why I aim for the rear flank. If I miss, the dart usually hits the ground."

"That's a big responsibility."

"It's the one part of the job I don't like."

"But you do it." He shifted toward her and studied her face. A few strands of hair drifted around her cheeks. He reached over and tucked them behind her ear. "You always find a way to surprise me."

She glanced down. "What do you mean? I'm just—"

"You're not 'just,'" he said, cutting her off. "I admire the way you don't let being scared get in the way. That's a rare strength."

"You're flattering me. I wish it were true. If you knew how many times I've been afraid."

He touched his finger to her chin and urged her to look

up at him. "Everyone is afraid. Most people let the fear win. You don't."

He smelled her perfume. It mingled with the warmth of her body, creating an essence that drew him closer. He wanted to kiss her full lips and feel the passion that had flared between them before. Instead, he traced the line of her jaw, then dropped his hand.

"Believe me, Faith. You're a hell of a woman."

She dismissed him with a shrug. "If I'm so damn strong, why am I scared of opening a snow-leopard breeding center? I think about it every day. I know it's the right thing to do. I have all the forms. I have the land. I can apply for permission to import two breeding pairs. If I packed up and moved today, I could be in business in less than six months."

"So what's stopping you?"

"Me." She set her soda on the ground. "I've never done anything like that. Edwina left me the foundation intact. I just have to keep it running. It's very different to start over from scratch."

He snapped off a blade of grass and toyed with it. "Once you were terrified of shooting a rifle. Now you're a marksman."

"I'm still scared. Every time I shoot a cat, I feel like I'm going to throw up."

"But you do it, anyway."

"I have to. They're depending on me."

"You'll move when you're ready," he said.

"I hope you're right." She wrapped her arms around her knees and stared into the distance.

Cort drained the last of his soda. It was peaceful out here. Faith didn't fill the quiet with chatter. She was easy to be with. He could talk to her or be silent with her. She wasn't afraid of hard work. She was a good leader. She'd given him instructions as to the care and feeding of the cubs, then left him to do the job. He knew she checked on him occasionally, but otherwise she trusted him to get it all done.

Cort used the same management style when he had people under him. Out in the field, there wasn't much chance for close supervision. He'd been alone when he'd been sent to South America. Why had he agreed to go? He grimaced. He knew the answer to that: Because it was his job.

"What's wrong?" Faith asked suddenly. "You look—" she leaned close to him and her mouth drew straight with concern "—as if you'd lost your best friend."

He jerked his head back and started to stand. She placed her hand on his arm. "Cort, don't turn away from me. I wasn't prying."

He hesitated, then settled back down. He hated to admit it, but he wanted to talk. To her, specifically. "I did just lose my best friend. Except for Jeff, my only friend." He looked at her. "Does that shock you? That I only had two friends in my life?"

"No," she said simply. "Not with what you do. Jeff's the same way. It's the job. You learn not to trust people."

"I guess you would understand. You live out here alone. You know what it's like to be on your own."

She turned until she was facing him, then sat cross-legged. "That's all I've ever been." She paused, as if considering her words.

He found it hard to volunteer information, but he wanted her to ask questions. He trusted her. It was risky to trust anyone, but Faith— It wasn't just because Jeff trusted her. It was because she was honest and dependable and strong.

"Have you remembered more of your last mission?" she asked.

"Some. I know where I was. I can't tell you the location."

"I understand." She smiled. "Classified. Can we narrow it down to a continent?"

"No." He laughed, then sobered. "I was supposed to check out an agent who might have gone bad."

"Had he?"

Cort stared past her into the trees. "Yes."

"I'm sorry."

He shrugged. "It happens."

"Is he dead?"

He looked at her. "Why do you ask?"

"I don't know. I just wondered." She spread her hands, palms up. "But he is, isn't he?"

Cort didn't answer.

She caught her breath. "Did you kill—"

"No."

"Then I don't understand why you're so troubled."

"I could have," he said sharply. He rose to his feet and started to pace in the clearing. "I could have been the one to kill him. I still don't remember enough."

"Did they tell you to kill him? Was that the mission?"

He hadn't wanted to admit it to himself, but he'd figured out the truth. "Yes."

"I've already told you I don't envy you your job," she said, standing up and leaning against the tree. "I wouldn't want to make choices about life and death, right and wrong. I know you've talked about fighting the good fight, but I don't understand the rules of your war. How do you know the enemy?"

He shoved his hands in his pockets. "You don't always. But I can't give up. That would mean they would have won."

"Who are *they?* That's what I don't understand. I guess I'm naive, but I like things to be black and white, or even in color. I couldn't live in your world of gray."

He stood in front of her and looked down at her open face. There were no secrets in her blue eyes, nothing artificial about her life. She lived in a world of defined choices.

Maybe that's what was wrong with him. Maybe it was the lack of color. Gray was cold and empty. It left him very much alone. He reached out to her, then dropped his hand. She saw the appeal and stepped close to him, wrapping her arms around his waist, burying her head in his chest. He hugged her tightly.

"I'm sorry I don't know how to help," she murmured.

"You've done more than you know."

He absorbed her warmth as if the heat itself would heal him. How long had it been since he'd allowed himself to hold another person? Not for sex, but because he liked the feel of her body next to his. He'd closed himself off because he couldn't let himself trust.

For what? He didn't know the who's and why's anymore. He didn't know anything. All he'd ever had was the good fight. Even that had been lost. He'd been sent to kill his friend. Circumstance had rescued him, but he knew he could have pulled the trigger. He had become the job.

He closed his eyes against the past and wondered if once, anywhere, he'd ever made a damn bit of difference.

William Thomas sat in a booth near the rear of the fifties-style diner. He'd barely had time to order coffee when a battered pickup pulled into the parking lot and a tall, bear-like young man stepped from the cab. Thomas allowed himself a small smile. Right on time.

Ken walked into the diner, looked around, spotted William Thomas and approached the booth. "Good to see you again," he said, holding out his hand.

"Young man." Thomas shook his hand, then indicated the empty seat opposite. "Please. Would you like anything?" he asked as the waitress returned with his coffee.

Ken slid in and smiled at her. "A cola, please." When she'd left, he turned to Thomas. "I've been really excited about what you told me. Is the job still open?"

"Of course. That's why I wanted to meet with you." Thomas smiled at the young man. "You're exactly what I'm looking for."

He wanted to reach across and grab the kid by the lapels of his ill-fitting sports coat and shake the information out of him, but he forced himself to go slow. Security had been tight at the party three nights ago. Too tight. He hadn't been able to get back into the building. Between the men patrolling and those bright lights they'd set up, he hadn't had a chance. But his life was on the line, so he'd come up with a new plan. And it all revolved around this college kid.

"You've worked at the way station how long?" he asked.

"Two years." Ken handed him a folder containing several typed pages. "Here's my résumé. As you can see, I have a lot of responsibility there. I know about the care and feeding of all the cats. Faith, uh, Faith Newlin—she's the lady who runs the way station—depends on me when she goes away. I'm sure I'll be right for you. Where did you say you were setting up your facility?"

"Texas," Thomas said, mentioning the first state that came to mind. He flipped through the pages without really seeing them. Before he'd left the party, he'd circled the compound one last time. He'd seen Ken putting a small, mean-looking cat into a cage and had struck up a conversation with the boy. The alternative to failing to get the cubs back was a .45 in the back of his head, so it wasn't too difficult to come up with a story to draw the kid out. He'd told Ken he was opening a way station of his own and was looking for someone to run it. The college student had taken the bait.

"I graduate in another month," Ken said, trying to hide his eagerness. "I was going to stay and work for the summer, but I'm sure Faith wouldn't mind if I—"

"What about security?" Thomas interrupted. "I noticed

a lot at the party. Is all that necessary? It was an expense I hadn't considered.''

''Don't worry about it.'' Ken leaned back in the booth. ''The extra security was for the party. Usually there's no one there but staff.''

''Usually?''

Ken straightened his jacket. ''Yeah, well, there's a guy there now, but that's because we have—'' He stopped suddenly and looked uncomfortable.

Thomas was silent. He learned long ago that most people couldn't stand silence. They would blurt out the first thing that came to mind just to fill the empty air.

''There's some rare tiger cubs staying for a couple months,'' Ken said. He paused. ''I'm helping another guy with security.''

Thomas didn't even have to look at him to know he was lying. One man. He smiled. Easy enough to take care of. He would simply drive in tonight and take the cubs.

He turned his attention back to Ken. He would continue with this mock interview. He didn't want to make the boy suspicious. A casual glance at his watch told him that he had plenty of time until nightfall. He would play out the game, then make his move.

Chapter 10

The absence of sound woke him. Cort sat up on his cot and listened. Normally the cats were active at night, playing, calling out to each other, roaring into the blackness. Nothing stirred outside his window, not even the wind.

He reached for his jeans and pulled them on, then slipped on boots and grabbed his pistol. The hallway was dark. First he checked on the cubs. They were sleeping in a bundle in the middle of their cage. Since the party three days ago, he'd kept them in the windowless room. He felt better knowing someone couldn't break in through a window. He backed out of the room, then secured the lock. He moved quietly to Faith's room and pushed open the door. She slept in her bed, her brown hair spread out on her pillow. He allowed himself a heartbeat of appreciation, then eased the door shut and went to her office.

Sparky stirred restlessly at his entrance and padded over to greet him. His chain stretched taut from its hook in the wall. Cort bent down and released the animal. Instantly

Sparky raced into the hallway and toward the door leading to the compound.

Cort followed him. He wished he could ask the animal what he heard or smelled. He checked through the glass in the door, but couldn't see anything. In the faint moonlight, Tigger paced in his habitat. The other cats seemed equally restless, but silent. Sparky butted him, then scratched at the door. Cort opened the lock and let the cat slip into the night. Before following, he chambered a round of ammunition, leaving the safety on. He cracked the door and went outside. As soon as he stood in the compound, he could feel the presence of someone. He crouched down and moved swiftly to the cover of the trees. Sparky had disappeared, and he didn't dare call out to the animal.

Cort closed his eyes and forced himself to concentrate. Could it be a four-legged predator, rather than a man? No, Faith had told him the scent of the cats kept any other animals away. Someone was after the cubs. He crouched low in the brush. He could circle around the building, but that wasn't where he sensed his enemy. Why would anyone hide out around the compound? He thought about the clearing they'd found a half mile up the mountain. Were they trying to come in that way, rather than through the front? Damn. Since his last mission, he didn't trust his instincts. He paused, torn by indecision, then moved slowly toward the habitats.

It took him thirty minutes to circle through the facility. He moved silently around the cages, trying to stay downwind of the more vocal cats. Twice Sparky appeared at his side. The leopard seemed to be hunting, as well, and having as little luck. Neither found any signs of an intruder, and Cort never heard a car or a truck. When he reached the main building again, all feeling of someone being there had disappeared. He put Sparky inside, but didn't chain him, then got the Jeep and drove it down to the main entrance.

He stared at the closed gate. A light mist of dew covered the ground. He bent down and touched the dirt by the road. It clung to his finger. No one had driven this way tonight. They would have left tire marks. He stood up and brushed his hand on his jeans. Was he crazy? Jeff had told him to stay and do his job because he was the best Jeff had. Was that still true? How much of his edge had he lost in South America?

He got back in the Jeep and jerked the steering wheel around. When he'd parked the vehicle, he took one last look around the compound. The cats were stirring now, behaving normally. A couple played with the bowling balls in their cages. The familiar *thunk* of the heavy balls hitting steel bars should have made him relax, but it didn't.

He opened the door to the foyer, then blinked at the lights in the hallway. Faith appeared at the doorway to her office. The sight of her caught him like a fist to the belly. She stood in a pool of light, naked beneath her cotton gown. The thin fabric hung to her ankles but concealed little. He could see the shape of her breasts, the darker color of her nipples and the small triangle of shadow at the apex of her thighs.

Long hair tumbled over her shoulders. Her feet were bare. She wore no jewelry, no ornamentation save her faint smile. Sparky sat at her side. The black leopard contrasted with her white nightgown. Cort understood why ancient men had worshiped women. Primal female power called to him, and every part of his body longed to respond. Between her thighs he could forget all that troubled him.

"What happened?" she asked.

"I though I heard someone. I didn't find anything. Neither did Sparky."

She nodded. "He would have treed a stranger. He's done it before. He won't, as a rule, attack." She rested her hand on the cat's head. "What else is wrong, Cort?"

He forced himself to look away from her. "What if no one was there? What if I've lost it?"

"If you've lost it, we'll find it for you. I believe you're right. Someone was there, but now they're gone. Come on." She held out her hand. "I've warmed some milk."

He ignored the outstretched hand. "I'm not some child you can coddle after a bad dream." The sharp tone of his voice had often made green agents tremble with fear. Faith simply looked at him. Sparky yawned. Cort stuck his gun in the small of his back and wondered when he'd stopped being intimidating.

"I'd planned to put rum in it," she said, turning away. "You look like you need a drink."

She hadn't shown her feelings, but he knew he'd hurt her. "Dammit, Faith." He hurried after her, stepping over the leopard who had settled in the hall. "I didn't mean—" He grabbed her arm and forced her to stop. "I didn't mean it like that."

He held her firmly, yet without bruising. Faith stared at his hand, at the scratches from playing with the tiger cubs, then looked at his bare chest. There was a scar from a bullet on his right arm, and the scratch she'd treated over a week ago. Had he been here that short a period of time? It felt as if he'd always been in her life.

Taking a deep breath, she raised her eyes to his. "I know what you meant," she said. She pulled her arm free. "Come into the kitchen. You could use a drink."

When he'd settled into one of the straight-back chairs, she poured warm milk into two mugs and added a healthy dose of rum. After sprinkling nutmeg on top, she handed him one.

"Cheers."

He touched his mug to hers. "I shouldn't drink on the job. It clouds judgment." He laughed without humor.

"Hell, I don't have any judgment left." He sipped. "It's good."

"Thank you." She flipped off the overhead lamp and took the seat opposite him. Light filtered in from the hall and glowed from above the ancient stove. "What happened tonight?"

He shrugged. The movement caused muscles to ripple across his bare chest and down his arms. She clutched her cup to keep from reaching out to touch him.

"Something woke me up. It's crazy, but it was the silence that made me think there was a problem. You know how loud the cats are at night."

She nodded. "If they were all quiet, there was someone or something out there."

"Whatever it was, it's gone now." He took another sip. "I checked the gate. No one had touched it. Maybe it was just some camper who got lost. He took one look at the jaguars in those end cages and headed back for the hills."

"I'm sure you're right."

"Am I?" He set his mug down and leaned toward her. "I still can't remember everything. It's driving me crazy. I know forcing my memory only makes it harder to recall exactly what happened, but I'm tired of waiting."

A strand of gold-blond hair fell over his forehead. She wanted to push it back into place. It was difficult to sit here and carry on a conversation while he was half-naked. She glanced down at her thin nightgown and smiled. She wasn't much more dressed than he was, but Cort didn't seem to be noticing.

"You don't want to hear this," he muttered, staring at the Formica table.

"Of course I do." He looked at her. The haunted expression in his eyes made her want to cry out in pain. Instinctively, she reached for his hand and covered it with hers. "Tell me anything you want. It won't go past these walls. I promise."

He turned his wrist until their fingers entwined. She squeezed tightly, trying to tell him she would hold on as long as he needed.

"I still don't know how the mission ended. I only have Jeff's word that I didn't kill my friend." He shook his head. "It doesn't matter if you know his first name. Dan. His name was Dan."

"Why do you doubt Jeff?"

"He may think I'm not ready for the truth." He leaned toward her. "I didn't have to pull the trigger to have killed him. There are a lot of ways to die on an assignment. A misspoken word. A route not changed quickly enough. Did I do or say something to tip the bad guys off?"

"Stop making yourself crazy," she said. "You have to put it behind you and go forward."

"I can't."

He stared out the window into the black night. She felt his pain as surely as if it were her own. She looked at his strong profile, at his straight nose and firm jaw. The pang inside her shifted and she realized it wasn't all about his hurting. She had a few wounds of her own to wrestle with.

He made her lonely. As they sat here in the quiet, baring souls, he made her ache with a wanting that would never be eased. She'd convinced herself she would never find a man who could understand her life-style and love her enough to stay. But being with Cort, sharing things with him that she'd always done alone, caring about him, made her vulnerable to hope. It was futile, she knew. But that didn't stop her from dreaming.

When the mission was over and the cubs were in their new home, he would leave her. His good fight required that he travel without excess baggage. He wouldn't have the room or the desire to carry her heart along. Even if she tried to tuck it in his pocket unnoticed, he would figure out the truth and cast it aside.

She listened as he spoke haltingly about Dan and their first meeting at the academy. He mentioned Jeff and the good times they'd shared. She could resist the warrior. He intrigued her, but didn't call to her innermost self. But this man, the one who exposed his wounds, swept through her barriers. She could not resist his vulnerability. His strength had first attracted her. His weakness made her care too much.

"The hell of it was," he was saying, "Jeff went ahead and asked me to be best man at his wedding." He shook his head. "At first, I didn't understand why he got married. Then I saw him with Jeanne. I don't know." He rubbed the bridge of his nose. "Loving that woman almost killed him." He shook his head. "That's not right. Losing her almost killed him. Loving her..." He trailed off. "It was all a waste of time, if you ask me."

Loving her made him strong, Faith thought, silently finishing Cort's sentence. She stared at their clasped hands, at his long, powerful fingers curling around hers. The truth swept through her, with all the power of a hurricane.

She understood Cort's reluctance to get involved. She knew he believed emotions weighed a man down. She recognized his confusion about love and duty because she shared it. For days she'd thought she felt attracted to him because he reminded her of the cats. All wild, unholy beauty with an amoral heart. Now she knew the truth. She'd seen more than the cats in Cort. She'd seen herself. They were, in the most basic of terms, soul mates.

"I need to go back," he said.

"Why?" she asked, trying to keep her voice from shaking. Her discovery shocked her to the core of her being.

"I have to know I can make a difference. It's all that matters." He looked at her. "Does that make sense?

You—'' he swept his arm across the table ''—you make a difference every day. Every time you save a cougar or send a snow leopard back into the wild, it changes the future.''

She ached for him, for herself and what she had to say. ''If fighting your battles makes the world better, then go back and fight.''

''Does it matter a damn?''

''I don't know. Does it?''

He drained his mug and squeezed her hand. ''Sometimes,'' he admitted. He hunched over as if the weight of his responsibilities were too heavy to bear. ''When I know who the bad guys are, like now, yes, it matters. Other times—''

''You mean, when the enemy might be your best friend?''

''You see too much.'' He looked at her. His lips curved up in a faint smile. With his free hand, he stroked her cheek. ''You are so beautiful.''

The compliment surprised her. She knew what she looked like, and while she didn't have to run around with a bag over her head, she wasn't anyone's idea of a beauty. She covered the hand on her cheek with her own and pressed his large palm against her skin.

She saw it deep in his gold-flecked eyes. He wanted to forget. And she was the easiest road to oblivion. He didn't love her; he never would. His heart had been given away long ago to a woman who hadn't bothered to appreciate the gift. Faith wanted to find the woman and demand she return Cort's heart so that someone else—someone like her—could have it.

Not likely. She knew her failings as well as her looks. She wasn't the kind of woman that men stuck around for. But the wanting in his eyes was a temptation. It would be easy to allow him to forget, if only for a night. She didn't give her body lightly, but this was Cort, and she could deny him very little.

Cort didn't regret the compliment. He'd spoken without thinking, but now, looking at Faith, he knew his words to be true. In the evening light, with compassion filling her eyes and her hair down on her shoulders, she was beautiful. It wasn't about the shape of her face, or her breasts almost visible under her gown. It was about the woman herself. All cats were gray in the dark, he'd told himself. But with Faith, he wanted to keep the lights on and know he was with her.

The itch that needed scratching, the desire to get lost, required a specific cure. It wasn't about any woman. It wasn't about the heat in his groin. It was about her. He needed *her*.

The realization scared him more than any sniper's bullet. He pulled away from her and stood up.

"Cort?" she asked quietly from her place at the table.

"This doesn't make sense," he grumbled. He walked over to the counter and leaned against it. "I'm sorry."

"Don't be." She rose to her feet. "I understand completely."

"I wish *I* did." He looked at her, at the shape of her body, at her honest face. "Go back to bed, Faith."

"I don't mind talking." She hovered beside her chair, not moving closer, but not going away, either.

"Maybe I don't want to talk."

She took a deep breath and moved to stand in front of him. "Maybe I don't mind that, either."

Her calm statement made his mouth water. His gaze swept over her. He told himself she couldn't possibly mean it. It was just the night or the circumstances. She was Jeff's friend and he'd promised his boss he would take care of her. Sex wasn't part of the package. Still, that didn't stop him from wanting her. He deliberately tortured himself by examining the shape of her generous breasts and watching her nipples pucker under the thin fabric of her gown. He felt the heat of her body so close to his. When he looked down at her feet, he almost groaned aloud.

She painted her toenails. Bright red. A completely, uselessly feminine flaunt in an otherwise utilitarian life. How the hell was he supposed to resist that?

He grabbed her by the arms and hauled her close. Her soft curves flattened against him, making his ache harden. "I need you," he said. "You're all I have to keep me sane."

She stared up at him and licked her lips. Deep inside, a powerful hunger snowballed through him, blocking out all rational thought, all pretense, leaving only the need.

"Cort, I—" She reached up to touch his face. Her fingers slipped against the stubble on his cheek, making a rasping sound. Her thumb brushed across his mouth. He touched her sensitive pad with the tip of his tongue and made her gasp. She tasted salty and sweet. Her blue eyes darkened, and she nodded as if coming to a decision.

"I feel it, too," she murmured. "And I don't mind if you pretend. I know it's about her."

He jerked his head away from her touch. "What are you talking about?"

"The woman. The one who broke your heart. I know you're remembering her. You can pretend she's the one—" She broke off and glanced down. She seemed to gather her strength together. She shook her hair away from her face and smiled faintly. "You can turn the light off."

Passion turned bitter and made him sick to his stomach. He'd told himself he'd lied so he wouldn't make Faith feel badly, but the truth was he'd lied to hide the blackness of his soul. Now it was coming back to haunt him.

He stared at her. She was the most open, honest person he'd ever known. He had, through the twisted hollowness of his life, turned her into a replica of himself. She was willing to let him pretend. But a woman like her wouldn't give herself lightly. He would go to a special place in hell for having reduced her to thinking she could only be a substitute when, in fact, she would have been the best thing that had ever happened to him.

"I'm so sorry," he said, knowing the words weren't enough.

She smiled. "Don't be. I couldn't help but notice how you were feeling. It makes perfect sense."

"No, it doesn't. I'm not the right one for you."

She flinched as if he'd slapped her. Her eyes flashed with the pain of rejection. "You don't want me." It wasn't a question.

"It's not that."

"Never mind. I understand." She stepped back and folded her arms over her chest. He recognized the protective gesture and wished he'd never started this particular game. There was no woman for her to remind him of. *She* would assume he was thinking of someone else, while he would only be thinking of her. But he couldn't tell her the truth without hurting her more.

"You can do better than me," he said, trying to ease her discomfort.

"Funny, that's what they all say."

"Faith." He reached out to her. She took another step back. "I'm just some guy who can't remember his past. You need to look beyond this to something better."

She walked over to the table and braced her arms against one of the chairs. "You mean *someone* better."

That one stung. "Yes."

God, he wanted to tell her the truth. He wanted to explain there never had been another woman, never would be. He didn't have relationships, didn't know how. Faith was the closest he'd come to caring. But telling her would mean admitting the lie, and the blackness in his soul.

"Faith, I—" He ran his hands through his hair. "Good night." He walked out of the room.

He was willing to admit he cared about Faith. But that wasn't his job. He was supposed to protect her. Better for him to remember that and not try to be her friend. Dan had been his friend, and look what had happened to him.

In the hallway he paused long enough to wonder when he'd changed. He wasn't the man he used to be. If only he could figure out if that was good or bad.

Cort blinked at the bright sunlight and bit back a groan. Last night, after Faith had gone back to bed, he'd taken the bottle of rum and finished almost half of it. Not only hadn't he been able to forget the accusing look in her eyes, he'd woken up with the mother of all hangovers.

By the time he fed the cubs and cleaned their cage, the pounding had subsided to the rhythm and volume of a jackhammer. His stomach lurched every time he thought about food, and he wondered if he could ask Faith to simply shoot him and put him out of his misery.

Just the thought of her made him feel worse. After last night, she would probably enjoy taking a shot at him, but she wasn't likely to make the end merciful. He slumped down against the building and shaded his eyes from the sun. He would sit here another minute, then he would crawl back to his room.

Sparky appeared at his side. The black leopard sniffed his face, gave him a rough lick on the cheek, then settled down next to him, laying his massive head on his thighs.

"Just don't purr loudly," Cort muttered, stroking his large, rounded ears.

"Hey, Cort!"

Cort flinched at the call. Ken jogged over and squatted in front of him. "You feeling all right?"

"No," Cort answered, being careful not to shake his head.

"Can I talk to you for a minute?"

There was something in the kid's voice that sounded a warning bell. Cort straightened. "What is it?"

Ken shifted and sat on the ground. "It's probably nothing, but I got to wondering, and what with the cubs and all—"

"The point," Cort said, then rubbed his head.

"I met a guy at the fund-raiser. He asked me about the cats and offered to interview me for a job." Ken looked up at him. "It's tough to get any work with big cats. The zoos don't have a lot of openings, and private facilities like this don't usually hire."

Faith had told him much the same thing. "So you're leaving?"

"No. Not yet." Ken shrugged. "I met with him yesterday and gave him my résumé. Only last night I realized I'd left out a letter of recommendation. So I called the hotel where he was staying. They didn't have anyone under that name registered there. Bowmund only has two hotels. I called the other one, then phoned around a few of the local motels on the mountain."

"And?" Cort asked, but he already knew the answer.

"Nothing."

"What's the guy's name?"

Ken flushed. "John Smith."

"You have a business card?"

The kid shook his head. "Guess he wasn't offering me a job, was he?"

Cort pushed Sparky out of the way and stood up. He ignored the pain in his head and looked at Ken. "Doesn't sound like it. Did he ask about the cubs?"

"I think so." Ken rose and shoved his big hands into his jeans pockets. "I know he asked about security. Cort, I'm sorry. I didn't mean—"

"I know you didn't. These people are pros. There's no way you could see what was happening. You were just looking for a job. Did you recognize the guy? Has he been at other fund-raisers?"

"He didn't look familiar, but I don't spend that much time with the guests."

"We'd better go talk to Faith." Cort led the way into the building.

Faith sat at her desk poring over official-looking forms. She glanced up as they entered the room.

"We may have trouble," Cort said.

She looked from him to Ken. "You'd better both sit down."

Ten minutes later she was going over the guest list. "I know most of the people personally," she said. "The description could fit a couple, I suppose, but there were about thirty guests I'd never seen before. There was no John Smith at the party, which means he probably used a false name to get in. You've seen the tape of everyone who came in the building the night of the party. Did you recognize him, Ken?"

Ken looked miserable. "I don't think so. It's dark and the tape only shows people from the back. Maybe. Oh, I don't know."

"Don't sweat it, kid," Cort said. "You did the right thing by telling us. If this guy approaches you again, be polite, but keep your distance. Tell him you can't talk now, and let me know right away. Whatever you do, don't play the hero."

Ken nodded.

Faith smiled at him. "Try not to think about this. Why don't you exercise Tigger for a while?"

"Okay, thanks." He left.

Faith closed the folder in front of her and sighed. "Was it one of the men after the cubs?" She didn't dare glance up at Cort. He looked awful and she didn't want to know why.

"Yes. I'm going to put a call in to Jeff. Apparently they've found out we're holding the cubs here. We need extra security around, and I want him to get those tigers moved as soon as possible."

"I don't like the idea of strangers—"

He cut her off. "You don't get a vote. I'm the security expert. I wasn't kidding when I warned Ken not to play the hero. Don't you be one, either. We need a team of at least six guys."

"Six!" She made the mistake of really looking at him. He hadn't shaved. The dark stubble made him appear even more dangerous. His eyes were red and had dark circles under them. "You look like hell."

"I feel like hell." He picked up the phone and punched in the number.

While he spoke with his boss, she toyed with her pencil. She would have to say it. Last night she'd lain awake and stared at the ceiling. The words had circled around and around in her head. She had to thank him.

He hung up the phone. "All set." He perched on the corner of her desk. "They'll be here by tonight."

"Thank you," she said.

"Just doing my job."

"No." She bit her lip. "Thank you for last night."

"Faith, I didn't mean—"

"I really appreciate your not taking advantage of me. I'm not promiscuous, and I might have regretted it later."

He stared at her oddly for a moment, then nodded. "You're welcome."

That was it? That was all he was going to say? She felt

as deflated as a popped balloon. Somehow she'd hoped for a little more from him. Something about how *he'd* lain awake wishing she were in his bed. Even a flicker of regret. She tossed her pencil on the desk and glared at him. He didn't seem impressed. As she studied him, she felt her body start to quiver. Despite his rejection and the other woman in his life and everything that was happening with the cubs, she still wanted him.

"You're a brave woman," he said.

"What does that have to do with anything?"

"It doesn't. The thought just occurred to me."

Great. She didn't want to be brave. She wanted to be irresistible and feminine and all those things she would never be. She laced her fingers together on the desk and allowed herself to think the truth. For once in her life, she wanted to be enough.

He rose and walked to the door. Before leaving, he turned back to face her. "Courage is a learned behavior, Faith. Who taught you yours?"

She frowned. "I'm not especially brave."

"That's the whole point. It's facing the fear that makes you strong."

Chapter 11

Thomas eased his dark sedan to a stop in front of the entrance to the university parking lot. He was not having a good day. He'd been awakened by a phone call informing him he had one week to complete his mission.

"Or we will be forced to discontinue our association."

Thomas grimaced. He knew what that meant. Association, hell. It was *him* they would be discontinuing. Damn.

He stared at the college students walking toward their cars. A quick call to the registrar's office had given him Ken's schedule. He knew what time his classes ended and had decided to wait by the entrance to the parking lot and intercept the student as he was leaving for the day.

He needed a way into the compound. Last night had been a complete failure. The gate had been too sturdy for his car to break through, and a study of the equipment used to open and close it had convinced him any tampering would result in an alarm sounding somewhere up at the compound. He'd been forced to drive up the mountain and hike into the facility.

Thomas grimaced as he shifted in the seat. His arms and legs were a mass of scratches from the underbrush and trees. With only a quarter moon and a flashlight to illuminate the way, it had taken him almost two hours to get near the place. Before he'd even gotten close to the main building, the security guy had been out walking around. Thomas would have taken him out, but then he'd seen the black leopard patrolling the cages. Jesus. A shiver rippled through him. What kind of crazies kept something like that for a watchdog?

To add insult to injury, his car had gotten a flat. He'd had to roll it down the mountain in neutral. He'd barely made it back to his room by dawn. He had to find a better way inside.

He was going to get the kid to let him in the gate. It was the only approach that made sense. If the kid didn't want to cooperate, he would force him.

The flow of students had subsided some, but now a large group of young people were making their way toward the parking lot. Thomas watched intently. There. Behind the blonde with the big chest. Thomas eased the sedan forward until he blocked the main path. Kids moved around the car, giving him dirty looks.

When Ken passed in front of him, Thomas opened the door and stepped out.

"Ken," he called, forcing himself to smile. "How are you?"

Ken froze in his tracks. He looked startled, then scared. "You? What are you doing here?"

Thomas didn't like the expression in his eyes. He had a bad feeling about this. He casually reached under his jacket for his gun. "I had a few more questions. You got a minute?"

The last of the students walked toward their cars, leaving Thomas and Ken alone at the edge of the parking lot. Ken shook his head. "Leave me alone." He started to walk away.

Thomas sprinted two steps and caught him by the arm. "Not so fast, buddy."

Ken jerked free. "Don't 'buddy' me. We're on to you, man. You're not going to get away with it."

Thomas felt the fury build up inside him. This little piece of trash had ratted on him. He grabbed Ken again and pulled him close. They were almost the same height. Thomas eased the gun out of its holster and pressed the barrel against Ken's stomach.

"Don't make a sound," he growled. "You hear me?"

Ken glanced down at the gun and caught his breath. He made a strangled noise in his throat. "Don't hurt me."

Thomas pushed him toward the door. "Get in."

Ken's face paled. "What are you going to do with me?"

"Just ask you a few questions."

The kid had nailed him, he thought with disgust. The whole facility was probably on alert. He cursed. Could it get any worse? He shoved Ken in the back seat, then reached in the glove box for a pair of handcuffs. When the kid was secure, Thomas started the car and drove off around the parking lot.

"Where's your truck?" he asked.

"Over there." Ken nodded in the direction.

Thomas stopped behind the truck. The kid would have a remote control device to control the gate. He could make use of that. It would take a couple of days to come up with a foolproof plan to get the tiger cubs. Before he made another attempt, he had a lot of work to do.

First he was going to find out everything Ken knew. Then he was going to get rid of his problem.

Faith slammed down the phone. Two days. Ken hadn't shown up for two days. She'd put a call in to his dorm room but no one had seen him. Any worry she'd felt disappeared when Ken's roommate informed her that Nancy, Ken's girlfriend, had gotten an assignment in Las Vegas. No doubt Ken had taken off with her and was currently having the time of his life.

She slowly turned her chair until she was facing the window and could see out into the compound. For the last few months, Ken had been completely irresponsible. The incident with the reporter had been the final straw. But since she'd warned him to straighten up, he'd been doing a good job. What had happened? When she got her hands on him...

She clutched the arms of her chair as a cold ribbon of fear curled up her spine. John Smith, or whatever his name was, had approached Ken and talked to him. Was it possible something had happened to the young man?

She watched Beth playing with Samson. The bobcat chased after her, catching her easily and gently taking her arm in his mouth. No, not that, she told herself. Ken *had* to be fine.

"You look pensive," Cort said.

She turned her chair until she could see him. He held the smaller of the tiger cubs in his arms. Little crawled up his chest and nuzzled his neck.

"I'm just cranky," Faith said, wondering why on earth she envied the cub's place in Cort's arms. She'd put her desire behind her the night he'd turned her down. She wasn't interested in him. She didn't care about Cort Hollenbeck at all. She sighed. Yeah, right.

"One of those days?" he asked.

She shrugged.

He came into the office and sat on the chair in front of her desk. The cub sat in his lap and blinked at her. Sparky trailed in, took one look at the cub and walked over to Faith, deliberately turning his back on the younger animal.

"You're jealous, aren't you?" she asked softly, scratching his ears. He humphed at her. She pointed at the cub. "How are they doing?"

"Eating, playing." He held up his arm, showing her a long red scratch from his elbow to his wrist. "Learning to wrestle."

She shook her head. "I told you to wear gloves when you play with them. They do require social interaction, but there's no need for you to pay for it with a pound of flesh."

He grinned. "Social interaction? Faith, these are tiger cubs, not children."

"They still have needs. As the surrogate parents, we have responsibilities that can't be ignored. If we don't take care of their social needs, they won't be well adjusted enough to spend time with other tigers and breed."

He scratched Little under the chin but stared at Faith. There was something about the expression in the gold-flecked eyes that made her want to squirm.

"Why are you looking at me like that?" she asked.

"I was thinking that the snow leopards are very lucky cats."

She busied herself adjusting Sparky's collar. "Don't be maudlin."

"I'm very serious. You're a dedicated woman."

"I'm still not sure I'm going to be able to pull this off."

He dismissed her with a shrug. "You'll open your center. You'll find a way to get the money and handle the permits. I have every confidence in you." Little nibbled on the buttons of his shirt. He pushed her away. She wiggled to get comfortable on his lap and shifted onto her back, exposing her white belly. Cort rubbed her soft fur and skin, making her squirm with pleasure. Bright blue eyes blinked sleepily. She grabbed his hand in her front paws and gnawed on his thumb.

Faith stared at the small cub and fought down fierce jealousy. Cort handled the baby and her needs with a combination of competence and affection that left her breathless. She wouldn't have thought one of Jeff's warriors would so easily adapt to the ways of the real world.

She smiled and glanced around at her dilapidated office, at the compound visible through the window and the black leopard sitting at her feet. Okay, so maybe this wasn't a normal situation, but it was much more domestic than he was used to. Perhaps his ability to adapt was what made him so good at his job. To think about tying him down would be as cruel and inhuman as caging a wild panther or snow leopard. Only domesticated creatures belonged in polite society. Even if he had been emotionally available to her, she couldn't, in good conscience, chain him to a life of mortgage payments and dinner at six.

Foolish dreams. He wasn't available to her. And she wasn't the kind of woman who could hold a man. Her own father hadn't loved her enough to stick around, and she'd been his only child.

Sparky flicked his tail and stared into her eyes. "You love me, don't you, baby," she said softly. He rumbled deep in his throat and shot the cub a malicious stare.

"Where's Ken?" Cort asked. "I haven't seen him in a couple of days."

She hesitated. "It's probably nothing, but I just got off the phone with his roommate. They haven't seen him, either."

Cort straightened in his chair. The quick movement caused the cub to roll onto her side. She mewed her protest, but he didn't notice. "What do you mean they haven't seen him? He's missing?"

Faith shook her head. "No. Nancy, his girlfriend, had an assignment in Las Vegas. His roommates think Ken went with her, and I agree. It's not the first time he's taken off without saying anything to me."

Cort reached forward and grabbed the phone from her desk. He pulled it toward him.

"What are you doing?" she asked.

"Calling the police."

She bit her lower lip. "Jeff had already checked out the guest list, and everyone was cleared. The guards checked ID at the gate. No one tried anything funny. I find it hard to believe one of the guests is involved with stealing the cubs."

"Maybe one of your guests wasn't who he pretended to be. There was no John Smith at the party, but we don't know the guy's real name. Or if he used a stolen invitation to get in."

She hadn't thought of that. "Is Ken in danger?"

Cort's call connected and he didn't answer her. He spoke to the local police and explained Ken might be missing. They agreed to contact the authorities in Las Vegas and try to locate Ken's girlfriend.

"Now what?" Faith asked when he hung up.

"Now we wait. I want—"

A knock on the door interrupted him. One of the security guards stuck his head in her office. "Cort, Andy told me to let you know the trailer's arrived. They're setting it up beside the Big House."

"That's fine." He motioned for the man to come in the room and handed him his walkie-talkie. "I want to change the frequency on these today. Tell Andy when he's done, I want to see him. We may have a missing employee."

The man stepped forward cautiously. He was in his late twenties, shorter than Cort by several inches and not nearly as muscular. He kept his pale eyes fixed on Sparky. When he reached out to take the equipment, the leopard raised his nose and sniffed. Before Faith could grab him, he spun on his huge paws and roared at the security guard. The man turned white and started to run. The tiger cub jumped at the sound and tried to bury herself in Cort's belly.

"Freeze," Cort commanded.

The man froze.

Sparky flinched slightly, and Faith cuffed him on the shoulder. "Mind yourself," she told the leopard.

The cub stared up at Cort, not sure which way to run. He picked her up in one hand and pulled her against his chest. "Sorry, Little," he said, petting her reassuringly. After studying him for several seconds, she mewed and nestled against this chin.

The guard stood trembling by the door. Cort rose and faced him. "Never run from the leopard. He won't hurt you unless you provoke him."

The guard nodded, looking unconvinced. Cort handed him the walkie-talkie. "You can go now."

The man left without saying a word.

Cort took his seat and shook his head. "You're going to have to keep Sparky chained up."

"I won't."

"Faith, if I hadn't been here, the guard would have shot him."

She touched Sparky's back protectively. "How do you know?"

"His hand was resting on his holster. It's an instinct. The men here are trained to react to danger. They perceive a large black leopard as danger. If nothing else, letting him roam free distracts them."

"I can't keep him chained up twenty-four hours a day. That's cruel."

"Let him roam this building at night, if you want. But other than that, he can only go out on a leash."

"I hate these changes," she said. "There are too many strangers here. There are cars running around the compound. The cats are restless. It's not good for them. This

morning when I spoke to Jeff, he said he'd have the cubs
moved by the end of the week. That's only four more days.
What can happen between now and then? Is all this necessary?''

Cort leaned forward and placed the cub on her desk. ''I
didn't question you about your instructions regarding the
cubs. Trust me to know my job and to do it right. I'm going
to keep you and them safe.''

She sat back in her chair and drew one leg to her chest.
''But six men? Is that necessary?''

''Two men per eight-hour shift isn't excessive.''

The cub sniffed at the papers on her desk, then batted at
a pen. It went flying off onto the floor. Little raced to the
edge and looked down. Sparky turned toward the kitten.
Their eyes met. Little arched her back, her hair raising on
end, and spit wildly at the leopard, then ran to the In-basket
and dove into a pile of papers.

Cort moved around the desk and stood in front of Faith.
He held out his hand and pulled her to her feet. ''What's
really the problem?'' he asked.

She shrugged. ''I'm out of sorts. Don't *I* get to have a
bad day?''

But it wasn't the day at all, she thought glumly. It was
the man. Time was ticking away. Her phone conversation
with Jeff had upset her more than she'd realized. Only four
more days until the cubs were gone, and Cort with them.
He was healthy now. He'd remembered most of his last
mission. It was probably enough to get him cleared to go
back to the field and do what he loved. But inside, deep in
the place where dreams hid, she felt a restless longing. It
was about more than being with him physically, although
she wanted that, too. It was about caring for someone and
having him care back.

''Are you sure there's nothing wrong?'' he asked, staring
into her eyes.

She reached out and touched the scar on his chin. The cut had healed completely, but the line from the corner of his mouth down across his chin still looked raw. He'd gained weight since he'd arrived and the hollows in his cheeks didn't look so gaunt. He walked without a limp. Truly there was nothing to keep him with her.

"Faith?" His gold-flecked brown eyes filled with concern. A lock of hair tumbled onto his forehead. Broad shoulders blocked out most of the overhead light. He was every inch a powerful alpha male, and she wanted to be his mate.

"What are you thinking?" he asked.

Something incredibly foolish, she told herself.

A loud squawk cut through the silence and drew her attention away from him. The tiger cub had jumped from the desk onto Sparky's back. She clung tenuously, digging her claws into his fur. Sparky shook like a wet dog, trying to dislodge her, but every jerk of his body made her dig in more.

Faith started to laugh. Sparky glared at her and growled. Cort leapt toward the pair. Little howled. Cort accidentally snagged the chair with his foot and started to go down. Faith grabbed his arm with one hand and the chair back with the other. She felt herself being pulled forward, but couldn't stop laughing. Sparky jumped toward them, knocking over the trash can in his haste. The metal container fell right where Cort stepped.

"Dammit, cat, get out of my way," he grunted, jerking sideways to avoid the container and losing his balance. Sparky spun in a circle, trying to pull the cub from his back. Faith released her grip on Cort and fought to hold on to her balance. The chair fell to the ground. Sparky's rear caught her behind her left knee and she went down, hitting her leg on the trash can and landing across Cort's midsection.

The "ooph" of his sharply exhaled air whistled by her ear. As Sparky circled by, desperately trying to pull the tiger off by grabbing her tail, Faith reached for the cub. Little dug in one more time, then released her claws and scrambled against Faith. Sparky made a beeline for the corner and curled up in a tight ball beside the file cabinets.

Faith was still laughing. She pushed herself into a sitting position, using Cort's stomach for leverage. He groaned as she pressed down against him. The cub slipped from her grasp and fell on Cort's chest. There she promptly collapsed and mewed in his face.

"You okay?" Faith asked, gasping for breath. She moved off his legs and onto the floor.

"No."

He sat up slowly, grabbing the cub by the scruff of her neck. Little instinctively curled up her back paws and looked expectantly at him as if saying, "Where are we going, Mom?"

Cort shook her gently. "You're a pest." Little meowed happily, and he dropped her onto his lap.

Faith leaned against her desk and surveyed the damage. Only the chair and the trash can had hit the floor. Not bad.

"Feeling better?" Cort asked.

"Yeah, I am. Are you going to tell me you planned that just to make me feel better?"

He shook his head. "No, but I'm glad you're smiling again."

She stared self-consciously at her lap. Cort leaned forward and placed his hand on the back of her neck. "Forget about all this," he said. "Ken, the cubs, the security. You've done all you can. I'm going to put this monster in with her brother, then take Sparky for a leisurely walk around the compound. You head up to the Big House for a long, hot bath. I don't want to see you back here for at least a couple of hours."

He kneaded the tense muscles in her neck, and she leaned into the relaxing pressure. "Is that a direct order?"

"You bet. And I expect it to be obeyed."

She told herself not to, but she couldn't help looking at him mouth. Those firm lips had once claimed hers with an amazing passion. She still remembered the fiery need that had raced through her at the first touch of his tongue. Her fingers curled toward her palms as she recalled the feel of his hot skin and the tight curve of his buttocks. Would he join her in her bath?

Before she even thought about collecting the courage to issue an invitation, she pushed the fantasy aside. He'd already turned her down once. She wasn't going to be foolish enough to ask a second time.

She stood up and reached for the cub. "I'll put her away. You see to Sparky. Can you check his back and make sure she didn't break the skin?"

"Not a problem." He looked at the black leopard glaring at the tiger cub. "We're buddies."

She held Little close to her chest as she left. The small bundle of fur wasn't enough to fill the ache she had inside. It would take a man in her life to make that need go away.

"Life is never fair," she murmured to the kitten before tucking her into her cage. "And loving someone can be very dangerous."

It was past midnight when Sparky padded into Cort's room. Cort sensed more than heard the animal as he silently slipped through the blackness. Cort raised up on one elbow.

"What is it, boy? What do you hear?"

The leopard grunted low in his throat and left the room. For the second time in a week, Cort pulled on jeans and boots, then reached for his gun. After making sure the cubs were in their cage, he backed out of the room and locked it behind him. Sparky hovered close by, following when he went to wake Faith.

He pushed open her door. "Faith, I think I—" He stared

at the empty bed. Where had she gone? He glanced down at the leopard, but Sparky simply stared back. After checking the other rooms in the building and making sure they were empty, he verified that the front door was locked, then stepped to the rear door leading out to the compound. Sparky butted his knee.

"No you don't," he told the leopard. "You're staying in here. It would be too easy for one of the guards to accidentally shoot you."

The leopard growled and tried to slip past him. Cort dragged him back to the office and secured him to the chain. Sparky glared his anger. Cort ignored him. "Nobody's dying while I'm in charge," he muttered. He collected his walkie-talkie as he moved past his room.

At the rear door, he looked through the glass before stepping into the night. As they had before, the cats paced silently in their cages.

He scanned the compound. The jeep wasn't where it had been parked when he went to bed. One of the guards must have taken it on patrol. The rule was that the two guards on duty were never to leave the area together. Someone was to stay by the main building at all times. But he couldn't see the second guard, or Faith. Yet someone was out there. He could feel it.

He spoke softly into the radio. The unit crackled, but there was no response. Low in his gut, a sense of unease grew. He spoke again. Still nothing. Cort chambered a round into the gun and put his thumb on the safety. He began moving toward the cages on the far side of the road to the Big House. He crouched low as he walked, constantly looking for signs of the intruder.

He was almost to the first cage when a flash of white caught his eye. He glanced up and saw Faith coming out from behind the habitat at the end, the one that housed the first of the two wild jaguars. He inched toward her and spoke her name. She turned toward him.

She wore black jeans and boots, but her white T-shirt made her visible in the night. He motioned for her to get down. She didn't see the gesture and continued walking toward him. The hairs on the back of his neck bristled. He didn't dare call out his instructions and alert whoever was out there.

Cort broke into a jog. A sixth sense caused him to look up ahead, where the compound bled into the trees. A glint of something metal made his heart pound in his chest.

"Get down," he called, not caring that the man behind her could hear him.

Faith stopped walking toward him and stared. "Down," he yelled as he jumped toward her. She hesitated a second, then hit the ground. He landed on top of her, just as he heard the distinctive *pop* of a silenced gun firing. He didn't bother waiting to catch his breath; he simply got to his feet, grabbed her arms and pulled her along with him, between the second and third habitats.

He counted six more shots fired at them as he and Faith came to a stop between an empty cage and one of the jaguars. The flat-faced cat growled and stuck its paw out by the front corner. Cort pulled Faith out of the way. He scrambled on his belly toward the walkway and fired into the bushes where the intruder had been.

The sound of his Beretta cut through the night. In the distance, he heard the trailer door bang open and the four other security guards run out toward the compound. Nothing stirred in the brush, and he knew the man was gone. Only then did he realize Faith hadn't said a word to him. He returned to her side and touched her face. "Faith. Are you hurt?"

She didn't answer. He pulled a penlight from his jeans pocket and shone it on her body. Blood seeped from her arm and collected in a pool on the ground.

Chapter 12

Faith's eyes fluttered open. She blinked several times, then raised her hand to push the light away.

"Don't move," Cort said, grateful she was conscious. "I think you've been shot."

"What?" She glanced down at her left arm. "Oh my God, I'm bleeding."

"Is that the only place that hurts?" He began to feel along her legs, then moved up to her torso.

While he was running his hands along her thighs, she raised herself up to a sitting position and stared at her arm. "I can't be shot. It doesn't hurt that badly."

"Shock," he muttered, slipping his hands under her T-shirt. When his palm brushed her bare midsection, their eyes locked. Despite the danger, electricity raced between them. He forced himself to ignore the sensations and quickly explored her chest and back. "Seems to be the only injury," he said, sitting back on his heels. "The bleeding is slowing."

The guards ran into the compound. "What happened?" Andy asked. "The Jeep is gone and neither of my men are answering."

"I know." Cort stood up. "Have Mike take her inside and stay with her. Tell Ralph to take a truck down to the gate and stay there. Don't let anyone out. You and Tom, come with me. I want to catch the bastard who did the shooting." He looked down at Faith. "Are you going to be all right?"

One of the guards stepped forward and gave her a hand up. "I'm fine. Go." She waved Cort off.

He drilled her with one more hard look, then gave directions to the men and jogged toward the bushes.

Once in the forest, it was difficult to find a path. He paused to listen. The two guards with him fanned out. Within five minutes he knew they didn't have a prayer of finding anyone tonight. Not unless the shooter tried to make a break for it. With only a quarter moon for light, and all the trees and leaves blocking that faint glow, he could barely see two feet in front of him. He pulled out his radio and told the two security men to head back to the main building. One of them was to guard the structure, the other was to join Ralph down at the gate. Cort turned around and took a step forward.

Time bent and ripped with an almost audible wrenching sound as he was flung into the past. An explosion roared through the night. He felt it lift him up and toss him aside like a rag doll. He hit the floor of the warehouse. Smoke and heat filled his lungs. And something else. Salt air. He could smell the ocean.

He tried to move, tried to escape, but his body refused to obey his commands. His head throbbed. Someone tugged on his arms, pulling him away from the flames. He was dragged from the burning building and tossed into the back seat of a car. He blacked out for several minutes and regained consciousness on a bumpy dirt road. The vehicle drove on, speeding through the night without even headlights to show the way.

Who was driving? Where were they going? Who had saved him? He forced himself to sit up and lean forward. There was only one other man in the car. The driver. He squinted his eyes and peered into the darkness. "Dan?"

His friend didn't turn around. "I'm glad you're awake. There's a nasty bump on your head, buddy. I was afraid you were out for good."

"What the hell happened?"

"Someone blew up the warehouse."

He had a hard time concentrating through the pain. "Was it you?"

Dan didn't answer for a long time. "Why are you here, Cort? Have you come to take me back?"

Now it was Cort's turn to be silent.

"I get it," Dan said at last. "I'm not supposed to come back. Don't worry, buddy. Going home to the good old U.S. of A. wasn't part of my plan, either."

He turned into a long, narrow field and cut the engine. Cort gingerly stepped out of the car and stared around him at the familiar landing sight. "What are we doing here?"

"Getting you home. The gentlemen I'm doing business with are onto you." Dan came and stood beside him. "Have been since the day you arrived. You're lucky to be alive."

Cort sure didn't feel lucky. With one hand, he held on to the car for balance. He had moments of clear vision, followed by sensations of vertigo. With his other hand, he reached under his sports coat and pulled out his gun. The metal finish gleamed in the light of the full moon.

"You sold out," Cort said. "Why?"

"I would tell you it was for the money, but you wouldn't believe me."

"You got that right. What happened? Blackmail?"

Dan turned toward him. Cort slowly raised his gaze and stared at the familiar crooked smile of his friend.

"That would be easiest, wouldn't it?" Dan asked. He lit a cigarette, then blew out the match and dropped it on the ground. "You would like to think I was being forced into this. Anything else would upset your tidy ideas of right and wrong."

"Damn you." Cort raised the gun toward his friend. "I'm taking you back with me."

Dan shook his head. "That's not what your boss told you to do, Cort. You're supposed to get the proof, then make sure I'm never a problem again." He waved his cigarette toward the heavens. "Here comes your ride."

Cort turned and looked up. A fast-moving plane seemed to drop from the sky like a rock. It dove down toward the narrow field, the sound of its engine growing as it approached. When it was seconds from landing, Cort jabbed Dan in the side with his pistol. "Move."

"No." Dan took one last drag on the cigarette and dropped it to the ground. After stepping on it, he looked at Cort and smiled. "You can kill me, or you can let me go, but I'm not coming back to the States. I wouldn't like prison."

From behind them, headlights swept across the field and focused on the car. A low, dark four-door car raced toward them. Cort recognized the vehicle and the men inside.

"Looks like your friends found us," he said.

Dan surprised him by laughing. "Nothing goes right in this country. Come on." He started toward the plane, which was bumping its way across the rough field.

Cort ran after him, keeping low to the ground. He was about ten feet away from the wing when a bullet caught him in the leg. He went down.

Instantly Dan backtracked and crouched at his side. "You're not having a good stay here, are you?"

Cort grinned, despite the pain. "Hell of a vacation. Get me on board that plane, you lazy bastard."

Dan hoisted him up over his shoulder and carried him to the open door. From inside, someone reached out to pull him to safety. Cort grabbed Dan, but his friend jerked free.

"I meant what I said. I'm not coming back." Dan had to yell to be heard above the plane's engine. The men on the ground started shooting at the plane.

"They'll kill you," Cort shouted.

"Better them than you. I'm not coming back." The plane started moving forward, gathering speed for takeoff.

"No! You can't stay. Stop!" Cort screamed to the pilot. "We've left one on the ground." But no one listened. He tried to jump out, but the men inside started hauling him away from the door. He leaned out and stared back at Dan.

His friend gave him a jaunty salute, then spun to face the men racing toward the plane. They were all firing at the small craft. Dan pulled out his gun and shot at them. Two went down. The remaining three turned their weapons on him. Cort stared in disbelief as they pumped Dan's body full of bullets. His friend hit the ground without a single scream of pain.

The plane rose above the field and the surrounding trees, then angled north for the trip home. Cort let himself be pulled inside, and the door was secured. The pain in his head increased with each heartbeat, and he felt the blood flowing out his leg. Then he closed his eyes and willed himself to forget.

The sounds of the past receded slowly, the plane engine fading until all Cort could hear were the night creatures and an owl in a nearby tree. He sank to the damp ground just outside the way station compound. He'd remembered it all. The hell of it was he just wanted to forget the whole damn thing.

Dan had known Cort had been sent to verify that he'd

betrayed his country—and if Dan had, Cort was to keep him from being a problem again. Yet Dan had saved Cort, sacrificing his own life in the process.

Why? It didn't make any sense. Why had Dan sold out in the first place? It wasn't about the money. Dan had never cared about that. He'd claimed it wasn't blackmail. Cort fought the memories. He'd gotten what he'd wanted most— he was fit to return to duty. But for what? Did any of it matter anymore?

He stood up and started walking back to the compound. Every step made him more aware of what he'd almost done. He'd accepted a mission that meant killing his friend. What kind of man had he become?

He stepped into the clearing. One of the guards rushed up to him. "We've heard from the missing two men."

"What happened?"

"The Jeep's tires were slashed. When the second guard on went to go get help, he was knocked out and left tied up."

"Anyone hurt?"

"No. Andy put a call in to the police. We have to report the intruder and the shooting."

"Good." Cort shook off the memories clinging to him and jogged toward the main building. He needed to make sure Faith was going to be all right.

Thomas pounded on the steering wheel of the sedan and cursed out loud. Every damn thing that could go wrong had. If he'd believed in luck, he would swear his was all bad.

He eased up on the gas as he negotiated a rough patch of ground and headed for the paved driveway leading out of the compound. He'd left the gate open when he'd come through two hours before, in case he had to leave in a hurry. He reached over and grabbed the remote-control device he'd stolen from Ken's truck, fingering the open button. Someone might have closed it.

He hadn't even gotten close, he thought with disgust. Even going up the driveway and parking a couple hundred yards downwind of the compound hadn't helped him get in without being seen. Those damn cats had begun acting funny, spooking him with their silent appraisal. He hated animals. He'd have to come up with a better plan. Time was—

He rounded the last bend and cursed when he saw the two trucks parked in front of the closed gate. Two men took up positions on either side of their vehicles and pulled out guns. One reached for something. Thomas punched the "open" button on the gate remote at the same time he hit the gas. The dark sedan jumped forward. Just in time, he remembered the asphalt gave way to a bumpy dirt road that would destroy the underside of his car. He jerked the steering wheel hard to the left and bounced off the road. The rear end fishtailed on the soft ground, but he didn't ease up on the gas.

One guard raised a gun in his direction. Thomas ignored him. The gate continued to swing open. Tree branches scratched against his windows. He smiled. The jerks had parked their trucks too far away from the gate. They hadn't planned on anyone going around. He would be able to slip through easily.

A bullet hit the passenger door.

"Amateurs," Thomas muttered. He jammed on the brakes as the car rolled onto the bumpy road. Turning sharply to the right, then left, he drove between the gate post and the trucks. The rear of his car just grazed the smaller vehicle. Two more bullets hit his car. One popped through the rear windshield and stopped in the passenger seat.

Sweat popped out on Thomas's back. Maybe he'd been

too quick to dismiss them. Then his front wheels rolled onto smooth public road. He floored the gas pedal and went screaming down the highway without looking back.

Fifteen minutes later he pulled into an abandoned barn and turned off the engine. If the guards had followed, he'd lost them when he'd left the highway and turned onto the backroads. But he couldn't keep playing around like this. Obviously he wasn't going to be able to steal the cubs without someone seeing, so why worry about subtlety? It was time to bring in reinforcements.

"Anything else you can add, ma'am?" the police officer asked.

Faith shook her head. "No. I'm sure they were after the white tiger cubs, but I don't know the name of the people interested in them. I've given your detective the phone number of the man in charge of this case." She reached up and rubbed her eyes. They, along with almost every other part of her body, hurt. "Jeff didn't bother to tell me names, and quite frankly, I didn't want to know who they were."

"Thank you." The officer smiled politely and left.

Faith leaned forward and rested her arms on her desk. It was almost two in the morning. The police had arrived an hour before and had combed the compound, searching for clues and asking everyone questions that couldn't be answered. Of course the man had been after the tiger cubs. But Cort and his team had handled the situation. She just wanted the police gone.

"How are you holding up?" Cort asked.

She raised her head and saw him standing in the doorway of her office. Sometime in the last hour he'd pulled on a sweatshirt. But his hair was still rumpled from sleep, and he needed a shave. He looked wonderful.

"I'm surviving," she said. "Are they almost done?"

"Yeah. Look at this." He moved into the room and held out a small plastic bag. A flattened slug rested in one corner.

"What is it?"

"A bullet. They found three altogether."

For the first time since Sparky had awakened her with his restless pacing, she smiled. "You'll have to forgive me if I don't share your enthusiasm. Finding bullets is rarely the highlight of my day."

"I'm having the police forward Jeff one of the bullets."

"What does he make of all this?"

"He's out of the country for the next two days. Nobody knows where he is. I can't get ahold of him."

"Don't look so grim. We'll be fine."

He settled on the corner of her desk. "I would like to pack you and the cubs up and get the three of you out of here until Jeff gets back and can make other arrangements."

She shook her head. "Don't even think about it. I can't leave the other cats. If it makes you feel any better, I'm going to call the kids and tell them not to come in to work until Saturday. That way there are fewer of us to guard. It's only a couple more days until Jeff moves the cubs. With you and your security team here, we'll make it."

"I wish I had your optimism." He shook his head. "Because this isn't an official operation, I'm going to have trouble getting more security. In the morning I can call in a few favors and see what happens. I just wish I knew where Jeff was."

"There's nothing you can do about it now." She reached up to touch him, then winced as pain shot through her arm.

Cort glanced down at the blood on her T-shirt. "You get anyone to look at that?"

"It's just a scratch. I think a piece of wood or something caught me. I'm fine."

He grabbed her good arm and pulled her to her feet.

"Where are we going?" she asked.

Instead of answering, he led her into the examining room, placed his hands on her waist and lifted her onto the high metal table. "Wait right here," he told her, then disappeared.

She heard him ushering the police out of the building and giving instructions to the security guards. The back door closed, and she heard the sound of a lock clicking into place.

"Is everything all right?" she asked.

"Yes. I've left two men on for the rest of tonight. Nothing is going to happen for the next few hours." He frowned. "I'd feel better if I knew where Jeff had run off to."

After washing his hands and collecting supplies, he stood next to her and gently tried to push up her T-shirt sleeve. Pain shot through her as the dried blood peeled off her skin. She flinched.

"We'd better take this off," he said, fingering the T-shirt. "One way or the other, you're going to have to pull it over the wound. Might as well be now."

She fought the instinct to cross her arms over her chest to protect herself. With the rush to figure out what Sparky was so upset about, she hadn't bothered to put on a bra. Was this how Cort had felt when she'd told him to take his shirt off? She bit back a smile. No, she didn't think he'd had quite the same reservations.

She pulled up the hem and slipped her good arm out of its sleeve, then tugged the shirt over her head. He took it from her and gently peeled it down the wound and dropped the T-shirt on her lap. The air felt cool on her breasts and she knew her nipples were puckering.

She glanced at Cort, but he was looking at her with all the interest of a vet looking at a sick cat. He stared at her wound and nothing else. She'd really impressed him with her feminine charms. Casually, she drew the shirt up in front of her and covered her bare chest. He didn't notice that, either.

"I don't see any fragments," he said. "Looks like a deep cut. I'll clean it up and bandage it."

He reached for the cleaning fluid and thoroughly doused her arm. She studied his familiar face and the focused look in his eyes. There was something about the set of his jaw. Lines of pain straightened his mouth. He looked like a man who had gone ten rounds with the devil and lost.

"Is something wrong?" she asked.

"No, why?"

"You look—" She paused, not sure how to explain it. "Did something else happen tonight? Something you're not telling me?"

Cort moistened sterile cotton with antiseptic. She took a deep breath and nodded. The flare of pain in her arm caused her muscles to stiffen. She forced herself to relax.

"Nothing to worry about," he said. "Whoever was out there made a run for the gates."

"Andy told me. I'm glad no one was hurt."

Cort peeled the protective covering off the bandage and pressed the dressing firmly against her wound. "Good as new."

She glanced down. "First you get hurt in the arm, then it happens to me. Does that mean I'm going to take a bullet in the leg next?" He didn't smile at her attempt at humor. There *was* something bothering him. "What is it?"

"Nothing." He collected the medicines and put them away.

"Cort, what's going on?" She slipped off the table, clutching her shirt in front of her.

"I told you everything is fine. Go to bed, Faith."

He stood with his back to her. She could practically see the pain radiating from him, but she didn't know how to make him talk to her. What had happened to him tonight?

"I'm going to take a shower," she said at last. "If you need me, I'm—"

He cut her off. "Good night."

She left because she couldn't think of any reason to stay. She took a quick shower, careful to keep her bandage dry, and changed back into the oversize T-shirt she was sleeping in. Then she turned off the light and crawled into bed. But instead of lying down and trying to sleep, she leaned against the headboard and stared into the dark.

She could hear Cort pacing restlessly up and down the hall. It stopped long enough for him to take a shower as well, then resumed. She heard him speak softly to Sparky, then a grunting "humph" as the big cat settled down in her office. The minutes ticked by.

Ten minutes, she thought. She would give him ten minutes, and if he didn't stop pacing and go to bed, she was going to demand he tell her what was going on.

She actually waited fifteen because she chickened out twice before finally throwing back the covers on the queen-size bed and stepping onto the floor. Her bare toes curled against the cold wood. She opened her door and stepped into the hall.

She found Cort in her small kitchen. He stood beside the Formica table, leaning against the window, staring out into the dark forest.

He'd brushed his hair away from his face, and the dampness made the gold-blond strands look darker. Jeans covered the lower half of his body, but his chest and back were bare. His muscles bunched under his skin as if he was steeling himself against whatever troubled him. He hadn't bothered to shave, and stubble outlined his jaw. He braced one arm up high on the window frame, the other hung at his side. Both hands were clenched into fists.

"Why aren't you asleep?" he asked without turning toward her.

He didn't sound angry. That gave her hope. She risked moving closer to him. She hovered by the counter before stepping toward the table and chairs. "Do you want to talk about it?" she asked softly.

Slowly he lowered his arm and turned to look at her. She almost cried out at the raw anguish in his eyes. "You don't want to know, Faith. Go back to bed and leave me alone."

"I can't," she said.

"I'm still just like one of your cats, aren't I? You can't bear to see any of us suffering." He shrugged. "I'm not bleeding anywhere for you to patch me up. Sorry."

He wasn't like one of her cats. He was far more dangerous. A man like him could leave her battered and broken, without ever touching her. That's because it was more than her body that was at risk; it was her heart. But he was right about one thing—she couldn't turn her back on his pain.

"Don't apologize," she said. "I heard you pacing and I want to do whatever I can. Would you like a drink?"

"I still haven't recovered from the rum."

"Oh." She twisted her hands together, not sure if she should leave. Obviously he didn't want to tell her what was wrong. "If you're sure I can't…" He didn't say anything. She drew in a breath. "Good night." She turned toward the hallway.

"Wait."

He'd spoken the words so softly, she wasn't sure she'd heard him. "What did you say?"

He pulled a chair back and invited her to sit down. "Don't go. Please. You're right. Something did happen."

She walked over to the chair and sat. He took the seat next to her. His elbows rested on his knees as he clasped his hands together. Cort studied his white knuckles and rubbed a scar at the base of his thumb.

"I remembered the rest of it," he said abruptly. "I got my memory back."

It took her a minute to figure out what he was talking about. "Your last mission? That's terrific. Now you can—"

"No." He cut her off. "It's not like that. I—" He swore. "I told you I was sent in to take care of a rogue agent? That he'd turned?"

Faith shifted in the hard-backed chair and pulled her T-shirt down until it reached her knees. "Yes, but you didn't kill him. You told me that, too."

"I was prepared to. When he refused to come back with me, I had my gun out and was ready to get it over with."

She swallowed the sudden bitter taste in her mouth. She was sorry now that she'd pried. She knew whatever he said was going to haunt her for a long time.

He raised his head and looked at her. Despair and self-loathing swirled in his brown eyes. Pain deepened the lines by his mouth. "He died for me. To save my useless butt. And I don't know why."

"Why he turned in the first place, or why he saved you?"

"Both. Either. I don't care. I want answers and I can't get any."

"How did it happen?" she asked.

"The bad guys showed up just as our rescue plane landed. I took a bullet in the leg." He jerked his head toward his healed wound. "Dan hauled me out to the plane, but refused to come on board. He stood there like some hell-bent hero and shot at them. While they pumped his body full of lead, we got away."

She leaned toward him and gently touched his cheek. He didn't pull back. She stroked the warm skin, her palm rasping against the stubble. "Maybe he knew he had nowhere to go. If he came back here, he would have been tried and sent to prison."

Cort laughed without humor. "Dan would rather have died than go there." He stopped suddenly. "That bastard. He died anyway."

"But this way, he gave his life for something good. He saved you."

He looked up at her. "Hardly a fair exchange." He straightened up. Her hand fell away and she clutched her arms to her chest.

"It used to be easy," he said. "We knew who the enemies were. Now the lines are blurring. Jeff keeps telling me to come in. Maybe I should. Maybe it's clearer if you have the big picture. Maybe it's too late for any of it. All the good guys are dead."

"Was Dan one of the good guys?"

He leaned back in his chair. "You like asking the tough questions, don't you?"

She shrugged. "Just trying to be a friend."

"Are we friends, Faith?"

"I hoped so."

"I'm not sure you need a friend like me."

She wanted to tell him that she needed a friend *exactly* like him. More than that, she needed a man like him. This night, the trouble with the cubs, the passage of time, Cort's leaving getting closer and closer, all reminded her how tenuous everything had become. In a few short days, her life would revert to normal. Cort would be nothing but a memory.

His pain was as tangible as the man himself. It radiated out from him and surrounded her, seeping inside until she wanted to weep for his suffering. It wasn't because he reminded her of her cats and she wanted to heal his wounds. It was more than that. She had come to care for this man. More than was safe.

She wanted to blurt out that fact, but knew he wouldn't take comfort in her feelings. Instead she risked speaking a smaller truth.

"I do need a friend like you," she whispered.

His brown eyes glowed as if lit with a fire. "Not as much as I need you."

The flame of his desire stirred her own to life. His uncharacteristic admission gave her courage. Without giving herself time to think, she rose to her feet and held out her hand.

He stared at her. "I don't think this is a good idea."

"Don't think anymore," she told him. She bent down, took his hand in hers and tugged him to his feet. He rose slowly, towering over her.

"You tempt me," he said, his gaze locking with hers.

Her knees trembled; he made her weak and yet at the same time, incredibly strong. "Good. I want—"

She never got to say what she wanted.

Chapter 13

Even as his mouth came down on hers, she clutched at his shoulders for balance. His skin was hot beneath her fingers. The anticipation of their kiss left her dizzy. She remembered the passion that had flared between them before.

The moment his lips pressed against hers, she felt as if her bones were slowly melting. Firm lips, soft pressure and hard, hard heat molded to her. Instantly, she parted to admit him. His tongue swept inside. She tasted the faint mint of toothpaste and something else. Something heady and sweet that could only be Cort himself. She met his caresses with slow sweeping strokes of her own. His stubble prickled her skin, adding to the deluge of sensation. She clung to him as her world narrowed to this moment. Her muscles quivered, and she feared she might collapse right there on the kitchen floor.

His hands moved up and down her sides, each pass raising her oversize T-shirt higher and higher until her midriff was exposed. He caressed her bare stomach down to her panties, then moved behind and cupped the curve of her buttocks.

She angled her head to deepen the kiss, and at the same time pressed her hips against him. His jeans felt rough against her belly, and his hardness strained against his button fly.

She moved her hands up his neck to the silk of his gold-blond hair. The short strands slipped through her fingers, their coolness a delicious contrast to the heat flaring between them.

He raised his head slightly and gazed down at her. Passion drew the lines of his face taut. His mouth was moist from her kiss, his lips slightly parted. His bare chest rose and fell with each breath he took.

"Faith." He spoke her name softly.

The sound whispered against her skin. She lowered her hands until they rested on his arms. Beneath her fingers, his muscles tightened, the sinewy length defined and powerful. Their eyes met. She saw the wanting there, and the affection. In his way, he cared for her. It was enough.

He squeezed her derriere. The need between them rose to an unbearable pitch. She could hear it filling the room, pressing against her until she could barely breathe. She felt as if she had wanted him forever. She'd needed him for even longer. She had been waiting for the right moment, the right man, to risk sharing her heart and her body again. And now she wanted to be a part of him, joining in the ancient ritual of love.

At the exact moment he bent down to kiss her again, she reached up to pull him close. Their mouths joined in a conflagration of tastes and pressures. She licked his lips frantically as if he were her only source of sustenance. He grasped the hem of her T-shirt and pulled. They parted long enough for him to draw it over her head. He paused to slide it gently over the bandage on her arm. When he'd freed the garment, he tossed it aside and reached for her breasts.

She swelled under the onslaught of his tender touch. Strong hands cupped her curves, weighing them in his palms, moving across her hard nipples. She moaned her pleasure as he swept his fingers over and around her breasts. He bent down to take her in his mouth. Sensation shot through her, reaching to her fingertips and toes, then collecting between her thighs.

He stepped back enough to pull her panties down to the floor, then grabbed her by the waist and lifted her onto the kitchen table. The tabletop felt cold on her bare derriere. She gasped at the contact. He grinned, then moved between her legs and urged her to lie back. His strong arms protected her from the table, while her position raised her exposed chest to him and thrust her breasts forward. He nibbled at her jaw and neck, moving lower, leaving a wet trail across her throat and her chest. His stubble rasped delightfully. His hands supported her head as he took first one, then the other nipple in his mouth. He dueled with the puckered tips, sucked them deeply and raised up far enough to blow on the trembling, damp skin. He rubbed his fingers through her long hair, massaging her scalp, easing tension even as his mouth sought to increase it.

She arched against him. Her bare femininity brushed against his jeans and his hardness. She rocked her hips gently, teasing him as well as herself, but it wasn't enough. The wanting grew. She stretched her arms out to undo the first button, but couldn't reach it, so she brushed her hands on his arms and continued to move herself against him, trying frantically to ease the ache. He groaned softly with each flexing of her body.

He pulled her upright and kissed her hard. Their lips pressed together. Her heart pounded and her lungs burned for more air, as her blood surged through her body. Pressure and hunger built inside her. There was no time to think or analyze. She could only feel. Spreading her legs wide, she urged him closer. His jeans stood between them. She reached for the buttons and quickly popped them open. His hands clutched at her shoulders. His fingers bit into her as she freed him. She pushed the jeans to the floor and touched him.

He filled her hand. All long, hot maleness. So ready. She stared up at his face. He stood with his eyes closed, his expression savage. There was no pretense in their mating. It was primal and necessary. If she didn't have this man, if he didn't ease the ache within her, she would perish.

She stroked his length. He groaned, then opened his eyes and looked at her. His gaze dropped to her hands holding him. Immediately she started to become aware of herself and began to pull away. He put his hand over hers and refused to let her go. Their eyes met. He kept his hand over hers and urged her to move back and forth. Beneath her hand, he felt hot and smooth and hard. Above her hand, the calluses of his palm rubbed her knuckles, and his fingers slipped between hers.

With each stroke, the fire in his eyes grew brighter. The pulse at the base of his throat thundered in time with her own. Between her thighs, moisture collected in anticipation of her release. She rocked her hips, wanting to ease the ache. At last he pushed her hand away and moved closer to her. He probed her moist center, rubbing his tip against her most sensitive place. She arched her back and let her eyes drift shut.

Up and down, yet barely moving at all, he teased her until she could do little but writhe at his command. She strained forward, toward her peak. At last, when the release was as inevitable as the tide, he plunged inside of her. Her breath escaped with an audible sound. He pulled her legs tightly around his hips and began to plunge back and forth.

Her hands clutched at him; his reached for her breasts and touched her hard nipples. She became lost in the journey, focusing on nothing but the sensation of him driving in and out of her. Deep inside, the pressure built and built until she had to give herself up to his rhythm.

He let go of her breasts and hauled her up against him. As his mouth claimed her, as she touched his tongue with hers, she plunged into the madness. It swept her along, rippling her muscles around him, as he surged deeper and his release joined hers.

The fires faded slowly, and she returned to normal. The night was silent except for the sound of their ragged breathing. When Cort tried to ease her back, she clung to him, burying her face in his chest. Now that she'd been sated, sanity returned. She didn't want to look at him and see what he must think of her. She'd acted like an animal, mating with him like that. She'd had no time to question her actions, she'd simply reacted. She squeezed her eyes shut. They'd done it on the kitchen table!

But he refused to be put off. He drew her arms from around his neck and brought her hands to his mouth. After kissing each of her palms, he slipped out from between her legs.

She kept her eyes tightly closed. "Cort, I—"

"Hush," he murmured. She felt him reach under her thighs and behind her back, then he was lifting her.

Her eyes opened. "What are you doing?"

"Taking you to bed." He smiled down at her. "It's a little more civilized, don't you think?"

He didn't look shocked by what they had done, she saw with some relief. Maybe, just maybe, he'd felt the incredible passion, too.

When he placed her in the center of her mattress, she tensed, waiting to see if he would leave her. She need not have worried. He slipped in next to her and pulled the covers up over both of them. She turned on her side, and he snuggled up behind her, fitting his body around hers. One of his arms rested on her waist. She pulled it between her breasts and laced his fingers through hers. She felt soft kisses on her shoulder.

"Thank you," she whispered.

"You're welcome. Thank *you*."

She smiled. "It's never been that...that wild before." She bit her lip. "You probably think I'm silly."

"Never." He raised up on one elbow and pressed on her shoulder until she half turned to look at him. His gold-flecked eyes still glowed from their inner fire. He touched her swollen mouth with his finger. "It was extraordinary and extremely powerful." He gave her a rueful grin. "Too powerful. I never thought to ask about protection. I know it's a little like closing the barn door after the horse has left, but were you protected?"

"Yes."

"Good."

Cort lowered himself back down onto the bed. He waited for the tidal wave of relief to sweep over him. It had been stupid as hell to make love with Faith without checking to see if she could get pregnant. For once, though, the thought of being tied down with a relationship and a child didn't send him reaching for his jeans and car keys.

It was just exhaustion, he told himself. That and the fact that Faith's bed was a lot more comfortable than his cot. Or maybe it was the scent of her body. He leaned close to her back and sniffed. She smelled of sex and French perfume.

The lights he'd set up in front of the building shone through the window blinds. He could just make out the four parallel scars on her shoulder and down her arm. He touched his mouth to those puckered lines. She wiggled against him. Her round derriere brushed against his groin, stirring him back to life. Slowly, he traced the scars with his tongue. The contrast of textures, rough and bumpy on the scars, smooth and silky on her skin, intrigued him. He licked them again.

"I knew it would be like this," she murmured.

"Why?"

"The alpha male always makes the best mate."

He smiled against her. "Am I the alpha male?" he asked, then trailed kisses down her back.

"Uh-huh." She sounded distracted.

He ran his tongue up every bump in her spine, then pushed her long hair aside and nibbled on the back of her neck. She moved her hips back toward him. Need surged between his legs and he felt himself growing harder.

"What makes me the alpha male?" he asked.

"Size, courage. The a-ah—"

He sucked on her earlobe. "Go on."

"The ability to lead the pack. Acceptance by others."

"Including the female?"

He leaned over and kissed her throat. She tilted her head to expose herself more. "Especially the female."

Her eyes were closed. She looked as relaxed and pliable as a cat getting her ears scratched. But he wasn't interested in her ears.

He trailed more kisses down her spine, then tossed back the covers exposing her bare buttocks and legs to view. She gasped when he nibbled the sensitive skin behind her knees. She parted her thighs when he slipped his hand between them and stroked her damp center. She raised her hips back toward him when he nibbled the round curves of her rear. He was already hard and throbbing. He could feel her moistness.

He bent over her back and kissed her neck. Then he bit her, hard enough to make her jump. A shiver ran through her. With one hand, he reached between her thighs and found her waiting wetness. He touched her sensitive core, and she spread her legs farther. He bit her again, then pressed his hardness against her and plunged inside.

She moaned and pushed against him, until the backs of her thighs pressed against the front of his. He continued to rub her center, matching the rhythm of his strokes. With his other hand, he reached around to feel her breasts. They bounced with each thrust, the hard nipples brushing against his hand. He squeezed gently. She cried out, and he felt the quick pulsing of her orgasm.

When her contractions had stopped, he withdrew, turned her onto her back and thrust into her again. Her eyes were wide and unfocused. She grabbed at his shoulders, pulling him down close, then kissing him hungrily. She bit his lower lip, sucked it in her mouth and soothed the hurt. She grabbed his buttocks and pulled him so close he thought he might explode inside of her. She clawed at his back and tossed her head from side to side.

He felt the pressure building inside him. She moved her hips faster and faster. As all his energy collected between his legs in preparation for that moment of release, he felt her contractions begin again. She lifted off the bed and clutched at him. Her eyes met his. He saw the pleasure in her face even as he felt her body quiver around his.

And then he couldn't think at all. He could only feel and stare at her, knowing she saw the same ecstasy in his expression. The climax went on and on, draining him of all thought, all coherency, until he could only collapse on the bed and pull her down next to him. Tremors shook their bodies. Sweat-slicked skin slid on the cotton sheets.

She touched his face, then leaned close and kissed the bullet wound on his arm. He touched his lips to the scars on her arm. They stared at each other in silent understanding. He had never felt this contentment, this connection, and it scared him to death. He pulled her close and shifted so she could rest her head on his shoulder. He didn't want her to see the fear in his eyes.

Cort held her in his arms until she fell asleep. He brushed her hair from her brow and stroked her cheek. Unfamiliar tenderness welled up inside of him, stretching his heart into new and painful vulnerability.

When Faith sighed and rolled away from him, he slipped out of the bed and looked down at her. The light from outside illuminated her long hair which flowed over her bare shoulders. He could make out the four scars across the back of her arm. The scent of her perfume mingled with the pleasing aroma of sex and animal heat. He pulled the covers up around her and walked silently out of the room.

In the kitchen he found his jeans and slipped them on. While he made coffee, he put on boots and a sweatshirt. Then he filled a mug and carried it to his bedroom, where he collected his gun and made his way to the foyer. He sat on the worn vinyl couch by the door and waited.

His muscles ached pleasurably from their lovemaking. He was tired, but he wouldn't sleep. Not until he knew Faith was safe. Pictures filled his mind. Pictures of her and the way she gave herself completely to him. Of naked female flesh, full breasts, long legs. Of the expression on her face as she lost herself to pleasure and forced him to do the same.

He smiled slightly and sipped his coffee. The smile faded as the pictures changed, mingling past and present, and he remembered how Dan had died in a field, shot down by arms dealers in the dead of a South American night.

He would never know why Dan had decided to go to the other side. Just as he would never know if he could have killed his friend. He'd been so sure at first, confident he could have done what was asked of him. He'd told himself it was just another mission. Now he knew better.

The comfort of a job done well mattered little in the cold hours before dawn. He suspected blackness had filled his soul many years ago. It was a price of his occupation, one he'd paid without question. The state of his soul had never mattered before. But Faith had reminded him to look past the obvious to what was important.

Cort chambered a round into his Beretta and checked to make sure the safety was on. Sparky padded down the hall and sat down beside him. The large black leopard rested his head on Cort's thigh. Cort scratched the animal's ears and listened to the sounds of the night. The big cats outside paced and called out; all was well in their world, if not in his.

Yet, if given the chance to do it all again, he would change nothing. Not the suffering he'd seen, not the questions, not even what he had tried to forget. Sparky leaned heavily against him and huffed out a sigh. Cort rested his hand on the animal's powerful shoulders.

Better to have seen hell and survived, he told himself, better to have a dark, empty soul, because he knew what he was capable of. He knew all the variations of the game, and he trusted his ability to keep Faith and the cubs safe. In the past, his missions had been a battle of wits—him against the enemy. This time the stakes were much higher.

Sparky stretched out and rested his head on his paws. Cort welcomed the company on his vigil. He knew the leopard shared his desire to protect. Whatever it took, Cort would pay the price. He was the best at what he did, and he would give his life before he would let anything happen to Faith.

At first light, Thomas backed the car out of the abandoned barn and returned to the main road. He drove past Bowmund and on to the next town. There he left the rental parked on a side street, walked to another car rental agency and got a good-sized van using one of his false IDs. The police would find the black sedan and notify the other rental company, but Thomas didn't care. He hadn't used his real name there, either.

He drove back to Bowmund, collected his belongings and checked out of the motel, paying the bill with cash. He got in the van and started driving.

He'd had a lot of time to think about what went wrong last night. His goal had been to collect the cubs without anyone knowing. But why was that necessary? All the stealth was getting in his way. Last night, those damn cats had spooked him. So much so, his shots aimed at the woman had gone wide.

He was no closer to getting the cubs than he'd been a week ago. Time was running out. The people guarding the cubs weren't stupid. Now that he'd shown himself, they were probably making plans to move the cubs. He had to get the job done tonight. But he couldn't do it alone.

He drove to a liquor store next to an alley. The store was closed. Parking the van close to the building, he went to the public phone on the outside wall and dialed a number.

"Yes?" a man answered.

"It's Thomas."

"You have the cubs?"

"No."

The man on the other end was silent. Thomas would have preferred him to get angry. Despite the cool morning, sweat collected on his back and his upper lip.

"I need men and supplies," he said quickly. "I want to take the cubs tonight."

"I'll send what you need," the man said. "But this plan must work the first time. Our mutual employer returns tomorrow."

Thomas fought down a flash of panic. "He's early."

"He would have arrived today, but there has been some

unpleasantness with the federal government. It will be straightened out by the end of the day. You must get the cubs.''

"I understand." Thomas quickly explained his needs and made arrangements for a meeting at four o'clock that afternoon. By the time he drove up the mountain it would be dark. He would wait until around ten, and then go in and take the cubs.

"Do not fail," the man told him.

"I won't," Thomas promised, and prayed he wasn't lying.

Chapter 14

Faith shifted in her bed. Her hand bumped something hard and flat, and she heard the rattle of silverware. She opened her eyes and saw Sparky leaning over the bed, eating off a tray beside her.

"What on earth...?"

The leopard looked up briefly, then reached over and lapped up a pile of scrambled eggs with a single swipe of his tongue. The toast followed in a quick gulp.

Faith grinned and pushed herself into a sitting position. She leaned against the headboard and brushed her hair out of her face.

"I don't think that's for you," she told the cat. He didn't look chastised.

Faith heard footsteps in the hallway. She pulled the sheet up to her shoulders. Sparky grabbed all three strips of bacon and made a beeline for the door.

"What the hell?" Cort said as the leopard sprinted past him. He entered the room, took one look at the tray and spun around to chase the animal. "You bring that back here." His voice faded as he jogged down the hall.

Faith giggled and used the moment to duck into the bathroom. With every move, unfamiliar muscles reminded her of what had gone on the previous night. She didn't regret what had happened. How could she? Cort had shown her things, made her feel sensations, she'd never imagined. Their bodies had reacted as if they'd been specially formed to bring each other pleasure. The trick was going to be whether or not she could keep Cort from figuring out she'd given him more than a night of pleasure. Sometime between hot hungry kisses and sweat-slicked thrusts, she'd also handed over her heart.

She stared at her face in the mirror. She didn't look especially different. Her eyes seemed a little brighter this morning, her mouth smiled easily. Her lips were still swollen from his kisses and the abrasion from his stubble, but other than that, she had no outward evidence that she was in love.

Love. She leaned against the sink. A big mistake. Cort was like all the other men she had known: He would leave her. This time however, she had only herself to blame for her heartbreak. She'd known from the beginning that his stay in her life was temporary. So why had she let herself care?

She heard him enter her bedroom and knew she couldn't hide out in the bathroom forever. Better to face him and get it over with. When she'd washed her face and brushed her teeth, she pulled her robe from the back of the bathroom door and slipped it on. She paused with her hand on the doorknob and reminded herself Cort had admired her for her courage. She couldn't let him down.

She drew in a deep breath and opened the door, then breezed across the hall to her bedroom. Cort was stretched out on the bed, on top of the covers, his arms folded behind his head. Worn jeans and a white shirt outlined his lean body. His tanned skin accentuated the gold flecks in his brown eyes. One lock of hair tumbled onto his forehead. After last night, she probably had the right to sit on the edge of the bed and brush it back with her fingers. No doubt he wouldn't even blink if she then leaned forward and kissed him. He might even respond.

But as she hovered by the foot of the bed, shyness gripped her. It had been a long time since she'd had to face the awkwardness of the morning after. It hadn't gotten any easier with time.

"I meant to surprise you," he said, pulling back the covers and patting the bed. "That cat ate your breakfast. I'm sorry."

"Don't be." She smiled hesitantly. "I appreciate the thought."

"Come here." He motioned for her to come closer.

She took a step in his direction.

"No, here." He touched the sheet. "I want to say good morning."

She moved forward and gingerly sat on the edge of the mattress.

He raised himself up on one elbow. "Don't," he said, taking her arm and pulling her close to him. "Don't regret last night."

"I don't. It's just—"

He didn't let her finish. He drew her closer and then claimed her mouth with his. The kisses demanded little from her. He pressed his lips fully on hers, then slid them back and forth until she parted to admit him.

His tongue swept over hers, gently, slowly, as if this sweet contact had nothing to do with the tempest from the night before. Without breaking contact, he lowered her onto the bed. She let her eyes drift shut and gave herself up to the feel of him.

It was different this morning. In the light of day, after admitting her feelings to herself, she felt raw and exposed in his presence. And yet she needed to be with him, to be held by him. The one man who would cause her heartache was the only man who could comfort her.

But it was more than comfort. He moved closer to her and loosened her short cotton robe. He tugged on the belt until it gave way, then parted the edges. She felt the cool morning air on her bare skin. Before she could open her eyes or even think about protesting, he cupped one breast in his hand.

She moaned. Their loving last night had left her tender. He seemed to know that instinctively, for he cupped her curves with the gentleness of a man handling priceless crystal. He barely grazed her nipples with his fingertips, yet electricity shot through her.

She reached up to slip her fingers through his hair, then moved down to grip his shoulders. He kissed her lips once more before moving to her neck, then lower to her breasts, where he sweetly sucked her into mindless passion, then lower across her belly. His fingers led the way, seeking her most sensitive spots. His mouth followed, loving the places that made her tighten and writhe and toss her head from side to side. Closer and closer, until he kissed her most secret place. He touched her with the tip of his tongue, making her jump. She drew her knees up and parted her thighs. He tasted her fully, then cupped her buttocks and gently assaulted her center, moving in a slow rhythm that threatened to drive her mad with passion before allowing her to seek her release.

It built slowly at first, like a single spark beginning a fire. The embers caught and grew, glowing hotter and hotter. Her skin burned as if lit from within. Her breasts swelled, and between her legs the flames enveloped her. Her heart pounded in her ears. From outside, she could hear the guards talking, the cats as they played and called to each other. Yet that world wasn't real. All that mattered was Cort and the magic he plied between her thighs. The flames grew and grew, pushing her higher with each flick of his tongue, yet the explosion surprised her.

She found herself tossed to the wind, carried aloft by the heat, then brought back to the real world, caught safely in Cort's arms. He held her tightly in his embrace as her body quivered in aftermath. Oddly, her eyes burned and she fought the need to cry. She wasn't sad or in pain. It wasn't her nature to give in to tears. She wondered why he was able to reduce her to such raw, exposed need.

He shifted until her head rested on his shoulder. "That was because Sparky ate your breakfast," he said as he stroked her hair.

She sighed in contentment. "What do I get if he eats my dinner?"

He chuckled. She heard the sound and felt the vibration in his chest. "You'll just have to wait and see."

She reached down and cupped the hardness straining at the button fly of his jeans. "You deserve a reward for going to all the trouble of cooking my breakfast."

He lifted her hand and brought it to his lips. "Later," he promised and kissed her fingers one by one.

She pulled her arm back and gazed at him. "Cort?"

"It's all right." He smiled. "I pleased you. That's all I want right now."

"But you, ah—" she glanced at his crotch "—obviously—"

He cupped her chin in his hand. "Yes, I am aroused. Yes, I could make love to you right now and it would be great. This was a different kind of pleasure. Let me enjoy it."

The tears she'd fought moments before threatened again.

She blinked several times, then nodded and rested her head back on his shoulder.

"Thank you," she whispered.

"You're welcome. How do you feel?"

"Are you fishing for compliments?"

"I don't have to," he said smugly. "How's the arm?"

She rotated her shoulder. "I'd almost forgotten. It feels fine."

"Maybe you should try take to it easy. You didn't get a lot of sleep last night."

"Neither did you."

He shrugged. "With everything that's going on, you need your rest."

Something in his tone caused a vague feeling of discomfort to steal over her, dissipating the lingering glow of their lovemaking. She raised herself on one elbow and looked down at him. "If I didn't know better, I'd say you were trying to keep me in bed this morning."

"Is that so bad?"

Yes, because it was completely unlike him. "What's wrong?"

Cort hesitated long enough for her stomach to lurch. "Nothing specific," he said at last. "I don't like the fact that Ken is still missing and I can't get ahold of Jeff. I've called a couple of friends and we'll have a few more security people here by nightfall."

"Are the cats all right?"

"Fine. I fed them earlier and I was about to start on their cages."

"I can do that," she said, sitting up and reaching for her robe. "They're my cats. I'm responsible for them."

"I wish you'd consider spending a couple of days in L.A. or San Francisco."

"No." She rose to her feet and tied the belt at her waist. "This is where I belong. I'm not afraid."

Cort shrugged as if to say he'd done the best he could, then he stood up and started toward the door.

"Is that—" She stopped talking long enough to clear her throat. She didn't want to ask, but she had to know. When she spoke again, she forced her voice to come out level, so he wouldn't know she was trembling. "Is that what this was about?" she asked, glancing at the bed. "Were you trying to distract me?"

"Faith, no." He crossed the room in three strides and gathered her close to him.

She hated herself for the weakness that invaded her body, knew she would regret clinging to him as if she was drowning and he was her lifeline, but she couldn't help herself.

"Never," he murmured, touching her hair, her back, her arms, then cupping her face and tenderly kissing her mouth. "I'd never hurt you."

Deliberately, she thought, mentally voicing the unspoken word. Because he would hurt her—he would leave.

"And I'll never abandon my cats," she said, disentangling herself from his embrace. "Go on, get out of here so I can get dressed. I'll meet you at Tigger's cage in ten minutes."

He kissed her once more, then left the room. She stood there, alone. By the end of the week, the cubs would be gone and Cort along with them. She touched her fingers to her mouth. She could almost taste the heartbreak.

Faith stared at the pile of forms on her desk. She'd sorted them by category, dividing them into federal, state and local agencies. Several had to be sent off to her attorney. About a third of them were finished. Those she slipped into envelopes and put in an empty box. The rest still had to be filled out. She fingered the two-inch-high pile. Could she do it? Could she not?

Sparky strolled into her office, followed by Cort. Despite

spending the morning helping her muck out cages, he still looked good, she thought, staring at his face. His hair had grown since he'd been here, and reached about a half inch past his collar. She liked it longer. Faith shook her head. Who was she trying to kid? She liked everything about him.

"Now what are you working on?" he asked, plopping down in the chair in front of her desk.

"More forms."

"So you've decided to go ahead with the snow-leopard project?"

"I guess."

He grinned. "That doesn't sound too enthusiastic."

"I'm not convinced I'm going to make it, but I've realized I have to try."

His gold-flecked eyes flickered with something that might have been respect. "I always knew you would."

She leaned forward and grabbed the top form. "While you're expounding on your precognitive powers, why not give me a little peek into the future and tell me how it's all going to turn out? You could save me dozens of sleepless nights."

"I have every confidence in you."

She tossed the form into the air and watched it flutter back to her desk. Sparky settled in the corner and yawned. She envied the big cat his simple, boring life. Right now, boring looked pretty appealing.

"Why are you so sure it's going to happen?" she asked.

He crossed his ankle over his opposite knee. "Because I know you. I know what you're capable of. Remember when we went shooting?"

She nodded.

"You told me you used to be afraid of guns, but you learned how to handle a rifle. Now you're a marksman. You're the best kind of team player, Faith. You're not afraid to get the job done."

His compliments made her want to do something foolish, like blush and stammer. Or worse, tell him how she felt about him. She took a deep breath and did neither.

"I'm still afraid," she said.

"What do you need that you don't have?"

"Aside from these forms and permits, I need—" She stood up and walked over to a map she'd pinned up on the wall. It showed the northeast section of North Dakota reduced to a two-foot square. She'd highlighted the land she'd bought. "I need a road from the state highway up to where I want the breeding center to be. I need to find a vet who wants to learn all he or she can about snow leopards. I need habitats and buildings and a source of food. I need six breeding pairs, but I'd settle for two. I need employees." She touched the map, trying to remember how beautiful and rugged the land had been when she'd visited it last year. "I need a house to live in and a room of some kind, big enough for fund-raising parties." She looked back at Cort and smiled. "Not much, huh?"

He raised his eyebrows. "What's your bottom line?"

"How much money?" She shrugged. "Interesting. I'd need enough for all that I've mentioned, plus the snow leopards. Of course, getting them is a lot more about government forms and legalities than it is about money. Altogether?" She did a couple of mental calculations. "Five million dollars. That would keep me up and running for a year."

Cort let out a low whistle. "I was going to offer to float you a loan, but the spy business doesn't pay *that* well."

"Thanks for the offer, but I wouldn't have accepted, anyway."

"Why? I thought we were friends."

"We are, it's just—" She paused. "What *do* spies spend their money on?"

He stood up and grinned. "Life insurance." He walked over to the map. "How much have you already raised?"

Faith leaned against the wall. "Once I set up my own foundation, the way station will give me a million and a half."

"So you're a third of the way there."

"If I get it all together." She looked at him. "I only have a two-year college degree. I know cats, but I don't know business."

"That's what lawyers are for, Faith. And business managers. Hire someone."

"Edwina always did it herself."

"You're not Edwina. You have other goals."

"I know you're right. I'm just—"

"Scared." He reached out and touched her cheek.

"Yeah. See, I'm not the strong woman you thought I was." She tried to smile, but she could feel her lips quivering and she let it die. Cort stared at her with an intensity that made her uncomfortable. She wanted to lean on him and let him tell her that she could do it, but she knew she would be foolish to start that particular habit.

"What about you?" she asked brightly, stepping away from him and returning to her desk. She perched on the corner. "When Jeff has the cubs moved on Friday, are you going back in the field? Fight the good fight and all that?"

He surprised her by shaking his head. "I'm not sure I can go back."

"Why?"

"What's waiting for me there? Another situation like the one with Dan? How many more friends am I going to be asked to kill?" He laughed harshly and without humor. "Who am I kidding? Except for Jeff, I don't have any friends."

"I'm your friend," she said softly.

"It's a risky proposition. You might want to rethink it,

Faith. I could be after you next.'' He walked across the room, turned and paced back.

''I don't plan on doing anything illegal.''

His slight smile gave her hope. She had always been so good at reading her cats when they were in pain. She concentrated and tried to do the same with Cort.

''I belong out in the field,'' he told her, shoving his hands in his pockets.

''There are other options.''

''Come in, you mean? Take that promotion Jeff's been offering me? You think I haven't considered that? But I'm a field man. Jeff had a reason for coming in. I don't.''

Jeff's reason had been his wife. Cort had no one. Faith told herself she was foolish to hope, and yet she remembered how tenderly Cort had held her and made love to her last night and this morning. He might still be in love with that other woman, the one who had stolen his heart, but maybe, just maybe, he was starting to care about her, too.

''Maybe you don't have to have a reason to come in,'' she said. ''Maybe it's just the best thing for you to do. You can't punish yourself forever. You have to let go of the past and try to recover. It's been long enough for you to forget.'' If only he *would* forget.

He came to stop in front of her. ''Long enough? It's been less than a month.''

''A month? You said it had happened years ago.''

Cort's eyebrows drew together. ''Dan died on my last mission.''

''Dan? I was talking about that woman you loved. The one who broke your heart.''

Cort turned away and swore.

''I'm sorry,'' she said quickly. ''I didn't mean to bring up the past. I respect the feelings you had for her. She was a big part of your life, and it's never easy to let something like that go. It's just that I was thinking, you and I...''

He started to walk out of the room. Faith swallowed and told herself she'd made a huge mistake. Of course he hadn't recovered from his past. Of course he wasn't interested in a woman like her. It was stupid to imagine otherwise. She wasn't the kind of woman who made men want to stay. She wasn't the kind of woman men loved.

"I shouldn't have said anything." She stared at her hands and twisted her fingers together. "I'm sorry."

Cort slammed his hand against the half-open door. Faith jumped and Sparky half rose to his feet before peering around the room, then settling back down.

"Why do women do this?" he asked, turning to face her. She could see the rage in his eyes. "Why? Can you explain it? I respect you. I care about what happens to you. I had a hell of a good time in bed with you. Why isn't that enough?"

Embarrassment flooded her body, and her cheeks flushed. "I didn't mean—"

"Yes, you did. You want to know about my past, Faith? You want to hear every detail?" He walked over and stood directly in front of her. "I met this girl in college. A few laughs, nothing long lasting. I knew what I wanted, and it wasn't a wife. So one day she says she's pregnant." He planted his hands on his hips. "Great way to mess up a life. Turns out she was just late. As soon as I found out she wasn't pregnant, I took off." He shrugged. "No mess, no broken heart."

Her horror grew with each word of his story. Dear God, she'd ached for him, for a heartbreak that had never existed. "Why did you lie to me?"

"Because you wanted me to. You said you wanted to hear the *real* reason why I wasn't married or involved, but you didn't *really*. You wanted the female fantasy. The truth is, Faith, love is a lie. I never cared about that woman or any woman."

"You never cared about me," she said numbly.

"You're a job. I do my job damn well."

"Especially in bed. I'll have to mention that in my thank-you note to Jeff," she said, then pushed past him. She ran down the hall and out into the compound. Once in the bright sunshine, she paused to catch her breath. Her chest felt tight, as if she'd been running for miles.

Funny how he'd almost made her cry this morning. His tender words and gentle embrace had left her exposed. But this ugly truth didn't make her want to cry. It hurt too much for tears. The hole inside, the place that had been formed by years of her father's abandonment, and later by the man who had left her in college, doubled, then tripled in size in the face of Cort's betrayal.

It was worse this time, because she had known better. Life had taught her the reality of relationships. She'd stopped believing. But Cort had caused her to hope. He'd laid it all out for her to see, all the ugly scars of his past. By spinning his convincing tale, he'd made her think he'd truly loved before. And knowing he had loved once had made her hope he could love again. That was the irony of the situation. He had reminded her of how much she had to give. But it was a gift he didn't want.

She stumbled along the path in front of the cages. Behind her, she heard Cort call her name. She couldn't face him now. She ducked between the two wild jaguars in their cages, narrowly missing being clawed by one of them, and doubled back through the trees. She came out behind Cort, ran into the building and locked herself in her office.

Sparky looked curiously at her as she took Cort's place pacing the room. She wanted to lash out at someone—at the man who had caused this ache. It felt as if her insides were twisting together into a tight knot. She wanted to be comforted and held, but the only person who could make it all go away was the one person who had caused the problem in the first place.

As she approached the wall, she saw her map and the shaded area of her land. She saw the carefully sketched drawing of the habitats and the house. She glanced at the forms piled up on her desk.

With a cry of despair, she picked up her metal trash can, and with one long sweep of her arm, she pulled the forms into the trash. Then she jerked the map from the wall and balled it up. It would never happen. She didn't have the experience or the education. She had nothing but a stupid dream.

She collapsed to the floor and pulled her legs up to her chest.

"Faith!" Cort pounded on the door. "Let me in."

She rested her head on her knees and ignored him. Sparky walked over and nosed her. She ignored the black leopard, too. He bumped her on the shoulder, as if telling her he would always be there, then he laid down next to her and began to purr.

It hurt, she thought, barely able to breathe through the pain. It hurt more than she'd imagined anything could. It wasn't just knowing she'd lost Cort. It was that he wasn't the man she'd thought him to be. She'd lost something that had never existed. The death of a dream. Of hope. He'd played her for a fool, handing her a line he used on all his women. That's what she was, just another woman in a long line of broken hearts. Nothing special at all.

Sparky sniffed her arm. She leaned down and cuddled the big cat, listening to his heartbeat. Cort continued pounding for a few more minutes, then he went away. When the ache in her chest became manageable, she let her gaze drift over the small room. She could be happy here, she told herself. She had been in the past. She could go on with what she was doing, keep the way station successfully. No one expected more.

She looked up at the photos on the wall and saw the two of the snow leopards. She remembered her joy when she'd found out they'd survived after she'd rescued them. She shifted and pulled the trash can close and stared at the forms.

No. She couldn't give up and walk away just because her heart was broken. She couldn't take the coward's way out. She was stronger than that. Due to God or fate or whatever controlled the world, she was in a unique position to make a difference. She might fail, but she had to do her best first. She had to try.

Faith collected the forms and stacked them back on her desk. She smoothed the map flat and pinned it on the wall. Then she took her seat and picked up the top paper. For a second, she couldn't figure out why the lines and words seemed to be blurring, then she touched her cheek and felt the tears. She blinked them away and bent over to complete what she had begun.

Chapter 15

Cort stood beside the police car and watched the entrance of the main building. Faith followed the security guard out into the parking lot. She glanced around at the two police cruisers, searching through the small crowd collected next to the vehicles, until she found him. Their eyes met briefly. She stopped in midstride.

She'd pulled her hair back in a ponytail, exposing her face to view. The blue T-shirt she wore clung to her torso, outlining her breasts, breasts that he had touched and tasted. The haunted look in her eyes and the quick steeling of her backbone was the only sign she gave that not two hours before he'd behaved like the worst kind of bastard and had deliberately hurt her.

If it had been in his power to do so, he would have called the words back. He would gladly have paid whatever price to forever erase the look of pained humiliation on her face as he'd blurted out the ugly truth of his past. He had no right to treat her that way. Not just because

Faith was his responsibility or because he respected her, but because no one deserved that kind of slap in the face. In a moment of anger, he'd selfishly allowed himself to lose his temper. He'd wanted to lash out at her specifically because she was the one who had made him question the very fabric of his existence. She was the one who asked about the good fight and his role in it. She was the one who made him wonder if doing his job well was enough to show for his life.

He was no better than her father and the other men who had hurt her. He shook his head. That wasn't right. He was worse, because he'd known what he was doing as he'd spoken the deadly words, and he'd gone ahead and said them, anyway.

His only excuse was that in the moment of her confession, when she'd hinted that their relationship didn't have to end just because his assignment was over, he'd wanted to stay. The need to put down roots scared the hell out of him. Sometime when he wasn't looking, Faith had burrowed her way into him. Cutting her out would leave a hole inside. Fear of the pain had made him lash out to scare her away. The excuse was meaningless in the face of what he'd done, but it was all he had.

Cort walked around the uniformed officers to where Faith hovered on the edge of the crowd. He saw her swallow as he approached. She glanced at the ground, then tossed her head back and stared straight at him.

"What's going on?" she asked, her voice calm and even.

She looked pale. He couldn't tell if she'd been crying, and the knot in his stomach jerked tighter. He hated knowing he might have made her cry. Not Faith. Not because of him. He'd always loved her strength best. Damn his sorry soul to hell.

"I'm sorry," he said.

She glared up at him, her blue eyes flashing rage. She motioned to the police officers around them. "This is hardly the time. What are they doing here?"

"I am sorry about before," he said. "But that isn't what I meant. Faith—" He took her arm. She tried to pull away from him, but he wouldn't release her. "Ken is dead."

Her eyes grew wide. She made a strangled noise in her throat and covered her mouth with her hand. He started to pull her close to him, but she jerked away and stood alone.

"What happened?" she asked.

He tilted his head toward the officers talking together. "They found his body earlier today. He'd been shot. They're checking, but they think it's the same gun that was used here last night."

"Someone killed Ken because of the cubs?"

He nodded.

"Oh, no." She folded her arms over her chest as if to ward off the bad news. "That poor boy. Not Ken. He was finally getting it all together." She glanced around wildly. "He has no family. And now he's gone? That's not fair."

"Faith, I'm sorry." He reached for her.

"Don't touch me."

He shoved his hands in his pockets and fought to ignore the bitter taste on his tongue. "The police have a few questions."

"Are they sure?" she asked. "Maybe it's not really him. Maybe it's a guy who looks like him."

"His girlfriend, Nancy, identified the body."

She seemed to fold in on herself. Her hands clutched at her arms and her shoulders bent forward. He wanted to comfort her, but she didn't want to have anything to do with him. He couldn't blame her.

She turned away and walked over to the police officers. The detective in charge pulled out a notebook and began asking questions. Cort had already told them what he knew. He'd asked the cops for extra protection for the way station, but they didn't have the manpower to do more than patrol the area.

He looked at Faith one more time. She stood with her back to him, speaking softly. The detective asked another question, and she nodded. Cort hovered nearby for several minutes. When it became obvious she wasn't going to acknowledge him or accept his offer of help, he went into the building to try and contact Jeff.

He entered her office and was greeted by an irritated Sparky. With all the activity around the compound, the leopard was chained up during the day. Sparky walked to the end of the chain and tugged, then sat down and humphed in disgust. Cort scratched the cat's ears and turned toward Faith's desk. A flat white box sat on the chair he normally used. It was stacked with mail. He picked up the top letter and stared at the address. Then he looked at the second and the third. He felt the weight of the envelopes. Every piece of correspondence was addressed to a government agency. He saw the stack of forms on her desk had been reduced considerably. There was a large pile rubber-banded together with a big note reading "Ask Attorney." A notepad contained a list of contractors. The area code next to the phone numbers was unfamiliar to him, but he would bet money it was for North Dakota. She was going to do it. She was going to open the snow-leopard breeding center.

Pride welled up inside of him. Pride for her and her gutsy nature. There weren't many people, male or female, who would be willing to risk it all for an endangered species. It wasn't just that she might face difficulties in handling red tape and funding and the unique problems of raising the leopards themselves. She was giving up so much. A normal life. Home, family, things most women wanted. She was willing to put her needs aside for the greater good.

He cursed under his breath. He had to forget about what had happened with Faith and get on with his job. He sat in her chair and picked up the phone. After punching in the familiar number, he waited.

It was answered after the first ring. "Markum."

"Where the hell have you been?"

"Hello to you, too, buddy," Jeff said, sounding weary. "I've been chasing the bad guys."

"Did you catch them?"

"No. He slipped through our fingers at the last minute." Jeff exhaled wearily. "What can I do for you?"

"We've had a shooting up here. Faith was injured. And one of the kids working here turned up dead."

Jeff was quiet for a minute, then he said, "Start from the beginning."

Cort brought him up to date. He finished his story by telling him about the police showing up that afternoon with news of Ken's murder.

"The men after the cubs will make their move soon," Jeff said.

"I know. That's why I was trying to get ahold of you. You have to get the cubs out of here. We can't wait until Friday."

"You're right. Ironically, I was chasing the guy responsible for buying the cubs in the first place. That's why I took off. I didn't have time to let you know, but I knew you would handle it. How's Faith doing?"

For a second, Cort thought he meant because of what had happened that morning. "She seems fine, but Ken's death shook her up."

He heard Jeff tapping his pen on his desk. His boss cleared his throat. "I'll have a team in there first thing in the morning. The cubs will be moved, but I'll leave the security in place to protect Faith. Can you hold out for the night?''

''Yeah. I made a few phone calls of my own while you were gone and called in some markers. I've already got four extra guys here.''

''That's why you're the best, Cort,'' Jeff said. ''I couldn't have left Faith in better hands.''

Cort didn't bother responding. His boss had that one a hundred and eighty degrees wrong, but there was no point in bringing it up now. Jeff would find out the truth soon enough.

''I'd feel better if Faith wasn't at the compound tonight,'' Jeff said. ''Why don't you send her into town?''

''I've tried. She refuses to budge.''

''Try again.''

''I'll do my best. You think *I* want her here when the bullets fly?''

''I know she can be a very stubborn lady.''

''You got that right.''

''Anything else?'' Jeff asked. ''Are you and your men armed?''

For the first time since that morning, Cort smiled. ''We have enough guns and claw power to hold off an invasion from a third-world country.'' His smile faded when he remembered that Faith had been the one to use that example. It had been his first morning at the way station. Funny, he would never have guessed it would turn out this way.

''What about the rest of it?'' Jeff asked. ''What about you?''

With all that had been happening, it took Cort a second to figure out what his boss meant. ''I remembered everything,'' he said flatly, fighting the anger inside.

Jeff didn't answer.

''You didn't think I would, did you?''

''I knew you'd remember,'' his boss said finally.

"You don't sound very happy, Jeff. Can't say as I blame you." He thought about the moment when he'd come face-to-face with Dan and pulled a gun on his friend because that was his job. "When this business with the cubs is over, you and I are going to have a talk about what happened down there."

"I look forward to it," Jeff said quietly. "You deserve some answers."

It wasn't the fight he'd been hoping for, but it would have to do. "Get the men here as quickly as you can," Cort said. "We'll hold down the fort until then." He hung up without saying goodbye.

He left Faith's office and headed toward the foyer. Once there, he pushed open the front door and stepped out into the parking lot. The police cars were pulling out. Faith stood watching them.

"Faith?"

She didn't bother turning around. "He's going to come here, isn't he? The man who killed Ken. He's going to come for the cubs and he doesn't care who stands in his way."

"Yes."

She nodded once. "At least you have the decency to tell me the truth about that. I appreciate it. We better get ready." She spun on her heel and started toward the building. As she brushed past him, he grabbed her arm. Immediately, she jerked away from him. "Don't touch me."

Something hot and wild flared from her eyes, but it had nothing to do with passion and everything to do with betrayal. Intellectually he'd known he'd hurt her, but until this moment, until he saw the raw emotion in her eyes, he hadn't known how much. Her agony caught him like a bullet to the gut.

"I'm sorry," he said.

"'Sorry' doesn't cut it."

"I know. For what it's worth, I never meant to hurt you."

She looked at him for a long moment. "It's not worth a damn." She pulled open the door and stepped inside.

He followed her. "Faith, wait. We have to talk. Not about this morning, if you'd rather not, but about what's going to happen tonight."

She stopped so quickly, he almost plowed into her. She balled her hands into fists and looked at him. "How dare you?"

"Stop it. I'm not talking about sex." This time when he grabbed her arms, he held on tight enough to bruise. She twisted away from him, but couldn't break free. "Listen to me. That man *will* come back. He's already proved himself a killer."

She stopped struggling. Fear invaded her eyes. "What are you going to do?"

"My job."

Faith flinched, but didn't look away. "What can I do to help?"

"Leave." He shook off her attempt to interrupt him. "I mean it, Faith. It would be a hell of a lot safer for all of us if you weren't here. You're not a pro. I don't want you to get hurt. I spoke to Jeff, and he's going to move the cubs, but he can't do that until morning. I want you to drive to town and check into a hotel. Two of the security guards will go with you and make sure you're safe."

"No."

She gave one last pull and he released her. He saw a red mark on each of her arms. It darkened into the shape of a man's hand.

"I won't go," she said. "Beth and Rob can't come to work. Who's going to take care of the cats? You're going to be busy. Someone has to look out for the animals. The guards are terrified, and if you sent one of them in to clean a cage, you would be asking for a bloodbath. You're the best. Jeff told me. So keep me alive. It should be easy enough.''

She pushed past him and walked down the hall, stopping at the small room used to hold supplies. By the time he'd joined her, she'd unlocked the weapons locker and had pulled out a .22 rifle. She reached in and removed a small revolver and two boxes of ammunition.

She looked up at him and smiled faintly. "As you can see, I'm perfectly capable of taking care of myself."

"I never doubted it for a minute." A single strand of hair floated against her cheek. He wanted to tuck it behind her ear and stroke her soft skin. He wanted to taste her lips and love her into a passionate frenzy until she remembered nothing except the magic they'd shared with their bodies.

She wore no makeup. Her T-shirt wasn't particularly new or stylish. Her jeans had a rip above one knee. Sensible work boots covered her feet. There was nothing glamorous about Faith. Yet he'd never seen her look more beautiful. Her plain clothes, her lack of artifice, made him ache. She'd never pretended to be more than what she was. He was beginning to see he'd destroyed something very precious.

He remembered the addressed envelopes in her office. "You made up your mind," he said. "You're going ahead with the snow-leopard project."

She tilted her chin up. "Yes. There's nothing to keep me here."

He wondered if that was a jab at him, but he didn't ask. Better not to know. "You'll be a success."

She didn't answer. Some of her pain had faded, along with the fear. Strength and determination shielded her emotions. She tucked the pistol into her waistband at the small of her back, closed the locker and picked up the rifle.

"Make sure no one gets trigger-happy and shoots one of the cats," she said, brushing past him. "And stay out of my way."

He couldn't let it end like this. "I know there's nothing I can say to excuse what I did."

She froze in the doorway, her back to him. "You're right about that."

"I never meant to mislead you. I don't know why I lied, except that it was easier than telling the truth. You're right. I *was* treating you like all the other women in my life. But by the time I figured out you were different, I didn't know how to fix it. I'm sorry."

She looked at the ground. "What are you sorry for, Cort? That you never loved that woman? That you said things to hurt me? Are you sorry I'm upset?"

"Yes." He stepped up behind her and took the rifle from her. Slowly, so she wouldn't run away, he turned her until he could look at her face. "All those things."

But he knew something was terribly wrong. She didn't look any happier. Her mouth trembled slightly. The knot in his gut gave another twist.

"You still don't get it," she said. "That's not what matters. Why did you take your last assignment?"

What did that have to do with anything? "It was my job."

"Dan was your friend. Someone else could have gone to bring him back. Someone else could have handled the situation. But you agreed. Why?"

"I'm the best."

She nodded slowly. "And that's all you'll ever be. Damn good at your job." She closed her eyes and drew in a deep breath, obviously struggling for control. It didn't help. A single tear escaped and rolled down her cheek.

He couldn't have been more surprised if she'd pulled out her pistol and shot him. Faith wasn't the type who cried. Cort touched his index finger to her cheek and swept the tear away. The moisture clung to his skin. He curled his hand into a fist, but he could still feel that tiny spot of salty moisture.

She opened her eyes and blinked away the tears. "Fight your fight, Cort. Be the best. Make it enough. Hold on to that, because everything else in your life is meaningless. You want to know why I think you went to South America?"

More than anything, he wanted to disappear and forget the entire conversation. This wasn't what he'd planned. But it was like a car-accident scene. As much as he wanted to, he couldn't make himself look away. "Why?"

"You went because you didn't care about Dan. What kind of man voluntarily puts himself through that kind of hell? I don't think you've cared about anyone, ever. Not even yourself."

"That's not true. Dan was my friend."

"I'm supposed to be your friend, too. Were you as kind to him as you were to me?"

Her verbal blow landed right in the center of his soul and knocked his facade askew. There was nowhere to hide from her words. He could run to the other side of the world, but her voice would follow, screaming out from his mind.

"That's not—"

"Fair?" she asked, staring at him. "Don't talk to me about fair. Were you fair when you let me believe you were the kind of man who knew how to love? I'd just confessed my heart's desire to you. No one ever loved me, no matter what I did. You rewarded that confidence with a lie. You let me believe and hope you were different." Another tear slipped down her cheek, but this time she was the one to brush it away. "You let me believe you might be the one."

She took the rifle from him and rested the butt on the ground. "You have taught me one thing. I'm a strong and determined woman. I'm going to start that breeding program and I'm going to make it work. I'm going to pour my whole being into it, and it's going to be a success. You know why?"

He sensed she was about to deliver the death blow. He stiffened to prepare himself. "Why?"

"Because I was ready to give you my heart, but you weren't interested."

She picked up the rifle and walked away.

He watched her go and knew in a blinding flash of truth that he'd lost her forever. Worse, he'd never known he had the chance to have her. He'd been too caught up in his war against faceless enemies to realize there was more to life than battles. Even warriors needed a home to return to.

He had found the one thing he'd been searching for all his life, and now she was gone. He had killed her love for him, as surely as he'd killed Dan.

Faith spent the rest of the afternoon making phones calls to potential donors to the way station. She spoke to Jeff to see if he could help her with her application for two breeding pairs of snow leopards. By tacit agreement, neither mentioned the cubs, the danger they faced, or Cort. If Jeff heard the catch in her voice, he didn't say anything. He promised to contact several friends he had in Washington and gave her a few more names of possible donors. For minutes, even tens of minutes, she was able to forget what had happened. Then it would all come crashing in on her. Ken, the cubs, Cort. Her mouth would grow dry and the hole inside her would get bigger.

As dusk settled on the compound, she told herself she couldn't hide out in her office forever. She had to face

Cort. Of course he would leave in the morning, along with the cubs. In theory, she *could* avoid him until then.

She straightened the papers on her desk. It was so easy to be a coward, but it wasn't *her* way. She might be shaking in her boots, but she would face down the fear and do the right thing. She would go out there and deal with Cort and the cats and the danger.

But what about the things they'd both said? She remembered how she'd angrily told Cort everything that was wrong with him. She'd lashed out like a wounded animal, seeking to inflict as much or more pain on her tormentor. She sighed. That wasn't fair. Cort hadn't tormented her. He'd hurt her, but she was as much to blame. She'd known from the beginning how it all would end. If the truth be told, she respected his life-style choice. After all, compared with the battle of good versus evil, how important was her heart?

She glanced at Sparky. The leopard looked bored after being chained up all day. "Come on, boy," she said, going over and unhooking him. "Let's go scare the guards."

Sparky leapt to his feet and followed her to the door. He made a beeline for her apartment, rushing with a haste that told her Cort must have already put out his dinner.

The small living room was empty, but a light shone from the kitchen. Dear God, she didn't want to face him in there. Not with the memories of their lovemaking so fresh in her mind. But there wasn't any escape. She drew in a deep breath and forced herself to walk in calmly.

Cort stood at the stove. Two pots and a pan sat on lit burners. The table was set.

"I thought you might be hungry," he said without turning around. "I've made chicken curry."

So they were going to pretend it never happened. She could do that, too, even though it felt dishonest. "It smells great. Can I help?"

"Why don't you go tell the guards we're letting Sparky out." He jerked his head toward the pantry. She could see the leopard's long tail flicking back and forth as he consumed his dinner.

"Sure," she said, wondering how she would get through this last evening. She would almost rather fight with him than pretend they were strangers.

But she didn't get her wish. The meal was long and awkward, with starts and stops of conversation, avoided glances and unspoken feelings hovering like unwelcome guests. It was as if they'd never laughed and talked together. Too much pain, she realized. Too many truths. As soon as they'd finished, she shooed him out of the room and took her time doing the dishes. When the last pot was clean, she wiped the counters, then carefully folded the dishcloth over the edge of the sink. She turned to leave and saw Cort standing in the doorway.

He had his arms folded over his chest. "A truce," he said. "For tonight."

"Why? Is something going to happen?" With all the emotional upheavals, she'd been able to put aside her fear, but now it returned.

"I don't know."

She nodded slowly. "All right, Cort. A truce."

He walked over to her and placed his hands on her shoulders. "I didn't mean to—"

"Hush." She looked up at him. "We both have regrets." His fingers felt warm and comforting as he touched her. "This has been hard on us. You have to worry about security. I feel responsible for what happened to Ken."

"You're not responsible. If anyone's to blame—"

"It's not your fault, either."

He studied her solemnly. "You're a hell of a woman, Faith Newlin."

"You have your moments, as well."

"Gee, thanks." He put his arm around her shoulders and led her out of the room. "What are the chances of you quietly going to bed and sleeping until morning?"

She told herself to step away from him. The casual contact was exquisite torture, reminding her of all the things that would never be. "What are *you* going to do?"

"Sit guard."

"I thought the expression was 'stand guard.'"

"Only if there's no chair."

She gently punched him in the side. "Then I'm going to sit guard with you."

"Somehow I figured you'd say that." He stopped in front of her bedroom door and looked down at her shirt. "You need to dress in dark colors. Long sleeves would be best. Get changed, then meet me in the foyer." He grinned. "You any good at poker?"

"I've never played much."

His grin got broader. "Good."

Somewhere close to midnight, Cort picked up his radio and made a routine call to the two men down at the gate. Faith listened to the crackling static and stifled a yawn. The spy business was pretty boring. They'd spent the evening sitting on the vinyl couch in the foyer of the main building, playing cards. So far she'd learned how to play blackjack and *Siguiendo la Reina*. The latter consisted of a series of changing wild cards that made the outcome of each game a surprise. She and Cort had avoided mention of anything personal, which left very little to talk about, so they'd concentrated on the game.

He spoke into the walkie-talkie again, this time louder. She looked up. "Anything wrong?" she asked.

"They're not answering." He stood up, walked over to the light switch and flipped it off. The room plunged into darkness with only the outside light filtering through the windows to ease the gloom. He tried to raise the other men.

Faith's boredom vanished and apprehension took its place. She wiped her suddenly damp hands against her black jeans. As Cort had requested, she'd changed into a long-sleeved dark shirt. He wore black pants, sweatshirt and athletic shoes.

After several seconds of static, she heard a man speak. She reached for the guns positioned next to them on the floor. She tucked her revolver in her waistband at the small of her back, and handed Cort his Beretta. He spoke for a minute, listened to the reply, then issued instructions and clicked off the equipment.

"None of the six men on duty are answering," he told her, his expression grim. "There were two guards at the gate and four positioned around the perimeter. Andy and three others were sleeping. They're going to surround the compound and start looking for the missing men."

"What are you going to do?"

His answer was cut off by a low whistle. Faith wasn't even sure she'd heard it, but Cort instantly sprang into action and headed for the door. "Stay here and lock the door behind me," he told her as he slipped out into the darkness.

"Wait a minute," she said, about to complain, but she was talking to herself. As she debated whether or not she should follow Cort, she locked the door. But before she could make up her mind, someone or something bumped against the back door.

Her heart leapt to her throat and her palms grew damp. She drew her gun and held the weapon out in front of her.

"Who is it?" she called quietly.

"Cort. I've got an injured man. Open up."

She stuffed the pistol back in her waistband and pulled

the door open. Cort stood in the shadows, holding one of the guards.

"Oh my God." She helped him carry Ralph into the examining room. While Cort slid him onto the metal table, she made sure the blinds were pulled tight, then clicked on a single light directly above the wounded man.

Blood coated the upper half of his body and stained his khaki pants. Faith swallowed hard. She'd seen lots of wounded cats before, but never a person this badly hurt. She washed her hands and grabbed the tray of antiseptic and bandages that she'd set up earlier.

As she unbuttoned Ralph's shirt, Cort checked his eyes. "They're dilating," he said.

She pushed the shirt aside and saw a wound in his left shoulder and another in his right arm. Cort glanced at the holes. "Small-caliber bullets," he said. "Doesn't look fatal."

"Glad to hear that," Ralph mumbled, shaking his head.

Faith pressed gauze to the wounds to stop the bleeding. "How do you feel?"

Ralph started to sit up, then dropped back with a groan. "Like I'm going to pass out."

"What happened?" Cort asked.

She reached for wide tape and secured the dressing on the guard's arm, then started to work on his shoulder. Having something to do took her mind off her fear.

"They came out of nowhere."

"You were posted by the gate?"

"Yeah. I thought I heard something. A truck or a van. I stepped out into the road, then bang, they shot me. Never saw where they were hiding. Next thing I know, I'm eating asphalt." Faith wrapped tape around his shoulder. When she was done, he gave her a shaky smile. "Thanks. When I came to, there wasn't any sign of intruders or the other guard on duty. I'd dropped my radio, but the Jeep was still sitting there. I drove up here right away."

"Where's the Jeep?"

"In the bushes."

Cort gave a curt nod. "Good work." He looked at Faith. "Call the police and get an ambulance up here."

She hurried to the extension on the wall and picked up the receiver. It was dead. She tapped the button several times, but nothing happened.

"There's no dial tone."

Cort swore. "They've cut the lines. The trailer has a two-way radio." He pulled his walkie-talkie from his pocket and spoke into it. He instructed Andy to have one of the men call for help and informed him of the guard's condition.

When he was finished, he looked at Faith. "Unless there's a patrol car already on its way out in this direction, it'll be about a half hour until help arrives. You lock yourself in here and—"

"No! I'm not staying here. I'm a good shot, Cort. I can help."

"You've never been in a combat situation. Stay here with him."

Ralph raised himself up on his elbow. "I'm fine."

"They're my cats," she said, determined to make him listen. "My responsibility. You're going to need all the help you can get. I'll just follow you, anyway. Unless you plan on tying me up, you're stuck with me." With that, she covered the wounded man with a blanket, gave him a quick smile and doused the light. "Let's go."

Cort hesitated. "Damn fool woman."

"Yell at me later."

He stepped into the hall, paused, then went back and gave his walkie-talkie to the guard. "Call if you get into trouble."

"Right."

Cort closed the door behind him, locked it and motioned for Faith to follow. "Do exactly as I say," he told her, his voice quiet.

"I will."

"If you don't, you'll die."

The fear returned, but she refused to give in. "I understand."

He went first, leading the way out the back door and around the right to the underbrush. She kept low to the ground, imitating his crouching run. When they stopped in the cover of several bushes, she pulled out her revolver.

"We can't see the front from here," she said. "How will we know when they get here?"

"They won't come up the front."

"How do you know?"

Cort grabbed her arm and pulled her farther back into the brush. The bushes rustled with each movement. Small branches scratched at her arms, and she was grateful for the long sleeves of her shirt.

"If they were coming up the driveway, they would already have arrived. They're probably going around the long way, up by the Big House."

She glanced to her right. The narrow road from the Big House to the compound was barely visible through the leaves.

"That means they'll come out right here."

"Exactly."

It was as if her questions had conjured up their enemy. First she heard the muffled sound of an engine. It grew louder, then there was silence. Seconds later a large dark van moved along the road and rolled to a stop just before entering the compound. The driver's door opened, and a man stepped out. Faith caught her breath in her throat.

They were so close, she could smell the sweat of his body and see the gleaming black leather of his boots.

In front of her, Cort motioned for silence. She nodded her assent; she had no intention of making a sound. She placed her hand on her chest and prayed they couldn't hear the pounding of her heart.

The men collected on the opposite side of the van. She heard the door slide open and the distinctive clinking of rifles banging together. Then the men stepped out in front of the van and fanned out. There were four altogether. Three went toward the building, and the fourth moved up the compound, keeping close to the cages.

Cort leaned close to her. "Stay here. If they try to get away, wait until they're in the van, then shoot the tires. But don't leave the cover of the forest."

"Don't be crazy," she whispered heatedly. "You can't go out there alone. It's four against one."

In the blackness of the night, with only the moon to light his face, she saw him smile. His eyes glinted with the knowing confidence of a born predator. "Even odds," he said, and he disappeared behind the van.

Faith shifted until she was sitting on the ground. The dirt was still warm from the heat of the day, and although she was scared, her nerves were finally settling down. Cort could handle it, she told herself, hoping her belief made it true. He had four guards of his own out there. He would simply call and tell them that—

She rose to her knees. He couldn't call for help; he'd given the wounded man his walkie-talkie. She started to stand, then remembered he'd told her to stay put.

"Now what?" she muttered, torn by indecision.

Then she recalled something that made the fear return. Her stomach clenched tight and her palms grew damp. After dinner, she'd never bothered to chain Sparky. He was loose in the building, and armed men were about to invade his territory.

Chapter 16

Cort stepped across the narrow road, then slipped behind the van and into the forest. For a split second he wondered if he should have brought Faith along with him. She would have slowed him down, but he didn't trust her to follow directions.

Damn. He should have tied her up and left her locked in a closet in the main building while he had the chance. At least there he would know where she was. Concern weighed on him. She would follow instructions as long as it was convenient, and there wasn't anything he could do about it.

He paused by an old maple tree and faded into the shadows. Closing his eyes, he drew in a breath and pushed all thoughts of Faith from his mind. He couldn't afford the distraction, not if they were both going to make it out of this situation alive. He concentrated on his prey, focusing until his hunter instincts hummed with readiness. He heard a low growl from one of the jaguars and began moving in that direction.

When Cort was behind the last cage, he peered around it toward the main compound. He saw the stranger staring warily at the jaguars in their separate cages. He stood about three feet away, just inside the protective chain. The cats paced angrily, eyeing him, resenting the intrusion. But they hadn't lashed out yet. Cort allowed himself a slight smile.

He bent down. Never taking his eyes off the man, he felt for small rocks and clumps of dirt on the ground. When he had a handful, he moved behind the cage, slipping silently, until he was between the two wild cats' cages. He tossed two pebbles at the metal base of the cage. They made a small pinging sound.

As Cort stepped back to fade into the darkness of the forest, he saw the other man lean toward the sound. One of the jaguars came to investigate the noise, the other stayed at the front of the cage.

Come on, Cort mouthed silently. *Just a little closer.*

Thomas stopped in front of the main building and motioned for his two men to wait. He listened, but there was only the quiet restlessness of the cats.

So far the mission was progressing well. They'd taken out a total of six guards. Two had been shot, another four tied up. If only he knew how many were left. So far there'd been no sign of the woman. He could only pray the cubs were still here.

He stepped forward; the two men with him followed close behind. No lights shone out from the building. Thomas gripped his pistol tighter. His assistants carried rifles, but he preferred a smaller weapon. Tucked in his jacket pocket were two bottles of tranquilizer and a needle. The cubs had been difficult to handle when he'd tried to smuggle them into the country.

"Stay here," he said softly to one of the men. "Don't let anyone in."

The man took up position beside the door. Thomas reached for the knob and pulled. The door opened slowly. He motioned for the second man to go in first, then followed him into the building. His heart was pounding with excitement and fear. He couldn't afford to fail.

As he stepped into the foyer, the glow from the lights out front illuminated the shabby furniture and part of the hallway. He knew the room the cubs had been in before. He turned and headed in that direction. He paused and sniffed. Mint? He inhaled again. What the hell…?

Cort held his breath as the man stepped closer to the cages. He willed the jaguars not to lash out at their prey, but to let him get close enough to step between the cages. He tossed another rock and it bounced off the cage.

The jaguar closest to him growled low in its throat. Cort ignored the cat and watched the man. A rifle gleamed in the faint moonlight. Cort didn't want any of the cats getting hurt. He lifted his pistol and took aim. He would rather take prisoners, but if that wasn't an option, he would kill him before risking the jaguars, or any of the cats.

When he had the stranger in his sights, Cort stepped back and deliberately snapped a twig. The man started at the sound, then took the last step that put him in between the two cages. Cort ducked down, raced toward the cage and banged into it hard. The jaguar by him roared and lashed out with a huge paw. Cort rolled out of the way and came up on his feet.

The second cat reached through the front of the cage and caught the man's arm with a swipe of its paw. The man screamed and dropped his rifle. It slipped between the bars and into one of the cages. The stranger clutched his arm and ran toward the rear of the cages. The jaguar by Cort snarled, stuck its paw out of the corner and clawed at the air. The man froze. He spun, but there was no escape. A large cat waited at each end of the narrow corridor. He moaned softly, then sank to his knees. Cort turned and jogged toward the main building.

Faith stopped in her tracks when she heard a man scream. Please, God, let Cort be all right. Her stomach lurched. She listened again, but there was only the sound of the cats pacing restlessly. One of the jaguars howled its frustration.

Faith wasn't sure which way to go. She would never catch up to Cort in the undergrowth. The moon provided some light, but not enough. Outdoor lamps illuminated the front of the building, but little of their glow spilled into the back. She peered into the darkness and bit her lip. She had to make up her mind; she couldn't just stand here forever.

She clutched her pistol tighter in her hand and turned toward the main building. Keeping close to the ground, she circled in front of the bushes, ducked behind the van and came out fifty feet from the man on guard. She moved slowly, cautiously, never taking her eyes from his dark form. He paced restlessly, like one of the cats; but unlike them, he was afraid. She could smell his fear. It made her feel better. When she was twenty feet away, she stepped up onto the porch. Her work boots scraped against the wood, and the man spun in her direction. She thrust her arms up in front of her, her pistol aimed.

"Freeze," she called. "And drop it."

The man stared at her as if he'd seen a ghost. Then he took a step toward her. "Lady, you're going to hurt yourself." He eased his rifle off his shoulder.

"I'll shoot," she said, and in that second, wondered if she could. She started shaking. The gun in her hand wobbled slightly.

"Come on," he said, taking another step. "No one is going to hurt you."

"I mean it," Faith said. She drew in a calming breath. He wasn't giving her a choice.

He started to raise the rifle, then he jerked his head and looked behind her. Faith resisted the instinct to turn around.

"Drop it," she said again.

He ignored her. She took aim, held her breath and pulled the trigger.

The gunshot echoed loudly in the compound. Several of the cats roared at the noise. Faith stared as the man slumped to the ground. His rifle went spinning on the porch. As she reached down to pick it up, someone grabbed her arm.

She turned to fight, then drew in a gasp of relief when she recognized Cort.

"I thought I told you to stay put," he growled, taking the rifle from her and opening the breech. The ammunition spilled onto the ground.

"I couldn't," she said. "I remembered that Sparky isn't chained up. They might hurt him."

"They might *kill* you."

"I couldn't leave him."

"That bitch shot me," the man on the ground spat out. He cursed several times.

Cort thrust her the rifle, then went forward and bent over the man. "You got him right through the knee. What were you aiming at?"

"His knee."

He looked up at her and grinned. "Good shot."

She smiled back, then felt the adrenaline begin to leave her body. Her legs wobbled as her muscles threatened to give way. She leaned against the building.

Suddenly the lights on the other side of the building went out. Then she heard a thumping noise from inside.

"Cort?"

Cort reached in the pocket of his black jeans and pulled out a thin rope. "One of them cut the power to make it harder for us. The other one is breaking open the doors we left locked. We don't have much time." He secured the bleeding man's hands behind his back.

"You can't leave me here," the man protested.

Cort didn't answer. He pulled a cloth out of his other pocket and used it to gag the man, then he dragged him to the far end of the porch and into the brush.

"Stand near him," Cort said. "Make sure he doesn't try anything. And stay out of trouble."

Another man came running across the compound. Cort raised his gun up toward him, then lowered it to his side. "Andy, what's going on?"

"I heard a shot. Are you—"

"We're fine. How are the other men?"

"We've found three of the six missing guards. They were tied up."

Cort jerked his head toward the building. "One is inside. Wounded, but he'll make it. I'm going in the building. Stay out here with Faith." He glanced at her. "Don't let her do anything foolish."

"Fine." Andy reached for her arm to draw her away from the building.

Faith hesitated, then allowed herself to be led toward the cages. "Don't forget about Sparky," she said. "I don't want anything to happen to him."

"I won't." Cort moved toward the building and paused by the door. He listened intently, then pulled it open and disappeared inside.

"And take care of yourself," Faith whispered when he was gone.

Cort let his eyes adjust to the gloom. Here, in the building, there wasn't even the faint light of the moon to guide him.

When he could make out the shape of the couch by the

front door, he knew it was time to move. He listened to the silence and tasted the air, waiting to see where his enemy hid. His senses became hypersensitive. Every muscle tensed in readiness. At last he felt it—a crawling sensation on the back of his neck. He turned and started down the hallway on his right, away from the cubs.

The first three doors stood open. The fourth was shut, but not locked. He waited two heartbeats, then pushed it open and ducked inside.

Immediately, he hit the floor and rolled silently to a crouched position. A single gunshot pierced the wall inches from where his head had been. He scanned the darkness, waiting for a sign of movement. There. Under the window. The shape of a man. Cort crept forward until he was inches from him, then he reached out and pulled his left arm hard against the guy's throat.

The man struggled, but Cort hung on. The man fought to bring up his gun. Cort raised the Beretta and pressed it against the man's temple.

Instantly his prisoner went limp and dropped his weapon to the floor. It landed with a thud.

"I thought you'd see it my way," Cort said, tucking his gun in the waistband at the small of his back. He reached in his pocket for the rest of his rope.

He was tying the last knot when he heard a sound from outside in the compound. He froze. The sound came again. It was Faith calling his name.

No! He grabbed his prisoner's gun and jogged down the hall toward the foyer. No, not Faith. Panic threatened, and was doused by rage. If that bastard tried anything—

He pushed opened the door and stepped outside. The glow of the moon illuminated the tableau in front of him. Andy lay on the ground unconscious. Blood poured from a cut on his head. A medium-sized man stood holding Faith as a shield in front of him. He had a gun pressed to her cheek.

Cort forced himself to ignore her and stare only at the man.

"Throw down your weapon," the man said quietly. "You try anything and I'll blow off her pretty face."

Cort did as he was asked. He still had his Beretta, but the man couldn't see it. Patience, he told himself. He'd get this bastard yet.

"I want the cubs," the stranger said. "Bring them out."

"I told him," Faith said desperately. "They've already been moved."

Cort allowed himself a quick glance at her. Her wide eyes showed fear, but she didn't plead for help. The determined set of her mouth and her squared shoulders told him she wanted to play this game out. Even now, with her life on the line, she was able to think on her feet. He felt a flash of admiration.

The man jabbed her cheek with the barrel of the weapon and she cried out. "Don't lie to me. I know they're here. Bring them out."

"They're not here," Cort said evenly, stalling for time.

"Don't play with me," the man warned.

"They're up at the Big House."

Faith stared at him as if he'd lost his mind, then she got it. She wiggled against the man holding her. "Don't tell him. I won't let them take the cubs back."

She was convincing, he thought, realizing in that moment exactly what he'd lost when he'd turned his back on what she offered.

"Okay, lady, let's go. You—" he jerked the gun at Cort "—lead the way. Don't mess with me. I'm not squeamish about killing women."

Cort started to turn when he saw a low black shadow moving around the side of the compound. He glanced over his shoulder. When he'd come outside, he'd left the door open.

"Move," the man said, not noticing the menacing shape silently slipping closer.

Cort took another step and prepared himself to lunge toward the man. He looked at Faith, trying to communicate with her. She followed his gaze, looked surprised, then nodded faintly.

"Now," the man ordered, tightening his hold on her waist.

She cried out, louder than necessary, then twisted in his hold. "Let me go," she demanded.

The shadow froze, then leapt up toward the struggling pair. Cort jumped toward them, too. Sparky landed on the man's back and sank his claws through the layers of shirt and jacket down to the skin. The man screamed and dropped his gun. Cort grabbed Faith and pulled her behind him, then pulled out the Beretta.

Sparky held the man's shoulder and bit hard. The man screamed again.

"Let him go, Sparky," Faith said shakily. The leopard raised its head and looked at her. "Sparky, come," she said, and collapsed to her knees.

Sparky bent down, gave the man a shake, then padded over to her. Cort moved next to her and held his gun on the intruder. In the distance, he heard the faint wail of a police siren.

Two weeks later, Faith was at her desk when she saw the sleek sports car stop just outside her office window. She ran down the hall and out into the compound.

Jeff had driven in the back way, and he parked by the narrow road. He got out and grinned at her. "You don't look too bad for a lady who faced down armed bad guys."

She gave him a quick hug. "I've had time to recover from the shakes." She smiled. "It's good to see you."

He looked around the compound. "I meant to get here sooner, but work got in the way. Here, I brought you these." He reached in the car and pulled out several photos. "They're doing great."

She glanced at the snapshot of the tiger cubs. "I can't believe they've grown that much in two weeks."

"They miss you."

"No." She shook her head. "They miss Cort. He was the one who took care of them."

She glanced over to where Cort was playing tug-of-war with Sparky. He'd barely looked up when his boss arrived, but she sensed his tension. She knew he wanted to talk to Jeff about Dan. Not that he'd bothered to tell her. In the last two weeks they'd done little more than work long days and stay out of each other's way.

Behind him, most of the habitats stood empty. The California zoo people would take possession at the end of the week. The jaguars had been returned to their zoo. Samson and Tigger had been moved to a way station in the high desert of Southern California, and the other cats had been shipped off to different facilities across the country. The last two cougars were leaving in the morning, but she wouldn't be here to see them go. She would already be on her way.

She handed Jeff back the pictures. "Thanks for all your help."

"Hey, you did the hard part." He draped an arm around her shoulders and led her toward the main building. "I'm sorry about all the trouble."

"You've apologized about fifty times. It's okay. None of us expected those men to show up like that to take the cubs."

"I'm just glad it's all over. Once we arrested him, William Thomas spilled his guts, and we've finally got his boss indicted.''

"When did that happen?''

Jeff held open the door for her. "Last week.''

"So why did you leave Cort here?''

"He was still on medical leave, and I wasn't sure one or two of his men might not try to get a little payback. The security couldn't hurt. But we've rounded up the last of them.''

She led the way into her office. As she moved to go around her desk, she stepped out of his casual embrace. Her feelings for her friend were warm and pleasant, but nothing like the sweeping passion and heart-stopping love she felt for Cort. It was like comparing a house cat to a tiger. She glanced at the bare walls of her office. Or a snow leopard.

Jeff took the seat on the other side of her desk, in the chair she thought of as Cort's. Cort would be leaving, as well. But not with her. Jeff would give him a lift into the city, and then he would go back to wherever spies went in between assignments.

"So you're really going to do it,'' Jeff said.

She glanced around at the packed boxes stacked at the side of the room. "Sure looks that way. Edwina's foundation has assured me I'll get the promised funding. They even came through with a little extra money. I have an attorney in Washington and another in North Dakota working with the necessary government agencies. It'll take months to get the final approval. In the meantime, I have meetings with contractors scheduled the week after I arrive. I should be up and running by the end of the year.''

"This may help with those start-up costs.'' Jeff reached into his suit jacket pocket and pulled out an envelope. He handed it to her.

She glanced at it, then at him, taking in his blond surfer good looks and the haunted expression that never left his eyes. She wished there was something she could say to take away his pain, but she knew words wouldn't help at all. She felt that same emptiness herself. Her chest tightened every time she thought about Cort leaving.

Since the cubs had been taken away, she'd thought of little else. What was she going to say? How could she tell him what he meant to her without embarrassing him or making him feel he owed her something? Maybe it would be better to say nothing at all. She should simply let him go. Fancy last words wouldn't make a difference. His leaving was going to devastate her.

She opened the envelope. The first piece of paper was a check for one million dollars. She glanced up at Jeff and raised her eyebrows. "You've been saving your pennies."

He smiled. "I did get a raise with my promotion. Actually, it's from an environmental group. Not one of the ones doing the calendars and mailings, but a smaller organization, funded by a handful of very wealthy patrons. I gave them a copy of your proposal and a list of your credentials. They were quite impressed."

"You didn't have to do that."

"I wanted to."

She felt herself getting weepy, so she scanned the other sheets. They contained names and addresses.

"Potential donors," he told her. "I've met a few people."

"Oh, Jeff." She stood up and came around the desk. He rose, and she stepped into his embrace.

As his arms pulled her close, she fought an overwhelming sense of sadness. If only they could have cared about each other the way they had cared about their respective soul mates. But it wasn't to be.

She looked up at him. "You're the best friend I've ever had."

"You're some lady yourself." He tapped her nose and smiled. "When are you leaving?"

"Right after you. The movers are coming tomorrow, and Beth is going to oversee all of that. I'm just taking some personal things."

"And Sparky."

"Of course. What else could I do with him? He's my family."

Jeff's blue eyes met and held hers. "What about Cort?" She tried to pull out of his embrace, but he wouldn't let her go. "I thought something had happened between the two of you."

"You thought wrong. Cort's healed completely and ready to go back to fighting his wars."

Jeff cupped her face in his hand. He studied her, then slowly nodded. "I'm so sorry," he said softly, and kissed her cheek.

"I'll be fine."

He stepped back. "You know what, Faith? I believe you will be. I admire that."

"You don't have to mourn forever, either," she said.

"I don't know how to do anything else." He turned toward the door. "I'll try to get up to visit in the next couple of months."

"I'd like that," she said, then watched him go.

When Cort saw his boss leave the main building, he released his grip on the thick towel. Sparky immediately took off for the telephone poles and climbed up, holding his prize in his massive jaws.

As Jeff approached, he pulled several photos out of his jacket pocket and held them out. "I thought you might like to see how the cubs are getting along. Faith says they've really grown."

Cort folded his arms over his chest. "You've got a hell of a lot of nerve."

"Oh? Something tells me you don't mean the extra time you've spent up here."

"Not quite. What the hell were you thinking of, sending me after Dan? Jesus, Jeff, he was my friend. You sent me to kill him."

Jeff tucked the pictures away. "I didn't see any other way."

Cort narrowed his eyes. "The hell you didn't."

"The director wanted Dan taken care of. I disagreed. I thought Dan deserved a chance. So I sent you in to solve the problem. You were my ace in the hole. I knew you couldn't kill your friend."

Cort stared at him, dumbfounded.

Jeff gave him a slight smile. "I trusted you to find another solution."

"Yeah, I got him killed by his new associates." Cort leaned against the telephone pole.

Jeff's smile faded. "That wasn't your fault. If you hadn't been shot, you would have forced him onto the plane. Once he was here, the director couldn't have done anything about it. Dan would have been alive."

"And in prison. Not much better than being dead," he muttered, but most of his anger had faded. Jeff's plan might even have worked.

"He would have had a chance," Jeff said. "Everybody deserves that."

"You could have clued me in on this."

"I didn't want to interfere. If I told you the plan, it would be my decision, not yours. You were the one going out in the field. What if Dan had to be killed? Only you could make that determination. Plus, I was breaking all the rules. If it all hit the fan, I didn't want you to take the fall with me."

Cort stared past him to the empty habitats. Once it had been easy to know the bad guys. Now the lines blurred. "Why did he do it?"

"I don't know. Maybe for the challenge of seeing if he could. We'll never know for sure."

"Hell of a way to make a living."

"So do something else."

"Like what? This is all I know."

Jeff started toward his car. "We're starting a task force with the Canadians to help deter terrorism in both countries. I don't have anyone to run it yet. It's a promotion. Interested?"

For the first time, he was tempted by one of Jeff's offers. Cort shoved his hands in his pockets. "Maybe."

"You would have to travel a lot, but you wouldn't need to live in D.C." Jeff pulled open his car door. "I have to make a decision by the first of the month. Let me know." He stepped into the car and shut the door. Then he rolled down the window. "You can still fight the war from the inside, Cort. Sometimes it helps to see the big picture. Think about it."

Cort watched him drive away. It was only when the dust settled and the sound of the engine faded that he realized he'd meant to bum a ride with Jeff. Cort looked up at the main building. Who was he kidding? He couldn't leave without saying goodbye. The problem was, he should have left here days ago. He just couldn't find the right words to let Faith go.

He'd hung around for two weeks pretending to handle security, when the truth was that he couldn't bear to leave. He'd been hoping she would say something, or even walk into his room naked one night. Any hint would have been enough. But she'd been all business, and he'd been—scared. He wanted her to know that he'd finally figured it all out.

He cared about her. But would she believe him? Had he left it too long or hurt her too much?

The door opened, and Faith stepped out. She stared at him. "I thought you were gone. Wasn't Jeff going to take you to town?"

"I guess he forgot."

Faith held a leash in her hand. She started past him and called for Sparky.

"Wait," he said, touching her arm.

She stopped. Now. He had to tell her now. Only, the words stuck in his throat. They would all sound stupid, anyway, and she was so tough, she probably didn't need him at all.

"I'll be happy to take you into town," she said, clenching the leash tightly in her hands. "You can rent a car and drive wherever it is you're going." She didn't look quite as in control.

"Where are *you* going?" he asked.

"North Dakota. I told you."

"Alone?"

She drew in a breath and glanced at him. "With Sparky."

He could practically feel the tight grip she had on herself. The effort it took her to act normal gave him courage.

"What is this all about, Cort? What do you want from me? A tearful goodbye? I'm not like your other women. I can't cry on command."

"You're so damn feisty," he said, and smiled. "No, don't cry. I couldn't stand it if you did that. I *would* like you to tell me you love me, though. Just once."

She stared at him as if he'd told her to shoot one of her cats. "Are you crazy?"

"No." He shrugged. "I'm scared as hell. Jeff offered me a job."

Her eyes narrowed. She wasn't going to make this easy on him. "You *have* a job."

"This one would be inside. I'd have to travel, but—"

Her anger faded. The lines of pain around her mouth softened. A few strands of hair escaped from her braid and drifted around her face. He reached out and tucked them behind her ear. She didn't flinch from him.

"But what?" she asked softly.

"I could live anywhere."

In her worn jeans and pale yellow work shirt, she wasn't anyone's idea of a beauty. He smiled. That wasn't true. She was his idea of the perfect woman. Strong and faithful, and incredibly sexy. She drew herself up to her full height, then nodded as if she'd come to a decision.

"All right. What have I got to lose? I love you, Cort."

He was surprised the words affected him. His throat tightened, and deep in his chest he felt an answering flood of emotion. "Just like that. Doesn't anything scare you?" he asked.

"You scare me. Here's my heart. Are you going to trample it again?"

He thought he saw her tremble, but he wasn't sure. He thought about the price he'd paid to fight his good fight and about how few times anyone got a second chance.

"No, Faith," he said. "I'm going to keep your heart with me always."

She looked hopeful, but wary. "Why?"

"That's easy. I love you, too."

She stared at him, then flung herself into his arms. He held her tightly against him, and the cold darkness around his soul cracked, allowing a little light to creep in. It hurt, but in a good way. Nothing had ever felt this right.

"Think I'll be the only spy living in North Dakota?" he asked.

"I'm almost sure of it."

"Think we can make this thing work?"

"Absolutely."

"Good, because I'm not letting you go."

He cupped her face and bent down to kiss her. She met him more than halfway, and passion flared between them. The rightness of their embrace, the feel of her body pressing against him, that damn French perfume, all called him home.

He felt something nudging his leg. He tried to ignore it, but the next nudge practically knocked him off balance.

Faith stepped away and laughed. He petted the black leopard. "Yes, Sparky, I care about you, too." Sparky rumbled deep in his throat. The purring sound floated out into the afternoon.

"Come on," he said, taking the leash from her and attaching it to the leopard's collar. "Let's get going. We've got a long drive ahead of us."

"But don't you have to report to work?"

He took her hand and started toward the building. "Jeff said he didn't need an answer until the first of the month. That gives us enough time to stop off in Las Vegas and get married." He glanced at her. "Unless you want a big wedding?"

"Married?" She stared at him. "We're getting married?"

"Don't you want to?"

She grinned. "Of course. I'm just surprised. Next thing you'll be telling me you want kids."

"Why not?" He held open the door for her and followed her through the foyer and out to the front. A large truck sat in the driveway. In back was a special cage for Sparky. Cort loaded him in and secured the latch. "I mean to do this thing right. I want a whole litter of kids. What is that— maybe five?"

"Five?"

He held open his arms and hugged her close. "One, five,

whatever you want.'' He stared down into her blue eyes. ''I'll love you forever. I swear.''

''I believe you,'' she whispered, drawing his head down closer to hers. This time she *could* believe. He would cherish her with the same unswerving loyalty with which he'd fought his battles. She trusted his honor and his love. Cort was the most special of creatures—a man who mated for life.

*   *   *   *   *

SHATTERED VOWS
Rebecca York

Chapter One

Eddie Cahill flexed his leg, feeling the reassuring tautness of the knife nestled between his sock and his clammy flesh. The weapon had cost him plenty, plus a few promised favors once he was on the outside. Which was going to be in twenty minutes if things kept clicking along according to plan.

In the prison kitchen the weapon had been a harmless butter spreader. Long, clandestine hours of sharpening had given it a deadly edge. But the knife was only part of the elaborate sequence of moves Eddie had been making since the day they'd locked him up.

His glance strayed from the soap-filled sink where he was washing pans from dinner. For a fraction of a second he caught Lowery's eye. The man nodded almost imperceptibly.

The poor geek. In a world where inflicting pain and suffering was a major recreational activity, Lowery came in for more than his fair share. But Eddie had seen the advantage of becoming buddies with a man who suffered from grand mal epileptic seizures. Now he was so pitifully grateful that he'd do anything for his one friend.

"All right, you bums, finish up so that you can close the place for the night," a guard barked.

Eddie began to scrub harder. He looked sullenly industrious, but every muscle in his body was tensed for flight. Rinsing the pan, he set it on the drainboard with a noisy clatter.

Behind him Lowery moaned. That was the signal, and Eddie's heart began to pound inside his chest. It was now or never.

A guard started cussing. With everyone else in the room, Eddie turned toward the disturbance. Lowery was already on the floor. His arms and legs jerked violently. His eyes rolled back in his head. His jaw opened and closed. Eddie had seen his fits a couple of times before. Only this evening it was all a put-on.

"Quick. Get somethin' under his tongue," he shouted as he edged toward the door to the garbage room. "'Fore he bites it off."

Nobody looked at Eddie. All eyes were riveted to the man on the floor.

"Jeeze," someone muttered.

Two guards knelt beside Lowery. One held his head; the other inserted the handle of a wooden spoon between his teeth. Eddie didn't stay to watch. In an instant, he was out the door and into the garbage area.

The guard inside whirled at the unauthorized entry. But Eddie was ready for action. Before the guy could unholster his gun or push the alarm buzzer, he plunged the knife into the man's heart. The guard went down with only a gurgle. Eddie took the gun and stuffed the body into the dumpster. Then he climbed in after him and began pulling refuse over both of them.

All the time his ears were tuned for the sound of the garbage truck. If it didn't come on schedule, he'd just iced a man for nothing. Too bad the odds of getting another chance were about a gizillion to one. For several heart-stopping moments, he was sure he'd lost the bet. Then the truck came grinding to a halt.

He waited in the foul-smelling darkness while the dumpster was lifted onto the huge truck. Then the vehicle was rumbling down the service road in back of the kitchen.

He almost blew his supper as he waited for the gate to open. Finally it did. Then the truck was speeding down Route 175. Eddie let out the breath he'd been holding and settled back to wait. He was out. That was the important thing for now. But he had plans. The first thing he was going to do was get even with the women who'd put him in the cooler.

SOCIETY PARTIES weren't exactly her scene, Jo O'Malley thought as she backed her Honda Civic out of the garage and pressed the remote control to close the door. Actually, she conceded with a little laugh, she'd really rather be on a stakeout wearing beat-up clothes with a hat to hide her red hair. Tonight her strawberry-gold ringlets had been coiffed by the Beauty Connection. She'd even sprung for a fifteen-dollar manicure to shape and polish her short nails.

She looked down at the Royal Persian polish, thinking that if Abby Franklin weren't one of her best friends, she would have politely declined the party invitation—except that you could hardly back out of the prewedding festivities when you'd already agreed to be the matron of honor.

As she headed up the Jones Falls Expressway, she turned the radio to her favorite country station, hoping the music would occupy her mind. WPOC was just starting a newscast, and she almost turned the dial. Then the name from a lead story leaped out at her like a ghost from behind a gravestone.

Eddie Cahill.

Jo's foot bounced on the accelerator making the car shoot forward and then slow. Behind her, a truck horn blared, and she struggled to proceed at a steady pace while the newscaster wiped out her sense of security.

"...both Cahill and a guard are missing from the maximum security penitentiary in Jessup, Maryland. Cahill may be armed and is considered extremely dangerous."

Realizing her hands were fused to the wheel, Jo made an effort to unclench her fingers.

Eddie Cahill. She'd thought he was safely behind bars. Now she remembered the terrible scene in the courtroom just after the judge had pronounced sentence. The prisoner had swiveled around, and his glittering black eyes had sliced into her, making it impossible to move. Then he'd fixed his wife and the prosecuting attorney, Jennifer Stark, with the same menacing look. A hush had fallen over the courtroom as every spectator caught the tension.

"No prison can hold me, and when I get out, you three bitches are gonna pay," Eddie had snarled with the voice of a witch doctor delivering a curse.

Jo was rarely spooked, but the absolute confidence of the threat had made her blood run cold. She'd never been so relieved to see a man handcuffed and hustled off to prison.

Now Eddie had made good on the first part of the promise. He'd escaped. Was he going to come after her first? Or was it going to be Jenny or poor Karen?

It had all started when Karen had hired private detective Jo O'Malley to prove that her husband was cheating on her. He'd been cheating, all right. But the infidelity had been like an oil slick floating on top of a polluted river. Eddie had been deep into drug distribution. When the police had closed in on him, the evidence Jo had uncovered had played a crucial role in his conviction.

Jo sucked a shuddering gust of air into her lungs and willed her pulse to slow. She would not let this get to her. Eddie couldn't know where she was. Not so soon. Not tonight. Yet all at once the prospect of spending an evening in the middle of a noisy crowd was very appealing, she realized as she turned in at the long driveway that led to the estate the Franklins used when they weren't at their retirement home in Florida.

Tonight the two-story Moorish-style house was ablaze with lights, and baroque music drifted into the night. Probably there wasn't a parking place near the front door, Jo decided with a sigh, as she pulled into a space near the gate.

She'd assumed her velvet suit would be warm enough. She hadn't counted on a long, cold walk up the tree-lined driveway. Jo folded her arms and hunched her shoulders against the November wind. Above her the remaining leaves on the tall oaks rustled ominously like dried-up decorations left over from Halloween.

A perfect place for an ambush, she reflected with a shiver, as she quickened her step. Someone who wanted to pop out from behind the boxwoods and grab her wouldn't even have to muffle his footsteps.

Her mind clicked back to Eddie Cahill and the evil look on his face that day in court. Only now he was waiting in the inky blackness beyond the circles of light that lined the driveway.

Jo managed a feeble laugh at her overactive imagination. With any luck, the police had already recaptured the man. Escaped criminals didn't stay on the loose for long. She let her mind spin out pictures of roadblocks, squads of uniformed officers on a manhunt, the final capture in a field near the state prison.

"Can I help you, miss?"

The movie in her mind vanished and private detective Josephine O'Malley jumped several inches off the ground. As she came down, she realized she was being addressed by a man in a maroon uniform.

Sheez. He probably thought she was some kind of loony. "I'm here to attend the Franklin-Claiborne party."

He looked around in puzzlement. "Did you arrive by taxi?"

"My car is at the end of the driveway."

"I would have been glad to park it for you, miss."

Jo realized she'd already made her second faux pas in less than a minute. The Franklins had hired parking attendants. But how could you expect a girl from the mountains of western Maryland to know that?

"I'll let you get the car when I leave," she promised as she started up the steps. Moments later she was bathed in the sparkling light of the crystal chandelier that graced the Spanish tile foyer. Stepping out of the night into the brightness had a transforming effect on her mood.

Or perhaps it was her first sight of a radiant Abby Franklin. She was standing with a not-quite-so-comfortable-looking Steve Clairborne greeting guests. Her sweater-topped sequined gown seemed as natural on her as the tailored suits she often wore to work. While her fiancé was ruggedly handsome in a tuxedo, Jo suspected he'd like to rip off his bow tie and open the stud at his neck.

When he saw her, he grinned and shook his head. She smiled back and gave him a thumbs-up sign. Probably they were the only two people here who wished the Franklins had thrown a crab feast instead of a formal party. Except that it was the wrong month for crabs.

They embraced warmly. Jo had helped Abby save Steve's life six months ago when he'd come back to Baltimore from the Far East to investigate his sister's mysterious death.

He pretended to do a double-take as he inspected her expensive outfit, makeup and hairdo.

"Who is this mystery woman?" he teased.

"You didn't think I had it in me, did you?"

"Of course we did," Abby interjected.

"It's a lot different from your usual tomboy-next-door image. But I like it," Steve continued. "I think Cam will, too."

"Who's Cam?"

"Our best man. I'll introduce you later," Abby promised.

After a few more minutes Jo moved aside so others could talk to the happy couple. As she wandered from drawing room to conservatory to dining room, Jo looked for Laura Roswell. She, Abby, and Laura all had their offices downtown in a turn-of-the-century building at 43 Light Street. Abby was a psychologist, Laura a lawyer. The three women often helped each other out on tough cases. More than that, they were the kind of friends who could be counted on in a crisis.

Jo was on a first-name basis with very few of the glittering society crowd who filled the elegantly furnished rooms. But she'd seen a number of the faces on TV or in the newspapers. Most were in small groups talking and enjoying the hors d'oeuvres being passed on silver trays by elegantly dressed waiters.

She couldn't help feeling more of an observer than a participant as she snagged herself a tiny quiche. Finally she spotted Laura and was heading across the drawing room when she felt the fine hairs on the back of her neck prickle. Someone was watching her. She could feel it. Like the malevolent eyes of Eddie Cahill boring into her the last time she'd seen him.

It took all of her willpower to keep from whirling around and confronting the menace behind her. Instead she turned slowly and casually surveyed the room. A waiter gave her a half smile. No one else seemed to be paying her any special attention.

Stop it, she told herself sternly. *The Franklins didn't invite the bogeyman to the party.*

With a too-bright smile plastered on her face, she grabbed a glass of champagne and took several swallows before starting back toward Laura. But her path was now blocked by a knot of men recounting the details of a golf game.

She was debating another route when she felt something hard press into the small of her back.

"Don't make a move, sister," a sinister voice hissed. "I've got you covered."

Her body, already tensed for action, jerked. The champagne she was holding splashed onto the front of her green velvet suit.

"Oh, brassafrax," came a muttered exclamation. "Jo, I'm sure sorry." She recognized the voice, and relief flooded through her. Turning she found herself staring into the apologetic brown eyes of Lou Rossini, the former shipyard worker who was now the superintendent of 43 Light Street. His gnarled index finger was extended like the barrel of a revolver.

"Lou. What—?"

"Just a stupid joke. You ain't usually so jumpy."

When he tried to dab at the front of her suit with a cocktail napkin, she shook her head. "That'll just make it worse. I'd better go see what I can do."

A hair dryer would take care of the wet mess that spread across the front of her green jacket, Jo thought as she went to seek out her hostess. She met Abby first, who directed her up to the master bedroom and told her she'd find the appliance in the vanity in the dressing area.

After a quick thank-you, Jo scurried up the stairs. At the end of the hall, she stopped for a moment to gape at the elaborate bedroom that looked as if it had been transported from the royal palace in Madrid.

The hair dryer was in one of the deep drawers of the marble vanity.

Although Jo had never been particularly domestic, she had some dim idea that she should try to get the stain out with water. Wetting a hand towel, she dabbed at the front of the jacket and succeeded in making the nap of the velvet look like a cat after a swim.

Behind her in the bathroom, someone else was also running water. When the door opened, a tall, dark-haired man stepped into the dressing room.

In the mirror, her eyes collided with those of Clark Kent behind a pair of gray-rimmed glasses. He was the image of Christopher Reeve. Did Abby's family know him? They hadn't mentioned it, but it could be possible.

As she studied his reflection, she began to pick up differences. The features were a bit more angular. The hair was a little curlier. The eyes were gray instead of blue. Yet the face had that same irresistible quality that had made her heart flutter when Superman had taken Lois Lane for that first magical flight over Metropolis. She wondered if this guy would look as good in tights and a cape.

He seemed just as intrigued with her face as she was with his. Then his gaze dropped to the inland sea that spread across the front of her jacket and the washcloth in her hand. "You're going to ruin that."

"No kidding."

Reaching briskly inside his tuxedo jacket, he pulled out something that looked like a slightly flattened flashlight. Instead of a light bulb behind glass at the end, there was a cone-shaped opening.

"What's that?" Jo asked.

"The prototype for an ionization spot remover. It lifts out foreign matter by changing the charge in the fabric from negative to positive. Want to give it a try?"

"Do I get a money back guarantee?"

"Sure." He threw a switch and the device began to purr.

She'd expected him to hand it to her. Instead he crossed the three feet that separated them and began to run the cone-shaped end of the gadget back and forth across the front of Jo's jacket.

"Turn a little to the side." His other hand went to her shoulder. Both hands were long and tapered and almost graceful for a man. As he moved the device back and forth a quarter inch above the suit front, he pushed a rapid combination of buttons on a key pad along the top of the instrument.

"What are you doing?"

"Augmenting the rapid recovery factor. But I'd better separate the alpha and the delta functions."

"Right. Sure."

Jo rarely sat by and let other people take charge of situations. Now a combination of curiosity about the device and curiosity about the man kept her immobile.

Clark Kent's gaze was intense as he bent to the work. In fact, his absorption was total, as if his mind was capable of filtering out any extraneous elements—like the fact that his face was now in close proximity to her chest.

Searching for something to occupy her own attention, she noted that his nose was perfectly proportioned with the rest of his features. His lips were narrow and pressed together as he concentrated on the task at hand. Through the glasses, she saw that his lashes were long and dark, quite striking really.

Wondering why she'd gotten caught up in such details, she shifted her regard to the suit jacket. To her astonishment, she saw that the wet spot had almost vanished and the velvet fabric had recaptured much of its former luster.

"Hey, that thing really does work. Where'd you get it?"

"I invented it."

The strong fingers on her shoulder shifted her to a different angle, bringing her body more tightly against his. She was starting to feel hot. In the next moment she realized why. The fabric over her chest was steaming.

"Ouch."

"Sorry. Let me get it away from your skin." His attention was still on the stain removal operation. Without hesitation, his free hand slipped inside her jacket.

Jo was rendered temporarily immobile as his warm flesh came in contact with the silky fabric of her blouse. As his fingers shifted to press against her breast, she sucked in a quivery breath.

The other hand, which was still moving back and forth with the stain removal instrument, paused in mid-stroke. He raised his head, and his gray eyes locked with her green ones. For several heartbeats, neither one of them moved.

Clearing his throat, he withdrew the offending hand. "Sorry."

Was he?

"Listen, uh—thanks. It's almost as good as new, really," she was surprised to hear herself stammering. Snatching her evening purse from the vanity, she turned and made a swift exit from the dressing room.

Jo was halfway to the stairs when she remembered she hadn't planned to go directly back to the party. Now that her jacket was back to normal, there was a call she should make. Hopefully it would set her mind at ease. If it didn't, she'd know what she was up against.

She found a phone in the upstairs den. The number she wanted was in the address book she always carried, even in an evening bag. One of the things Jo had learned from her deceased husband, Skip O'Malley, was that the right contacts can make the difference between cracking a case and going down in flames.

Now she thumbed through the well-used book and found Sid Flowers's number. A senior administrator in the Maryland prison system, he was bound to know what was going on.

"Flowers here," he answered crisply.

"This is Jo O'Malley."

"Jo, where in the hell are you? I've left messages on your answering machines at work and at home."

"I'm at a party."

"I assume you know about Cahill."

"Can you give me the scoop, Sid?"

"The details are confidential."

"Understood."

"As near as we can figure it, he persuaded a fellow inmate to fake an epileptic seizure in the kitchen. Then, while everybody was watching the Academy Award winning performance, he slipped into the garbage room and killed the guard. Unfortunately, the truck went right to the Howard County dump. If we'd intercepted it fifteen minutes earlier, we would have had him in custody again."

"Then he's still on the loose, I take it." Jo was amazed at how steady her voice sounded when she could feel her nerves jumping like bullfrogs on a hot plate.

"It's only a matter of time before we pick him up."

"Meanwhile, I'd better watch my back." There was an electronic click and the line was suddenly stronger.

"Did someone hang up your extension?" Jo asked the correction officer.

"I'm here alone."

"Well, maybe somebody here picked up the phone and got hooked on the Cahill drama."

Flowers laughed. "If they're still on the line, they're under arrest."

Jo laughed too, but she felt the hairs on the back of her neck flutter again. Had someone been deliberately listening? No. Why would they?

"If anything else breaks, I'll let you know."

"Thanks."

"Jo…" Sid's voice was edged with concern. "Maybe you ought to consider taking a vacation until they catch up with Eddie."

"Don't be silly. I've got a business to run."

"Guess you do. This will probably blow over in a few

days anyway. Either Cahill's in Wilmington by now, or they're gonna scoop him up PDQ.''

"Have you talked to Karen Cahill or Jennifer Stark?''

"I'm working on it.''

There were more reassurances proffered and accepted. But when Jo got off the phone, she closed her eyes and took several deep breaths. No matter what Flowers said or how tough she tried to sound, she wasn't going to stop looking over her shoulder as long as a psychopath like Eddie Cahill was on the loose.

Right now, however, her immediate problem was getting through the evening without any more mishaps. Piece of cake, she assured herself. How bad could an engagement party be compared to a killer on the loose?

Chapter Two

The ground floor was even more crowded when Jo came back down. For a moment she stood near the foot of the spiral staircase surveying the guests. Which one had been listening to her conversation with Sid Flowers, she wondered. Had it just been an innocent mistake? Or was someone interested in her personal business?

Laura Roswell's voice broke into her thoughts. "Jo. I've been looking all over for you."

"Likewise." They smiled at each other, two women from very different backgrounds who were closer than family now.

The blond lawyer was wearing an ice-blue beaded gown that could have been part of the Nancy Reagan designer loan program. With Laura's long legs and gentle curves, it looked much better on her than it would have on the former first lady. But it wasn't a loaner. Jo was pretty sure that Dr. William Avery, Laura Roswell's husband, invested in his wife's clothing as a reflection of his success.

"Where's Bill?" Jo asked.

Laura's expression tightened. "He's known about this party for weeks, but he decided at the last minute that he just had to attend an Internal Medicine meeting in Atlanta."

Jo heard the mixture of annoyance and hurt in Laura's voice. Were her friend's marital problems building to some sort of crisis? She'd mentioned several times that things weren't going well with her and Bill.

"I'm sorry," Jo responded.

"One way or another, things are going to shake out," Laura predicted. "But I'm not letting it get me down right now. This is Abby and Steve's night."

Before they could continue the conversation, Abby's mother joined the pair. A tan, slender woman in her late fifties, Janet Franklin looked fit and attractive. If her mother were any indication, Abby was going to age gracefully, Jo thought.

"So there you are," Mrs. Franklin said. "We're taking a few pictures in the library. And we'd like to photograph Jo with Steve's best man, Cameron Randolph."

With that name he was undoubtedly another Baltimore blue blood, Jo thought. Was he a maverick like Steve, or had he carved himself out a comfortable niche with his silver spoon?

The matron turned to Laura. "We'd like shots of everybody who's going to be in the wedding party."

When they entered the room, the photographer was just finishing a series of romantic poses with Steve and Abby. The bride-to-be looked relaxed. Her intended looked as if he'd rather be back running guns into Afghanistan. When he saw Jo, relief washed over his face. "Your turn," he called out, stepping out of the lights and tugging Abby along with him. The photographer was about to object, but she shook her head.

"I think he's reached his limit."

Steve gave Abby a grateful hug.

"Okay, we can move on to the matron of honor and best man."

Jo quickly glanced down at the front of her jacket. It would pass inspection. As she positioned herself in front of the fireplace wall, a tall, rangy man who had been standing in the shadows stepped into the light. When his gaze encountered hers, she knew he'd been aware of her from the moment she'd stepped into the room.

Her stomach did a triple somersault.

"Jo O'Malley, I'd like you to meet Cam Randolph," Abby made the introductions, not realizing she was already twenty minutes too late. "I'm sure the two of you are going to get along famously."

"We've already met," Cam told Abby. "She was a reluctant guinea pig for one of my new inventions." When he spread his expressive hands, palms up, Jo remembered the feel of his warm flesh against hers.

"As a matter of fact he took the stain off the front of my suit," she added hastily. "Otherwise I'd be running away from the camera."

"Sounds intriguing," Steve interjected. "Are you going to tell us about it?"

"No," came the simultaneous response.

Abby looked from Jo to Cam. Before she could comment further, the photographer interrupted.

"Stand right here." He maneuvered Jo and Cam together. She slid him a sideways glance. His tall frame was stiff, his hands awkwardly clasped in front of him. So he wasn't quite as cool as he was pretending to be, she thought, secretly pleased.

The photographer stepped behind the camera and snapped off two shots. "Come on, you guys. Make it look like you're having fun."

Jo turned to Cam and gave him an exaggerated grin. "Play like you just won the Nobel Prize for stain removal."

He grinned back. "Right."

The photographer was able to snap off several pictures of a smiling couple. "Much better. Thanks, guys."

"Don't go away," Abby said as they stepped out of the lights. "We need you for the group shot."

They moved to a quieter corner of the room while the photographer selected his next victims.

"So how do you know Steve?" Jo asked, making an attempt to normalize diplomatic relations.

"We were at McDonough together."

Well, I was right, Jo thought. One of the city's most prestigious prep schools. Cam Randolph was definitely out of her league.

He must have read her doubtful expression. "I promise I won't spring any more inventions on you tonight."

"It's not you. It's the guy who escaped from prison this evening that I'm really uptight about." It was sort of a relief to joke about the danger.

"What are you talking about?"

"Eddie Cahill. A drug dealer I got mixed up with last year. Apparently the prison system couldn't hold on to him."

"How did a nice girl like you get mixed up with a drug dealer?" Cam sounded as if he suspected she might be pulling his leg.

"On a case. I testified against him."

"Are you with the police?"

"Private detective."

"Oh." His eyes narrowed and his expression closed.

Jo suddenly wished she'd kept her big mouth shut. It had a habit of getting her into trouble. "You have something against private detectives?"

"It's nothing personal." He cleared his throat. "If you're worried about escaped criminals, you should have a good home security system."

"I have one of the best. The Centurion from—"

"—Randolph Enterprises," he supplied.

Jo realized her mind hadn't made an important connection. "Your company?"

"Yes. And my design."

"Well, I love the auto-delay feature. And the tone sequence selector."

"It definitely gives you more for the money. But I try to build special features into all our products."

"Have you always been in the design department?" Despite herself, Jo was impressed. She'd seen the Randolph Enterprises catalog and knew the company offered a wide range of innovative merchandise.

"I had to take over management for a couple of years."

Jo caught a hint of tension in his voice but suspected he wasn't going to elaborate.

She was right. He changed the subject. "I'm back in the lab now."

"Do you have a lot of inventions?"

"Thirty-seven patents."

Jo whistled. "Maybe we weren't joking about the Nobel Prize."

"Not likely. Only a small percentage of inventions can be brought to market as profitable products. Since we don't have unlimited resources, sometimes I have to rely on Phil Mercer's judgment on where to put our priorities."

Again she caught an undertone of acerbity. "Who's Phil Mercer?"

"Our CEO. He was my father's right-hand man."

"Your father retired?"

"He died a few years ago."

The answer was clipped, and Jo understood why he might not want to pursue the topic. When you loved someone, it was hard to reconcile yourself to never seeing them again. Even after three years it still hurt to think about Skip.

They were called over for the group shot of all the participants in the wedding. Then dinner was announced. Jo pretended she'd agreed to eat with friends and joined a group of young professionals. As she picked at artichoke hearts vinaigrette she couldn't shake the tension headache

Eddie Cahill had generated. Only a desire not to let Abby down kept her at the table, barely holding up her end of several sporadic conversations. Finally, just before dessert, she gave up the struggle and slipped away.

Outside Jo gave her keys to the parking attendant. Once he had a description of her car, he disappeared, and she was left standing alone under the arbor that spanned the circular drive. A tiny circle of light enclosed her. Beyond it the concealing darkness hovered. At least she didn't have to march out into the night again.

It had gotten colder during the evening, and the wind's icy fingers probed through her jacket. Once more she wrapped her arms around her shoulders to ward off the chill, yet she knew the wind and cold weren't the only reasons she was shivering. It was impossible to shake the awful sensation of being watched. She'd felt as if someone had been keeping tabs on her all night, playing hide-and-seek in the crowd.

Last time she'd played it cool. Now she whirled around, her eyes probing the windows on either side of the door. No one was peering back. But that hardly lessened the tension in her neck and shoulders.

She felt some of the strain melt away when she saw twin headlights cutting through the dark. As her car pulled in front of the door, she hurried around to the driver's side. Once behind the wheel, she gunned the engine and roared off down the drive.

She thought of Abby and Steve wrapped in the warmth and love of friends and family. But more importantly, they had each other. She remembered the feeling. Just for a minute she let herself wish there were someone around to take care of her—or someone at home who would breathe a sigh of relief when she walked in the front door. Then she shook her head. Except for the few years she'd been married to

Skip, she'd always taken care of herself. There was absolutely no reason she couldn't continue.

Not until Jo was several blocks away did she stop to consider the uncharacteristic panic that had sent her hurtling down the Franklin drive like the Tokyo Bullet. She never acted like this. She was a woman who was perfectly capable of handling dangerous situations. That was what she did for a living. But something about the house or the party or the company had thrown her badly. Or perhaps it was just the threat of Eddie Cahill hovering over the proceedings.

As she drove back toward Roland Park, she went over each element of the evening but couldn't draw any firm conclusions. However, her mind kept coming back to Cam Randolph.

He was part of what had thrown her. In a man-woman way. But she wasn't looking for a relationship. And if she were, it wouldn't be with someone like him. They were worlds apart socially. Not to mention that he was one of the smartest guys she'd ever met. What in the heck were they going to talk about until the wedding was finally over?

She was still trying to puzzle that one out when she turned onto her street and reached for the automatic garage door opener. After the door had shut behind her, she got out of the car and punched in her I.D. code on the security system's key pad. The box played back a little tune that told her everything was as she'd left it. Suddenly she realized she wasn't going to be able to hear that melody without thinking about the inventor. She wasn't sure whether she liked that or not.

THE STASH HAD BEEN right where he'd left it, in the Eternal Friend Pet Cemetery on Route 1. Early Sunday morning had been a good time to disinter the grave marked Rambo. Back when Eddie had buried the little casket, he'd said he was putting a beloved poodle to rest. The watertight box had really contained twenty thousand dollars in small bills. Eddie had put the bread aside for an emergency when he'd been riding the crest of a wave of successful drug deals. He hadn't had any specific catastrophe in mind, but now he was damn glad he'd had the foresight.

Last night he'd stolen some coveralls off a Howard County clothesline and hitched a ride with a trucker to Jessup. At the cemetery he'd found a shovel in the groundskeeper's shed and dug up the dough. Then he'd checked into a rundown motel in Elkridge, where he'd scrubbed the garbage smell off his body. After that, he'd watched accounts of his escape on the evening news and gone to sleep with the guard's gun under his pillow.

The next morning he was feeling rested, refreshed and ready to settle a few scores. As he watched the news again, he chuckled. The money was going to make all the difference. Without it he'd just be a poor schmuck on the run. With it, he could buy what he needed and lay low until some of the heat was off.

Over an Egg McMuffin and a cup of black coffee, which he brought back to the motel room, he considered his options. First on the agenda were some decent clothes and some wheels. Then he'd think about the tools he needed. He already had a gun. Adding an assault rifle to his arsenal wouldn't be a bad idea.

Jo O'Malley woke up determined to look on the bright side. As she retrieved the fat Sunday paper from the front walk, she counted her blessings. She owned her rambling old Roland Park house free and clear, thanks to Skip's mortgage insurance. She was self-supporting. And the police had probably already recaptured Eddie Cahill, although she wasn't going to spoil her Sunday morning by calling them until she'd eaten breakfast—just in case.

On weekdays Jo just grabbed a bowl of cereal and instant

coffee in the morning. On Sunday she continued the ritual that she and Skip had started. Baking-powder biscuits, country ham, fresh ground coffee. They made her think of home and warmth and love. She did so in a positive way. There was no point in dwelling on what was missing from her life.

First Jo whipped up a batch of biscuits, then she opened the *Sun*. Since she'd been a kid in western Maryland, she'd always read the comics first. Usually her only concession to adult responsibility was to scan the headlines when she opened the paper, but this morning she read the article on Eddie Cahill. It had less information than she'd gotten from Sid the night before, so she turned to her favorite comic— The Far Side. Talking cows again. She grinned.

Her good mood lasted through two cups of coffee and a plate of biscuits smothered with butter and her mother's wild raspberry jam. Not a very low cholesterol breakfast, she thought as she went out to empty the trash. But one of the joys of living alone was eating what you wanted.

Halfway down the steps to the backyard, she stopped and uttered a rather unladylike imprecation. The trash cans lay on their sides, and the refuse looked as if it were scattered as far as the Baltimore County line.

Standing with her hands on her hips, she did a slow burn. Then she got a pair of garden gloves out of the toolshed and started picking up the debris from her well-tended yard. After Skip had died, she had assumed the upkeep of the three-quarter acre that surrounded the house would be a chore. Instead she discovered she liked pulling up weeds and planting flowers. She even had a garden down near the alley where she grew tomatoes and zucchini.

Muttering under her breath, she pulled a soup bone out from under the forsythia and a wad of clothes dryer lint off her favorite tea rosebush.

Mac Lyman, the retired postman who lived next door, came out to commiserate. Jo liked Mac. He reminded her of the honest, hardworking folks she'd grown up with in Garrett County.

"I guess those good-for-nothin' dogs got you again," he said as he began picking up scattered papers.

Jo stuffed a juice carton back in the can. "'Fraid so. Did they mess up your yard, too?"

"Not this time."

"You're lucky." Trying not to get her bathrobe dirty, she edged under a hydrangea to retrieve a plastic meat tray.

"Funny thing," Mac mused. "Usually I hear barkin' or somethin'. Not this time."

"You didn't see anything?"

"Zippo. No details." He waited for a moment. "Don't you get it? Details. Tails."

She forced a laugh. "Yeah. Right." She hadn't heard any barking, either. And she hadn't slept particularly soundly. Maybe it hadn't been dogs. But what else could have made such a godawful mess?

Jo tightened the belt of her bathrobe. All at once it was easy to picture a short, wiry man with Eddie Cahill's ferretlike face prowling around her house.

Come on, O'Malley, she chided herself. *What's happened to your deductive reasoning? If Eddie Cahill came after you, he wouldn't get much of a kick from scattering a little bit of garbage. He'd be scattering buckshot at the very least.*

With Mac's help, the trash was cleaned up in less than fifteen minutes. Jo thanked the old man warmly and went back inside to shower. Hot water washed away the outside chill, but it couldn't quite reach the cold feeling that had sunk into her bones.

WHEN CAM was deep into a new project, he couldn't stay away from the lab, even on Sunday morning. So after his regular five-mile run, he showered and pulled on a pair of jeans and a sweatshirt.

The outfit was modest. His Cross Keys Village town house was small but comfortable. The sleek red Lotus in the garage was one of the few luxury items he'd acquired. Although the Randolph fortune would have bought a life-style full of upscale perks, in general, material items didn't mean much to Cam.

He cared more about intellectual challenge and about having built Randolph Enterprises back up the Forbes' hot list.

Electronics was one of his true passions. So was maneu-vering the Lotus down narrow Baltimore streets with the skill of a race car driver.

He hummed along with the radio as he made the twenty-five-minute ride from Cross Keys to Owings Mills. Pulling into the executive parking lot, he noticed Phil Mercer's Mercedes nearby. So the CEO was catching up on business again on Sunday, too.

Cam sighed. With any luck he wouldn't run into him. Phil was a good manager, excellent at handling day-to-day operations. It was just that the man had strong opinions about which projects to push. Often his decisions were driven by monetary considerations rather than the love and challenge of innovation.

In the workroom behind his private office, Cam brought up the computer specs for the little electronic spot remover. The thermostat was definitely out of whack, he thought as he typed in instructions for a two-minute simulation of the cleaning cycle.

While the results plotted themselves out on the screen, he realized he wasn't thinking about the temperature curve. He was recalling the soft curve of Jo O'Malley's breast under his hand.

Randolph, you've been buried in the lab too long, he told himself sternly, *if all it takes is a little inadvertent canoo-*

dling to make you react like a teenager at his first strip show.

But even as he mentally tossed off the self-deprecating thought, he acknowledged that the response had been more than a case of overloaded circuits. There had been something very appealing about Jo O'Malley. The bouncy red curls, the impish blue eyes, and the slightly sassy manner. Most of the women he met were impressed with his money. He'd known instinctively that Ms. O'Malley didn't give a damn. In fact, the Randolph millions probably meant as much to her as mildew in the corner of the shower. He hadn't met many women like her, and he hadn't been sure how to parry her thrusts. Yet he'd enjoyed her unpredictability and the natural sex appeal she projected.

Being with her generated the same excitement as the start of a new lab project. You had a definite result in mind, but you didn't know how or if things were going to work out.

Just what kind of result did he want with Ms. O'Malley, he asked himself. As several very graphic pictures leaped into his mind, he fought to rein in his runaway imagination. *Slow down,* he ordered himself. *There isn't any hurry.*

He and Ms. O'Malley were going to be spending a good deal of time in each other's company over the next few weeks. There wasn't going to be any problem getting to know her.

He forced himself back to work, but after another forty-five minutes he realized it wasn't going to be a very productive Sunday morning.

Getting up from the computer, he pushed a button that dispensed the right amount of instant coffee, water, creamer and sugar into a mug. After a robotic arm stirred it all together, the finished product slid toward him.

He took a sip. Perfect. His department had done a great job of programming the machine, but marketing had never gotten it into mass production. It was one of those products that had fallen through the cracks a few years ago when Randolph Enterprises had been on the brink of disaster.

That was a time he'd promised himself he wasn't going to think about. Now his Adam's apple bobbed painfully as memories came flooding back. It had all started when Dad had hired a private detective to find out who was responsible for the industrial espionage robbing Randolph of its most promising designs. The espionage had stopped, although there had never been any definite proof of who was responsible. But the price had been too high. Cam still blamed the detective who had exceeded his instructions when he'd dug into the mess.

Cam found his hand was clenched around the coffee mug. With a sigh, he relaxed his fingers, set the mug down, and walked to the window where he stood staring out at the parking lot.

His mother had died when he was only seven, and for years the three males in the Randolph family had been a close-knit unit. At least until Collin had— He clenched his teeth together and willed away the painful memories of surprise and shock. He loved his brother and would have stood by him. But Collin hadn't given him the chance. Shock had followed shock. Within the month, Cam had lost what remained of his immediate family—both his father and his brother. Ultimately, the only way to deal with the grief had been to shove the whole pitiful mess into a locked compartment of his mind. But there were times when the locked door came bursting open, and he'd be so enraged that only climbing into the Lotus and taking the precision machine up to 120 miles an hour could wipe out the need for retribution.

Why was all this coming back now when he was usually so efficient at keeping his dark emotions under control? He sighed. One thing he did know, mental connections didn't pop up at random. They were triggered by data stored in the brain—even if you didn't understand the correlations. However, there might be a way to get at the information.

Sitting down at the keyboard, he accessed the industrial espionage file his father had carefully kept. All at once, the grim facts flashed to life on the high-resolution screen. Documentation on the stolen development plans. Financial loss estimates. Status reports on the investigation. A couple of letters of reference on the detective Dad had hired. His name was Skip O'Malley.

Cam's eyes narrowed. Skip O'Malley. His conscious memory had deliberately lost the name. But it had been buried in his subconscious like a corroding container of nuclear waste.

He'd even talked to the man a couple of times, he remembered now. He'd been tough, experienced and in his forties. Now additional details were coming back to him. Several months after being dismissed from the Randolph case, Skip O'Malley had been killed in a waterfront shootout. Was Jo a relative? Perhaps she was the daughter who had taken over his business.

Although he didn't have a copy of the obituary, it was easy enough to retrieve it from one of the on-line data bases Randolph subscribed to. Five minutes later he was scrolling through the relevant section of the *Baltimore Sun*.

Cam's fingers froze on the keyboard. It was worse than he'd suspected. The little redhead who'd been occupying his thoughts that morning wasn't Skip O'Malley's daughter. She'd been his partner. And his wife.

He pushed back his ergonomically designed chair and meshed his fingers behind his neck. Well, this certainly put a different perspective on things, he mused, picking up a pencil and tapping it against his lips. Fate had handed him an opportunity, and he was never one to turn down that kind of gift.

The pencil began to seesaw between his fingers as his

formidable intellectual powers kicked into overdrive. There were exponential possibilities, but he'd better consider his strategy carefully.

He was just starting to explore a promising plan of action when there was a perfunctory knock. Almost immediately, the doors to the lab swung open. Cam's head jerked around, and he found himself staring at Phil Mercer. The trim, gray-haired executive had a thick sheaf of papers under his arm.

As he advanced toward Cam, the scientist quickly blanked out the data on the screen. Theoretically he and management should be entirely open with each other, but he knew damn well that Mercer had his quota of hidden agendas. So did he, for that matter. The digging he'd been doing this morning was private—not something he wanted to share with the CEO.

"Glad I caught you today," Mercer was saying. "I've got some questions about your expenditures for the next fiscal year."

"I don't think they're out of line."

"I have the feeling you're not taking the present economic slowdown into consideration."

Cam sighed. Now he was in for a two-hour lecture on the delicate balance of profits versus R&D. Just when he was itching to start digging into the background of one Ms. Josephine O'Malley.

Chapter Three

Jo stopped by Laura Roswell's office Monday morning before unlocking her own door.

"How are you doing?" Jo asked Laura's secretary as she pulled off her ivory knit hat and gave her red curls a little shake.

"Fine." Noel Emery cut off the personal conversation to answer a phone call, which was interrupted by the second line. As she smoothly handled both conversations, she held up two fingers indicating that she wouldn't be long.

Noel ran Laura's office with top-notch efficiency. But it hadn't always been that way. When she'd first come to 43 Light Street, her self-esteem had been at rock bottom.

Jo had wondered why Laura had hired a secretary who lost messages and misfiled important briefs. All Laura had said was that the young woman needed the job.

It had been months before Noel told Jo what had happened at her last place of employment. Her boss, a partner in one of the city's most prestigious law firms, had pressured her into dating him. Next he'd tried to get her into bed. When she'd refused, he asked her to work late one night and raped her on his office sofa.

Noel had threatened to call the police, but he'd laughed and asked who she thought they were going to believe.

She'd quit her job without a reference, and Laura Roswell had hired her when she'd been at the end of her rope.

With the encouragement of the other women at 43 Light Street, Noel had pulled her life back together. She was going to night school, and by day she guarded Laura's waiting room with the loyalty and tenacity of a bulldog.

Jo listened to Noel reading the riot act to a father who'd called to say he had no intention of coughing up child support payments. As she hung up, she rolled her eyes. "Laura's not in this morning. She's in judge's chambers on a custody case."

"Too bad. I wanted some free legal advice on canine vandalism."

Noel consulted her boss's schedule. "It looks like she has an opening around two. I'll give you a call if she can see you."

"Thanks."

Jo took the elevator up to her office. For a moment she stood in front of the frosted glass door panel that still proclaimed the occupants "O'Malley and O'Malley." It wasn't just sentiment that kept her deceased husband's name on the door and in the Yellow Pages. There were clients who still wouldn't hire a female detective. If they didn't ask about the other member of the O'Malley team, she'd let them assume he was an active partner in the business.

She smiled as she remembered back to when she came to Baltimore years ago. Like Noel, she'd been looking for a better job than she could find in rural western Maryland. Skip O'Malley, who'd been in desperate need of a secretary, had quickly discovered Jo didn't have much talent for office management. He'd fired her three or four times but always hired her back—because her insights often helped solve cases.

She'd become his de facto partner in six months and a real one in a year. A year after that, he'd given up fighting his attraction for a woman fifteen years his junior and married her.

Skip had taught her everything he'd learned in his twenty years of private investigation. More than a mentor, he'd been her best friend and lover as well. It would take a hell of a man to replace him. Certainly not Cameron Randolph, she told herself, and then wondered why she'd even entertained the idea.

Turning her attention to the blinking red light on the answering machine, she cleared a place on her desk, grabbed a yellow legal pad and a pencil and hit the button.

The first call was from Sid Flowers—but it predated their conversation of the night before. The second was from a prospective client who wanted to know if Jo worked on a contingency basis. "Sure," she muttered. "Plus up front expenses." She didn't take down the number. If the man wanted to call back, she'd explain her fee schedule.

The machine clicked again, and she raised her pencil to take notes.

"Hi there, Jo. Sorry I didn't catch you in." The words were friendly enough, but the voice was electronically distorted as if it might have been generated by a computer. Had those blasted direct marketing companies finally figured out a way to personalize their greeting, she wondered.

"You've got a gorgeous little body, angel face, you know that?"

Jo's head snapped around toward the machine. What kind of product were they selling, anyway?

"Just thinking about what I'd like to do to you makes me hot all over, baby. The problem is, I can't decide whether I want to give you a poke with my sugar stick or stick you with a hot poker." The observation was followed by a high-pitched laugh made shrill by the electronic distortion. The noise was like the buzz of malevolent insects. Jo felt them surrounding her, descending, crawling on her skin. Dropping her pad and pencil, she rubbed her arms as if that would rub away the invasion.

"Get the wordplay? But when you and me play, baby, it ain't just gonna be with words."

Jo continued to stare at the machine. Then she shook herself free of its spell. "Just who do you think you are, buster?" Still, her hand reached out and pushed the save button, a silent acknowledgment that the message had disturbed her more than she wanted to admit.

It was this damn Eddie Cahill business, she told herself vehemently. When she let her guard down, he had her feeling as if she were balanced on the edge of a razor knife.

Had he made the call?

She forced herself to think analytically. Whoever it was had used her first name, which wasn't in the agency's telephone listing or on the directory board in the lobby. It had to be someone who knew her—either personally or professionally.

That didn't mean it was necessarily Eddie. Over the years her job had put her in conflict with a fair number of people. But who would pick this method of getting even? If this was Eddie's little joke, maybe she'd lucked out. But she couldn't quite convince herself he'd be satisfied with long-distance vengeance. Not after the look he'd given her in court.

Was there some sort of clue to the caller's identity in the recording? Before she could change her mind, she replayed it, struggling to blot out the crawling feeling from the electronic distortion and listen dispassionately as she cataloged details. The caller sounded vaguely masculine, yet she knew that someone speaking into the right electronic equipment could make his voice sound like anything from Donald Duck to Darth Vader.

She ran through the tape one more time, listening for background noise. If the call had been made from a phone booth, there might be traffic sounds. She couldn't detect any. On the other hand, she thought she heard music in the background. Radio? Television? There was no way to tell. What would that prove, anyway?

Well, the last thing she was going to do, she told herself, was blow the whole thing out of proportion. There was no point in jumping out of her skin over a crank call. What she would do was get busy.

First she put in another call to Sid Flowers. He didn't have anything more to report—except that Jennifer Stark, the Assistant D.A. who'd prosecuted Cahill, was vacationing with her husband in the Virgin Islands.

"Lucky her," Jo muttered.

Flowers agreed.

Since the police weren't making much progress on the case, Jo decided to see if she could lend a hand.

Cahill. *C.* She opened the top file drawer and began shuffling through folders. Once she'd had the bright idea of color coding cases to make everything easy to find. Red for active, blue for deep freeze, green for paid up. Except that she'd gotten tired of transferring materials. So most of the folders were still red.

Cahill should be between Cable and Callahan. But the file was missing. Had someone been riffling through her papers? Before she could investigate, the phone rang.

It was Sandy Peters at the *Baltimore Sun.*

"Jo, the Carpenter family you were telling me about. My editor's interested. If you can get me those pictures and documents this morning, I think I can swing a feature for you on Sunday."

"You've got it. I'll meet you in fifteen or twenty minutes."

The Carpenters had been a family of five siblings. When the parents had died thirty years ago, the kids had been separated. One of the younger brothers had hired her to try to locate the rest of the family. Jo had posed as a social worker to get access to adoption records and had found two sisters and another brother. Then she'd started calling Maryland newspapers to see if they'd run a picture taken of the children when they were little—along with a human interest story on the search.

When she reached the lobby, Lou was cleaning the glass on the directory. Purple-blue light from the transom above the door pooled around him like a soft spotlight. "Some party last night, huh?" he observed.

"Right."

"You shoulda seen the baked Alaska flamin'."

"I had a little indigestion and went home early."

He gave her a closer inspection. "You do look kind of peaked."

"Thanks." Jo hesitated for a moment. "You haven't—uh—seen any strangers hanging around, have you?"

"Nobody any weirder than usual. Why?"

"There's this guy who escaped from prison last night."

"The one whose picture was in the paper?"

"Yes. I'm not on his Christmas card list."

"He's got a grudge against you or somethin'?"

Jo hated broadcasting her troubles. Yet in this case, she reasoned, the more people who knew about Cahill, the better. "I helped arrange for his state expense-paid vacation."

Lou whistled through uneven teeth. "Want me to keep an eye on the hallway outside your office?"

"If you happen to be up there."

Lou casually stopped his polishing and ambled to the door after Jo. She knew he was watching as she strode across the street to the garage where her blue Civic was parked. Beneath his crusty exterior, he was a real softy, she thought. He wasn't just someone who took care of an office building for a living. He cared about the tenants of 43 Light Street as if they were his children.

Lou watched Jo's back until she'd disappeared into the shadows of the parking garage. Perhaps if he'd waited until after her car pulled out, he would have noticed the gray van that drifted down the street in back of her.

The driver of the van wore workman's coveralls. A painter's cap partially hid his face. He looked like a handyman, but his talents were far more sophisticated. The interior of the van rivaled an FBI surveillance unit. There were directional mikes that could pick up a whispered conversation from across the street. And the computerized tracking system and racks of radio receivers, recording equipment and spectrum analyzers weren't found in any standard electronics catalogs.

He whistled an old Billy Joel song as he drove. His foot was light and easy on the accelerator as he kept the van several hundred feet behind Jo. He didn't have to keep her in sight. The directional finder he'd put on her car this morning was working perfectly.

He slowed down as Jo turned in at the fenced lot of the *Sun* complex and spoke to the guard at the gate. Instead of pulling in after her, he drove on by the redbrick building. No way was he going to explain his business to some rent-a-cop. But he did activate the directional mike and caught the second half of her conversation with the guard. She was dropping off material for a missing persons story. The coincidence made him laugh. The high-pitched sound echoed around him in the van, and he stopped abruptly. He hated it when his voice went all high and piercing like a dolphin in distress.

He checked his reflection in the rearview mirror. He looked like he was perfectly in control. And that's what he was. He swung around the corner and headed back toward the downtown area. He had time for a cup of coffee and a doughnut with cherry icing and sprinkles.

THE TWO-STORY LOBBY of the Sun Building with its black-and-white marble and stylized murals always impressed Jo, since the office of the weekly newspaper back in her home-town looked as if it hadn't been renovated since the Civil War. When you stepped through the glass-and-metal doors of the *Baltimore Sun*, you felt the power of the Fourth Estate. Which was just what she wanted, because the more people who saw the story on the Carpenters the greater the possibility of bringing the scattered siblings back together.

Sandy Peters thanked Jo warmly for bringing the file over so quickly. Getting out her notepad, she asked a few more questions about the case. "Can I quote you as the detective conducting the investigation? Or do you just want to be background?"

"Oh, what the heck. Go ahead and quote me. It can't hurt business."

There were so many aspects of detective work that churned up dirt and muck. It was nice to play fairy god-mother for a change, Jo mused as she drove away from the newspaper building.

The sharp blast of half a dozen car horns made her body jump. With a sizzling bolt of awareness she realized she'd just turned the wrong way on a one-way street. Her car was facing four solid lanes of traffic—all coming toward her!

She did a quick U-turn on the wide avenue and sped back toward her office, pretending that the drivers in back of her weren't staring and that she didn't feel like an utter idiot. She'd sworn she wasn't shaking in her shoes over Eddie Cahill—and that she hadn't been rattled by the message on her answering machine. Obviously she was wrong.

Well, work was the best way to get back on track. Fifteen minutes later she was at her desk with the Cahill file, which she'd found stuck in the middle of another folder. She opened it just as the phone interrupted.

"O'Malley and O'Malley," she answered brusquely.

"Hello, Jo." The voice was thin and raspy and instantly flashed her back to the obscene call on the answering machine. In reaction, her scalp tingled.

"I called you, but—" the sandpaper voice continued. Jo cut him off before he could get any further.

"I will not tolerate being harassed," she spat into the phone. "If you try something like that again, buster, you're going to regret the day you ever messed with me." As she finished the warning, she slammed the receiver back into the cradle.

Fifteen seconds later, the phone rang again. Jo snatched it up ready to do battle again.

"Jo?" The same raspy voice inquired. This time she took a few seconds to make a rational judgment. It wasn't the electronic distortion she'd heard on the answering machine.

"Who is this?" she demanded.

The caller made an effort to clear his throat. "Cameron Randolph."

"Cam?" After she'd ducked out of the party, she hadn't expected him to call.

"I woke up with laryngitis."

"Oh, sheez. Cam, I'm sorry." A wave of relief mixed with chagrin washed over her. "I thought—"

"I take it you've been getting some—uh—offensive phone calls," he croaked.

"Just one. It's no big deal. How are you feeling?" She wasn't planning on talking about her problems to him.

"I'll live. This happens sometimes."

She pictured him in bed, alone, with no one to comfort him. "My mom used to give me honey and lemon when my throat was sore," she said softly.

"I've been using lozenges. Maybe I'll try your remedy."

"Do you need anything?"

He was silent for a moment. "I sound worse than I feel. Anyway, I should be all right by Thursday."

''Thursday?''

''You know, the party my aunt's giving for Steve and Abby. You didn't say whether you were coming.''

Jo cringed. Maybe he thought she hadn't responded because of him. That wasn't the problem. She remembered getting the invitation weeks ago and sticking it somewhere safe. She'd simply forgotten to R.S.V.P.

For a moment she flirted with the idea of admitting her oversight and adding that she'd bought tickets to the Baltimore Blast indoor soccer game, for that night. The excuse never made it to her lips.

''I was planning to come. Unless it's too late.'' Maybe circumstances would decide for her.

''No, no. We're all looking forward to seeing you. Especially me.''

The last part wasn't very loud but it sent a shiver up her arms. Had he really said it? She certainly couldn't ask for him to repeat it. ''I guess I should get directions,'' she muttered.

He cleared his throat again. ''Why don't I pick you up?''

''I don't want to put you to any trouble.''

''No trouble. Tell me where you live,'' he requested as if he hadn't already checked out the location of her Roland Park house.

Jo gave him directions.

''Then I'll see you around six-thirty on Thursday.''

''Fine.''

Jo hung up, surprised that she was actually looking forward to the party but still feeling a bit uncertain.

Cam hung up feeling slightly guilty, slightly nervous, and more than a little excited about the prospects for Thursday night.

JO DIDN'T HAVE TO WAIT until the afternoon to talk to Laura. She ran into her friend at the deli in the office building across the alley. Jeff and Mutt's specialized in upscale sandwiches like turkey with avocado slices and chopped liver with bacon. But when Jeff saw Jo come through the door, he slapped her usual hamburger onto the grill and lowered a basket of onion rings into hot oil.

Laura was just paying for a shrimp salad sandwich on five-grain bread. "Noel said you stopped by," she told Jo. "I was going to call you as soon as I got back to my desk." She looked down at her sandwich. "But a conference in judge's chambers always makes me ravenous."

"How did you do?"

"We got custody. But we're still working out the child support. What did you want to discuss?"

"I need your advice about a neighborhood problem."

Laura looked out at the clear blue sky. "I was going to eat at my desk. But it's gotten so nice and warm this afternoon. There won't be many more days like this before winter sets in. Why don't we walk down to the harbor?"

"Sounds good."

As they strolled past the parking garage on their way to the refurbished inner harbor, neither woman was aware of the activity inside. The man who had been following Jo that morning was fine-tuning the modifications he'd made on her car. His tracking device was going to cause her some future problems. On the other hand, because he was otherwise engaged at the moment, he wasn't eavesdropping on the conversation between Jo and Laura.

Ten minutes later, the women arrived at the waterfront. Not so long ago the area had been littered with decaying factories and warehouses. Now luxury hotels, glass and steel pavilions, and plush office buildings proudly proclaimed the inner city's rebirth.

The pleasure craft that crowded the harbor in summer had departed, but the U.S. *Constellation*, the oldest ship in the

U.S. Navy, still waited for the lines of children who came regularly on school field trips.

Half the downtown work force was taking advantage of the unseasonable weather. Jo and Laura were lucky to find a bench along the brick quay.

"What's on your mind?" Laura asked as she poked her straw through the top of her can of lemonade.

"Dogs. I'm thinking of strangling some," Jo quipped, aware that she was channeling her other anxieties into this particular problem.

"As your lawyer, I'd advise against it."

Jo laughed. "It was just a passing fantasy, but seriously, I do have a problem." Succinctly she explained about Sunday morning's backyard activities.

Laura commiserated. "But you can't accuse any dog owners unless you have proof."

"What do I have to do—stake out the area?" Before her friend could answer, her face lit up. "I've got it. I'll rig a camera with a motion detector."

Laura grinned. "I'm impressed. You really know how to do that kind of thing?"

"Piece of cake." She told Laura a bit about the technique.

"I could help you set it up this weekend."

Jo regarded her friend. They were closer than family but if Laura wasn't going to explain why she wasn't spending the weekend with her husband, she wasn't going to press, not when they only had a few minutes to talk.

"Great. At least that's one problem I can solve," she said instead.

"You have others?"

"Nothing I can't handle," Jo murmured.

"If you need help, you've got it."

"You, too."

Back at the office twenty minutes later, Jo finally reviewed the Cahill file. The notes brought back memories of the risky operation where she'd infiltrated the Baltimore drug culture to get the goods on him. If Eddie really was hanging around plotting to get someone, the person in the most danger was his ex-wife.

Karen was blond, beautiful, delicate, and not very independent. She'd been horrified at the chain of events that she'd set in motion by trying to prove that her husband was cheating on her. All she'd wanted to do was get out of the marriage with some of the money Eddie was throwing around like confetti at a New Year's Eve party. Instead she'd ended up testifying against him at a drug trial that had been page one news for weeks.

When Jo called Karen Cahill's home number, the phone just rang and rang. She was able to locate the woman on her next try—at her mother's Highlandtown row house.

"Jo, how did you figure out where I was?"

"I'm a detective, remember."

Karen clicked her teeth nervously. "If you can find me, Eddie can, too."

"You haven't heard from him? Or seen him?"

"No, thank God." Karen's voice quavered. "But he said he was going to get me. What am I going to do?"

Jo considered what advice to offer. Giving false assurances could be dangerous. On the other hand, she didn't want to make the woman panic. "It might not be a bad idea to get out of town until they recapture him."

"I just started dating this real classy guy. He's not going to like it if I disappear."

He won't like it if you get killed, either, Jo thought but didn't voice the sentiment.

"If you're going to stay in town, talk to the police about taking precautions."

"What precautions?"

"Don't go out alone. Check the locks on your doors and

windows. Keep the curtains drawn at night. Let the police know if Eddie gets in touch with you.'' She went on to enumerate several other suggestions.

''I don't know whether I feel better or worse,'' Karen said. ''I can't live my life like a prisoner. Tyler likes to go out at night. Dinner and dancing. You know.''

Jo struggled with exasperation. This woman couldn't have it both ways. ''Karen, just be careful,'' she advised.

''I wish I'd never met Eddie.''

That was one point they agreed on, Jo observed silently. ''Good luck,'' she offered instead.

''You, too.''

After she hung up, Jo cupped her chin in her hands. Karen hadn't been much help. In fact, the woman had her priorities all screwed up. Talking to her had served an important purpose, however. It had made the danger more real.

Unlocking one of the bottom desk drawers, Jo brought out the snub-nosed .32 she rarely carried. After checking the action and loading the weapon, she put it into her purse.

Chapter Four

Jo kept several changes of clothes at the office for the various roles she needed to assume in her work. Over the years, she had played everything from a cocktail waitress to a nun to get information. Today after donning jeans, a plaid shirt and a bulky sweater, she inspected herself in the mirror. She'd do.

The solid weight of the gun felt reassuring as she left the office again. This time she was headed for Lucky's Cue Club, a pool hall just off Dundalk Avenue. Eddie Cahill had hung out there before he'd made it big, and from time to time he'd come back to hustle games and brag about his success.

Jo knew there had been a fair amount of jealousy among the old crowd in Eddie's former working-class neighborhood. In fact, a couple of his former buddies had testified against him. Probably they had a bet going on the time and hour he'd be picked up. If anyone at Lucky's had a lead on Eddie, perhaps they'd share the information. For a price.

In the garage across from 43 Light Street, Jo turned the key in the ignition and backed out of her parking space.

The moment her engine turned over, a warning signal sounded in a workshop ten miles away.

The man monitoring the alarm typed in a sequence of commands on his keyboard, activating a satellite link. Al-

most instantly, the high-resolution computer screen trans-
formed itself into a grid map of the downtown area. The
garage was at the center of the grid. As Jo's car began to
move, the map changed so that a red blinking dot could
follow her progress through the city. She was heading up
Eastern Avenue. Where was she going?

LUCKY HADN'T SPENT much on exterior frills since the last
time Jo had been to the pool hall hustling information about
Eddie. The *L* on the neon sign in the window was still out.
It had been joined in death by the *Y*. Now the sign simply
said "uck." Which was a passable description for the dimly
lit interior.

At two in the afternoon, the large room was just beginning to fill. A group of kids hooking school were in the
back at the game machines, and the bar was lined with men
in leather jackets and work boots. A lot of them were on
unpaid vacation from the local auto plant.

The only other women in the place looked as if they
weren't there to hustle pool. Ignoring the speculative stares,
Jo bellied up to the bar and asked for a Miller Lite.

Before she'd taken more than a couple of sips, she was
joined by a slim, dark-haired fellow who had been hidden
in the shadows at the far end of the bar. He had the wolfish
look of a ladies' man, but the broken veins in his face made
him unappealing. Jo remembered him. In addition to
women, he also liked his booze.

"What brings you to downtown Dundalk, beautiful?"

"You tell me."

His eyes flicked over her petite figure. "You're looking
for a little action."

Jo stared back. "Guess again."

He changed tactics. "You're tryin' to get a line on Eddie
Cahill." Apparently he also remembered her.

"Bingo."

"Eddie's too smart to show his puss around here."

"Is he still in town?"

The wolf man shrugged elaborately.

Jo pulled out the twenty-dollar bill she'd tucked into the side pocket of her purse.

Her companion studied the bill. Jo was pretty sure he wasn't trying to get a make on Andrew Jackson.

"You heard anything?" she asked.

Before he could answer, a younger guy who'd been listening to the conversation joined the group. His hair was shaved on the sides, stuck up on top, and hung in a long lock down the back of his neck making him look like an Indian chief. She liked his looks even less than the wolf man's. But she only wanted to talk to him; she didn't have to date him.

"Heard something about Eddie from a buddy of mine," he ventured.

"Yeah, what?" the wolf man demanded.

"This is between me and her." The newcomer glanced at Jo.

She nodded, and he lifted the twenty from between her fingers. The wolf man gave them a sour look before sauntering off.

When he had disappeared back into the shadows, the informant leaned toward Jo. "This friend of mine, Dick Petty, gets cars for people at the auction out at the fairgrounds. And other ways."

Jo didn't inquire about what the other ways might be.

"Eddie got in touch with him. Said he wanted a car. Nothing flashy or hot. But it has to be reliable. Said he'd pay cash."

"Did he give Petty a phone number?"

"No. He said he'd be back in touch."

"How can I get a hold of your buddy?"

"He's around, you know, but sometimes you can find him at Arnold's Gym up on Holabird."

"Appreciate it," Jo told him. If the information was true, it meant Eddie was still around town, and he had some cash. That was bad news.

At the door of the pool room, she turned and looked back at the man. He was drinking her beer.

Starting toward her car, she dug her keys out of her purse. At the corner of her vision, she saw a figure push away from one of the form-stone buildings and start toward her. She had a quick impression of spiked hair, black jeans and a black jacket with iridescent colors. Another punk.

She didn't want to stare; she didn't want to look intimidated. Yet something about the purposeful way he moved made her step briskly as she turned the corner and headed toward her car.

There was no one else on the side street, no one to help her, she realized as she bent to insert the key into the lock. A burst of movement and the instinctive knowledge that she had become a target made her turn and reach inside her purse. But she was a split second too late. Before her fingers could close around the butt of the gun, the leather strap over her arm fell away.

Cut, she thought, even before she saw the knife blade glint in the sun. Reflex took over.

The keys dropped from her hand. Fast as a whip, her foot lashed out with the technique she'd practiced in martial arts class. It caught her attacker in the thigh. He cursed. Then the knife was slashing down toward her arm. The blade sliced the knit of her sweater and pierced her forearm.

The slash sent a scream tearing from her throat. The stakes had escalated.

They were face-to-face: hers drained of blood, his covered with bumps and red splotches.

She was backed up against the car, and he had the knife.

His fist grasped her purse. Why didn't he run? What else did he have in mind? Jo wasn't going to wait and find out.

"You slimebag," she shrieked as she launched her hundred-and-eight-pound frame toward him.

For a moment he seemed dumbfounded by the attack and her fighting skill. The two-second hesitation allowed her to kick the knife out of his hand. Now it was an even fight, she thought. Her brains and his strength.

She tried to wrestle her property out of his grasp, but she hadn't counted on his desperation. With one hand he clasped her purse against his neck.

Her fingers scrambled and clawed down his face. In the scuffle she vaguely heard her keys fall through the nearby storm drain.

With bone-jarring force, he slammed her back against the side of the car. As her knees buckled, he turned and ran.

Jo sat on the sidewalk, struggling to catch her breath. Now that the fight was over, she was aware of a burning pain in her arm. Looking down, she saw blood soaking into her sweater.

"Sheez!" No car keys. No purse. Cut and bleeding and sitting like a drunk on the sidewalk. She needed help, but she'd rather die than go back into Lucky's bar.

"You want an ambulance? Or the police?" someone asked.

She looked up to see an old man squinting at her from the front stoop of a house a few doors down.

"Could I use your phone to call a friend?"

"Yeah."

Jo grimaced as she pushed herself to her feet. In his living room, she called Abby and quickly explained her problem.

"Can you pick me up?" She gave the address. "Honk and I'll come outside."

"Sit tight," Abby said. "Help is on the way."

THE PURSE LAY on the passenger seat begging him to drag
it over and riffle through the contents. He couldn't give in
to the siren call until he'd pulled the van onto a side road
where he knew he wouldn't be disturbed. Even if a car
happened to pass, there was no reason to connect him to
the mugging. When he'd used the transmitter to lead himself
to his quarry, he'd parked well away from the pool hall.
And Detective O'Malley had been in no shape to follow
him back to the van.

Yet, as he made a sharp turn, he could feel his thigh
throb. She'd studied self-defense. That's why she'd been
able to get in a few licks. He'd be ready for that next time.

He was glad the windows were smoked glass as he unwrapped a cleansing pad and began to wipe off the makeup.
She'd smeared the stuff, but he was sure she wouldn't recognize him in a police lineup. Only after his face was back
to normal did he reach across the console and spill the contents of the purse out on the seat.

The pistol captured his attention. He thought she'd
reached for a can of mace but she'd been going for a gun.
The bitch could have shot him.

The brush with danger sent a little thrill down his spine
like the caress of a lover's fingers. He sucked in a sharp
breath.

Instead of just taking her purse, he could have bundled
her into the van and taken her then. But that would have
cut out half the fun. He wanted her to know he was after
her. He wanted the terror to build until he was ready to
strike.

The more you knew about a person, the easier it was to
freak them out. And there were so many ways to collect
information. With stiff fingers, he set the gun aside and
began to poke through the rest of her stuff. Not much
makeup. Just a lipstick. In one of those dumb colors women
liked. Warm melon. He caressed the tube, raised it to his

nose, smelled the faint cosmetic scent—and the scent of her body clinging to the cold metal. It made him feel close to her, very close. Just like her comb did. Pulling a bouncy red strand from the teeth, he wound it around his finger like a wedding band.

Her wallet was the biggest treasure trove. Baltimore Shopping Plate, phone credit card, VISA, gasoline cards, insurance, AAA, professional organizations. There was also a snapshot of a man. For several seconds he stared at the smiling image. Then he crumpled the photo in his fist.

He was going to make her sweat. She deserved it. Then, when he was ready, he'd strike with the coiled speed of a rattlesnake. Only there wouldn't be any rattle to give her warning. The thought made him giggle.

OUTSIDE A CAR HORN honked. Jo struggled to her feet, thanked her host once more and opened the front door. Shock had enfolded her injured body as she huddled in a faded wing chair. Now she grasped the railing to keep from toppling down the marble steps of the old row house.

A car door opened and someone rushed toward her. Not Abby Franklin. Cameron Randolph.

"What are you doing here?"

"Abby couldn't get away. She called me."

He was staring at her, taking in her white face, her tangled hair, the blood soaked through the arm of her sweater. His own face drained of color.

"My God, Jo. What happened?" As his hand gripped her good arm to steady her, his voice was edged with more than the hoarseness she'd heard earlier.

"A mugger. I'm okay. I just need—"

Her knees belied her words. They gave way unexpectedly, and she pitched against him. His body absorbed the shock as if it had been designed for that purpose. When he caught her and held her upright, one arm at her waist, the other across her back, she had the odd sensation of having come home.

Jo's head fell against his chest, and her eyes fought a losing battle to stay open. Walking down the steps had been a bad idea. She was on the verge of blacking out.

"I'm taking you to the hospital." Cam left no room for protest. For a moment, she gave in to his care, shocked at how good it felt. Even as he spoke, he was carrying her to the sports car and settling her in the seat.

She leaned into the comfort of the sun-warmed leather, only peripherally aware of him climbing into the driver's seat. In the next moment, the car accelerated like a jet going through the sound barrier.

"Are you sure I'll live to make it to the hospital, Mr. Sulu?" she managed in a weak voice.

"Is there ever a situation when you can't come up with a smart remark?"

"A few."

She cast him a sidelong glance as he wove expertly in and out of traffic. She would never have imposed on him like this. Yet when Abby had called him, he had come charging down here to help her as naturally as if they'd been friends for years. No, more than friends.

"I thought you were sick," she muttered, still not quite acclimated to his presence or the situation or her reaction to him.

"I'm better."

He had her to Francis Scott Key Medical Center in record time.

"Can you stand up by yourself?"

"Of course I can stand up!"

But her steps were still none too steady as he escorted her in from the parking lot. When she reached the desk, she realized she had a big problem. "Damn."

"What?"

"No medical insurance card, no ID and no money."

"I'll take care of everything."

"Cam—"

"We'll settle up later."

The admitting nurse had called the police, so while Jo waited for treatment, she made a brief report. She and the officer agreed that there wasn't much hope of getting her personal property back.

Finally her name was called, and she was ushered into a curtained-off cubicle. It was still half an hour before a nurse practitioner came in to stitch and bandage her wound.

She had told Cam she didn't need him anymore. He was sitting in a hard-back chair watching the doorway. As she came back into the waiting room, he jumped up.

"How's the arm?"

"I'll live."

Wordlessly, he took off his jacket and draped it around her shoulders. Now that the emergency was over, they faced each other uncertainly.

"Thanks," she murmured.

"I'd better get you home."

When they stepped out the door, she was astonished to find that it was dark. She'd been here for hours.

As the car headed northwest, she found she was almost back to normal—except for the throbbing of her arm and the oddly tight feeling in her chest as she sat next to Cam Randolph. It was because she didn't like being helpless or dependent, especially with him, she told herself. Well, it was only for another fifteen minutes. Ignoring the pain and the man beside her, she started cataloging the things she'd have to do: call her insurance company about the credit cards, get some money from the bank, talk to the DMV, report the theft of the gun...

The car had pulled in at a shopping center on Cold Spring Lane. "What are you doing?" she asked in surprise.

"Getting dinner."

"Cam, really, you don't have to do that."

"I want to. Do you like Chinese food?"

"Yes, but you don't—"

He got out of the car before she could argue any further. She sat with her arms folded, less and less pleased with the way he had taken charge. It was one thing to come to her rescue. It was another to— She stopped herself. The least she could do was accept his offer graciously.

When he returned fifteen minutes later and she caught the scent wafting from the bag he carried, she felt her stomach rumble.

Minutes later, they pulled up at her door, and she hurried up the front walk. However, when she reached the door, she stopped abruptly. No key.

"You're going to have to get the locks changed."

"Not unless that son of a gun digs them out of the storm drain. That's where they landed in the scuffle."

"At least you don't have to worry about his breaking in. But *we* might have to."

"There's a spare key at my neighbor's. I'll be right back."

After Jo opened the door, Cam didn't immediately follow her inside. She turned and found him studying the control panel for the security system. It wasn't the kind of thing she'd expect from most guests. But then the man had designed the thing, she told herself.

"It's a B9N8-150. We don't make that model anymore."

"Doesn't it work right?"

"Of course it works right! Correctly. It's just that we've incorporated some new features."

"Like throwing unwanted visitors off the porch?"

He laughed. "You need the inventor around to do that for you." He looked at her disheveled appearance. "Want to clean up before we eat?"

"Yeah."

"Are you up to sitting at the table? I could bring you up a tray."

"No! I'll come down," she answered quickly.

"I'll put the stuff in the microwave."

Upstairs she stripped off her clothes and washed away the street grime as best she could without getting the bandaged arm wet. Anything she put on was going to hurt. She settled for one of Skip's old sweatshirts over a pair of jeans. It was too much effort to pull on shoes and socks so she stuffed her feet into her bunny slippers.

Cam was in the living room when she came back downstairs, looking through Skip's collection of twentieth-century fiction. Her husband had been into Faulkner and Hemingway. She read the detective stories.

When he heard her footsteps, he turned. "Are you all right?"

"Do I look all right?" The minute she'd said the words, she was sorry.

She'd invited his inquisitive eyes to make an inspection. He started with the hair she'd quickly combed and progressed to the oversize sweatshirt and worn jeans. It ended abruptly at the bunny slippers. She'd thought the outfit wasn't in the least bit sexy; somehow his look of male appreciation made her feel otherwise.

In the car, she'd deliberately turned her mind to practical matters. Now that they were alone in her house, she was conscious that he was her first male visitor in a long time and that her hands were trembling slightly. She shoved them into her pockets.

He cleared his throat.

Her gaze swept up to meet his gray eyes. Men in glasses weren't dangerous, she'd always said. Who was she kidding? She knew he was just as aware of the sudden intimacy of the moment as she.

She took a step back, then quickly turned and headed toward the scent of Chinese food drifting in from the kitchen.

He watched the back of the baggy sweatshirt disappear into the kitchen. The way it swallowed up her slender form was endearing. The effect shouldn't be sexy but it made his body tighten. Maybe stopping to buy dinner was a mistake, after all.

The shirt was probably her husband's, he realized, and felt an unexpected stab of something he didn't want to label as jealousy.

Uncertainly he followed Jo down the hall. When Abby had called him, he'd decided she was handing him a golden opportunity to check up on Ms. O'Malley. That was before he'd seen her as pale as death and soaked with blood. Or before she'd pitched into his arms and he'd caught her slender form against the length of his body.

Jo moved a new Dean Koontz novel and a stack of bills off the kitchen table and onto the radiator and then got plates and cutlery.

The clutter made her self-conscious. At the moment everything made her self-conscious.

The house and furnishings had been Skip's. They were both comfortable in a warm, unconventional way. When she'd first seen the place, she'd assumed he'd acquired furniture on a need-to-use basis. There wasn't any particular style and nothing much matched. Most women would have launched a reform movement, but she hadn't cared enough about home decor to make any major changes. Besides, it was luxurious compared to the rural poverty in which she'd grown up.

Cam had turned to study the old-fashioned chestnut cabinets she and Skip had kept when they'd put in new appliances.

''The furnishings don't look very—'' He searched for the right word. ''Coordinated.''

She laughed. ''My husband's special brand of decorating.''

''Oh.''

They both busied themselves pulling out cartons and inserting spoons.

Eating, that should keep them out of trouble, Jo thought.

''I hope you like it hot and spicy.'' Damn, he hadn't meant it to sound that way.

''Um. But Skip had ulcers so we could never share any Szechuan dishes.'' As she finished the sentence, she realized she'd just mentioned her husband two times in as many minutes. It didn't take a Freudian analyst to figure out that subconsciously she was trying to warn Cam off.

She looked up to find the man in question studying her again. Their eyes searched each other. She was the first to lower her gaze.

''He was a lot older than you were.''

Somewhere in her mind, the remark registered with more than face value. She was too off balance to grapple with the implications. ''Fifteen years,'' she clarified.

''Did he teach you a lot?''

There was more than one interpretation to the question. ''Like what?''

He watched her bite into a piece of chicken and then couldn't tear his eyes away as she flicked out her tongue to remove a bit of sauce from her lip.

He needed to know how deeply she'd been involved with Skip's cases. He couldn't stop himself from wondering about the sexual side of their relationship. How had the difference in their ages affected that? ''Detective stuff,'' he clarified, his voice a shade raspier than before.

''He taught me everything I know.''

''You worked closely with him?''

"Usually. Sometimes we had our own cases." She could remember a couple of times when he'd told her it was best for her not to get involved in what he was doing. She didn't see any need to go into explanations with Cam.

They were both silent as they concentrated on the food. Jo chewed and swallowed a mouthful of crunchy meat. "This is good."

"Crispy beef. In Chinese cuisine, the beef dishes are usually the least rewarding. But if they make this one right, it's wonderful."

"Do you know a lot about Chinese cooking?"

"I didn't mean to sound pedantic. It's just that when I get interested in a subject, I tend to go a little overboard."

"It's okay. Skip was like that, too, sometimes."

Cam wasn't sure he liked being compared to her late husband. "He made a study of Chinese gastronomy?" he asked stiffly.

"No. He knew everything there was to know about firearms and baseball."

The man on the other side of the table didn't reply.

"What do you—uh—do for fun?" she asked.

"The same thing I did when I was a kid. Tinker with stuff. Only now I'm designing new products instead of taking apart the family appliances or fixing things that don't work."

"That doesn't sound too relaxing."

"Well, in the evening I've got a stack of mysteries beside the bed."

Her eyes lit up. "Me, too. I like the women detectives best."

"I'm more into police procedurals. The logic appeals to me."

It would, Jo thought. She considered telling him that she was thinking of writing a book herself. But he'd probably just laugh.

As they finished the meal, they continued the literary discussion, both relieved that they'd found a safe topic.

Jo was reaching for a little more crispy beef when she saw the carton was almost empty. They'd put away an awful big meal.

"I never thought of Chinese food as a substitute for chicken soup." She grinned.

"Chicken soup?"

"Didn't your mother bring you bowls of chicken soup when you were sick?"

"I hardly remember my mother. Dad and Collin weren't much into cooking."

"Your mother—"

"Died when I was seven. Dad and my older brother, Collin, raised me." As he delivered that last piece of information, his face was watchful.

"I guess I'm not the only one who had it rough," Jo murmured. She didn't elaborate. Neither did he. Instead they both got up at the same time to start clearing the table. His hand brushed against her sleeve and she winced.

"Sorry."

"You should have told me it was still hurting."

"I'm okay."

"Did they give you anything to take?"

"I don't need anything."

He reached out and gently grasped her shoulders. She glanced down at his strong, lean fingers on her sweatshirt.

"If you need to take something so you can get to sleep, go ahead and do it. You don't have to tough out the pain."

She looked away, embarrassed that he'd read her so accurately.

"You're not used to having someone take care of you."

"I'm out of the habit."

"I never got into it."

She might have asked why. He hurried on. "You didn't

like my showing up instead of Abby to take you to the hospital.''

"She's already seen me at my worst. I guess you have, too—now.''

"I like you at your worst as much as I liked you all spiffed up for Abby's party.''

"Sure.''

His hands dropped back to his sides. "Listen, I should probably let you rest.''

"Well, thanks—for everything.''

"See you Thursday.''

"I'll be looking forward to it.'' As soon as she'd said the words, she knew they were true.

"I will, too.''

They stood regarding each other for a moment. She saw his gaze drop to her lips. Seconds stretched or was it only her imagination that drew the moment taut. Then he turned abruptly.

She followed him down the hall and locked the door behind him.

The unexpected dinner with Cam had been edged with a man-woman awareness Jo didn't really want to examine too closely. They'd each been reluctant to reveal too much about themselves—except just before he'd left when she'd found herself admitting things she usually kept to herself. Jo was too worn out to ponder the implications.

Fifteen minutes later she had settled down in bed with the book she was reading. The phone rang, and she automatically picked up the receiver.

"Hello.''

"Hi there, angel face. I'm glad I caught you. It's about time we got a little more up close and personal.''

That voice! It was him again! Jo's spine tingled as if icy fingers were walking down her bones.

"Who—who is this?'' she demanded.

The high-pitched laugh assaulted her again like swarming bees. This time, their stingers penetrated all the way to her marrow.

"Want to meet me at the Giant Food Store at the Rotunda Mall? We can see if the bananas are ripe."

"No!"

"You didn't tell me you liked M & M's. They're one of my favorites, too."

"Who are you?"

"Someone who's going to have his way with that gorgeous little body of yours," the caller continued. "It's going to be a lot of fun. We'll smear warm melon lipstick on your mouth, and you can leave love marks all over my skin. Unless you'd rather use those little white teeth of yours."

"No!"

Jo slammed down the phone. Her whole body had begun to shake. She felt physically assaulted. Invaded. Not just by the sexual threats, but by the mundane details of her life he'd tossed out at her. To keep her teeth from chattering, she clamped them together.

Ten seconds after she hung up, the phone jangled again. She let it ring. When the answering machine clicked, she shut that off too. Pressing her hands over her ears, she squeezed her eyes shut, drew up her knees under her nightgown, and huddled in a ball under the covers. Yet now she couldn't blot out the awful knowledge that the first call to the office hadn't been a fluke. This one was to her home number. Someone was stalking her. And he knew exactly where to find her at any minute of the day or night.

Chapter Five

Before going to bed Jo unplugged the telephone jack in her room. But she wasn't able to sleep. Questions with no answers circled in her head like caged animals desperate for freedom.

Who was calling her? What did he want?

She tried to stop thinking about the threatening words. They were burned into her brain tissue. The caller had mentioned the Giant. Had he seen her buy M & M's? And he knew the color of her lipstick. Was he someone who had been watching her? Or was he talking about the lipstick that had been in her purse? Did he have her Giant check-cashing card?

Panic jerked her to a sitting position. As chill air hit her shoulders, she clutched the covers up to her chin. The sudden movement jarred her injured arm, and it began to throb.

She'd been mugged this afternoon. When she'd clawed his face, his splotchy complexion had come off on her fingers. He'd been wearing makeup. Could it be the same man who was calling her? Was it Eddie Cahill? Was that why he'd been disguised?

She'd certainly baited him by invading his territory. If he had her purse, now he knew a whole lot more about her. Driver's license. Credit cards. Medical ID. Insurance. Oh God, he had everything. Except her keys.

Suddenly it was impossible to sit there in the dark, and she switched on the light beside her bed. For a few moments she squinted in pain. Then her gaze shot to the curtains that were pulled across the window. He could be out there now. Did it give him a charge to know she'd turned on the light? Was he laughing at her?

Stop it, she told herself firmly. *You're making more out of this whole thing than it's worth. The calls and the mugging probably aren't connected. Nobody's out there in the night under the hydrangea bushes watching your house.*

The ludicrous image called forth a brittle laugh. At least she could still joke about it, Jo told herself. That was a good sign. Getting out of bed, she crossed to the bathroom on legs that weren't quite steady, turned on the water, and filled the glass that sat beside her toothbrush holder. A few swallows of cold water made her feel better. Compromising, she left the bathroom light on when she returned to bed. She didn't fall asleep until just before dawn.

The face that greeted her in the bathroom mirror showed the effects of the sleepless night. Grimacing, she vowed she was going to take control of the situation.

Jo dug out her spare set of car keys and called a cab to take her to the Department of Motor Vehicles for a duplicate driver's license and registration. With that taken care of, she tackled her next problem—getting her car, although the thought of going back to Dundalk was as appealing as a trip to the dentist for a root canal.

Marching to the phone, she called another cab. After she'd slid into the back seat and given the driver the address, she leaned back and closed her eyes.

"You okay, lady?"

"Fine." Jo sat up straighter and pretended interest in the business establishments along the highway. She was actually picturing faces. Eddie Cahill the way he'd looked at her before they'd dragged him off to jail. The mugger with his punk haircut and makeup. She couldn't make the two images match up.

"What address did you say?"

"In the next block. You can pull up in back of my Honda." As the cab drew abreast of the spot where she'd been assaulted, she felt a hundred fists clench in her stomach. She knew the fear was ridiculous. The mugger wasn't hiding around the corner.

"Would you mind waiting until I check my car?"

"I can't stay long."

She slapped another five-dollar bill into his hand. "Indulge me."

First she peered into the storm drain. As far as she could tell, the keys were probably in the Chesapeake Bay by now. Then she turned to her car, inspected the tires for slash marks and started the engine. When she was satisfied, she gave the driver the high sign and roared out of the parking space at Cameron Randolph velocity. It felt good to put distance between herself and the scene of the crime.

But she still hadn't regained her equilibrium. The closer she got to her office, the more she found herself picturing the answering machine crouched on the bookcase like an animal poised to spring. Relief flooded through her when she saw that there weren't any messages waiting.

Flipping through her Rolodex, Jo found the number of the employee at the Chesapeake and Potomac Telephone Company business office who'd been helpful when she'd handled harassment cases for clients.

"Haven't heard from you in a while," Sheila Douglas replied to her greeting. "I guess you're still in the detective business."

"Yes. But this time I'm not making inquiries for a client. I've gotten a couple of nasty calls myself."

The woman made sympathetic noises.

"I know you ask customers with harassment complaints

to keep a log for a week. But assuming the calls continue, I want to understand my options.''

''Are there any distinctive specs?''

''Yes, the voice was electronically distorted. I got one message on the answering machine and one in person.''

''An answering machine. That's not typical. Usually telephone harassers want a live reaction on the other end of the line. Let me try a couple of searches of our new computer base.''

In a surprisingly short time, Mrs. Douglas was back on the line. ''I did find some incidents that might be related. But it's not procedure to give out that kind of information without written authorization. I'll need to check with my supervisor.''

''I'd appreciate that.''

''Meanwhile, we do have some new tools to fight telephone misuse. Maryland is one of the states where you can get a caller ID phone that displays the number from which a call is placed.''

Mrs. Douglas launched into an enthusiastic sales pitch for the new equipment. ''Or, if you think the problem is serious enough to bring in the police,'' she went on, ''you can take advantage of the new tracing option in the system. After the call is completed, you dial a special number that initiates the trace. The results are sent directly to the police department.''

''I guess I'd like to start with a caller ID phone.''

''We don't sell the equipment, but I'll give you the number of the company that does.''

After thanking Mrs. Douglas, Jo phoned the supplier and found she could get the attachment on her business and home lines by early the next week. She hung up feeling optimistic.

There were several more things she should take care of. Yesterday she'd been ready to go over to Arnold's Gym and look for Mr. Petty. Now she reconsidered the idea. After a silent debate with herself, she admitted that Jo O'Malley, P.I., wasn't too enthusiastic about putting herself in danger again. Instead she called Sid Flowers, who promised the police would follow up on the lead.

Over the next couple of days, Jo felt steadily better. She'd planned to talk to Abby about the psychological profile of telephone harassers. But there weren't any additional phone calls, so she didn't bother her friend with the problem. There also hadn't been any more news about Eddie Cahill. Perhaps he'd decided to cut his losses and get out of town after all. Maybe he'd even left the country. Or the planet!

Wednesday night Jo crawled into bed early, determined to catch up on some of the sleep she'd missed lately. Her light was off by ten forty-five, and she was asleep by eleven.

She dreamed of Cam. They were at a dance, swaying together to the music, their bodies drawing closer and closer. Her arms circled his neck. She tipped her mouth up to his. Their lips met, and she felt a warm surge of pleasure. Then he and the dance floor were gone, and she was alone in an endless park.

She was hurrying among beds of bright columbine, searching for him, when the flowers caught her attention. She had thought they were real; now she saw they were made of tiny wires, little filaments, electronic parts. Bees flitted between the blooms. Jo gasped as she took a closer look. The bees weren't what they had seemed, either. They were miniature robots with tiny glowing electric eyes like digital displays. Their silicon wings were veined with printed circuits.

But it was their mechanical hum that made her scalp crawl. *Bzzzzzzzzz.* It was the sound of danger. The laugh from the answering machine. Slowly, afraid to run, lest she attract their attention, she began to back away.

It was no good. Her skin prickled as more and more of

the bees stopped moving among the grotesque flowers and hovered like toy helicopters—their green eyes all locked on her.

Fear choked her throat now. The fear swelled as the tiny robots rose from the flowers, circling and buzzing in a huge swarm. They poised in the air, the sun reflecting off a thousand beating wings. The whirring grew louder.

Desperately she turned to run. But too late, too late. Giant metal spikes sprang up to block her way. The bees were swooping toward her.

For what seemed like an eternity, she fled for her life, dodging the spikes. Her feet pounded the ground. Her breath hissed in and out of her lungs. But it was no use. She couldn't outrun them.

They overtook her, buzzing, whirring, diving for her arms and face, stinging her flesh, choking off her breath.

Scream after scream tore from her lips. Then she was sitting bolt upright in bed, heart hammering, sweat pouring off her body.

It took several moments to convince herself she was safe in her own room. But the noise hadn't stopped. Then she realized what she was hearing. It was the buzz and whir of the automatic garage door opener. Opening and closing, opening and closing by itself. The sound must have triggered the awful dream.

It was a relief to focus on reality. The damn door was on the blink. Or maybe it had been activated by an airplane radio frequency. Unless—

No. It must be a plane, she assured herself. The problem had occurred once before, and Skip had had to change the frequency on the opener. Tonight she'd have to turn it off.

The clammy fabric of her nightgown clung to her body as she eased out of bed. Stripping it off, she tossed it on the chair and found another in the drawer. Then she donned her robe and slippers.

In days past she wouldn't have hesitated to investigate a weird noise in the middle of the night. Now she couldn't afford to take any chances. Before going downstairs, she slipped Skip's .357 Magnum into the pocket of her robe. Then she turned on every light she encountered as she moved through the house.

Her ears were tuned to any unusual noises. She almost expected to catch the sound of insects buzzing. But all she heard were her own footsteps creaking on the old floorboards. Even the malfunctioning door had stopped whirring.

When she reached the entrance to the garage, she hesitated, picturing an intruder crouched in the shadows.

First she turned on the garage light. Then she shouted a warning through the door. "The police are on their way. And you'd better get the hell out of there." No response came from the garage. Still, she was holding the gun in a police assault stance as she threw the door open.

It took only a few seconds to determine that the garage was empty—except for her car. Even after she'd turned off the door and gotten into bed, she lay awake staring into the darkness conjuring up an electronically distorted laugh. Or was it the buzzing of a thousand bees?

JO HAD PLANNED to come home early Thursday afternoon to get ready for the party, but a new client walked into her office at four-thirty. The woman was in tears because her husband of three months had cleaned out their joint bank accounts and skipped town. Jo spent an hour and a half calming her down and getting as many facts as possible. However, there was nothing she could do about starting to trace the man until Monday.

By the time Jo got home, she was running late. She was about to dash upstairs when she remembered the mail. Along with the usual assortment of letters and bills was a package wrapped in brown paper. A note from her neighbor Mac Lyman was attached.

"A catalog company was offering a special on these things. They're guaranteed to keep unwanted animals out of your yard. If it works, we won't be picking up any more trash."

Jo smiled. That was certainly sweet of Mac to have ordered one for her. She'd have to insist that he let her pay him. She wanted to open the package and take a look at the device. But right now she'd better get ready. Or Cam was going to come over and find her still dressed for work.

After a quick shower, Jo used the blow dryer on her red curls and put on a little makeup. But she'd always been a sucker for gadgets, and the package downstairs kept tugging at her curiosity. Maybe she could spare a few minutes to open it. If it wasn't too hard to operate, she might even be able to get it set up outside before she left. But she'd better do it before she got into her dress.

After shrugging into Skip's robe, Jo padded downstairs in her bunny slippers. Bringing the package to the couch, she sat down and began to undo the wrapping. The unmarked cardboard carton inside was held together by two thick rubber bands.

Jo slipped the bands off, and the packing material fell away. She found herself sitting with a box about the size of a five-pound bag of sugar. Hefting it, she noted that the weight was about right, too.

Danger. Her intuition screamed a warning. She pictured herself hurling the box through the window. In her mind she saw it smashing against the sidewalk. But her body didn't carry out the command.

As far as her senses could detect, nothing happened. There was no noise from the box. No odor. No change in temperature. No flashing lights. No electrical discharge. No explosion.

But she felt as if an explosion had gone off inside her head. Somehow she *knew* that the box was the source of the sudden terrible pain.

Get away, her brain screamed. With a superhuman effort, Jo stood up. Her legs were no stronger than flower stems. Before she could take a step, her knees buckled, and she collapsed to the floor. As the box bounced beside her on the carpet, shock waves reverberated in her head. She tried to scream. No sound came out. The agony was locked inside her throat.

Get away. Arms and legs twitched. They wouldn't obey her commands. She lay on her side, helpless, disoriented, a prisoner in her own body—and more terrified than she'd ever been in her life.

TWENTY MINUTES later when Cameron Randolph rang the bell, there was no answer. He rang again and, to deny his own feeling of nervousness, waited with tuxedo-clad arms folded across his chest. When he still didn't get any response, he turned and looked back toward the street but didn't see Jo's car. It could be in the garage. Or maybe she had forgotten about the party. His stomach tightened with a mixture of disappointment and annoyance. He'd already told himself all the reasons why he shouldn't be attracted to Jo O'Malley. This was one time when his emotions didn't yield to logic.

He could see a light on in the living room. Cupping his hands against the glass, he peered inside. A figure lay crumpled on the rug in front of the couch. Through the window he saw a man's robe. Below it protruded the bunny slippers he remembered. Above it was flaming red hair. Jo. Her hand was stretched toward a black box that lay beside her. The box was sickeningly familiar.

"Jo," he called and banged on the glass. "Jo."

He couldn't see her face. She didn't stir, and he felt a

knot of unexpected fear tie itself inside his chest as his eyes riveted on her limp body. My God, he hadn't anticipated anything like this! How long had she been lying there?

His first impulse was to smash through the window. He stopped himself. In his pocket was the new tool he'd been working on to test Randolph Electronics security systems. It wasn't designed as a lock picker, but he could use it that way.

It took less than ten seconds to electronically retract the bolt. As soon as he threw open the door, the dials on the instrument in his hand went haywire. Something inside the house was generating a powerful electromagnetic pulse.

He knew what it was. His eyes swung to the black box on the floor beside Jo. Guilt drove all shreds of common sense from his mind. When he took a step forward, readings on the meter doubled. At the same time, a wave of nausea swept over him, and he struggled to stay on his feet. It took all his remaining strength to struggle backward out of the field. When he reached the door, his head stopped spinning.

The box was small. It couldn't affect a very large area. From the door he calculated the distance to where Jo lay sprawled in the living room. Only eight feet, but it might as well have been eight miles. If he got any closer, he'd crumple before he reached her.

But he had to get her out of there. Before she— His brain wouldn't let him finish the thought.

Was there something he could use to shield his head? Wildly he looked around the porch and saw nothing that looked remotely useful. Then he spotted the garden hose still connected to the outside faucet. If his luck held, Jo hadn't gotten around to turning off the water for the winter.

When he opened the spigot, the hose stiffened and water spurted erratically from the nozzle. Tensely he waited to see if he was just getting leftover water from the pipes. Seconds later, he muttered silent thanks as the flow steadied.

Running back to the door, Cam adjusted the nozzle to produce a narrow stream and aimed at the box. When the force of the water struck the target, the box jumped as if it had been hit by a bullet. Water sprayed the room but the box was taking the brunt of the dousing. It sparked, crackled, and finally gave out a shuddering wheeze.

There was no other apparent change inside the room. But Cam checked the meter and saw that the room was now safe. Twisting the nozzle to shut off the water, he flung the hose onto the porch. Before it hit the wide boards, he was sprinting inside.

He knelt on the wet carpet beside Jo. *Not set to kill. Not set to kill.* The words were like a chant in his mind.

Gently he turned Jo over. For some reason, he was shocked to see that the rough fibers of the rug had pressed a pattern into the skin of her cheek. He was even more shocked by how deathly pale she looked.

With trembling fingers, he reached to find the pulse in her neck. Panic seized him when he couldn't find it. Finally he located the steady beat and breathed a sigh of relief.

At his touch, Jo stirred and moaned.

"It's all right. You're going to be all right," he murmured, praying that he spoke the truth. He didn't have much experience giving first aid. Or tending to unconscious females, for that matter, he thought, as he scooped her up and cradled her against the pleated front of his dress shirt. Even wearing a half-soaked robe, she was feather light in his arms. Under the bulky fabric her body felt fragile and very feminine.

Her color was returning.

"What?" she muttered, still not quite awake.

"You're all right," he repeated. This time he was pretty sure it was true.

He bent and pressed his cheek against hers. He was about

to set her on the sofa when he saw that the cushions were wet.

Damn! Now that the immediate danger was passed, he could see that he'd made a mess of the place.

Still holding Jo in his arms, Cam turned toward the stairs. There was no problem figuring out which room was hers. The rest of the house leaned toward dark colors and sturdy furniture. The first bedroom on the right was an oasis of feminine warmth and country charm. The cabinet pieces were pine and oak including a carved armoire. Instead of a chest of drawers, there was a pie safe against the opposite wall. The curtains and chair cushions had been made from a matching blue and peach print.

Drawing back the antique quilt, he laid Jo on the four-poster bed. When he opened the front of the sopping robe, he forgot to breathe for a moment. She was wearing only a delicate bra and lacy panties that hid almost nothing.

He would have jerked the robe back in place except that his mission hadn't changed—he had to get her out of the soggy thing. When he tried to slip the garment from her arms, he didn't make much progress—probably because his fingers were now too clumsy to function properly.

Sitting down on the edge of the bed, he pulled her up and forward. But her body was boneless. She collapsed against him, the air whooshing out of her lungs.

As her head drooped against his shoulder, the air rushed out of his lungs as well. For a moment he couldn't move. He'd been fantasizing about her. Now he was held captive by the pressure of her breasts against his chest, the silky feel of her skin, and the wildflower scent of her hair.

His arm came up to cradle her body protectively against his. At that moment, she was so sweetly vulnerable that he felt as if his heart would burst if he didn't kiss her. Turning his head, he pressed his lips against the soft skin where her cheek merged into her hairline.

He was confused by the strength of his emotions. But he wasn't the kind of man who took advantage of unconscious women, he told himself firmly. Letting out an unsteady breath, he forced his attention back to the job at hand. He'd just removed one of her arms from a sleeve, when he heard her murmur.

"Coming home…"

"Jo. Thank God."

Her body jerked as if she'd just realized what was happening.

"What in the hell are you doing this time?" she demanded. Her words were slurred but the message was clear.

"Your robe is soaked. I have to get it off."

"Soaked." She shifted and seemed to become aware of the sodden fabric—and also the proximity of her body to his.

When she pushed away from him, he didn't try to hold her. "From the hose," he mumbled.

"I was out in the yard?" As she spoke she shrugged off the wet garment and pushed it onto the floor. For a moment she sat there as exposed as a butterfly newly emerged from its chrysalis, the scar on her arm still a vivid red. Then she snatched at the quilt and pulled it up to her chin.

"No." He managed.

"No, what?"

"You weren't in the yard."

"The box," she muttered, sinking back against the pillow.

Cam reached for her hand. "How do you feel?"

"Weak. Confused." Her fingers gripped his as if she could draw strength from him.

He fought the urge to take her in his arms again. "Do you think the box came from your escaped con?" he asked instead.

She shrugged. "I don't know. It was with the mail. There

was a note from my neighbor saying he'd ordered it from a catalog. It's supposed to be an ultrasonic pest repeller.''

"That thing's no pest repeller."

"What is it?"

He wished he hadn't been so emphatic. "I had to douse it with the hose to short the circuits.''

"What is it?" she repeated.

He sighed. She wasn't going to be sidetracked so easily. "My guess is that it generates an electromagnetic pulse.''

"Something like an electromagnetic field? I've heard of them.''

"No. Something different."

"What?"

"A crowd control device, I think. I'll take it back to my lab and check it out.''

Jo pressed her palm against her forehead as if the gesture would help her brain function. The box would be evidence if she decided to call the police. After what it had done to her, however, the thought of having it in the house made her cringe. What if it went off again?

"How did it make you feel?" he asked, as if he had read her mind.

"Sick. Shaky. Frightened. Gonzo headache."

"I'm sorry."

"It wasn't your fault."

She missed the culpable expression that flashed across his face and the way his gray eyes were squinted in momentary pain.

There were a lot of things he wanted to ask. But she was in no condition to come up with explanations. Besides, he couldn't start raising questions until he'd gotten some answers of his own. "I'm going to get you some aspirin.''

"Okay. It's in the medicine cabinet. There's a glass on the sink.''

As she watched his tuxedo-clad back disappear through

the bedroom door, she remembered what he was doing here. They were supposed to be going to a party at his aunt's house.

Thank God he'd come to pick her up. If he hadn't, she'd still be lying in the living room with that thing microwaving her brain. The image sent a massive shudder through her body, and her mouth went as dry as chalk as she realized what a close call she'd had.

He was gone longer than it should have taken. Maybe he was giving her time to collect herself. When he handed her the glass, she took a gulp. Then, self-conscious, she swallowed the aspirin.

He sat down in the rocker by the window. "This room's nothing like the rest of the house. Did you redo it after your husband died?"

"We had our own bedrooms. I brought a lot of these things from western Maryland. My grandmother made the quilt. The pie safe was hers, too."

"You and Skip had separate bedrooms?"

"Yes. I—we—" She flushed.

"You don't have to explain anything to me."

"I don't want you to think we didn't—" God, she wondered, why was she fumbling around like this? It must be the aftereffects of the box. But that didn't explain why she cared what he thought. "He used to read until three or four in the morning. The light kept me awake." The explanation ended on a slightly defiant note. "Where are your glasses?" She changed the subject.

Now he was the one who looked slightly embarrassed. "I thought I'd wear contacts tonight."

"You didn't have to go to any special trouble on my account." She started to push herself out of bed, until she remembered she wasn't exactly dressed for company.

"The party. We're supposed to be at your aunt's house right now."

"I hardly think you're up to it."

"Yes, I am!" Even as she issued the protest, a wave of dizziness swept over her.

"I'll be downstairs. You get some sleep and we'll talk about it in a couple of hours."

Perhaps to forestall further argument, he got up, strode to the door, and turned off the light. She heard his footsteps on the stairs.

When she closed her eyes, she knew she didn't have a prayer of going to sleep. She'd been too confused to think straight. Now the implications of what had happened were starting to sink in. If the box wasn't a dog control device, then Mac hadn't sent it. Which meant it had come from someone else—someone who wanted to hurt her. Had they set the whole thing up? Had they scattered the trash in the first place? Was that why Mac hadn't heard any dogs barking?

Under the covers her body went rigid, and her heart began to thump. She could feel sweat beading on her upper lip.

She was in her own bed, but suddenly she felt like an animal in the forest—an animal being stalked by some unseen predator. Only it wasn't a beast coming after her through the underbrush. It was a person. Someone who was poking and prying into her life and using the knowledge to terrify her. He knew her neighbors. He knew where she shopped. What candy she liked. Did he also know what soap she used? What cold capsules? Was he going to empty them out and fill them with cyanide?

Stop it, she told herself. But she couldn't halt the awful speculations.

Who? The same person who'd been calling her on the phone? Eddie? Had he trashed her yard the night he'd escaped from prison? Or was it someone else?

If she kept on like this, she was going to unravel like the

slashed sweater she'd thrown away earlier in the week. She wasn't going to let it happen.

Since childhood, Jo O'Malley had had more gumption than most full-grown men.

After her father had died in a logging accident, there hadn't been much money. Her mother had supported the family by clerking in the country store down the road. The five kids had pitched in to keep the garden going; her brothers had supplemented the family diet with small game they brought home from the surrounding countryside.

As a child Jo had learned to mend a pair of jeans or a pair of shoes on the old treadle machine in the dining room. At twelve, she had gotten a job after school working as a maid at one of the ski resorts that dotted the mountain area. In summer the operation switched to boating, fishing, riding and the like.

Jo had learned three things very quickly. She wasn't cut out to be a maid. There was more than money that separated her from the vacationers. And education was going to be the key to a better life.

Teachers at the local high school had admired her determination and her ability and had tried to curb her natural proclivity for getting into trouble. They'd helped her win a scholarship to the University of Maryland. But when Mom had been laid up after an automobile accident, the family had needed money. Jo had quit school and gone looking for a job.

She hadn't counted on falling under the spell of Skip O'Malley. Now she knew that part of the attraction had been his age—and his ability to take charge. He became the stable male influence she'd never had. And something in him had responded to this girl from the country who had needed taking in hand. The relationship had been good for both of them. She'd played Eliza Doolittle to his Henry

Higgins. But like Eliza, she'd outgrown the student-mentor relationship and matured into her own woman.

Now she pushed herself to the side of the bed and swung her legs over the edge. For a moment she swayed and had to steady herself against the nightstand. Then the spasm passed.

Somehow she walked across the floor to the bathroom. Somehow she ran the shower and got under the hot water. It seemed to have a restorative effect. Or perhaps it was a combination of the hot water and her determination to feel normal.

By the time she dried her hair for the second time that evening she was feeling almost human. To compensate for her still-pale complexion, she put on a bit more makeup than usual. Then she donned fresh underwear and the dress she had planned to wear to the party.

When she came downstairs, Cam was stamping on the fifth towel that he'd used to blot the rug. It still wasn't dry, but it was a whole lot better.

Hearing a noise in the hall, he spun around in surprise. When he saw Jo standing in the doorway, his jaw dropped open.

"I guess you forgot your spot remover."

He smiled. "This is too big a job, anyway."

"Then let's go to the party," she suggested.

"But you can't—"

"You can take me home early if I give up the ghost. Come on. We're already late."

Chapter Six

"Maybe I should call a doctor. The aftereffects of that EMP may be worse than I assumed."

The woman who stood rebelliously in the entrance to the living room stiffened her spine. "Do I look like I need a doctor?"

Cam studied the pint-size figure of defiance. From the top of her red hair to the toes of her black leather pumps, she looked ready to take on Baltimore's best. And the parts in between were definitely worth a second look.

The aqua silk dress she was wearing did wonderful things for her eyes and skin. The soft folds of the material played hide-and-seek with the curves he'd become acquainted with upstairs.

If she realized how much she turned him on, she'd probably use it to her advantage, he told himself. Better to get out of here while the getting was good.

He sighed. "You win. Let's go."

She seemed surprised and perhaps a little disappointed that they weren't going to do battle over the issue. He turned away so she couldn't see his grin.

The women he had dated would have slipped a fur coat over the silk dress. Jo pulled a trench coat out of the closet. On her the belted style was flattering and gave her an air of mystery.

But after they'd gotten into the car, he knew she wasn't quite as recovered as she pretended by the way she leaned back in the padded leather seat and closed her eyes.

"I hope you don't mind if we make a quick stop."

"Why?"

"Got to change my shirt. I was already dressed for the party when disaster struck."

"Oh—right."

The questions he wanted to ask about what had been happening to her hovered on the edge of his tongue. But he still didn't want Jo turning around with questions of her own, so he found a classical station and let the third Brandenburg Concerto fill the silence.

Cam pulled up in front of his Cross Keys town house.

"I'll be right back," he told her as he turned on a couple of lights and ushered her into the living room.

Jo melted into the comfortable cushions of an off-white couch and looked around with interest at the place where Cam lived. Even a girl from the mountains could see that the furnishings were very expensive. But the house certainly wasn't "decorated" in any high fashion sense, and it was a lot smaller than she would have expected. She didn't have much time to study the layout. As promised, Cam returned quickly. Then they were on their way to his aunt's nineteenth-century Mount Vernon residence.

As they ascended the steps, she fixed a smile on her face. When Abby Franklin greeted her inside the foyer with its fourteen-foot ceiling and carved mahogany woodwork, no one would have guessed that less than two hours before Jo had been flat out on her much more modest living room floor immobilized by EMP waves.

"I'm sorry we're late," she apologized to Cam's aunt. "But I had to see a new client just as I was getting ready to leave the office."

Cam watched the performance, amused and impressed

with how well Jo handled the situation. Her claim might be true but it didn't begin to explain what had happened a few hours ago.

Steve came into the hall, and he and Jo hugged each other warmly.

"Making progress setting up your stateside air cargo business?" she asked.

"Sure am. Some of those contacts you gave me look like they're going to pan out."

The three of them discussed Steve's business plans for a few minutes. Cam was glad to see his friend sounding enthusiastic. He'd been worried about how a modern adventurer was going to fit into a more conventional life-style. Apparently he was finessing the situation. Was Abby as delighted with the arrangements? Perhaps she had decided it was better to have her husband flying around on this side of the world.

Steve clapped Cam on the back. "You and Jo are two of my favorite people. I hope you're getting along."

"Oh, we are."

Cam took her arm and they moved into the drawing room. Now that he'd gotten to know Jo better, he would characterize her behavior as watchful. What was she looking for, he wondered. And would her state of alert make it more difficult for him to take care of an important piece of business? Was she watching him as well as everyone else?

Just after the sit-down dinner for fifty, he got his chance. One of his aunt's friends had gotten into a gardening discussion with Jo, and they were exchanging tips on dividing irises and the best compost mix.

Quickly he slipped away from the group and made his way up the curved Georgian staircase. In the guest bedroom he quietly closed the heavy paneled door. Then he picked up the phone and dialed the familiar number he'd been waiting all evening to call.

BY TEN-THIRTY Jo knew that she couldn't keep up the game much longer. She'd wanted to go to the party to prove to herself and to Cam that she was functioning normally despite her mishap earlier in the evening. She'd also decided it would be foolish to give up the chance to check out the guests.

A whole bunch of nasty things had started right after the last party. If they weren't the work of Eddie Cahill, then perhaps there was a connection with the circle of Franklin-Claiborne-Randolph friends. Much as she hated to entertain the possibility, she couldn't dismiss it. So she spent the evening gliding through the authentically decorated Georgian rooms getting to know people.

Last week she'd felt out of place in the society crowd. Once she'd decided to employ her detective skills on her own behalf, she found that she was no longer feeling at a disadvantage.

However, as she chatted with Abby's cousin Glen Porter, she found her attention wandering. He was about her age and had worked as an extra in a couple of the recent movie productions set in Baltimore. She must be in bad shape, however, if she was having trouble focusing on his stories about Tom Selleck on the job. The aftereffects of the box were finally catching up with her, she conceded.

As if Cam had tapped into her thoughts, he appeared at her side, her coat draped over his arm.

"I have an early day tomorrow. I hope you don't mind if we make our excuses."

"I can give her a ride if you want to go ahead and leave," Glen offered.

Cam's expression took on a look of male possessiveness.

"No, I'm ready to go home," Jo broke in, strangely pleased by her escort's sudden show of covetousness.

PRISON TAUGHT YOU patience, Eddie Cahill thought. If you planned a job down to the last detail and waited for the right moment before you struck, you were sure of success. He'd already had a busy evening. Now he was waiting in the shadows when the flashy Buick pulled up in front of his ex-mother-in-law's house. He'd staked out the place before—as well as most of Karen's other haunts. In a day or two, he'd be ready to grab her.

The car had pulled up under a streetlight, and the driver cut the engine. Eddie wanted to stride across the cracked pavement and wrench the door open. Instead he pressed farther back into the darkness of the narrow alley. His stomach twisted as he watched Karen say good-night to her new lover boy.

It hadn't taken sweet little Karen long to replace him, Eddie thought. While he'd been rotting in prison, she'd worked her way through a series of guys with flashy cars and money to burn. They all liked to walk into a restaurant or a club with a drop-dead, good-looking blonde on their arm.

The observation brought a mirthless laugh to his lips. When he finished with her, she wasn't going to be beautiful anymore. But she was definitely going to be dead.

Then after he took care of her, he was going to switch his full attention to that other bitch—Jo O'Malley.

CAM DIDN'T SPEAK until they were settled in his luxury sports car once more. "Maybe I was out of line. Did you want Glen to take you home?"

"Of course not."

She saw his hands relax on the wheel.

"How are you feeling? I was sure you were going to fold before the main course. You must be Superwoman."

Jo mustered a laugh. "And I thought I was out with Superman."

Cam looked startled.

"Hasn't anyone ever mentioned you look like Christopher Reeve?"

"No one else would dare." He turned onto Charles Street. For several minutes they rode in silence. "One thing about you, Jo O'Malley, I never know what to expect."

"A detective has to keep the opposition off balance."

"Do you consider me the opposition?"

"I guess I did at first."

"Why?"

"Your family probably served wine with dinner. Mine was lucky if we had root beer."

"So?"

"It's funny about the upper class. They take things as simple as food on the table or indoor plumbing for granted." In the dark, Jo worried a thumbnail between her teeth. She hadn't planned to dump her insecurities in Cam's lap. Now her tongue was flapping like a hound's ears.

Up ahead a traffic light flashed red, and Cam downshifted to a halt. "It sounds like you had a rough childhood."

"Rural poverty builds character."

"I guess that's true—if you're an example."

"What do you mean?"

"Don't you know you're an extraordinary woman?"

"Extraordinary? I'm just a simple country girl trying to survive in the big city."

"In my experience, most women fish for compliments. I try to give you one, and you throw it back in my face."

"A sexist compliment. That's a new twist."

"I hadn't thought about it that way." There was the hint of a grin in his voice.

Jo slid him a sidewise glance. A few minutes ago she'd thought she was too exhausted to put together a coherent sentence. Now she realized the conversation with Cam was having a stimulating effect. She suspected the reaction wasn't one-sided.

When they pulled up in front of her house, Cam cut the engine.

"You know, most guys don't care whether you have a thought in your brain," Jo said, turning his observation around on him as he escorted her to the porch. "They're more interested in figuring out how to make a move on you."

There was a long silence. "I'm not going to pretend I haven't had some thoughts along those lines. Does that bother you?"

Jo had been inserting her key in the lock when his words sank in.

"Yes...no."

The air around them was suddenly crackling with tension as though someone was beaming an entirely different EMP charge in their direction.

Superman moved quickly when he set his mind to it. Cam turned the key, whisked them both inside, and entered the security code that turned off the alarm system before Jo could blink. Then he was pulling her into his arms.

He'd been spinning fantasies about Jo O'Malley all week. Now, as his lips slanted over hers, he tried to hang on to the tattered shreds of his reason. He told himself he was conducting a scientific experiment. She couldn't possibly be as exciting as the daydreams that had been interfering with his work, and he was going to prove it.

Cameron Randolph had never been all that aggressive with women. When he'd been a kid in high school, the football stars—not the science fair winners—had made it big with the girls. After a couple of major disappointments, he'd told himself there were more important things in life than scoring. The tables had turned in college. In the right circles, intellectual prowess was a sexual stimulus. Being a good catch didn't exactly hurt, either. Without much real effort on his part, he'd found himself in the enviable position of picking and choosing the women who spent a few weeks or a few months in his bed. None of them had lasted very long, because none of them had claimed as much of his interest as his current lab experiments.

Things hadn't changed a lot in adulthood—even during the six months when he'd been engaged.

But now he held a woman in his arms who didn't give a damn about his money and who was a billion times more exciting than anything his fevered brain had invented. At odd moments all evening, he'd been torturing himself with mental pictures of the way she'd looked in her lacy bra and panties. Each time he'd felt as if he'd grabbed hold of a high voltage line.

His mouth moved over hers. Her lips parted on a bare whisper of a sigh. She was as warm as biscuits fresh from the oven. As sweet as homemade strawberry jam. As rich as fresh churned butter. Suddenly he was starving for the unaccustomed luxury of downhome cooking.

Experiment be damned! He knew the moment his lips touched hers that he had only been kidding himself. There was nothing experimental about the urgency of his need to feel her mouth open for him, nothing analytical about the shudder of excitement that raced through his body when her tongue met his.

Jo had told herself right from the first that she and Cam Randolph didn't have a damn thing in common. They were worlds apart socially, philosophically, economically. If she'd been capable of coherent thought at this moment, she would have acknowledged that none of it mattered.

They were male and female locked in the grip of a force older than time. When she felt his body shudder, she answered with an involuntary tremor of her own.

His lips moved over hers, changing the angle, changing the pressure, changing everything between them.

He muttered low, sexy words deep in his throat. The syllables were almost obliterated by the primitive assault of his lips on hers.

When his hands skimmed down her back and found the curve of her hips, she automatically raised on tiptoes, her body seeking the masculine hardness that fit so perfectly with her feminine softness. It had been years since she'd felt this way. Perhaps she never had.

But she was seeking more than simply physical gratification. Warmth, closeness. All the things she'd told herself she didn't long for.

"Coming home," she murmured. That was how being in his arms felt.

He shifted her body so that his hands could cup her breasts. They were small—but firm and perfect. Earlier when he'd taken off her robe, he'd seen the shadows of her nipples drawn to taut peaks from the cold water. They were taut now—from the heat he and Jo were generating between them. Through silk and lace, his thumbs stroked across the swollen tips, drawing a little gasp from deep in her lungs.

He ached with the need to go on touching her, kissing her, making love to her.

Instead he dredged air into his own lungs. He hadn't meant to go this fast.

"Jo, I—"

"Cam—"

They stared at each other, dumbfounded that they had traveled so far and turbulently. It was just a kiss, wasn't it? No, it was much, much more. Suddenly neither of them knew how to cope with the implications.

Her fingers trailed across her own thoroughly kissed lips.

"I'd better leave. Are you going to be all right?" he asked.

She nodded.

"I'll call you tomorrow."

Fingers still pressed to her lips, she watched him close

the front door behind him. Then she turned the lock. She stood there until long after he had driven away, her emotional equilibrium in tatters.

She'd known sexual satisfaction with Skip. She'd known love. She had never known this white-hot energy arcing between a man and a woman. The closest she'd come to this feeling, she thought with a little grin, was when Tommy Steel had slipped her some white lightning at a church social.

But she wasn't high on anything now except Cameron Randolph. Was it just the skill of his lovemaking? Even as she asked the question, she dismissed it. She'd dug a moat around herself after Skip had died. No one else had dared to stick his toe into the shark-infested waters. But Cam had waded right in and forged across the dangerous channel. He'd charged up the opposite bank and into the stronghold—sword drawn—ready to help her fight the dragons breathing fire down her neck.

She shook her head. She was doing it again, casting him in another super-hero role. Drifting down the hall, she was headed for the stairs when she noticed the answering machine light was on. Still slightly drunk from the aftereffects of the kiss, she pressed the button.

"Did you have a good time at Mrs. Randolph's party, angel face?" the frightening voice that had become so familiar asked.

Oh God, he'd been watching her again. Couldn't she make a move without his knowing?

Jo's euphoria metamorphosed into razor-sharp horror. She pressed her shoulders against the wall in an effort to remain on her feet.

"I'm surprised you went out this evening after your little taste of my power."

She fought to swallow her scream. But her knees gave up the struggle to hold her erect, and she slid down to the rug. It was still soggy. Instantly chilly water soaked through her silk dress. Her teeth began to chatter and her body started to shiver—as much from fear as from the cold.

"Now you know that when I turn the switch, you'll do anything I want you to." The observation was followed by the high-pitched laugh Jo had come to know and fear. Moments ago her skin had been soft and tingly from Cam's caresses. Now it crawled with the pressure of a thousand insect wings. Beating. Beating.

"I have a nice brass bed all ready for you. I'm looking at it now. I can picture your red hair against the white pillow, your silky skin waiting for my touch, your wrists and ankles strapped to the brass rails. You're going to get everything you deserve."

Jo gagged. Unable to take any more, she reached out and pushed the fast forward button on the machine. An electronic garble assaulted her ears. When it cut off, she saved the message.

Her fingers dug into the soggy fibers of the rug. It was something to grip, a fragile hold on reality. Helpless fear threatened to swamp her. She wouldn't let it.

"You bastard," she hissed through clenched teeth, breaking the spell. Ejecting the tape, she clenched the small plastic cassette in her hand.

"You've had your fun. But I'm going to get you. You're going to be damn sorry you ever messed with Jo O'Malley," she grated, thinking about the caller ID attachment that soon would guard her phone. Then she'd know who he was!

Pushing herself to her feet, she started for the stairs. Her foot was on the second tread when she stopped abruptly, all at once aware of exactly what Laughing Boy said. He'd told her he was the one who'd sent her the nasty little present this afternoon.

It could have killed her. Maybe that was what Eddie had in mind. If it was Eddie.

When he'd started with the phone calls, she'd doubted it was him because the revenge had seemed too tame. But he'd escalated from words to deeds. What was next?

Well, she wasn't going to wait around and find out. She was going to take control of the situation. First thing in the morning she'd call the police and tell them about the EMP attack. No. She'd better get the box back from Cam first or they'd never believe anything so farfetched. But there were other things she could do, too. Eddie—Laughing Boy— whoever he was—had given her a big clue about his identity. That box must have come from somewhere. Cam had said it produced an electromagnetic pulse. She needed to find out what the devil EMP really was. Then she'd see who manufactured the units.

The next morning she called Cam, but he wasn't in his office. Disappointment warred with other emotions as she acknowledged that she was having a morning-after reaction to their kiss. Last night she'd been so wound up with Cam that Skip O'Malley had been completely wiped from her mind. Now she couldn't help feeling a bit guilty and disloyal.

Jo had planned to go straight to her office. But as she dumped her soggy robe in the dryer, she remembered the clothes she'd dropped at the cleaners six weeks ago. She'd better pick the outfit up before they got pitched.

One was an apricot cocktail dress she'd planned to wear to a couple of the parties. Another was a tweed suit she often wore for initial interviews with clients when she wanted to look professional.

On her way downtown, she stopped at the cleaners. "My pocketbook was stolen, and I don't have the ticket," she explained to the woman behind the counter. "But my name is Jo O'Malley, and I brought the items in last month."

The woman behind the counter checked her records. "Our files show that those were claimed."

"Are you sure?"

"The ticket receipt is here."

How could that be? She hadn't picked them up. "Do you remember who collected them?"

The woman shrugged. "It was three days ago. There have been hundreds of people in here since then."

"Was it one of your regular customers?" Jo persisted, unable to squash the tight feeling building in her chest. It was happening again. Another invasion into her life. Or maybe the guy who'd gotten her purse was going to sell her clothes for ready cash. Maybe it wasn't related to the other stuff at all. "Can I talk to your manager?"

"Sure."

The most Jo could get was a promise that if someone realized they had the wrong laundry, she'd be called. If not, her homeowner's insurance would pay for the loss. She should have felt relieved that she wasn't going to be out the couple of hundred dollars, but she couldn't shake the foreboding hovering over her.

Still, there was nothing more she could do about the missing clothes. And there were more pressing matters to take care of. Back at her office, she flipped through her Rolodex until she found the name of Harvey Cohen, Ph.D., past president of the Institute of Electronics and Electrical Engineers, former Princeton professor, and author of *The Electronic Warfare Game*, an exposé that had rocked the Pentagon a decade ago. Antiestablishment money had set him up in a Columbia, Maryland, think tank where he nipped at the heels of government agencies eager to spend public funds without regard for public health and safety.

Jo smiled as she conjured up a mental picture of Dr. Cohen. He'd been in the thick of the sixties radical movement. Thirty years later he still wore his curly hair in a halo around his face and favored cords and turtlenecks instead of suits. A suit would have hidden the little potbelly that spilled over his belt buckle.

Jo had met him a year ago when she'd done some undercover work aimed at stopping the Defense Department from filling in Eastern Shore wetland and building a weapons plant. They'd both been dressed as duck hunters that morning at dawn when she'd taken him out in a small boat to tour the area. He'd asked her to call him anytime she needed his help. She was still surprised when his secretary put her right through.

"Jo! Glad to hear from my favorite sneak boat pilot. I assume this isn't just a social call."

"Very astute, Professor. I'm wondering what you can tell me about EMP."

"As in Operation Sleeping Beauty?"

"If you say so."

"That's the code name for one of the government's secret research projects. I assume you don't want technical jargon."

"Right."

"In a nutshell, the Defense Department is very interested in using EMP to disrupt the functioning of the body's central nervous system. Actually it could be a very effective weapon against terrorists who have hijacked an airplane. Once they're on the ground, you zap the plane with EMP waves and everybody inside starts throwing up or goes temporarily blind and deaf or keels over. Or if you want to turn up the juice, you could use focused beams of high-powdered radio-frequency waves to kill by literally frying brain cells."

Jo shivered. She'd felt as if her brain cells were being fried when the box had switched on. Obviously it hadn't been set to kill. Or she wouldn't be talking to Dr. Cohen.

"So it's all still experimental. Who's doing research in the field?"

"The Navy has a contract out. U.C.L.A. had something going at their Brain Research Institute."

Jo could hear papers being shuffled on the other end of the line.

"Hmm—let's see—there was a local contract that never panned out. With Randolph Enterprises. Wonder boy Cameron Randolph was supposed to be working on a prototype for the Army."

Chapter Seven

"Cameron Randolph?" Jo repeated carefully, hoping she'd heard Harvey Cohen wrong.

"Do you know young Randolph? Hell of an inventor."

Jo's mind tried to process the new information. "We've met," she managed.

"I'm a little vague on what happened with the EMP deal, but as I understand it, he reneged on the government contract. He paid back what they'd already given him plus a penalty, but there was some talk of suing him, anyway. I don't think it came to anything."

"Why did he renege?" It was hard to speak around the wad of cement that had wedged itself in her throat.

"The rumor was, he declined to test his prototype device on prisoner volunteers—said there was no way of knowing whether there were any permanent effects."

Jo realized that the hand gripping the receiver had turned clammy. Permanent damage. Did she have any permanent damage from that session with the box last night? Transferring the phone, she wiped her palm on her skirt.

"I can send you a summary of the current literature. You might want to take a look at an article in the I.E.E.E. Journal."

"Uh, thanks."

When Jo hung up, her heart was thumping around in her chest like a tennis shoe in a clothes dryer.

"Get a grip on yourself," she hissed between clenched teeth. "You've still got all your marbles." But her body simply wouldn't respond to the command. She wasn't just worried about her brain cells. Cam had lied to her last night. No, that wasn't exactly true. He'd simply forgotten to mention that he'd invented the device that had mowed her down like a field of tobacco in a hurricane.

What else had the man lied about? The possibilities were so hideous that her whole body turned clammy. Scary things had been happening to her ever since the engagement party for Abby. Last night she'd wondered if someone at the Franklin mansion was responsible. What if that someone were Cameron Randolph? The man who'd conveniently come along and rescued her. The man who'd made her feel as if Fourth of July fireworks were exploding in her body when he'd held her in his arms last night.

The phone rang, and she snatched the receiver from the cradle.

"Hello!" she barked.

"I was calling to find out how you were feeling. If I had to answer the question myself—I'd say belligerent."

"Cam."

"Jo, what's the matter?"

"Do you think you could come down to my office? I need to talk to you."

There was a long pause on the other end of the line. "Right now?"

"Yes."

"I'll be there in twenty minutes."

As she hung up the phone, Jo could hardly believe the brief conversation. The gut-wrenching need to confront Cam with her knowledge had banished any other considerations. She had to know what was going on. Now she wondered if she were stupidly putting herself in even more danger.

Opening her desk drawer, she made sure that the revolver she'd brought from home to replace the stolen one was loaded. Then she methodically began to clear the piles of folders and mail off her desk. She didn't make any attempt to sort the material. She simply swept it into stacks and set them on the floor of the closet. When the surface was clear, she pulled the two answering machine tapes from the middle drawer and placed them on the blotter. Then she positioned a tape recorder in front of them.

She had barely finished when a loud knock made her jump. Less than twenty minutes, she thought as she glanced up to see the male silhouette filling the rectangle of frosted glass. Had the man driven or had he flown through the air with his red cape streaming behind him? She got up and hurried across the room but stopped with her hand on the knob—suddenly remembering an important detail that had failed to penetrate her fogged brain last night. Cam had gotten into her house without battering down the door or breaking any windows.

What was she dealing with? Well, it was too late to change her mind now. If he wanted to get in, she couldn't stop him. When she flung the door open, they stared at each other. Jo was struck with a feeling of unreality. Friends? Strangers? Enemies? She didn't know. She couldn't trust her judgment.

As she backed away, he followed her inside and closed the door.

"What's bothering you?"

Jo circled around so that the large bulk of the desk was between them. Deliberately she sat down and positioned her hand near the desk drawer. Taking his cue from her, Cam pulled up one of the sturdy wooden armchairs.

Now that he wasn't looming over her, she was able to

study his appearance. He looked as if he'd gone home, changed out of his tuxedo and spent the night in a pair of gray slacks and a white cotton shirt. They were both rumpled. And his lean face was haggard and unshaven.

"You tell me what's bothering *you*." She turned his question into a demand.

"Last night at my aunt's I called Phil Mercer to get some stuff ready for me at the lab. I've been up all night running tests on that box that had you down for the count—and going through Randolph Enterprises records."

"And?" she prompted.

His Adam's apple bobbed. "That box. Jo, I'm the one who invented it."

She had pictured the way they'd play this scene. It wasn't following the script.

"I had the feeling you weren't being straight with me yesterday. Why didn't you tell me the truth?"

"I wasn't one hundred percent sure of the facts."

"How did your invention end up in my living room?"

"I've been asking myself that question for hours."

The look of anguish on his face made Jo's chest squeeze painfully, but she met his gaze squarely, studying his features. In her profession, she'd encountered her share of accomplished liars. All were natural performers, outgoing, charming people—not introverted research scientists. Liars betrayed themselves in all sorts of little ways. Flashes of emotion that revealed their real feelings. Lopsided expressions that were slightly stronger on one side of the face than the other. None of the signs were evident. She was willing to stake her reputation on the certainty that Cameron Randolph wasn't lying to her.

Jo clutched the knowledge to her breast like a child clutching a security blanket in the middle of the night. However, she needed to know more if she were ever going to trust him again. It wasn't a question of staking her reputation. It was more like staking her life.

"I think you'd better tell me about it," she prompted.

"Do you want to know why I took the government contract in the first place? Or the part about how the damn invention slipped out of my control?"

"Why don't you start from the beginning?"

He pounded his fists against the chair arms. "God knows I didn't need the money. In fact, the damn project ended up *costing* Randolph Enterprises a hell of a lot. When I first started investigating the concept, the intellectual aspects of EMP research excited me. That's why I put in a bid in the first place. When it came down to conducting tests on prison volunteers, I realized I didn't want to take that kind of responsibility."

Jo nodded. Without any prompting on her part, he was confirming what Harvey Cohen had said. He went on to tell her about canceling the contract and paying back the money. Then he stopped abruptly. His teeth were clenched together, and his hands gripped the arms of the wooden office chair. Jo felt her own tension leaping up to match his.

When he began to speak again, his voice was as brittle as a batch of semiconductors plunged into a vat of liquid nitrogen.

"I thought I'd closed that chapter of my life—until I found you lying unconscious on your living-room rug. When I got the box back to the lab last night, I took it apart and checked the circuitry. Then I checked my specs on the project. I hadn't realized it before, but the EMP files must have been some of the ones that were copied from us several years ago."

"Copied?"

"As in industrial espionage. All the original records are still there. But the box is a perfect replica of my design—

down to the casing. The only difference is that someone added a pressure trigger so it would switch on when the cardboard wrapping was removed.'' His gray eyes were hard. ''We had some other plans stolen before my father died. A couple of prototypes I developed ended up being marketed by other companies.''

''Who was stealing the plans?''

''We never found out.''

''But the problem stopped?''

''Yes,'' he clipped out. ''Jo, this is strictly confidential information.''

''I understand.''

Before she could ask him another question, he cut in with one of his own. ''You didn't get me down here because you knew anything about the espionage, did you?''

''No.''

He nodded, as if the answer satisfied some need of his own. Then he gestured toward the machine in the middle of the blotter. ''Are you recording our conversation? Or did you want to play a tape for me?''

The ghost of a smile flickered around her lips. It vanished almost at once. ''To play a tape. Cam, a lot of disturbing things have been happening to me lately. Not just the EMP stuff last night.'' Picking up one of the cassettes she inserted it into the recorder and pressed the button.

''You've got a gorgeous little body, angel face, you know that?'' the electronically distorted voice began. Jo had heard it before and thought she was prepared. Still, her palms dampened and her skin began to crawl. She shot Cam a glance. His expression was grim.

''*This* is the call you got the other day?''

''Shh. Just listen.''

''...what I'd like to do to you makes me hot all over, baby. The problem is, I can't decide whether I want to give you a poke with my sugar stick or stick you with a hot poker.''

Listening to that sort of smut in private was one thing. Now her cheeks heated as embarrassment overlaid her other reactions to the recording.

Cam muttered a curse. His expression had gone from grim to murderous.

''Get the wordplay? But when you and me play, baby, it ain't just gonna be with words.''

''My God, Jo—'' Cam began.

''There's more. Let me play the other one before I lose my nerve.'' Her hands were shaking now as she removed one tape and inserted the other one into the recorder.

''Did you have a good time at Mrs. Randolph's party, angel face?'' the distorted electronic voice that had become a part of her life asked once again. Unconsciously Jo wedged her shoulders against the back of the chair the way she'd pressed them against the wall last night when she'd first heard the message, but she couldn't stop her whole body from trembling. Her hands were clenched. Her fingernails dug into the palms of her hands the way she'd dug into the fibers of the rug.

Cam was out of his seat and around the desk before the caller delivered his next line. Pulling Jo up, he took her in his arms. Then he lowered himself into the chair and cradled her in his lap.

''I'm surprised you went out this evening after your little taste of my power.''

She felt Cam's body tense, heard him swear again.

''Now you know that when I turn the switch, you'll do anything I want you to. I have a nice brass bed all ready for you. I'm looking at it now. I can picture your red hair against the white pillow, your silky skin waiting for my touch, your wrists and ankles strapped to the brass rails. You're going to get everything you deserve.''

She'd sworn listening to the tapes again with Cam wasn't going to knock the props out from under her. Somehow his arms around her shoulders and his chin pressed to the top of her head shattered her fragile hold on equanimity. She'd been dealing with this alone. Now her teeth began to chatter the way they had when she'd collapsed on the wet rug.

He rocked her gently, waiting for the attack of fear to pass. In his embrace, the trembling subsided.

"Cam, I tried to call you this morning. When I couldn't reach you, I did some checking on my own. I knew you had invented an EMP prototype."

His body jerked. "I can imagine what you must have concluded. At least you picked up the phone instead of a gun."

Perhaps because of the tension in the room, the observation made her a little giddy. Turning around, she pulled open the desk drawer. "I wasn't taking any chances. The gun's right in here."

He whistled through even white teeth. "I'm glad we're on the same side."

"Who are we fighting? Was Eddie Cahill ever in a position to get into Randolph Enterprises files?"

"Eddie Cahill. The escaped con you told me about at the party? Last night I was wondering if he might have sent you that box."

"Me, too."

"What does Cahill look like?"

"There's a picture in my file." Jo slid off Cam's lap, opened the closet door, and went down on her knees to go through the folders.

"You keep your files on the closet floor?"

"About every two weeks, I catch up with them."

She brought a stack of folders back to the desk. A few minutes later she handed Cam several photographs of Eddie Cahill.

He studied the man. Slight build. Medium-length brown hair. Black eyes that were both defiant and watchful. A scar on the right side of his upper lip. "He doesn't look familiar."

"He was vain about his haircuts. He's probably making death threats against the prison barber, too." Jo closed the folder.

"Did he make a death threat against you?"

"Not those exact words." Jo sank back into the chair opposite the desk. Succinctly she filled Cam in on the history of her association with the drug dealer—ending with his courtroom curse.

"He could be the one making the calls. Even if he didn't steal the EMP plans, he may know the person who did," Cam conceded. "Maybe he bought the box. Maybe they've become a new intimidation device among Baltimore's criminal element."

"I think I would have heard about it. Unless I'm a test case."

Cam worried his bottom lip between his teeth. "You've only received those two calls?"

"Three. One was live."

"The guy on those tapes knows a hell of a lot about you."

"Why do you think it's a guy?"

"Would a woman say those things?"

"I guess not." Now that they had begun to discuss the problem, Jo found herself wanting to share some of her insights. It was just like the old days, when she and Skip had hashed over one of their cases. "I was wondering last night if someone at the party was responsible—since everything started right after the reception at the Franklins'."

"So that's why you were playing social butterfly. You were looking for leads."

"Yes. Cam, what if it's not Eddie at all? What if it's somebody else?"

"But who?"

She shrugged. "Someone else with a grudge against me. I don't know."

"Have you talked to the police?"

"About Eddie. And I reported the mugging. I was going to tell them about the box—but you took it away."

He looked chagrined. "Have you told them about the calls?"

"I've talked to the phone company. I'm getting one of those new caller ID systems. That's going to solve the phone harassment problem. When I have the evidence, I'll take it to the police."

"Don't you think they ought to have the whole picture now?"

"What do you think they're going to do? Put a twenty-four-hour guard on me? They don't have the manpower, and even if they did, private detectives don't call the police every time they get an obscene phone call."

He swore vehemently. "Did Skip O'Malley teach you that claptrap?"

She sat up straighter in her chair. "Skip O'Malley was the best. He taught me everything I know."

"He got himself killed on a case, didn't he?"

"How do you know that?"

"I checked some back issues of the *Baltimore Sun*."

"Why?" she demanded.

"I wanted to know more about you," he pointed out reasonably.

"You could have asked."

"When I want facts, I go look them up. Isn't that what you did this morning when you checked up on me?"

She glared at him. "I didn't know that checking up on EMP was going to lead back to you."

"Why is it," he asked slowly, "that when the two of us seem to be getting closer, Skip O'Malley steps between us?"

"He was my husband."

"He's been dead for three years and you're still wearing his ring."

Her eyes went to the narrow gold band she'd transferred to her right hand. "What's wrong with that?"

"Jo, I understand why you're on edge. Anyone would be after getting those calls. I even understand why I represent some kind of threat to your loyalty to Skip. Last night when I kissed you, you weren't thinking about Skip O'Malley."

She'd admitted as much this morning. Somehow when he said it, her defensive shields went up. "Of all the colossal male arrogance."

"Okay. You're not ready to talk about it. I'll call you in a couple of days. Or if you need me—"

"What I need is for you to get out of my seat so I can get back to work."

He got up as if he'd just realized whose chair he had confiscated. Sheepishly he headed for the door. When he reached it, he hesitated.

Jo didn't call him back. Long after he'd left, she sat staring at the frosted glass of the door. Damn him, she thought. Damn him. He was right. He was the only man who'd made her insides melt in the three years since Skip had died.

But that didn't mean she hadn't made a big mistake.

OUT ON THE STREET, Cam folded his arms across his chest. When Jo had summoned him down here, she'd sounded so upset that he'd dashed out of the office without a coat. Earlier he hadn't even felt the November chill. Now he did.

He thought about surprising Jo by marching back into her office, taking her by the shoulders and shaking some sense into her. Then he was shocked by his caveman thoughts.

Instead of acting on the impulse, he walked briskly toward the garage where the Lotus was parked. When he'd reopened Skip O'Malley's investigation, he'd thought he'd understood his own motives. Now his stomach knotted as he grappled with confusion. He'd always prided himself on his rational, scientific powers. Well, his cool detachment had been shot to hell.

He cared about Jo. A lot. Unfortunately his new feelings were at war with his old loyalties. He still hadn't told her everything. Perhaps that wasn't fair. His stomach clenched tighter. What had happened in the past had hurt him. He couldn't just let go. If he did, he'd be letting go of part of his life. Somehow he had to make it all come out right.

Jo DELIBERATELY kept her mind off Cam. Instead she called Mrs. Douglas at the phone company again. The woman had already talked to her supervisor. "It's highly irregular to give out information about harassing calls," she repeated, and Jo was afraid she wasn't going to get the names. "But under the circumstances," she continued, "I've obtained permission."

"I appreciate that," Jo told her sincerely.

When she came down to the office, Mrs. Douglas handed a sheet of paper across the desk. Jo scanned the names, addresses and now-unlisted home numbers—along with work numbers. There were also notations of when the calls had been received. Some were almost three years ago. "Thanks."

"If you get a lead on the caller, I assume you'll share the information with us."

"Of course," Jo agreed. "Is there an office I can use?"

Mrs. Douglas led her down the hall to a cubicle with a modular desk and set of phones.

"This will be fine."

The first woman she tried wasn't home. The second, Melody Naylor, worked at the Hairsport—a unisex salon on Route 40. She wasn't able to talk on the phone because she was giving a customer a perm. When Jo persisted, she said if the detective could stop by in the next hour she wouldn't mind answering a few questions.

Melody turned out to be a petite blonde in her late twenties who was wearing blue jeans and a fringed cowgirl shirt. Two pairs of dangling gold earrings hung from her small lobes.

"Yeah, I did get a couple o' calls about eighteen months ago," she told Jo as she expertly rolled and clipped sections of hair. "But, see, I figured it was my ex-boyfriend. We'd just broken up, and he wasn't taking it very well."

"Did you ever get him to admit it?" Jo asked.

She shrugged. "He just laughed when I asked him."

Laughed, Jo thought. That could fit.

"He left town about the same time the calls stopped," Melody continued.

"Why did you make a report to the phone company if you thought you knew who it was?"

"The jerk was calling me at work and tying up the line."

Jo was about to ask another question when the shop door opened. The women who entered fixed Melody with a sharp look. "My manager," the hairdresser whispered. "I thought she was gonna be out longer."

Jo followed her gaze. "I could get back to you later."

"No. There isn't much else I can tell you. The whole thing's been over for a long time, and I'd rather forget it, anyway."

Jo left wishing she'd gotten more information. Back at the office, she tried phoning several other names on the list. One of the women had moved. Another didn't want to talk about the incident.

With progress like this, she might have the case solved in a couple of hundred years, Jo thought on a discouraged sigh. She was about to go home for the day when the UPS man knocked on the door. To Jo's delight, he'd brought the caller ID attachments for the phone. Now she had a much more productive way of attacking the problem.

As soon as the delivery man left, she hooked up one box at her office. She'd plug the other one in at home. Then when that bastard called back, she'd nail him—and she wouldn't have to bother with a bunch of dead-end interviews.

All through dinner, she kept glancing at the phone. For the first time in days, she hoped it would ring. But it didn't.

After she washed the dishes, she called Laura.

"Do you still want to help me set up that special photo equipment?" she asked her friend. Initially Jo had thought she might get a shot of marauding dogs. Now she wondered if she were on the trail of bigger game.

"Why not."

"Is Sunday morning still okay?" she asked, noting that Laura's enthusiasm didn't match her own.

"Uh-hum."

"If you want to get out of it, I'll understand."

"Sorry. It's not you. I'm just kind of down."

"Want to tell me about it?"

"I'll bend your ear on Sunday."

Saturday Jo rented rug and upholstery cleaning equipment and spent the day putting the living room back in order.

Sunday she skipped her usual breakfast. Despite getting the house back in shape, she was feeling a little depressed, and she suspected her friend's visit wasn't going to elevate her mood—since Laura hadn't sounded very chipper, either.

But when the blond lawyer knocked on the door, she had an upbeat expression on her face. The People section of the *Baltimore Sun* was tucked under her arm. She pulled it out and waved it aloft.

"Hey, you're famous."

"Famous?" Then Jo remembered the article about the Carpenters. She hadn't even brought in the paper that morning.

They spread the section on the kitchen table. The Carpenter story was the lead feature article. On the top of the first page were two photographs—one of the Carpenters as children and one of Jo's client as he looked now.

Jo scanned the text.

"This sure is going to call attention to the family," she said with a note of satisfaction.

"Bet it'll bring in some business for you. The whole second half is full of words of wisdom from Detective O'Malley."

"Yeah. I didn't think Sandy Peters was going to quote me so much."

"You're quotable. And it's interesting to hear about your methods."

"I didn't tell her all my tricks." Jo gestured toward the motion detector and camera, which were also on the kitchen table—along with a wooden birdhouse. She picked up the house and removed the roof. "I thought we'd put the camera in here, to protect it from the weather and prying eyes."

"Clever."

"We'll run the connecting wire along the fence and attach the motion detector to the underside of one of the horizontal supports."

Although Jo could have done the work herself, she was glad to have the company and hoped that Laura would open up about what was bothering her. After they had set the equipment up, they tested it by taking turns entering the line of fire. They got a picture of Jo mugging as she lifted the lid of a trash can and one of Laura with her hands over her face like a murder suspect ducking the media.

"You didn't really need me," Laura commented as she washed her hands at the sink. "Nobody needs me."

"Oh, come on."

"Well, Dr. William Avery certainly doesn't."

Jo spun around. "What do you mean?"

"He told me he wants a divorce. Yesterday he moved all his stuff out of the house."

"Sheez, Laura, I'm sorry."

"Maybe it's for the bes—" The sentence finished on a little sob. Jo wrapped her arms around her friend, and they stood in the middle of the kitchen for several moments.

"I promised myself I wasn't going to break down," Laura sniffed.

"Just let it out," Jo said softly.

Laura couldn't stop the bottled-up tears from flowing. But in a few minutes she had control of herself again. Jo handed her a tissue, and she blew her nose.

"You definitely think it's over?" Jo questioned.

"I found out he's been seeing a physical therapist from the clinic. When he moved out of our house, he moved in with her."

Jo snorted. "I can imagine what kind of physical therapy she's giving him."

Laura laughed. "Yeah. Let's see how she likes keeping his dinner warm when he doesn't come home till nine. Or listening to fascinating gall bladder surgery details when she's dead tired and has to get up at six-thirty in the morning."

Jo chimed in with a couple of ridiculous suggestions, and they both started to laugh. Then the conversation turned serious again.

"The scary part is worrying about making it on your own," Laura admitted. "I don't mean financially. I guess I mean emotionally. Not thinking of myself as part of a couple."

"I felt that way when Skip died. I'd come home at night and there would be things I wanted to talk to him about. It was hard getting used to the empty house." She didn't mention the way she felt now. She and Cam could have become a couple. That wasn't very likely anymore.

"I've had months to get used to that. Bill's hardly been around." Once Laura opened up, she spent the next hour talking about the marriage. Finally she sighed. "I don't know what got into me. It's a wonder you're still awake."

"You can talk to me anytime. That's what friends are for." Jo cast around for a way to lift Laura's spirits—and her own. "Hey. I've got an idea. There's a great Sunday brunch at the Hunt Valley Inn. Omelettes, Belgium waffles, the best coffee in Baltimore. I don't know about you, but I didn't eat breakfast this morning. What do you say?"

It didn't take too much persuading to get Laura to agree. They spent a pleasant couple of hours avoiding references to the men who were the source of their anxiety.

"Thanks," Laura said as she dropped Jo back at her house. "That was just what I needed."

After unlocking her door, Jo stopped to check the answering machine. When she saw there were several messages, her body went rigid. Then she reminded herself that the caller ID service was in place. If he'd called her again, she'd know where to find him.

First she checked the phone numbers. None were familiar, so she wrote them all down. Then, almost eagerly she pressed the Play button. No electronically distorted voice. No threats. Did the perp know she was ready for him? No, he wasn't clairvoyant, she told herself firmly.

The messages were all from people who'd read the article in the *Sun*. Two wanted to hire her. One had information he thought might be helpful in the Carpenter case.

The day had gone well, and Jo was in a better mood than

before Laura had arrived. For dinner she microwaved herself a baked potato, slathered it with butter, and heaped it full of vegetables and cheese.

While she ate, she checked the cable schedule. She hadn't turned the TV on all week. But HBO was showing *Tin Men* again. Since she got a kick out of both Danny DeVito and the Baltimore locale, she decided to watch.

Just before eight she fixed herself a bowl of popcorn, changed into her most comfortable flannel gown, and settled down in bed. When she used the remote control to switch to HBO, the wrong movie flashed on the screen.

The scene made Jo cringe. It looked like one of those horror flicks where a guy with eight-inch steel fingernails chased a bunch of half-naked teenage girls around a high-school locker room before he started ripping out their throats.

Ten seconds of the mayhem made her gag, and she pressed the button to change the channel. The screen jumped for a second. Then the same scene snapped into focus. She pressed again. More gore.

With a muttered curse, Jo tossed the malfunctioning remote control onto the bed and marched over to the set. Reaching out, she grasped the channel knob, and a jolt of electricity shot through her body.

A scream tore from her throat as she jumped back. Rubbing her hand, she felt the pain ebb. Her eyes were fixed on the television picture. It took a confused moment to realize what she was watching. Instead of a high-school locker room, the scene had switched to the deep woods. Now a group of teenage campers was being ripped apart by werewolves.

Squeezing her eyes shut, Jo gave her head a savage shake. That didn't shut out the screams of the victims. She was reaching for the volume control when she snatched her hand back. It tingled with remembered pain. She couldn't risk that again.

Her gaze dropped to the plug. Pulling on it could be just as dangerous as touching the controls.

Jo was backing away from the television set as if it were an alien when a flicker on the screen made her freeze in place. For a split second, the image had changed to something even more frightening.

Mouth dry and heart pounding, she held herself rigid watching the mayhem in the woods. Twenty seconds later, it happened again, and she gasped. A quick cut to another scene. She was left with the impression of a woman tied to a brass bed. A red-haired woman.

Jo's bare toes dug into the rag rug in front of the television set so hard that they started to cramp. But she couldn't tear her eyes away. The little insert flashed again and again on the screen—interspersed with a dismemberment in a sawmill. Hardly able to breathe, Jo viewed the next intrusion. Now she could see the back of a man as he advanced on the helpless woman. A knife was in his hand. Next time the image appeared, the knife arched down toward his victim.

Jo screamed and covered her eyes with her hands. Somehow that broke the spell. Snatching up the brass barrel-shaped piggy bank that sat on top of the pie safe, she flung it at the television. The screen exploded.

Chapter Eight

It should be over. It wasn't. Although the picture was gone, the sound remained. It was as if a demon had taken possession of the set.

Turning, Jo fled the room. Sheer black fright nipped at her heels. She hadn't realized that the volume on the TV had been steadily escalating. Wails and screams followed her down the stairs. No. The sound was actually getting louder the farther away she ran.

When she reached the living room, she came to a screeching halt. The television. She hadn't turned that one on. But the horror she'd fled in the bedroom confronted her anew. Now it was on a twenty-five-inch picture tube. The sawmill. The helpless victims. And the woman on the bed. Only now her body was cut and bleeding.

On a choked sob, Jo sagged against the doorjamb. Terrifying calls. The EMP waves. Now this. Someone was trying to reduce her to a quivering mass of fear. Her hands balled into fists. She wasn't going to let it happen.

The circuit-breaker box was down in the basement. She could turn off the sets that way. The cellar stairs were rough. Slivers of wood dug into Jo's feet as she pounded down to the utility room. When she snatched open the electrical box, she thanked God Skip had been much more organized than she. Each circuit was labeled. Furnace. Air conditioner. Refrigerator. Bathroom. Dining room. Living room. Bedroom.

Throat raw, breath hissing in and out of her lungs, she stood with her hand hovered above the last switch. A shock from the power box could kill. But if someone had wanted to electrocute her she'd be dead already, wouldn't she? Gritting her teeth, she threw back the circuit. Her hand throbbed, but only with the anticipation of pain. After the living-room switch, she flipped the one from the bedroom. The house was plunged into blessed silence.

Jo stood beside the circuit box, gasping. When she'd caught her breath she tiptoed back upstairs. The living room and the front hall were dark and silent. So was her bedroom.

Someone had gone to a lot of trouble to scare the stuffing out of her. Was it all Eddie Cahill's doing? Was this how he'd decided to punish her?

Had he rigged the television sets while she and Laura were at lunch? Was he in here now? Suddenly her scalp began to crawl, and she cringed into the shadows trying to make her body small and inconspicuous. Then she got a grip on herself.

She hadn't watched television since last Sunday. He could have done this anytime during the week. And if he'd wanted to spring out of the spare bedroom and attack her, why hadn't he already done it?

What if the phone and the EMP generator had been just the first and second acts of his private little melodrama starring Jo O'Malley. This was the third. What had he planned for the fourth? Tying her to the railroad tracks?

Or was it more like tying her to a brass bed and— All at once she knew she couldn't stay in the house straining to hear a lock turn or a window rattle. By the time she reached her darkened bedroom, she was limping. There must be splinters all over the bottoms of her feet, she realized. She couldn't do anything about that now. From the pie safe she snatched a pair of sweatpants and a shirt. The orange pants and the turquoise top didn't match, but she wasn't going to stop and coordinate her outfit. Then she grimaced as she yanked on socks and thrust her feet into loafers. The shoes made the splinters hurt all the more.

Despite the pain, Jo made it across the garage and into her car in two seconds flat. After locking the doors, she activated the opener and started the engine. Roaring out into the driveway, she paused only long enough to close the door again. Halfway down the street she remembered that she'd forgotten to reset the security alarm. But what difference did it make if he'd already been in her house?

Taking a deep breath she put her foot to the accelerator and sped off into the night. For the first few blocks, she kept one eye on the rearview mirror just in case somebody was following. To her intense relief, no set of headlights tailed her around the twisted course of streets through which she drove. She didn't realize until she'd found herself on Jones Falls Expressway that she was heading for Cam's.

She didn't even consider his reaction to the unexpected visit until she'd rung the bell. Then it was too late. Before she could think of exactly what she was going to say, he'd thrown open the door.

His eyes widened when he took in her disheveled appearance. "My God, Jo, what's happened now?"

"Well, my television has a big hole where the picture tube used to be."

He seemed to know she was starting with the least important detail. "You'd better come in and sit down," he said gently.

She followed him into the living room and flopped onto the couch. He sat down beside her looking uncertain.

Jo squeezed her eyes shut and struggled to get a grip on her emotions. Now that she was in the warm, sheltered en-

vironment of Cam's town house, she was afraid she was
going to come apart.

"Do you want a cup of—uh—tea, or something
stronger?"

"Something stronger."

Cam poured brandy into two snifters. While he stood at
the bar in the corner, Jo willed the strands of her self-control
to knit themselves back together.

When her host turned around, she was feeling a bit more
composed. Yet she couldn't stop herself from gulping a
swallow of the brandy. The unaccustomed fire in her throat
made her cough. Cam waited patiently until the spasm subsided.

"Better?"

"I think so."

"Jo, are you going to tell me what really happened to
you tonight?"

"Someone's trying to drive me nuts," she repeated the
conclusion she'd come to earlier. "Or maybe the neighborhood Halloween committee is getting a jump on next year.
When I turned on the television set tonight, all I could get
was horror movies. When I tried to turn one off, it gave me
a hell of a shock."

"Oh, honey." Before she finished the account, he'd
crossed the two feet of space that separated them and folded
her into his embrace. She didn't resist. In fact, she went
almost limp in his arms.

His hands smoothed across her back. Her body absorbed
the comfort. When she'd seen him last, they'd both been
on edge with each other. Now it was as if the angry words
had never been spoken.

"Not just regular horror movies." She swallowed low
and slowly. "Interspersed with the commercial stuff was
another scene. I could only see it in flashes. This guy had
a woman tied to a brass bed. She was small, and she had

red hair. I guess she looked a lot like me. He came at her with a knife. And he—and he—'' Jo wasn't able to continue.

Cam gave her a few minutes to collect herself. "Tell me everything, honey," he finally murmured. "Everything that's happened to you."

"You know a lot of it."

"I want to understand the whole picture."

Jo gulped. "All right."

It felt surprisingly good to say it all. The longer she went on, the more convinced she was that everything fit into a pattern. While she talked, Cam held her close and stroked her back and shoulders.

"What do you think he's going to do next?" Jo finally asked the question that had been preying on her mind since she'd fled her house.

"I don't know. But one thing's for sure," Cam muttered, "you're not spending the night at home."

She nodded.

"And you're going to call the police and have them meet you over there so they can check this out."

"I already decided that."

Fifteen minutes later, they were heading back to Jo's. When the Lotus turned the corner onto her block, neither she nor Cam paid any attention to the van parked under the branches of a maple tree. Instead Jo's eyes were focused on her home. It was a strange experience viewing her house from the curb. Although it was after midnight, most of the lights were on because she'd flipped every switch she could reach as she'd fled the shrieks and cries blaring from the upstairs television set.

Jo stared at the windows as she climbed out of the car. Something wasn't right. Something— Then it hit her. She'd thrown the circuit breakers that shut off the electricity in the living room and her bedroom. Now the lights of both rooms blazed as brightly as those in the rest of the house.

"Cam! The lights. In my bedroom and the living room."

He'd listened intently to her earlier narration of events. Now his mind quickly followed her train of thought. His feet were already pounding toward the porch. "Stay out here," he ordered.

Ignoring the shouted command, Jo followed him down the front walk and up the steps.

He had halted at the front door. This time he hadn't come prepared with his lock picker. Jo produced the key. As soon as the door was open, they rushed inside. The living room was empty. Upstairs, floorboards creaked in rapid succession.

Cam took the stairs two at a time. Despite the pain from the splinters in her feet, Jo charged right after him. As Cam reached the second floor, he was greeted by the sound of shattering glass.

Something heavy hit the porch roof. By the time Jo made it into her bedroom, Cam was out on the roof. Jo was about to climb out when he came back into the room.

"Damn! He was out of here before I got upstairs. I couldn't even see where he went. If he broke in, I wonder why the security alarm wasn't blaring when we pulled up."

Jo looked down at her toes. "I, uh, forgot to reset it when I left."

Outside a car engine started with a grinding noise. They couldn't see the vehicle. But they heard it speed away into the darkness.

"He was here. Now I know the bastard was right here!" Jo spat out. She stared around her bedroom. The armoire was open. So was the pie safe. Along with the broken glass from the television picture tube, clothes were strewn around the floor.

"But I think he wasn't here long—because he'd only

gotten to the clothes.'' She hobbled across the room and sank onto the bed.

Cam noticed the limp she'd managed to hide when he was looking. ''What's wrong with your feet?''

''Splinters. From when I ran down the basement stairs.''

A heavy pounding on the front door sent her springing to her feet, and she winced.

''That must be the police,'' Cam told her. ''Too bad they didn't get here five minutes ago.''

He went down to answer the door. Jo hobbled after him.

The officer who took the report was Detective Evan Hamill. He was a big man with ebony skin, close-cropped hair and a face that sported a two-inch scar across his chin. Jo had never met him but she knew the type. A fifteen-year veteran who had grown up in the inner city. When she told him about the bizarre episode with the television set, he looked surprised. But he pulled out a pad and pen and took a report.

''I guess this guy wasn't from the customer service department of ComCast Cable,'' Hamill quipped.

Jo gave him a weak smile. At least the man had a sense of humor.

''Can either of you give me a description?''

''No. He was gone before we made it upstairs,'' Cam said. He had found a pan and filled it with hot water. During the interview, Jo sat with her sweatpants pushed up to her calves and her feet submerged. The wet heat felt good, and she shot Cam a grateful look. He smiled encouragingly at her.

''It's not just what happened tonight,'' he said. ''Ms. O'Malley has had problems over the last several weeks— ever since a man who she helped send to prison escaped.''

That got Hamill's attention. ''What's his name?''

''Eddie Cahill.''

''Yeah I saw the report. He's one mean dude. And cagey.

It looks like he started planning his escape the minute they slammed the gate behind him.''

Hamill fumbled in his pockets. Jo expected him to pull out a pack of cigarettes. Instead he removed a bag of smokehouse almonds.

''You mind? I missed dinner.''

''Go ahead.''

With Cam's moral support, Jo forced herself to go through the story of Eddie Cahill, the phone calls, the mugging, the EMP, and the television sets again.

''It sounds like you're a target, all right,'' Hamill agreed, wiping his hand on his pants' leg.

''What kind of protection are you going to give her?'' Cam asked, gesturing toward Jo.

''We don't have the manpower to keep someone with her twenty-four hours a day. About all we can do at this point is increase police visibility in the neighborhood and send more patrol cars past her house.''

Jo shot Cam an ''I told you so'' look.

''I think it would be a good idea if she spent the night somewhere else,'' Hamill continued.

''That's already been arranged,'' Cam muttered.

''I want to have the lab dust for fingerprints in the morning. Why don't we make an appointment for ten.''

''I'll have her back here by then,'' Cam told him.

When the detective had left, Jo closed her eyes. ''Cam, I don't think I can face the mess in my room. But I need some stuff for tomorrow.'' She swallowed, wondering exactly what he thought she'd agreed to when she'd said she'd accepted his hospitality. ''And a nightgown.''

''Um-hum.''

Their eyes locked for several heartbeats.

''I'll bring some stuff down.''

''Thanks.''

''Is there anything I can use to board up that window?''

"I think there's plywood in the basement. And my overnight bag should be in the top of my closet."

Half an hour later, for the second time that evening, Jo fled her own home. As she looked up at the plywood covering the bedroom window, she silently admitted to herself that she felt a whole lot better with Cameron Randolph next to her.

When they reached his Cross Keys town house, Cam opened the car door and swung Jo into his arms.

"I can walk," she protested.

"Your feet have taken enough punishment for one evening."

He set her down on the sofa where they'd first talked. "I'll be right back."

Jo nestled into the comfortable cushions.

When Cam returned, he was carrying a first-aid kit and a small lamp, which turned out to focus a narrow but powerful beam.

"We'd better get those splinters out before they get infected and you're really laid up."

"Yeah."

"Lie down."

When she'd complied, he sat down so that her feet were in his lap. Then he adjusted the beam of the lamp, swabbed her feet with a cotton ball soaked in antiseptic, and sterilized a needle and tweezers.

"That long soaking in hot water should help. But tell me if I hurt you." The tone was matter-of-fact, but the hand that grasped her ankle was amazingly gentle. So were the fingers that held the needle.

She peered up at Cam who was ministering to her as if they did this sort of thing all the time. A wave of warmth and gratitude swept over her. Out there in the night, someone had been stalking her. In here, she felt safe—and cherished.

Cam worked with precision, finding each splinter and easing it from her flesh with no more than a bad twinge or two each.

Several times he grasped one of her toes so that he could move one or the other foot to a different angle. There was a strange intimacy having him work on a part of her body that was usually covered up.

"I think that's the last of them," he finally announced. His voice told her that he felt the intimacy as much as she did.

Jo leaned back and closed her eyes. They blinked open again as cold antiseptic made her wince.

"Sorry."

"I don't think it can be helped."

Cam turned off the high-intensity lamp and set the first-aid supplies on the coffee table. But he made no move to get up. His hands continued to stroke Jo's ankles and to wander over her toes.

Now that the medical procedure was finished, she was free to enjoy his attentions. With one finger, he traced the arch of her foot, sending little shivers up her legs.

"Feet never turned me on before." Cam's voice was rough. "Did anyone ever tell you yours are damn sexy?"

"No."

He lifted one of her ankles, bringing her toes to his mouth. When he brushed his lips back and forth against the soft pads, Jo closed her eyes. When he started to nibble on them, she sucked in a surprised breath.

"Sorry," he repeated his earlier apology, quickly lowering the foot.

"That wasn't exactly a complaint. I didn't know feet were a turn-on, either."

When he'd brought her inside, she'd been exhausted and in pain. Now the air in the room had become erotically charged. They stared at each other for a long, breath-stopping moment. Then Jo held out her arms, and he came into them.

Stretching out beside her on the couch, he clasped her tightly. His lips skimmed along her jaw and over her cheeks before settling possessively over her mouth.

He kissed her for long, hungry minutes. She met each thrust of his tongue, each sensual movement of his lips with one of her own. When he finally lifted his head, they were both gasping for breath.

"Jo, honey. Oh Lord, Jo." He cradled her body against the length of his. "Friday when I left your office I told myself I wasn't going to call you again. I spent Saturday climbing the walls of my lab. Then tonight I called Steve because I needed to talk to someone who could give me a clue about how to handle you."

"How to handle me! What did he say?" She tried to pull away, but there wasn't much room to maneuver between his hard body and the sofa cushions.

"He told me to—uh—how can I put this politely—make love to you until you couldn't stand up."

"Sheez!"

Cam swallowed. "I'm not effectuating this very well."

"You and Steve Clairborne. I thought he was my friend."

"He is."

"He thinks sex is the quick fix for interpersonal relationships."

"No. If he did, he wouldn't have left Abby last spring and gone back to India."

Jo nodded slowly.

"He said he thinks you and I would be making a big mistake if we didn't give the relationship a chance. I think so, too."

Jo considered the words and the vulnerability she detected behind them. He had just offered her a chance to reject him.

She looked into his gray eyes, reading her own uncertainty but also an unspoken promise. Reaching out, she cupped Cam's face in her hands. "I think I keep littering the area with my emotional baggage. Then I get angry when you trip over it."

"Everybody has emotional baggage. If they've loved someone—and lost them. Or if they've been hurt by someone. Or if their childhood wasn't perfect."

"How do you know so much?"

"I'm smart."

"That's one of the things I like about you."

"What else?"

"I like the way you effectuate."

"Now you're making fun of me."

"I like the way you kiss, too."

"Gently or libidinously?"

"Every way." She relaxed in his arms once more.

Her words and the physical invitation drew him closer. He kissed her gently. He kissed her passionately. He kissed her tantalizingly. And while he kissed her, his hands began to move over her body.

His fingers slipped beneath her sweatshirt and inched upward. When his hand closed around her breast, the breath trickled out of her lungs.

They were lying on the couch facing each other. Ducking down, he caught the hem of the shirt with his teeth and edged it the rest of the way up. Then he began to caress her with his face and lips. "I could go mad from just tasting you."

When he began to tease one taut nipple with his tongue, a shaft of intense pleasure shot through her. She felt the madness, too, and her body arched into his.

Cam raised his head and looked into her eyes. "Could I

interest you in a tour of the upstairs, starting with my bedroom?''

Jo grinned. ''Yes, I think you could.''

Pulling her shirt back into place, he helped her up.

Arm and arm they climbed the stairs. The light from the hall filtered into the master bedroom through the partly opened door. Cam folded down the covers on the king-size bed. Then he turned back to Jo. Between kisses and murmured endearments he stripped off her clothes. She did the same for him.

Naked in his bedroom. The reality was overwhelming. His body was lean and tough and very masculine. Tentatively she reached up to touch the dark mat of hair on his chest, feeling her fingers crinkle the curly hairs.

''Don't be shy with me, Jo. One of the things I like about you is that you're so direct.''

She swallowed. ''This is different.''

''Jo O'Malley acting cautious. I never thought I'd see the day.''

''Don't tease me.''

''Honey, not holding you in my arms is teasing the hell out of myself.'' With a growl deep in his throat, he tugged her into his embrace, and they clung together.

When he lowered her to the mattress, it rocked gently.

''A water bed. I might get dizzy.''

''Then you'll have to hold on tight.''

She stared up at him as her arms circled his broad back, still half stunned just being here with him like this.

''I've fantasized about you naked in my bed,'' he murmured, echoing her thoughts. ''I thought I was going to go crazy if I didn't make love to you.''

Despite his statement, he didn't seem to be in a hurry. He enticed her with soul-searing kisses and tantalizing caresses until she was half out of her mind with need. And always he kept release just out of her reach.

But his body wasn't out of her reach. When her hand closed around him and began its own tender assault, she knew she'd tipped the balance.

She felt him shudder. "Jo, you're going to—"

"—have you inside me."

The hand that held him captive guided him into her body. They gazed into each other's eyes, acknowledging the moment's potency.

Then his hips began to move. He'd made a turbulent assault on her senses. Now he overwhelmed her with the power of a primitive male claiming his mate.

Her response was just as elemental. She moved with him, against him, around him, her fingers digging into his back as she reached the peak of sensation.

The tempest seized them both, racking their bodies with sensual spasms, sweeping away all reality but the two of them locked together in passionate fulfillment.

Little aftershocks of pleasure rippled over her as she nestled in his embrace.

He held her fiercely. Since the angry confrontation in her office, he'd come to realize that she was more important to him than what had happened in the past. Now there were things he had to tell her about his run-ins with Skip O'Malley.

Or maybe it was already too late for confessions. Maybe no matter what he said or did from now on, she was going to end up hating him.

No. There must be a way to keep it from happening. If she just got to know him better—to trust him—before she found out the truth, everything might be all right.

Chapter Nine

Out in the night, the man sitting in the driver's seat of the van banged his fists against the steering wheel. She was in there with that know-it-all, swell-headed Cameron Randolph.

Cam Randolph.

He'd taken her home so he could get into her pants.

A picture of the conceited inventor rolling on a bed with the little redhead leaped into his mind, and he spat out a stream of curses.

Once again, he got up and fiddled with the equipment in the van. With anyone else, he'd be able to hear what they were saying. Although probably they weren't communicating with anything more than sighs and groans.

He cursed again. Randolph must have some kind of electronic shielding around his town house. Just the way he had around his lab now.

The guy was a slow learner. But he'd finally caught on to the possibility that someone could be stealing his precious inventions.

In his spare time, he'd made a little study of Cam Randolph. The way he saw it, the lucky stiff had been born with the two big advantages in life—money and family. Sure he'd come up with some pretty good gadgets over the years. That didn't prove anything. Hadn't he gone to the best schools—gotten the best training money could buy. And he hadn't had to work for a living like everyone else. So he'd been able to shut himself up in his lab for as long as he wanted—until he'd gotten lucky a few times.

Everybody was always talking about how smart and how creative Cam Randolph was. Didn't they see the real reasons for his success? Didn't they understand what a cold-blooded bastard he was and that he never gave anyone else a chance?

FOR LONG MOMENTS Jo was content to just snuggle against Cam's chest, listening to his heart beat a strong, steady rhythm against her ear. "For years I told myself I didn't need this," she said softly. "You've changed my mind. But I never dreamed I'd get hooked up with anyone like you."

"You might say you have your hooks into me."

"That sounds painful."

"In a way it is. But then it's a new experience for me."

"You've never—"

"—cared enough about a woman to go after her like this."

Her eyebrows lifted.

"It's kind of nice to hold a woman in my arms who somewhere in the back of her mind isn't counting my money."

"Oh, come on. They've also got to be thinking that you're smart and good-looking and charming and a wonderful lover."

"Oh?"

The implications of her rash statement sank in. "You also have a habit of spouting big words when you're tense or embarrassed."

"I know. They're a kind of protective circumvallation."

They both laughed.

Jo was suddenly feeling better than she had in weeks.

She nestled her head against Cam's shoulder, and he clasped her to his side. "When I was a kid in that shack in the mountains, I kept a stack of library books beside my bed. I went through everything I could get my hands on. My favorites were the Oz books and the Narnia books because they were about a magic place where some lucky children had gone to get away from the real world. I dreamed about doing that."

"I think I can understand why."

"One thing I learned when I got older—there's no point in sitting around daydreaming. You make your life what you want it to be." She swallowed. "Except that from time to time, Fate throws you a wild card. Like your husband gets killed. Or a psychotic decides he's going to show you slasher movies—and then come slash you to pieces."

His arms tightened around her. "He's not going to do that."

"It would be a damn bad thing, just when I've gotten my hooks into this brainy, charming, sexy guy."

"Jo." His mouth found hers again. And for a little while, they both shut out the danger waiting to envelop them.

WHEN THEY PULLED UP at Jo's front walk the next morning, a police car was already parked in the driveway. Detective Hamill had arrived in a separate car, which was parked across the street. As they got out of the Lotus, he ambled around the side of the house. His jaw was working. More almonds, Jo thought.

"It looks as if the special TV programming was rigged through your cable hookup," he said.

"That was my hypothesis last night," Cam agreed. "But I didn't get a chance to check it out."

"By the way, what's the fancy photo setup out by the trash for?" the detective added.

"Photo setup?" Cam asked.

Jo explained to both of them, "I thought I was going to get a picture of some dogs. Maybe we got lucky last night." She went around back and checked the camera. The film hadn't advanced.

"Too bad," Cam said.

They all tromped back to the front porch, where Jo let the fingerprint crew inside. As they went upstairs to start in her bedroom, Jo headed straight for the living room. When she saw the answering machine was blinking, her body went rigid.

Cam was right behind her. "Let's find out who's left a message," he suggested in an even voice.

First Jo activated the recall mechanism on the caller ID unit. The number she wrote down definitely wasn't familiar.

Then she took a deep breath and pressed the Play button on the answering machine.

"Well, miss newspaper celebrity, I guess you think you're too important to have anything to do with me. I'm afraid you don't have a choice. How did you like the little movie show I set up for your personal viewing enjoyment?"

"He saw the article in the paper," Jo whispered, her skin growing clammy. God, she'd been a fool to put herself in the public eye like that. "I never should have let that reporter quote me."

Cam wrapped his arms around her and began to rub the goose bumps on her arms.

"That wasn't nice of you to bash in your television set like that. But I understand why you might have flipped out." The words were followed by one of his high-pitched laughs. Even the security of Cam's embrace couldn't stop the shudder from rippling over her skin.

"Easy, honey," he whispered.

She gave him a shaky little nod. This time she wasn't facing the voice and the threats alone.

"And it wasn't nice of you to go off with that slimebag

inventor,'' the voice continued on a harsher note. ''Don't tell me you let him play bouncy bouncy with you. After that has-been Skip O'Malley, you need to develop better taste in men.''

Jo's hands were balled into fists. With a look of helpless rage, she glanced around the room. ''How dare he. How dare he,'' she gritted.

''He's just trying to get a rise out of you,'' Cam said. But he couldn't quite keep the anger out of his own voice.

When the message finished, Hamill pressed the Save button. ''So that's the kind of trash you've been hearing,'' he muttered.

''I call him Laughing Boy,'' Jo told him.

''I can see why. Mind if I take the tape?''

She shook her head. ''You can have the other ones, too. They're down at my office.'' Her fingers sought and found Cam's. His almost crushing grip was like a safety line.

Hamill was already dialing a special number at the phone company. In a brusque voice, he spoke into the receiver. A few minutes later, he swore. Slamming the phone back into the cradle, he turned to Jo and Cam. ''It looks like we're not going to catch the bastard this morning.''

''Why not?''

''He used a phone booth off Charles Street.''

Solving the problem with something as simple as caller ID had been too much to hope for, Jo told herself. ''He was here last night,'' she reminded the detective. ''He must have seen the unit.''

''Damn!'' The exclamation came from Cam.

''If he called from a phone booth, how did he get that distortion in the transmission?'' Hamill wondered aloud.

''Portable equipment?'' Jo asked, her tone matter-of-fact now. She was going to think about this just like any other case. If she did that, the fear wouldn't swallow her up.

"I'd like to see what kind of setup he has," Cam mused. "EMP. Portable electronics equipment."

"Yeah." The police detective looked thoughtful.

"Do you think it's Eddie Cahill doing this?" Jo asked.

"I dug out the court records last night. You did some prime undercover work to nail Cahill. No wonder the mother said he was going to get you," Hamill answered. "But there's no hard evidence linking him to any of this."

"There's plenty of evidence that Ms. O'Malley's life is being torn apart." Cam looked toward the answering machine and back at Hamill. "Are you going to tell me you still can't commit yourself to protecting her?"

"I know you're worried—"

"Dammit, man."

"Cam, please," Jo whispered.

"I'll put everything I can into the investigation," Hamill promised. "And we've already increased patrols in the area. Basically Ms. O'Malley's doing the kinds of things I'd recommend. An alarm system. Good locks. Maybe she should put in some extra lighting in the yard," the police detective continued.

Then he turned to Jo. "Where can we reach you?"

"At my house," Cam answered.

She shot him a startled look. Helping her was one thing, making decisions for her was quite another. "Since when do you do the talking for me?"

"You sure can't stay here alone."

"I'm sure I'd be welcomed at my friend Laura's. She has a big house all to herself."

"Do you want to put your friend in danger?" Cam asked slowly.

"I—no."

Hamill cleared his throat. "I'd recommend taking Mr. Randolph up on his offer. He's likely to function as a deterrent. Whoever made the calls and rigged the TV stunt has been going after a woman living alone. He ran when Randolph discovered him in the house. He might give up if you had a protector.''

Jo snorted.

Cam tried not to look victorious.

They waited until Hamill had left before continuing the personal discussion.

''I'm not going to spend the day hiding at your place,'' Jo informed Cam.

''What are you going to do?''

''I'm going to go back to those phone company records on other women who had similar calls and see if I can find out if they have anything in common with me.''

''Would you mind if we stopped back at my place and had a look at your car? I'd like to check something out.''

The question and his conciliatory tone of voice astonished her. ''Cam, I'm not used to having a bodyguard.''

''I know.''

''I—things are moving so fast. I mean, with you and me.''

''Honey, when this is over, I'll send you flowers and take you out to dinner at the Conservatory. Right now, I want to make sure you're going to be safe.''

Jo nodded, unsure of how to act in this unfamiliar situation. ''Okay,'' she agreed in a barely audible voice.

''Okay, we can go check out your car? Or you'll permit me to help you?''

''Okay to both.''

Back at Cross Keys, Cam pulled into a parking place near Jo's Honda. She watched as he walked over to the car, stooped down and began to run his hands along the underside of the bumpers and under the chassis. When he reached a spot under the back bumper, he paused.

Seconds later he turned back to Jo. In the palm of his right hand lay a dull metal disk.

"What is it?"

"A directional transmitter. That's why he thought you were still at my house last night. He knew your car stayed."

Air wheezed out of Jo's lungs as the extent of her tormentor's scheme hit her. Her knees began to wobble and she sat down heavily on the curb. "He's been following me. Poking into my life. He's known where I was every second of the day and night because he's been tracking me."

"Yes." Cam was beside her, holding her.

"My God. What else has he been doing? If he's got a bunch of electronics stuff—he—he could have been listening to us." She gulped. "Like in your house last night."

"Not in my house! The place is shielded. Nothing gets in or out of that house without my knowing about it."

"Why?"

"I told you about the industrial espionage. Sometimes I take work home—or make business calls from there."

She nodded slowly and then raised an eyebrow in surprise as Cam got up and put the transmitter back where he'd found it.

"What are you doing?"

"I think we can lay a trap for the bastard." He worried a knuckle between his teeth. "Just let me think about how I want to set it up."

"Do me a favor. Let me help you think about it."

"Sure."

They drove in separate cars to 43 Light Street. While Jo waited in the back alley, Cam went down to talk to Lou Rossini. The building superintendent agreed to drive Jo's car to the vicinity of the pool hall where she'd been mugged. He'd take a cab back. Cam would park in a nearby alley and see who showed up at the car.

Before he left, Cam pulled Jo into his arms and gave her

a hard kiss. "Remember, you're not going anywhere without letting somebody know about it," he reminded her.

"Yes, Mother." She wrinkled her nose. She didn't like having a bunch of constraints. On the other hand, the careful arrangements were comforting.

Sitting at her desk, she drummed her fingers against the wooden surface. She'd pinned her hopes on the caller ID equipment. It had done her as much good as a tissue paper dress in a rainstorm.

Now what? Maybe it was time to go back to the phone company list of women who'd been harassed.

Again she had to dial several numbers before getting anyone at home. The third woman she called answered the phone with the kind of cautious greeting that had crept into Jo's own voice recently.

"Is this Penny Wallace?"

"Who is this? How did you get this number?"

"My name is Jo O'Malley. I've been receiving some threatening phone calls. Since I'm a private detective, the phone company has given me permission to contact other women who might have been harassed by the same man."

"I really don't want to talk about it."

"Please. I'll only take a few minutes of your time."

"Are you the detective who was in that article in the paper Sunday?"

"Yes."

"What kind of calls have you been getting?"

"From someone with an electronically distorted voice." She kept her tone as steady as possible. "He seems to know a lot about me. And he's been leaving messages on my answering machines as well as speaking to me in person."

Penny made a choking sound. "That's what happened to me six months ago."

"Could I come over and talk to you?" Jo asked.

There was a long pause. ''All right,'' the woman finally answered.

Jo got directions. When she hung up, she thought about the newspaper article again. The man stalking her had read it. So had Penny Wallace. On balance, the notoriety was probably more of an advantage than a disadvantage.

After locking the office, Jo went downstairs and started out the door toward the parking lot where she usually kept her car. Then she remembered the Honda was in Dundalk—and she'd promised Cam she'd stay at the office. Well, what Cam Randolph didn't know wasn't going to hurt him. Besides, this might be an important lead in the case. Going back inside, she called a cab and waited in the lobby until it arrived.

Penny Wallace lived in a redbrick row house in Catonsville. When she answered the door, the two women stared at each other in shock. They were both petite and both sported heads of short, curly red hair.

''You could be my sister,'' Penny said in amazement.

''That's just what I was thinking. Let's see if we can find out if we have anything else in common.'' Jo's voice brimmed with excitement. Finally she was getting somewhere.

Penny Wallace blew her nose and ushered her visitor into a small, neat living room decorated in a stark modern style. Well, taste in decor is something we don't share, Jo thought as she took off her coat and folded it beside her on the sofa.

''You're lucky you found me here. I've got a cold so I decided to stay home.''

Jo sympathized before getting down to business. ''When did the calls start?'' she asked as she took a seat in a low-slung leather chair.

Penny faced her on the chrome-and-leather sofa with a box of tissues at her side. ''May 15. I remember exactly because I'd just come home from Alice's wedding shower.''

"You were in a wedding?" Jo asked carefully.

"I was the maid of honor."

The words sent a strange chill sweeping over Jo's skin as if an icy finger had reached out and touched her shoulder. "My calls started a couple of weeks ago when I came back from an engagement party for one of my best friends. I'm the matron of honor in the wedding."

Penny leaned forward. "That's spooky."

"Yeah."

"I know what you're going through. He's making sexual threats, isn't he? And he knows a lot about you."

"He knows everything about me."

"It was creepy. Especially the way he laughed."

"Yeah." Invisible insects buzzed around Jo for a moment. She willed them away.

"If it's any consolation, the calls stopped after the wedding."

"That's definitely something to look forward to. But I'm not just dealing with this on a personal level anymore. I'd really like to nail the guy if I can."

"I just wanted him to leave me alone," Penny whispered. It was apparent that talking about the episode had brought the whole thing back to her.

"Is there anything else that might help me track him down?"

"The music in the background. It sounded like a band."

"Yes! What about the stuff he threatened?"

"My therapist said the best thing I could do was put this out of my mind."

"I understand." Jo could empathize with that. "Did he just call? Or did you have any physical contact with him?"

"Just calls."

"Are you sure?" Jo gave a brief account of the electronic devices that had been used at her house.

Penny's eyes grew round. "Thank God I didn't have anything like that. It was all over the phone."

They talked for about fifteen minutes longer but Jo didn't get any more facts. "I wonder where he got the names of the wedding attendants," Penny mused.

"He could be a wedding photographer. He could work for the caterer or the florist. Do you know who provided those services for your friend?"

"No. I'm sorry. I could ask Alice and get back to you."

Jo gave Penny one of her cards and then asked if she could call a cab.

"A private detective without a car?"

"It's a long story."

Back at her office, Jo tried some more numbers and got another one of the victims, Heather Van Dyke, who was at home because she ran a sewing business from her recreation room. Now Jo had a better idea about what to ask. This woman, too, was a redhead within an inch of her height who'd been the matron of honor in her sister's wedding.

As Jo put down the phone, she leaned back in her chair. Two redheads and a blonde. How did that add up? Was Melody Naylor an unrelated case? She wished she'd asked the woman more questions.

Then a crucial fact flashed in her mind like the payoff light on a slot machine. Melody Naylor was a beautician. A lot of beauticians change their hair color the way other women change dresses. Maybe she had been a redhead when she'd gotten those calls.

When she phoned the shop, Melody was on a break.

Jo reintroduced herself and explained that she'd been talking to some other victims of phone harassment and might have discovered a common link. "Was your hair a different color when you were getting the calls?"

"Gee—let me think. I change it so much," the woman said, confirming Jo's speculation. "I was using Champagne

Blond for a while. Then I decided to see if redheads have more fun, so I tried Fantastic Autumn.''

''Your hair was red?'' Jo clarified, her heart skipping a beat.

''Yeah. But I dyed it back just before Lucy's wedding because it didn't go with my pink dress.''

''You were in a friend's wedding?'' Jo asked, struggling to keep her voice steady.

''I was the maid of honor. And this real great-looking guy was one of the ushers. For a while I thought things were going t work out with us. Then he went back to his damn motorcycle racing.''

Jo made appropriate responses as Melody prattled on about her love life. But her mind wasn't on the conversation. Redheads. Weddings. She touched her own red curls. She had the link between her and the other women. Could she find out why—and then who?

Chapter Ten

With renewed energy, Jo picked up the phone again. The next name on the list was a Margaret Clement. An older woman answered.

"Who's calling my daughter?" she asked in a strained voice.

Jo went through her now-familiar explanation, adding that she'd already talked to several other victims.

For long moments there was a silence on the other end of the line. "Margaret was getting calls like that," the woman finally said.

"Is she a redhead?"

"Yes,"

"Was she the maid or matron of honor in a wedding?"

"Yes. Her cousin's."

"Did the calls stop after the wedding?"

"No. They got worse. He was calling every day and saying such horrible things. And she started getting weird packages in the mail. One was a Christmas angel with red hair. Another was an electric bell that started buzzing when she opened it up." Jo's gasp was drowned out by the choked sob on the other end of the line. "Then Margaret disappeared."

Jo's fingers clenched the phone in a death grip.

"Back in August," Mrs. Clement continued. "She left

her office to come home one afternoon, but she never got here. We haven't heard anything from her since.''

"Could she have run away to escape the harassment?" Jo grasped at an explanation.

"She didn't take any of her clothes. And she didn't leave me a note or anything like that.'' Mrs. Clement's voice rose. "Margaret wouldn't have left me to worry like this. I just know she wouldn't. Besides, where would she have gone off to on her own?''

Jo had thought she understood the pattern that was developing. The new information and the anguish in the other woman's voice made her throat contract. "I'm sorry,'' she managed. "What did the police say?''

"They've been looking. So far nothing's turned up." The woman hesitated. "Did you say your name was Jo O'Malley? Didn't I read something about you in the Sunday paper?''

"Yes.''

"I couldn't afford to pay you very much. But maybe you could help me find Margaret. She's such a good girl. Do you think he kidnapped her the way he said he was going to?''

"He made specific kidnapping threats?''

"Yes.''

Jo shuddered. "I'm investigating the man, Mrs. Clement. I'll do what I can. Would it be all right if I came out and talked to you in the next few days?''

"Just call and let me know when you want to come.''

Jo put down the phone. Her mouth went dry as she considered the new evidence. She'd been operating under certain assumptions. What if— She was saved from further speculation by a knock on the door. Her head jerked up, and she recognized Abby through the frosted glass.

"What's new?" she asked as Jo unlocked the door.

"Did Cam send you down here to check up on me?''

"Yes. It sounds as if you had quite an evening."

"And Cam told you all about it."

"Of course he did. Sweetie, the man has fallen hard for you. He can't keep from worrying himself sick over what's happening. Do you really blame him for that?"

"No," Jo admitted.

"You're under a lot of stress right now." Abby switched the focus of the conversation. "I'd say it's partly from the harassment and partly because you told yourself no one could take Skip's place—but you're beginning to wonder what a long-term relationship with Cam would be like."

Jo hadn't planned to discuss Cam. Now a sort of confession came tumbling out. "Last night, when he took me home, we made love. It was good, Abby." Jo's voice softened. "Not just good, better than…anything I can remember." The end of the sentence was as revealing for what it didn't say as for the actual words.

Abby crossed the room and put her arms around Jo's shoulder. "You're feeling guilty because being with Cam was warm and satisfying and made you feel cherished."

"How do you know it was like that?"

"I've gotten to know Cam Randolph over the past few months. At first I was sad for him because I thought here's a great guy, with so much to give the right woman—only he'd never found her. Then I started wondering if the right woman might be you."

"So you set things up."

"Not exactly. Steve wanted Cam for his best man. I wanted you for my matron of honor. But let's not get sidetracked from the real issue—your feelings."

"We sure wouldn't want to do that, Dr. Franklin."

"If you were in therapy, I'd make you work through things. But you're not. Jo, I've known you for a long time. I understand how you felt about Skip and what you went through when he died. You don't have anything to feel guilty about now. It's not a question of Cam's taking any-one else's place. It's a question of opening yourself to the possibilities of a new relationship.''

''What about all the questions of money and social class? That kind of stuff. I mean, we hardly—''

''If Cameron Randolph had wanted a society girl, believe me he'd have one.''

Jo nodded slowly. ''You've given me a lot to think about.''

''Good.''

''Can we talk about my other problem? Unfortunately it's just as pressing.''

''Fire away.''

''I need some insights into the psychological profile of a guy who goes after redheaded maids of honor.''

''Cam didn't say anything about that.''

''He doesn't know yet. I finally made a breakthrough with the list of women I got from the telephone company. One of them let me come over and interview her. Abby, it was spooky how much she looked like me. And she'd been the maid of honor in a wedding.'' Jo went on to summarize the rest of what she'd learned, including the conversation with Margaret Clement's mother.

Abby looked alarmed. ''That doesn't fit the usual pattern of a phone harasser.''

''Or of a guy that was in the state pen until a couple of weeks ago—not when the records I have from the phone company go back two or three years.''

''How do you think the wedding angle figures in?'' Abby asked.

''Well, I'm not the psychologist here. But if I had to make a quick guess off the top of my head, I'd say that a redheaded woman rejected the guy who's been calling and maybe married someone else, and now he's getting even.''

"And the caller is the same one who hit you with the EMP box and rigged your television sets."

"He told me he was."

"Oh, Jo. I hate to think that being in my wedding is putting you in danger."

"We still don't know for sure what's going on. Maybe Eddie knows about the wedding guy and is imitating his M.O."

Abby looked doubtful.

"Do you have any thoughts on handling the creep if he shows up in person?"

"I could tell you more if I heard the tapes."

"Two of them are still in my desk drawer." Jo pulled them out and popped one into the recorder. As she played the messages for Abby, she gritted her teeth and tried to evaluate them in light of the conversations she'd had with the psychologist.

"That man is seriously disturbed. He's not just trying to get a rise out of you with the sexual content. He's trying to terrorize you," Abby whispered when the second message had run its course.

"He's doing a pretty good job. What do you—uh—think about that brass bed? Didn't he make it sound kind of like a sacrificial altar?"

"That's stretching things."

Before she lost her nerve, Jo forced herself to spell out the terrible thoughts that had been in the back of her mind since she'd talked to Mrs. Clements. "He didn't just tell me about it. You know, I'm pretty sure that's what was flashing on the TV screen last night. Quick glimpses of a woman who looked a lot like me. Strapped down and help-less. In the early scenes she was wearing a long, white dress, then she was naked. I—I keep thinking," Jo gulped and made herself continue. "Maybe it was Margaret Clement.

Maybe he was actually going through some kind of ritual murder with her. And he filmed it.''

Abby's face had drained of color. She stared at her friend. ''Oh, Jo—''

''I could be right, couldn't I?''

Abby nodded slowly.

''So if I end up in his clutches, it would probably be a good idea to stay off that bed.''

''You're not going to end up in his clutches.''

''What if I do—''

''Yes. Stay away from the bed.''

BY THE TIME Detective Hamill came to collect the tapes, Jo was in control of her emotions. As if she were talking about any old investigation, she filled him in on what she'd discovered.

He was impressed with her detective work. ''We could use you downtown.''

''Don't count on it.''

''I'll go back and pull the files on those cases to see how it fits in with the Eddie Cahill stuff.''

''I'll get the names of the caterers and other service people each of the wedding parties used. Maybe there will be a name or address from their employee lists that will be some kind of link.''

''And we'll keep each other up-to-date on our progress,'' Hamill added.

By the time Cam called at four to say he was coming back, Jo was deep into information gathering. She hadn't found out anything startling. But doing the work gave her the feeling that she was accomplishing something.

When Cam explained in a disgusted voice that the stakeout hadn't turned up anything, she was quick to reassure him that the idea had been worth trying.

''I debugged your Honda,'' he said, when he came into

the office. "Then I put the transmitter in the garage across the street and stashed your car at Abby's apartment building." He stopped abruptly before continuing in a less confident voice. "If you wanted, you could see how Laura feels about a houseguest. I mean, if we made sure you weren't being followed, there wouldn't be any way he'd know you were there."

Cam wasn't pressing. He was giving her choices. That and the conversation she'd had with Abby tipped the balance.

Jo closed the file she'd been trying to make some notes in. "I'd rather go home with you," she said.

"I was hoping you would. Do you want to stop at your house and get some more clothes?"

For tomorrow or the next couple of weeks, Jo wondered.

As they drove up Charles Street, she told him about her new discoveries. His head snapped toward her when she came to the part about the redheads and the bridesmaids. "So maybe this isn't what we thought at all."

"I don't know how the new stuff fits in." Unconsciously she pulled her trench coat more tightly around her slender body, as if the fabric could protect her from more than the elements. "Do you think it's possible that two different people are involved?"

"God, Jo. I hope not."

"Then what?"

"We'll figure it out. Meanwhile, we'll keep you safe."

At her house she breathed silent thanks when she saw that the answering machine didn't have any messages. Then her mind reevaluated the implications. Laughing Boy knew everything else. Maybe he hadn't called because he knew she wasn't going to be home.

Wanting to spend as little time in the house as possible, she grabbed some clothes out of the closet and raided a few drawers. Then Cam was ushering her back out to the car.

He didn't drive straight to his place, and she knew he was making sure they weren't being followed. The way he handled the Lotus, only a stunt driver could have kept up with him.

Fifteen minutes later they pulled up in front of his door. Knowing that Cam's house was protected by every security device that was on the market or still in the development stages gave Jo a profound sense of well-being. Or maybe it was just being with Cam.

She wondered if he was feeling something similar. Once he'd closed the front door, he pulled her into his arms. At first it was enough to simply hold each other close. But as they stood in the hall, the feeling of comfort escalated quickly into sexual awareness.

They exchanged hot, hungry kisses. His hands were tracking up her back when they stopped abruptly. "When I get you in my arms, it's hard to remember about more mundane things."

"Like what?"

"Dinner, for instance."

"Oh, yeah. Dinner."

"I've got steaks, stuffed potatoes and green beans in the refrigerator," he told her. "So we don't have to go out to the store."

"Steak and potatoes," she said in a slightly dazed voice as she followed him down the hall to the kitchen.

Jo fixed the vegetables while Cam put the steaks on an indoor grill.

"We'll eat in the den," he said as he began to put plates and cutlery on a large tray.

He led the way into a comfortable room with sofas, a fireplace, and a thick shaggy rug. To her surprise, he set the food on a glass coffee table and pulled pillows off the couch. Then he used the built-in gas jets to start the wood in the fireplace. The dry logs were blazing in moments.

"Neat trick," Jo observed as he turned off the gas and let the wood take over. She wondered if she'd ever get used to that kind of casual luxury.

"I wish I had invented it," Cam remarked half seriously.

Jo, who had forgotten to eat lunch, tackled the food. "You grill a mean steak, Randolph. You're handier in the kitchen than you'd let on," she observed.

"It's just a basic bachelor skill."

"Before I married Skip he survived on meatball subs and frozen entrées. Then when we used to come home from work together, I was the one who had to get dinner on the table."

"Did you resent having to do all the cooking?"

"No. I grew up in a family that was pretty traditional. The women did the cooking and the cleaning. Of course, if Skip had offered to fix dinner once in a while, I wouldn't have turned him down."

She looked at Cam to judge his reaction. Apparently their relationship had progressed to the point where she could mention her late husband without the two of them automatically getting uptight.

"How about some dinner music?" Cam asked as he slid open a panel in the side of the table.

"Sure."

Jo expected Chopin or Mozart. Instead when the eight-speaker system sprang to life, it delivered a Kenny Rogers ballad about two teenagers whose love finally triumphed over the long arm of the law.

"I like Kenny Rogers."

"I thought you might."

"If you'd rather hear something else—"

"I've got eclectic musical tastes." Pressing some buttons, he adjusted the speakers. "The system can reproduce any size effects from a large concert hall to a small cabaret. What's your choice?"

She closed her eyes for a minute. "Let's pretend we've got lawn seating at Oregon Ridge."

He laughed. "You're a cheap date." When he held out his arms, she nestled against him as they listened to the rest of the song.

The smile curving her lips froze as the phone rang.

Jo's eyes riveted to the brass telephone on the end table. Cam followed her gaze. "It's all right. He's not going to call you here."

She nodded tightly.

Cam picked up the receiver. It was a business discussion, and her host was obviously uncomfortable talking in front of Jo.

"I'll clean up while you're busy," she mouthed.

He nodded. "Sorry."

Jo loaded the tray. In the kitchen, she put the trash in the compactor, rinsed the dishes and stacked them in the dishwasher. Cam didn't appear. To give him some more time, she made coffee. When she brought it in, he was just putting down the phone. There was a scowl on his face.

She set the coffee cups down. "Problems?"

"Nothing that can't be straightened out. I've got Phil Mercer working on it."

Instinct told her he was being evasive. "You didn't get to work at all today, did you?"

"No." He reached up and pulled her down beside him onto the thick rug.

"Is there anything I can do to help?"

"Yes."

His mouth slanted over hers with a kiss that should have driven every coherent thought out of her mind. When he lifted his head, she gave it one more try. "Don't get your priorities screwed up because of me."

"Honey, I'm not. I don't think I've ever had my priorities in better order."

He lowered her to her back, trapping her body between his hard length and the plush rug. The feelings that had been simmering between them during dinner came to a full, rolling boil.

She could come to no harm when she was in his arms. The knowledge was as liberating as it was arousing.

With primitive urgency they began to explore each other's bodies, twisting and arching together with the need to get closer and closer still. If there was a note of desperation in Cam's lovemaking, Jo didn't question its source.

SOMETIME during the evening they moved upstairs to Cam's bedroom. When Jo woke up at seven in the morning, she was naked with the covers down around her waist, and Cam was lying on his side, his gray gaze locked on her.

She reached down to drag up the sheet, but he pulled her back into a tight embrace.

"I thought guys slowed down after thirty."

"You do potent things to my hormones. Or maybe it's because I'm falling in love with you."

Her eyes flew open. "Are you teasing me?"

"I wouldn't tease you about something like that."

"Oh, Cam—I—don't know what to say."

"I'll let you get used to the idea."

He began to kiss her and touch her once more. Now there was a tenderness in his lovemaking that made her heart ache to be able to return his declaration. But it was too soon. She had to know that she wasn't just turning to him in a crisis. She had to know her feelings would stand the test of time, because if she ever got married again, it was going to be for keeps.

He seemed to sense her mood as she got dressed later and followed him downstairs. As they made breakfast, she saw his pragmatic, empirical persona slip back into place.

"I have to put in an appearance at Randolph Enterprises," he told her.

"You can't spend all your time chaperoning me."

"There's another car in the garage. A BMW. Why don't you drive that down to Light Street, and I'll meet you for lunch."

"If you can't get away, I'll understand."

"I'll get away."

"Do you mind if I make a few phone calls here? It's early enough so I might be able to catch some of the women who weren't home yesterday."

"Of course not."

Before Cam left, he gave her the keys to the car and the house and showed her how to set the security system—which was much more elaborate than hers. Then he gave her a bear hug. "Take care of yourself."

"I will," she promised.

Jo decided to use the phone in the den. As she sat down at Cam's desk, she was amused to note that all his mail was sorted into labeled cubbyholes. At least if she married him, he'd organize the clutter that swirled around her. Or would the disorganization drive him bananas?

She smiled, suddenly optimistic that they'd somehow work things out.

Just as she was reaching for the phone, it rang. Jo tensed. Until this was over, she was going to be suspicious of all incoming calls, she acknowledged. But it could be Cam with something he'd forgotten to tell her.

"Hello?"

"Angel face! Did you think you could hide from me?"

Her heart started to pound and she almost slammed the receiver back into the cradle. Then she realized Laughing Boy was handing her an opportunity. This was the first time she'd talked to him since she'd interviewed some of his other victims. "How did you get this number?" she asked, hoping her voice sounded calm.

"I have my ways."

"I've talked to some of the other women you've bothered."

He laughed. "So?"

"What have you got against redheads?"

"Wouldn't you like to know?"

His mood was different, Jo noted. He wasn't bombarding her with sexual innuendos. This time, even through the electronic filter, she detected a note of tension. Good. Maybe he was worried because she'd gotten somewhere with the phone company.

"I know something you don't," he taunted.

"What?"

"Something about Randolph."

Despite her resolve not to let him get to her, she clutched the receiver. "Cam?"

"There are some very interesting things your boyfriend would rather you not know."

"Are you going to tell me what they are?"

"No. I think it would be more fun for you to find out by yourself, miss hotshot detective. But I'll give you a hint to get you started. Go back to those old files of your husband's. The ones involving cases he didn't talk to you about."

"Which case?"

"Oh, I'm sure you'll figure it out." Before Jo could ask another question, the line went dead, and she was left with white knuckles clutched around the receiver. What possible connection could there be between Cam and one of Skip's cases?

Nothing! she told herself firmly. The jerk was just trying to rattle her. But now she had to crush the seed of doubt he'd planted—before it took root and started poisoning her mind. Instead of making phone calls to the other women on the list, she'd better go right to the office and check back through the files.

On her way to the garage, however, Jo hesitated for a moment. Laughing Boy had called and maneuvered her into checking her files. Was he outside somewhere waiting for her to leave Cam's house? Maybe this was just a ploy to get her out in the open where he could pounce. Cautiously she looked out both the downstairs and upstairs windows. As far as she could see, no one was lurking around. If he were around the corner, Cam's BMW could certainly outrun just about anything he had.

Her prediction about the car proved correct. It was fast and powerful and a joy to drive. After whipping around several blocks, Jo was sure no one was following her. But as she approached the garage on Light Street, she began to tense up again. Her tormentor knew where she was going. He didn't have to follow her to the office to scoop her up.

Jo circled the block, once more looking for suspicious cars or pedestrians. On a downtown street, it was difficult to determine whether the panhandler on the corner was collecting money for his next bottle of Wild Turkey or watching for her.

She hesitated at the entrance to the garage where she usually parked. Then instead of driving inside, she pulled up in the loading zone in back of 43 Light Street. From there it was only a few steps inside the building. In the basement she found Lou and asked if he'd mind parking the car. He was quick to oblige.

"I wish they'd catch the guy who's botherin' you," he muttered.

"They will," Jo assured him. As she took the elevator up, she sagged back against the wall and closed her eyes. Over the years she'd worked for a number of women who were being harassed or threatened. She'd been sympathetic, but she'd never really understood the sense of defenselessness—the growing terror as you lost control of your life. Now she did.

As she walked down the hall to the office, a man stepped out of the shadows. Jo stopped short, her heart in her throat. She'd been so careful, and he was already in the building waiting for her! She was about to turn and dash for the stairs when he called her name.

"Ms. O'Malley. Wait. It's Detective Hamill."

"I'm sorry, I thought—"

"I didn't mean to startle you."

"I guess I'm just jumpy this morning."

"I called you, but you must have left Randolph's house. So I took a chance on intercepting you here."

The grim set of his mouth and the tone of his voice put her on guard. "Something's happened."

"Yes. Can we go inside your office?"

As Jo unlocked the door and flipped on the lights, she felt her stomach clench. Turning to face him, she steeled herself for something unpleasant.

"We found Eddie Cahill's ex-wife early this morning. There's no way to put a good face on this, so I'll just give it to you straight. She was beaten and murdered."

Chapter Eleven

With all the focus on redheads and weddings, Jo hadn't been thinking much about Eddie Cahill's wife. News of her death was the last thing Jo had been prepared to hear.

A gasp escaped her lips. "Oh, poor Karen." Suddenly she knew her legs wouldn't support her. Before she could embarrass herself by falling on her face, she dropped into one of the visitor's chairs opposite the desk. Hamill brought her a drink of water from the cooler, and she sipped gratefully.

"I know it's a shock."

"I suppose Eddie did it."

"There's no hard evidence yet."

"What about Jennifer Stark? Is she okay?"

"The prosecuting attorney? I understand she's taken an extended leave of absence."

"Yeah." Jo sat numbly clutching her paper cup while the officer told her what they knew about the murder. Karen had been reported missing by her mother the night before. Under the circumstances, the department had mounted an extensive search. Her partially clothed body had been found near Loch Raven reservoir by a man walking his doberman that morning. "The dog pulled the guy off the path and into the underbrush," Hamill said. "There wasn't much attempt to hide the body. It was almost as if the murderer wanted it to be found.''

"Where does that leave me?'' Jo asked.

"We can keep a tail on you for a few days, and we'll certainly increase the patrols near your home and office and Mr. Randolph's town house. I'd also like to suggest putting a decoy in your house—a policewoman with your general physical characteristics.''

That wasn't Jo's usual style, but she agreed.

"You didn't think Cahill was going to make good on his threats, did you?'' she asked.

Hamill looked embarrassed. "You know what kind of constraints we operate under. When he wasn't recaptured immediately, there was no way we could put you or his ex-wife under indefinite surveillance.''

Jo nodded. That was what she'd told Cam.

"Do you have an extra key to your house?'' Hamill asked.

Jo produced one from her desk drawer. "I'll get a few more things I need this afternoon. Then the place is all yours.''

Hamill's visit left Jo feeling strangely lethargic—as if she hadn't slept in days and couldn't summon the energy to cross the room. Partly, she acknowledged, it was guilt. Last year she was the one who'd told Karen Cahill that she was going to have to go to the D.A. with the information about her husband's drug dealing. Now he'd killed her.

On the other hand, it was Karen who had come to her with the request for some ammunition she could use in a divorce case. At the moment, the circular reasoning was too much for Jo. Finally she forced herself to get out of the chair and go over to the large storage closet where she'd stuffed Skip's out-of-date records.

They were stacked in cardboard boxes, and the thought

of shuffling through all of them made her even more weary. But she forced herself to start the task.

It was too much trouble to carry the boxes to her desk. Instead she heaped them in a semicircle on the floor, sat down in the middle, and began to dig through them.

It didn't take long before she began to get interested in the project—particularly after she came across the first case she and Skip had worked on together. They'd both posed as street people and staked out Fells Point to catch the runaway daughter of an old Baltimore family.

There were other cases, many of which she'd worked on. Finally she came across a box that contained folders Skip had kept to himself. Some of the assignments had been before she'd come to work for him. Despite her protests, others had been jobs he'd considered too dangerous to involve his wife. And a few had been situations where clients had insisted on strict confidentiality.

As Jo thumbed through the last two categories, her eyes bounced off one of the names, and she stopped dead. Where her fingers touched the manila folder, they seemed to burn. The tab read Randolph Enterprises. Cam certainly hadn't mentioned anything about that.

With a feeling of dread, she pulled the file from the box and began to read Skip's carefully penned notes.

Morgan Randolph, Cam's father, had hired Skip to find out who was responsible for a series of disturbing incidents. Randolph products still in development were showing up in the commercial lines of competitors. That must be the industrial espionage episode Cam had told her about, Jo thought, with a little sigh of relief. He hadn't tried to hide that from her when she'd asked.

Yet he hadn't said a word about Skip being on the case. Hadn't he known?

She got her answer several pages down, when she found a carbon of a letter from Skip to Cam requesting a list of compromised projects. His detailed reply was clipped to the carbon. Jo leaned back against the wall.

So Cam *had* dealt with Skip. But most of her husband's contacts had probably been with the father. Perhaps Cam hadn't remembered the detective's name.

With shaky fingers, she turned more pages. There was also a memo from Cam's older brother Collin Randolph. Since he was in charge of personnel, he had listed employees he thought Skip ought to check. From Skip's subsequent reports, it appeared that none of those investigations had panned out.

Reading between the lines, Jo gathered that the elder Randolph had started pressing for results. Skip's next tack had been a background check on the members of the Randolph family. Jo breathed a sigh of relief when she saw that there was nothing questionable in Cam's background. About his only indiscretion had been to get drunk at a couple of parties in his freshman year at Dartmouth.

The next report was on Collin. He'd also been a model college student. Interestingly, he'd had hardly any social life when he'd lived in the dorm at Brown. Former classmates had spoken of him as not being particularly friendly. Things had changed when he'd come back to Baltimore to work in the family company. Sporadically at first and then on a regular basis, he'd begun frequenting gay bars. Jo paused as she digested that bit of information. According to Skip, Collin had hidden his homosexuality from his family, even when he'd developed relationships with several men who became more than casual lovers.

Skip had handled the revelations discreetly. He'd quietly gone to the older Randolph brother with the information and asked if there was anybody who might be taking advantage of him because they knew about his secret life. Collin had responded in a very flat, emotionless manner and had assured Skip that his private life would not put the company in jeopardy. Two days later, he had stuck a pistol in his mouth and pulled the trigger.

Jo's hands clenched the edge of the paper. How tragic. No wonder Cam hadn't wanted to talk about the case. It had inadvertently led to his brother's death.

She almost put the file away. But there were a few sheets of paper left. Under an obituary in the *Baltimore Sun* was an official letter from Morgan dismissing Skip from the case along with payment of $2,000 to cover his expenses to date.

The final entry in the file was the summary of a conversation Skip had had with Cameron Randolph a month later. Morgan Randolph had just died of a heart attack. An angry Cam had called to accuse Skip of destroying the family. According to Cam, Skip hadn't been asked to investigate family members. Furthermore, the dirt he'd dug up had driven Collin to suicide, and their father had never recovered from the shock of his son's death. Which meant that he was responsible for not just one but two deaths. Skip's notes added that Cam had threatened to put him out of business.

Jo closed the file and let her head flop back against the wall, fighting the sick feeling that had begun to churn in her stomach. Cam had never mentioned that he'd known Skip. But they'd certainly been acquainted. More to the point, he'd worked himself up into an irrational hatred for her husband. Now she thought back over all the subtle and not so subtle signals Cam had given off when Skip's name had entered the conversation. She'd assumed Cam was just jealous because she'd been married before. Viewed in this new light, Cam's behavior suggested open hostility to Skip. Just where did that leave her?

With fingers that felt as if they'd been numbed in an ice storm, she shuffled through the papers again, scanning disjointed paragraphs and sentences, somehow hoping that things would look different on a second reading. As she was skimming the paragraph on Collin's college career, a knock at the door made her jump. Her head jerked up. Through the glass she recognized a familiar silhouette.

When she got up and unlocked the door, there was a smile on Cam's lips. It quickly faded when he saw the grim expression on her face.

"What happened?"

She considered the question for several heartbeats. "Well, for starters, it looks like Eddie Cahill made good his threats against Karen. She was beaten and murdered."

"Oh, Jo— Honey, I'm sorry." He moved to fold her into his arms but she evaded his embrace. "What else is wrong?"

"I have the feeling you can figure it out if you really try."

He looked from her to the stacks of boxes and open folder on the floor. "You were going back through Skip's old files." On the surface his voice was flat but Jo could hear the edge of tension he was trying to control.

"And I've been reading his notes on the industrial espionage at Randolph Enterprises. Why didn't you tell me the whole story when we had our frank little discussion about the EMP?"

"It wasn't relevant."

"Not relevant! Sheez!" Jo stamped her foot, paced to the window and then whirled back toward him. "What wasn't relevant? That you blamed my husband for your brother's death—and your father's? Or that you were just getting close to me so you could figure out a way to put me out of business—the way you threatened to do with Skip?"

He winced as he faced her across the room. "I'd decided you didn't have anything to do with that."

"From your investigations of me, you mean?"

"Yes. And personal observation."

"How magnanimous of you."

"Okay, I admit it. Meeting you brought it all back." He swallowed convulsively. "All the sorrow and all the anger. Right after I realized who you were, I decided to see what I could find out about you—with some vague idea of settling the score."

She muttered something unladylike under her breath and folded her arms across her chest.

"Jo, I swear," he continued, "as I started getting to know you, I felt horrible about our relationship not being honest. Then when I realized that you were more important to me than anything that had happened in the past, I just wanted to keep from destroying what was developing between us."

"Did you think I wasn't going to find out about your letter to Skip?"

"I was going to tell you—later."

"Sheez!"

"I'm not very good at this sort of thing."

"You're right about that."

"Jo, please—"

She shook her head before he could finish the sentence. "It's pretty hard for me to operate on an open, honest level with someone who isn't being open and honest with me." Her eyes drilled into him.

The accusing look on her face would have made a lesser man drop his gaze. Cam held his ground. After several silent moments, it was Jo who felt too uncomfortable to continue the standoff. She looked away.

"Dishonesty isn't my strong suit," Cam said. "I knew I'd made a mistake. I was trying to work my way out of it—without losing you."

"Do you still think Skip was responsible for your brother's death? And your father's?"

"Jo, I—"

"Do you?"

"He wasn't authorized to go digging into our family."

"What do you mean he wasn't authorized? Your father hired him to find out who was stealing Randolph product designs, and he was conducting the investigation according to his best judgment. He was authorized to do anything he needed to do to get the job done. He hadn't turned up anything on the employees. The next logical step was to see if someone in the family was responsible."

"He should have cleared that with my father."

"What if your father was the one involved?"

"My father hired him, for God sakes."

"Weirder things have happened in this business. People torching their own warehouses to get the insurance money. Clients hiring a private investigator and laying a trail of clues leading to someone else."

"My father wouldn't have done that."

"Then let's go back to the facts and try to figure out what did happen. I gather from our previous conversation that the espionage stopped after your brother's death. That suggests that it did have something to do with him. Maybe one of his gay friends had threatened to go to your father if Collin didn't cooperate. Collin knew the revelation would crush your father, so he complied."

"That's preposterous. I won't have you besmirching my brother's memory."

"I'm drawing logical conclusions from the information in that file. You ought to understand that. You're big on logic, aren't you?"

He glared at her.

"Your father didn't let Skip continue the investigation after Collin died. Perhaps if he had, we wouldn't be standing here making guesses about what caused the information leak at Randolph Enterprises."

"You're a lot like Skip, aren't you?"

"If you mean logical, dependable, persistent, fair-minded, yes."

"Fair-minded!"

"A private investigator has to put personal biases aside when he takes on a case."

"And he or she doesn't care about who gets hurt as a result of the investigation," Cam grated.

"Of course we do. But facts are facts."

"Facts are facts," he repeated sarcastically.

"And while we're on that subject, what was it that you were trying to hide from me last night when Phil Mercer called? Or were you even talking to Mr. Mercer?"

"Certainly I was talking to Mercer. He was following up on an assignment I gave him. I was trying to find out how someone could have gotten into your house to screw around with your television set when your Randolph Enterprises security system was on."

"And?"

"I'm still working on it," he clipped out.

"Why didn't you want to tell me about it?"

"I was upset about the system failure and wanted to wait until I had some answers."

"But you didn't trust me enough to get my input."

"Trust wasn't the issue."

"Don't you think I have a right to be angry with you? And I'm not talking about the damn security system. It's the business with Skip."

"Yes. You have the right to be angry," he admitted in a low voice.

"At least we've reached a point of agreement."

Cam sighed. "Jo, I think we're both too upset to be having a rational discussion." He waited for some sign that might contradict the statement. When it wasn't forthcoming, he walked slowly toward the door.

Anger and Jo's need to defend Skip had kept her going during the argument. Now her throat was too raw with unshed tears to call him back. As he carefully closed the door, they welled up in her eyes. But the emotional release gave her no comfort. Deep inside she ached from a mixture of outrage, hurt and sadness.

THE MAN panhandling on the street corner across from 43 Light Street glanced up with interest as Cameron Randolph stalked out of the building. The defeated look on the inventor's face brought him an immense surge of pleasure. Jo had checked her late husband's files and discovered that mister rich-and-powerful Randolph wasn't such a nice guy after all.

He turned his head toward the rough brick wall and hunched his shoulder as if he were shielding his body from the wind. He was really hiding the smirk that had plastered itself across his features. He'd won a major victory this afternoon. He'd pried Jo O'Malley away from that smart bastard. It was only a matter of time before he got the rest of what he wanted.

He spotted a plainclothes policeman also dressed like a panhandler working the other end of the block across from Ms. O'Malley's building. The irony didn't escape him and he couldn't hold back a little giggle.

He wasn't stupid enough to try to scoop Denise up now when the heat was on.

He blinked and felt a momentary wave of confusion. Denise. No, this one was named Jo O'Malley. Or was she Denise? She looked like angelic little Denise. But she wasn't going to get the chance to hurt him the way Denise had. This time he was the one who was going to call the shots.

He wanted her to know how much power he had over her. Then he'd show her his brass bed in the wedding chapel.

OVER THE NEXT FEW WEEKS, Jo's life evolved into a strange motif. She felt as if she were simply going through the motions of living—without any rhyme or reason to her existence. Her further attempts to find out who had made the phone calls to the other women turned up nothing. Since she was barely capable of functioning, she wasn't surprised.

If the period before Abby's wedding was marked by anything for her, it was chiefly the lack of any regular routine. Jo varied the time at which she left for the office and when she came home. She wore a changing array of disguises that would have done central casting proud. She used the back entrance to 43 Light Street as often as the front. She rented a series of cars—never driving one for more than a couple of days. Some afternoons she gathered up a handful of the files she'd need and tried to work from one of her temporary homes. Devising and carrying out the precautions became a game on which she could focus. It was better than dwelling on the disappointment of discovering that the future she'd dared to imagine with Cameron Randolph was just a stupid fantasy.

As soon as Laura heard about what had happened, she quickly invited Jo to stay with her. Jo gratefully accepted—on condition that she minimize any danger to her friend by making arrangements at the last minute and never over the phone. She also found she could count on a warm support group ready to help her in any way they could. Noel Emery, Laura's secretary, and Abby's mother also volunteered to put her up. So Jo bounced between the extremes of a lumpy sofa bed in Noel's tiny living room and a plush suite in the Franklin mansion.

There were still wedding activities at which her presence would have been expected. But everybody understood that Jo could be in danger, which turned out to be the perfect excuse for ducking out. She skipped the mixed groups where Cam would be on the scene and only attended a couple of the showers and luncheons that were just for the female contingent. And she avoided getting into any serious discussions with Abby.

But the Wednesday before the wedding, Abby showed up at Jo's office with a bag from the deli.

"I brought us some lunch," she announced. "A hamburger and French fries for you and chicken salad with sprouts for me."

"Thanks."

"I need the company. Every time I'm alone, I start getting the jitters," the bride-to-be admitted.

"You?"

Abby unwrapped a straw and twirled it between her fingers. "No matter how much you think you love someone, getting married is a big step."

"Yeah."

"I missed you at the Stacys' reception last night."

Jo slowly chewed a bite of hamburger. "You know why I wasn't there."

"For two reasons. One of them is certainly valid. But you can't keep avoiding Cam."

"Sure I can."

"What about the rehearsal dinner Friday?"

"I can skip the dinner and just come to the walk-through."

"Jo, please."

The detective wadded her hamburger wrapper into a ball and pitched it at the trash can. It bounced off the edge and landed on the floor. "I don't think you have the jitters. I think you came up here with lunch so we could talk about how stupid I've been acting."

"Do you think you've been acting stupid?"

"No, Dr. Franklin. I think I'm being perfectly realistic about my nonrelationship with Cameron Randolph. It's over."

The psychologist sighed. "It's kind of a conflict of interest counseling both you and Cam. That's why I haven't brought up the heated conversation that ended with you ordering him out of your office.''

''Is that what he told you? Well, I didn't order him out of the office. He was the one who said he was going to leave.''

''Just seeing if I could get a rise out of you. Your emotions have been as flat as a loaf of pita bread lately.''

Jo sat up straighter in her chair. ''Just what the hell did Cameron Randolph say to you?''

''Do I detect a tiny spark of interest in your question?''

''No. All right, yes.''

''If Cam were a patient, I'd have to consider the things he told me confidential.''

''He's a friend.''

''A good friend,'' Abby agreed. ''He's also a man whose mother died when he was a little boy. His father and his older brother raised him. How do you think it made him feel when one of them committed suicide and the other had a fatal heart attack within a matter of weeks?''

Jo dragged a cold French fry through the catsup and laid it back on the paper plate. ''Bad,'' she murmured without raising her head.

''Devastated is more like it. The loss of his brother and his father one right after the other was the worst thing that ever happened to him—and that was coupled with the shock of finding out that the brother he loved had been hiding a secret life from his family.''

Jo's whole body was charged with tension, but the only sign was in the bloodless caps of her knuckles where she'd clenched her fingers.

''He had to find a way to deal with it,'' Abby continued. ''Unfortunately part of his coping mechanism was looking for someone to blame.''

"Too bad it was Skip. And me." Jo didn't allow her voice to reflect her churning emotions.

"Over the past few weeks he's had time to think about his own motivations—and about how his behavior affected your relationship."

"He hasn't called to share his insights with me."

"He's terrified to face you."

Jo laughed mirthlessly.

In contrast, her friend continued in a calm voice. "One thing about a man like Cam, when he chooses a course of action, it's hard to see things any differently. As he got to know you, the relationship cast a whole bunch of earlier assumptions he'd made in doubt. He had a terrible time dealing with that."

"If he'd come clean with me up-front, it would have been a lot better."

"Would it? Can you honestly picture him calling you up the morning after my parents' party and telling you he blamed Skip for the major tragedy in his life?"

Put that way, the suggestion was ludicrous, Jo admitted.

"Even if he'd waited until he knew you a little better, with your hot temper and your sense of loyalty to Skip, you would have given him the heave-ho."

Jo nodded slowly. "You're probably right. But there had to be some better way than what he did."

"Hindsight is wonderful, isn't it?"

Jo flushed.

"There's no point in speculating on what might have happened," Abby continued. "Now that you've both had a chance to cool down, why don't you talk about it? A lot of major misunderstandings between people could be cleared up if they'd just sit down and have a sensible conversation."

"I said some things he didn't want to hear."

"He said things you didn't want to hear."

"Yeah. Like about Skip."

"Perhaps you made him realize that his feelings toward Skip were a defense mechanism," Abby said gently.

"I did?"

"The only way you'll find out for sure is to talk to him about it," Abby reiterated.

Jo was silent for a moment. Finally, she took a deep breath. "You think he—uh—that he still—?"

"Yes." Abby's voice was full of encouragement.

"He hurt me—with the stuff he said about Skip."

"But how does he make you feel otherwise?"

"What if it was all wishful thinking on my part?"

"Do you really believe that?"

"Abby, I know it doesn't make perfect sense, but in a way, after Skip died, I felt like he'd let me down. I mean, I'd opened up and let myself lean on him. Then he pulled the rug out from under me." She looked pleadingly at her friend.

"A lot of people feel that way when a loved one dies."

Jo sighed. "I felt guilty about that for a long time. And then, you know, I was just getting to the point where I thought I could take a chance on Cam…"

"Sometimes you have to take a chance to get what you want."

The two women ate in silence for several minutes, neither one of them making much progress with the meal. Finally Abby wrapped up her half-eaten sandwich and stood up. "I'd better get back to my office. I've got a patient coming at one o'clock."

"Thanks for lunch. And for…provoking me."

Abby grinned. "No charge."

After her friend left, Jo sat staring out the window at the office building across the alley. For the first time in weeks, she felt the dark cloud that had been hovering over her begin to lift. She had only thought about certain parts of that last angry conversation with Cam. Now she allowed herself to remember the look on his face and some of the things he'd said. He'd talked about sorrow and anger, but she hadn't let herself react to the pain in his voice. When he'd said he'd been afraid of losing her, she'd been thinking that he already had.

Now she couldn't help wondering what it would be like to see him again. The more she wondered, the more she felt something tender and protective inside her chest swell with hope.

Abby had said you had to take risks to get what you wanted. Wasn't everything in life a risk?

What was the worst thing that could happen, she asked herself. That she and Cam couldn't work things out. Well, Abby had made her see one thing pretty clearly: they didn't have a chance the way things stood.

The wedding rehearsal would be neutral territory. Maybe if he didn't make the first move, she would.

THE NEXT EVENING as she stood before the ornately carved cheval glass in Laura's guest room, Jo surveyed her appearance with more interest than she'd shown in weeks. The strain of hiding and of being estranged from Cam had both taken their toll. She'd lost weight, and her face was pale. She'd compensated with a bit more makeup than she usually used. Earlier that afternoon she'd driven her rental car out to Columbia and found a silk shift at Woodies that helped camouflage her thin figure.

Dinner was in a private room upstairs at the Brass Elephant, an elegant restaurant in a restored town house on Charles Street. Its unusual name came from the brass fixtures throughout the building that were shaped like elephant heads. Steve had been pleased with the choice of location because he knew Abby was providing a little reminder of his years in India. The meal would be followed by a walk-through at the Greenspring Valley Church where Abby and Steve were getting married.

To minimize the risks to Jo, Abby had waited until the last minute to make firm arrangements for the party. It was understood that Jo and Laura would arrive a bit after the stated dinner hour and slip in a back door of the restaurant. Jo wasn't thinking about security as she and Laura drove down to Charles Street. In fact, she could hardly contain the keen feeling of anticipation that had been building ever since she'd talked to Abby that afternoon.

Her steps were quick as she hurried toward the little dining room several steps ahead of Laura. When she walked through the archway, she noticed two things almost simultaneously. The bride-to-be was looking anxiously toward the door. And Cameron Randolph was conspicuously absent from among the assembled members of the wedding party.

Chapter Twelve

The minute Abby spotted the maid of honor, she came rushing forward. "Oh, Jo, I'm so sorry. He called a few minutes ago to say he wouldn't be here." There was no need to name the man they were talking about.

Jo tried to keep the disappointment off her face.

Abby squeezed her hand. "I don't know what to say. I shouldn't have gotten your hopes up."

"It's not your fault." Jo turned quickly away toward the bar that had been set up in the corner. She didn't really want anything to drink. Still, she needed a few minutes to pull herself together before she faced the happy throng assembled to honor Steve and Abby.

Cam didn't show up for the actual rehearsal, either. Jo found herself playing her matron of honor role opposite an empty spot on the stone floor.

It was no less empty than the hollow that had opened up inside her chest. She'd gotten her hopes up, and they'd been dashed.

She went through the rehearsal in a daze, unaware that her friends had thrown a sort of protective net around her— both physically and emotionally.

But the man standing in the shadows at the back of the church with neck rigid and jaw clenched was very aware of what was happening.

Denise...

Jo O'Malley...

Denise...

They were together in church again.

The first time he'd seen her standing under the stained-glass windows, it was like a light from heaven had streamed in on both of them.

Watching her now, the feeling came back, strong and sure the way it had been in the beginning. He needed her again.

The craving to have her with him once more almost choked him, almost choked off all rational thought. Sudden energy surged through his body, and he almost started up the aisle. Then at the last minute, he caught himself. Not now when everybody was watching. But soon. He had the power. And when he chose to use it, no one could stand in his way.

IT WAS STRANGE, Jo thought as she stood in front of the inexpensive door mirror in Noel's hallway, how different she felt this morning. The dime-store looking glass reflected back a slightly distorted image, elongating the middle of her body as if to accent her recently acquired gauntness.

She tugged at her skirt. But that didn't make it hang any better over her bony hips. Two months ago when Abby had selected the elaborate blue velvet gown, Jo had simply felt overdressed in the rich creation. Now she was going to feel like an out-and-out fool walking down the aisle.

Except that no one was going to be looking at her, she told herself. They'd all be focused on Steve and Abby. Maybe she could even slip away right after the receiving line and come back here to lick her wounds.

She hadn't slept much. She hadn't been able to choke down more than a cup of weak tea for breakfast. And she hadn't been able to get her mind off Cameron Randolph.

After that talk with Abby, she'd been stupid enough to

be optimistic. Well, Abby had made a mistake in her analysis of Cam. Because she was in love and getting married, she'd blithely assumed that the rest of the couples in the world would work out their problems.

She made an effort to bring her mind back to the wedding. At least there was one thing to look forward to. Whoever was making calls to redheaded maids of honor almost always stopped as soon as the big event was over. After today, she'd only have to worry about Eddie Cahill, she thought with a grim little laugh.

All her cynicism evaporated, however, when she walked into the room at the back of the church where Abby and her attendants were waiting for the service to begin.

The bride looked radiant and excited and nervous in her taffeta gown studded with tiny pearls. When she smiled uncertainly at her, Jo crossed the room and embraced her friend.

"I'm so sorry about last night," Abby apologized again.

"It's all right. Really. Don't let anything spoil today." Jo took a step back. "You look beautiful."

"Thank you. So do you."

Jo stifled the automatic denial that sprang to her lips. If the bride wanted to entertain that kind of fantasy, why put up a protest?

Laura and two friends who'd gone to school with Abby fluttered around trying to make conversation. They were all a bit teary as they listened to the organ music drifting in from the chapel.

Finally one of the deacons and Abby's father appeared at the door and told them it was show time. He didn't look any too calm himself, Jo thought as his daughter took his arm and they started for the back of the church. Probably they were both glad they didn't have to walk down the aisle alone.

Which was not the case with Jo. The bouquet of rosebuds

and baby's breath trembled in her hands as she followed them out. She glanced at the private security guard stationed by the door. He was there for her, she thought and squeezed her eyes shut for a minute. *Don't let anything mess up Abby's wedding,* she prayed silently as she took her place at the central portal.

In front of her, the church was filled to capacity, the crowd waiting in hushed expectation.

Then, as the organ music reached a crescendo, Jo was marching down the aisle, her eyes fixed on the stained-glass window above the altar so that she saw the assemblage on either side of her only in her peripheral vision. The bridesmaids and ushers had already taken their places amid the red roses perfuming the chancel. Then the organist began to play Wagner's traditional wedding march. A minute later, Abby and her father joined the group in front of the altar.

The music stopped, and a door to the right of the choir opened. The groom and his best man stepped out. Jo knew she had been waiting for this moment. She was sure all other eyes were focused on Steve, but she couldn't take hers off Cam. Her breath caught in her throat as once more she was struck by how incredibly handsome he looked in a tuxedo. Except that now his face was pale and his features were drawn. Only his eyes held the energy she remembered. They seemed to glitter in the warm light of the chapel as they locked with hers. For a dizzying moment, some wordless communication passed between them.

"This is the day the Lord has made. Let us rejoice and be glad in it," the minister said.

Cam continued to watch her intently. She gave him an uncertain smile, and he nodded almost imperceptibly.

"God created us male and female, and gave us marriage so that husband and wife may help and comfort each other, living faithfully together in plenty and in want, in joy and sorrow..."

The words took on a special meaning as she and Cam stared at each other. In front of her, she heard Steve and Abby exchanging vows.

"Abby, do you take Steve to be your husband and promise before God and these witnesses to be his loving and faithful wife...?"

"I do."

Jo saw Cam's expression soften. Her hand reached out toward him. When she realized they were standing five feet apart, she dropped her arm back to her side. A current seemed to flow between them. Or was it just because she wanted to believe in the power of love?

When the service was over, the organ music swelled up as Steve and Abby kissed. At the same time, Jo felt emotion swell in her chest.

With radiant smiles on their faces, the newly married couple hurried back down the aisle. Cam's eyes were not on the bride and groom. He was staring at Jo. He caught her hand and simply held it for a moment as if he'd forgotten where they were. Then they fell into place behind Steve and Abby. As they reached the back of the church, the rest of the party automatically headed for the limousines waiting to take them to the reception. Cam looked around, and Jo had the feeling he was about to pull her out of the line. Then one of the deacons appeared and ushered them out to the waiting cars. They piled in beside Laura and another bridesmaid.

"We have to talk," Cam whispered.

"Yes."

But there was no opportunity for a private conversation as the car sped toward the exclusive Greenspring Valley country club where the reception was being held. And there was no chance to talk as they stood in the endless receiving line making polite conversation with friends and family.

Jo felt a thousand butterflies clamoring for attention in

her stomach. Beside her, she could feel Cam's tension building. Her own nerves were drawing as tight as an overwound clock spring. She shifted from one foot to the other as she gave Cam little sideways glances.

Finally he muttered something under his breath, grabbed her hand, and yanked her out of the line. "I think they can finish without us," he commented as he looked around for a place where they could be alone. The lobby was crowded with elegantly dressed guests, and heads turned in their direction as they made their way through the throng.

Cam didn't waver. His face set in determined lines, he pulled Jo through double doors and they found themselves in the serving pantry off the kitchen, surrounded by rolling carts of food destined for the buffet tables.

"I thought you knew where you were going," Jo observed.

Cam shrugged. "I'm through hiding from you. We have to talk. Now."

As they stood facing each other, words seemed to freeze in Jo's throat. And Cam wasn't doing much better.

Suddenly the ice jam broke and apologies came tumbling out.

"I didn't mean to hurt you."

"I should have called you."

"I don't know what I was thinking about."

"I—"

Before the sentence could be completed, the door flew open, and a man bolted into the room.

Startled, they both whirled to face him. Suddenly details registered in Jo's mind: the brown hair. The scar on the right side of his upper lip. The malevolent look in those dark eyes she remembered from that day in court.

Eddie Cahill.

From under his coat, he pulled a sawed-off shotgun.

"You thought you were so clever switching cars and

houses. But I've been watching you and I've got you now, Ms. Super Detective,'' he gloated, his voice seething with hate. ''When you play hardball with Eddie Cahill, you'd better watch your back.''

Time seemed to slow as Jo shrank away from the man who had been stalking her for weeks. He had killed Karen. He had said he was going to kill her, too. He was going to do it. Now. Just when she and Cam had found each other again. In his face, she saw how much he was enjoying her agony and his triumph.

Out of the corner of her eye, she detected a slight movement. Cam was edging toward Eddie.

No! The warning was frozen in her throat.

The gun wavered as if Eddie had suddenly become aware that he and Jo weren't the only people in the room. At that moment, her hip bumped against one of the serving carts. Another, heaped with shrimp and cocktail sauce, was immediately to her left. Acting on desperate reflex, she reached out and shoved it with all her might toward the man who had sworn to kill her. It plowed into his waist, and Eddie grunted just as the gun went off. The shot went wild. Plump shrimp and red cocktail sauce flew into the air—some of it landing on Jo's dress and the rest splattering to the floor.

Cam dived toward Eddie and wrestled him to the tile. There was another shot as they fought for the gun.

''Cam, Cam,'' Jo screamed, her voice at last unfrozen.

The shots had attracted attention, and moments later, the door flew open. Steve Claiborne bounded into the room, his face grim, his body primed for action. Behind him, moving more slowly, was one of the Franklins' security guards. He was staggering and holding his chin.

Jo barely noticed the intrusion. Her eyes were glued to the men at her feet. One of them had been shot. But who?

They stopped struggling, and a groan issued from the

tangled pile of arms and legs. Jo's whole body went rigid with tension. For several seconds, nothing happened. Then Cam slowly sat up. He was holding the gun. And Eddie Cahill was holding his side. Blood oozed from between his clenched fingers.

As Steve swiftly assessed the damage, Jo dropped down beside Cam. "Are you all right?"

"Yes."

"Thank God." She was reaching for him when his eyes riveted to the red splotch spread across her dress.

"Jo—what—are you—?"

She followed his gaze and noticed the stain for the first time. "Cocktail sauce."

Cam sagged with relief.

"Where were you?" Steve was looking pointedly at the security guard.

"He hit me. Afraid I was down for the count, but I'm all right now." All business, he knelt over the gunman. "Cahill's going to make it. But he's through harassing you."

"Good." Jo stared at the man sprawled on the floor. The attack had happened so fast. Her brain was just starting to catch up with the action. After Eddie Cahill had killed his wife, he'd been waiting for his opportunity to ambush her. The excitement of the wedding reception had given him the perfect chance.

The wedding! This was happening in the middle of Steve and Abby's wedding reception. Jo felt her face heat as she shot the tuxedo-clad groom a mortified glance. "I'm making a shambles of your big day," she muttered.

"Don't be ridiculous." Steve didn't miss a beat. "You've just livened up the occasion. The important thing is that the two of you are all right."

Jo looked at Cam. "You know, I was really looking forward to the shrimp. Too bad, I'm wearing them and the sauce."

"Damn! Another missed opportunity to field test my spot remover," he struggled to match her ironic tone.

A blond waiter pushed his way through to the front of the crowd that had gathered around them. Jo remembered him from the reception Abby's mother had given. "Let me give you a hand," he offered kindly. "I think I've got something that will take that stain out."

"Thanks."

She was about to follow him out of the room when Cam reached toward her. They clenched hands, and for several heartbeats she was caught up in the sensation of his strong fingers gripping hers.

Oh, Cam, don't ever let me go again.

"Come on. You want to get back to the party," the waiter urged.

"Yes. Right." Jo allowed herself to be led away, conscious of the tight hold on her arm. The man was gripping her as forcefully as Cam had. At the door, she hesitated.

"I'll meet you back here," Cam told her, and she knew that before they returned to the reception they were going to settle their own unfinished business.

"Yes."

The waiter gave her a little tug. "Hurry. Before the stain sets."

She nodded, vaguely confused and uneasy. Something was wrong. Something— But the experience she'd just been through had robbed her of the ability to think clearly.

They headed down the hall toward the employees' washroom.

"What's your name?" She tried to start a conversation.

"Art."

"I guess the staff has to be equipped for anything."

"That's right. I'm equipped for anything."

In the next moment she felt cold metal against her ribs.

"This time it's not your friend Rossini playing jokes. I've got a gun. Bring your hands together behind your back."

Jo briefly considered bolting—or screaming. The menacing jab of the gun against her side convinced her it was safer to play along. Seconds after she'd complied with the order, she felt metal cuffs clamp around her wrists. They were hidden from view by the man in back of her.

Panic welled up in her throat as she tried to shift her hands. Her chances of escape had just dwindled to near zero.

"Move it." Then he was shoving her through a door and into the parking lot.

Jo's mind scrambled for sanity—for rational explanations. Was this an accomplice of Eddie?

She stumbled. The man with the gun cursed as he jostled her down the sidewalk.

They were almost to a gray van. Panic and little flashes of mental clarity pinged through her mind with lightning speed. He was going to shove her inside and drive away. When he did, no one would know what had happened to her.

Was there anything she could drop? Some clue she could leave? Not with her hands manacled behind her back.

What about her shoe? No, he'd see it. Then she remembered the gold band that was still on her right hand. With her thumb, she worked it down her finger. As it dropped she held her breath. It didn't hit the concrete and give her away. It was on the grass.

The door of the van slid open. Once Jo was inside, her kidnapper's tense expression changed to one of confidence. As he secured the manacle to a ring riveted into the wall, a little giggle escaped from his lips. Her heart froze. She recognized the sound. The man on the phone! The man who had told her exactly what he was going to do to her.

A scream tore from her lips as the van pulled out of the parking lot.

ABBY, WHO HAD GONE searching for her new husband, joined the group in the kitchen.

"What happened?" she asked, aghast as she spotted the wounded man still lying on the floor.

"Eddie Cahill, the escaped drug dealer who was after Jo," Steve explained. "He's gonna live to serve out the rest of his term. On top of ones for murder and attempted murder."

"Where's Jo?" The bride's voice was still anxious.

"Cleaning up." Cam gestured toward the mess on the floor. "I'm afraid Cahill turned the kitchen into a giant shrimp cocktail."

Abby lifted her white dress away from the ruined party food, and Steve slung his arm around her shoulder.

As the groom recounted the action for the bride, more and more employees gathered to listen. But Cam hardly paid any attention to the narrative as he kept glancing at the door.

The police came to cart away Eddie Cahill, and he had to answer some questions.

"We'll need to talk to Ms. O'Malley, too."

"She'll be right back."

The minutes stretched.

"Where is she?"

"I'll get her."

Cam went out in the hall and glanced around, fighting the tension knotting his stomach. There was no sign of Jo or the waiter who had hustled her out of the room so quickly.

"Excuse me," he asked one of the passing busboys. "Did you see the maid of honor and one of the waiters?"

"The lady with the big red stain on her dress?"

"Yes."

"They went through there." The boy gestured toward a door and hurried off.

The knot tightened into a strangle-hold as Cam jogged down the hall and pushed open the door. He was only half surprised to find that it led to the parking lot behind the kitchen.

Nothing moved as he walked toward the catering trucks and employee vehicles. Maybe the busboy had been mistaken.

If his head hadn't been bowed in concentration, he would have missed a small piece of metal in the grass. It winked in the sunlight.

Cam stooped to pick it up. Jo's ring. The one she'd never taken off.

Oh, my God! What had happened to her? Clasping the ring in his fist, he dashed back toward the building.

WITH HER HANDS angled in back of her and secured to the wall, every sway of the van sent a painful jolt through Jo's arms and shoulders. And every jolt was like a stab of fear piercing her breast.

Get away. Escape, her mind screamed. *Before he— Before he—*

Physically flight was impossible. The temptation to shut down her mind, to withdraw to a deep, guarded place within herself where she'd be safe was overwhelming.

The vehicle jounced over a bump and a wrenching jolt of pain ricocheted down Jo's arms. It brought her back to reality.

She lifted her head. For the first time since she'd been shoved into the van, she took in her surroundings. The interior was filled with boxes and cartons of wires and circuit boards and tools—along with a small workbench. Racks of electronic equipment lined the walls.

The implications suddenly hit her in the gut like a street fighter's punch. The transmitter Cam had found on her car. The mystery of the malfunctioning garage door opener. The electromagnetic pulse. The television gone haywire. Eddie Cahill hadn't done any of that.

Her eyes shot to the man in the driver's seat. He didn't look back at her. But she could hear him muttering in a low, urgent voice.

The sound was no longer electronically distorted, yet the speech rhythms were the same ones she knew so well from the phone calls.

Now he had her. Just like—just like—Margaret Clement. *No. Oh, God no.*

Desperately she wrenched at the ring that bound her to the wall. She was no match for the thick metal.

Instead she forced herself to listen to the words spewing forth from the man driving the van. He was talking to himself. No, he was really talking to her. The same phrases over and over.

"Wedding party... Denise... Maid of honor... Like an angel... Redheaded bitch."

"Denise?" she gasped. "You have the wrong person. Let me go. Please, let me go."

He swiveled around and fixed her with an angry look. "I liked you, you know that? With your short hair and your slim little body, you reminded me of a boy. And I thought I could—I could..." His voice trailed off for a moment, and she saw his features tighten. "I could have done it!" he insisted, but there was an undercurrent of uncertainty in the assertion. "I asked you to marry me, and you laughed at me. You shouldn't have laughed, Denise. You shouldn't have laughed because I needed you. You could have saved me. You could have changed my life."

Even as she caught a note of desperation in his tone, Jo

cringed away from his piercing stare. "Please, I—I—don't know you," she stammered.

"Sure you do, Denise."

"Please—"

"Don't play games with me, angel face. You'll make me angry."

He turned back to the road.

CAM YANKED at the door that led back into the hallway. It was locked from the inside. He might have gone around to the front of the building, but he wasn't exactly thinking clearly. Raising his fists he began to pound against the metal barrier.

"Okay, keep your pants on," somebody shouted from the other side. Then a man in a white apron threw the door open.

Cam didn't stop to explain. Instead he pushed past him and sprinted down the hall to the employees' washroom. A startled salad girl looked up from the sink and then shrank away as he advanced on her.

"The woman with the stained dress?" he demanded sharply.

"Haven't seen her since she left the kitchen. And I came in here right after that."

She had hardly finished the last sentence before Cam was on his way back to the pantry area. Steve and the security guard were still talking to Abby. He'd been gone for less than five minutes. It just seemed like five hundred. The policeman who'd taken his statement had given up waiting for Jo and started interviewing some of the kitchen help.

"Cam, what's wrong?" Abby gasped when she saw the wild look on his face.

"Jo and that waiter have both disappeared."

"Maybe they're still in the washroom," Abby suggested.

"I checked. They're not there." Cam held up the ring.

"I found this outside in the grass beside the parking lot. It's Jo's. It couldn't have slipped off her finger. She had to have taken it off deliberately."

Abby stared at Cam. "But why? The danger's over. You got Eddie."

"Then where's Jo? I think the waiter hustled her down the hall and outside into a car."

Abby gulped. "The phone caller. Jo just about proved it wasn't Eddie."

"The waiter was at the Franklins' house. I remember him because I was thinking he didn't exactly fit in," Steve entered the conversation.

"The maids of honor...the ones Jo talked to..." Abby rambled. "One of them was kidnapped. And she hasn't been heard from again."

Hoping against hope, they dispersed to separate areas of the building to search for Jo. They were joined by the security guard and police officer still on the scene. By the time they'd finished, everyone at the reception had heard about the incident.

The grim news ended the party. The guests departed, leaving the bar fully stocked and buffet table loaded with food. The bride and groom and the best man hardly noticed.

Laura, Lou Rossini, and Noel joined the circle of anxious friends in the kitchen where Cam was drilling the staff. He found out quickly that the waiter's name was Arthur Thorp.

"What do you know about him?" Cam demanded.

Various staff members contributed bits of information, Thorp looked to be in his early thirties. He was a temporary employee of Perfection Catering Service who only worked at peak periods.

Another one of the waiters remembered that he hadn't known the business very well at the beginning. But he'd sure been a handy guy to have around. Several times he'd pulled Perfection's chestnuts out of the fire by stepping in to fix malfunctioning kitchen equipment.

Cam looked up from the middle of the interrogation to find Abby ushering Evan Hamill into the kitchen.

"I decided we need the detective who's been in on the case from the beginning," she explained.

"Yeah," he agreed, his voice grim.

Hamill's arrival put the situation into bleak perspective. Finding Jo wasn't going to be easy. And every second she was missing put her life in greater jeopardy.

Chapter Thirteen

Art opened the door of the van and unfastened the handcuffs from the ring on the wall. Lowering her arms brought a sting of pain to Jo's numb limbs.

She shrank away from his touch as he forced her out of the van. But he kept a firm hold on her biceps as he hurried her through a large garage.

They were parked next to a silver Toyota. He caught her glancing at it.

"Alternative transportation in case anyone's looking for my van," he explained. Then his voice changed as he hustled her past a workbench and machine tools. "We're going outside for a minute. If you scream, you're dead. Got it?" The gun barrel in her back emphasized the order.

"Yes," Jo whispered.

The air outside was cold and raw. It was a tantalizing hint of freedom that was quickly squelched as Jo's captor bustled her into a backyard full of weeds and screened with unclipped privet hedges. Jaunty music floated toward her on the wind. Something strident and jarring would have been more appropriate.

The upbeat tune persisted. It was being played by a band. The same one that she'd heard in the background on several of the phone calls.

She was ushered quickly up rickety steps that led to a

back porch. Her kidnapper paused to turn off a sophisticated security system that looked out of place in its seedy surroundings. A Randolph deluxe model, Jo thought.

The house was about the same vintage as her own Roland Park home, but no one had kept up the interior. In the dim light, she could see that the wood floors were unpolished and uneven, old wallpaper hung down in yellowing strips in several places, and cobwebs festooned every corner. The air of mustiness made it hard to take a deep breath.

The whole effect made Jo feel closed-in and queasy. She fought back her revulsion and ordered her detective's mind to store as many details as possible.

When she lingered, her captor gave her a shove down the hall. It was lined with several closed doors. He directed her toward the second one on the right. She breathed a sigh of relief when she saw he wasn't taking her upstairs where she'd have to climb down a drainpipe or something to get away. She stopped short when she saw the door was guarded by a separate security monitor.

Taking her arm, Art jostled her inside where she squinted in the bright light that contrasted so sharply with the rest of the interior.

He pushed her toward a narrow bed lined up against one wall. At least it wasn't *the* bed, the brass one in the video. But a ring and a chain dangled from the wall.

"Please…" Jo didn't try to keep the quaver out of her voice. Maybe if she played on his sympathy. "Please, my arms hurt so much. Don't chain me."

Art laughed. "You expect me to trust you? The day I snatched your purse, you kicked me."

"You—" The revelation numbed her to the bone.

"Sit down," he ordered.

Jo's glance flitted to the bed, which was covered with a homespun quilt, and then back to the gun trained on her chest.

Her captor followed her gaze. "I don't want to shoot you, but I will if I have to," he growled.

She sat gingerly on the very edge of the bed while he secured one hand to a cuff that dangled from a chain attached to the wall.

When he was finished, he stood over her for endless moments contemplating her slender frame. Jo steeled herself to keep from quaking like a sapling in a windstorm. She didn't raise her gaze to meet his. She didn't want him to see the horror in her eyes.

Now that he was completely in control, his voice took on a subtle note of satisfaction. "I worked hard to get things ready for you."

Crossing to the closet, he opened the door. Like a mouse dropped into a cage with a snake, Jo fought paralysis as she followed his movements.

When he brought out several garments on hangers, she gasped in surprise. Two of them were the suit and apricot cocktail dress that had disappeared from the cleaners. The others were slacks and blouses he'd stolen from her closet the night he'd rigged the television set.

There were other personal things, too, she saw, as she looked around the room. Novels that she'd read were on the bedside table. The lipstick from her purse was on the dresser, along with a number of the toilet articles she used. And then there was the quilt, so much like the one on her own bed at home.

Such simple, everyday objects. Yet because they were here in this room, terror threatened to carry her away in its undertow.

The room was like a carefully constructed stage setting. Unreal, yet with the appearance of reality. What drama was going to be enacted? She was pretty sure she knew what the director had in mind for the finale. Her only chance was to change the script.

"For dinner, I'll fix you some of your favorite foods. I looked in your trash and found out the kind of stuff you like to cook."

He'd been spying on her for weeks, collecting her things, dogging her every move. He'd even pawed through her trash! Nausea warred with terror.

Then she realized he might have made a fatal mistake. Her trash. If it was after the camera— No, she was grasping at straws. But if he had— If he had—

Jo tried to keep any hint of hope out of her voice. "You know so much about me," she whispered instead. "You must know who I am. I'm Jo O'Malley. I'm not the woman who hurt you. I'm not Denise."

"Shut up!"

Jo nodded. *Careful,* she warned herself. *You just made a mistake.*

"Denise," he repeated, staring at her, his eyes slightly out of focus. "Denise. You were going to make an honest man of me. And then you slapped me. You shouldn't have done that. Do you understand?"

"Yes," Jo whispered. She fought to keep her teeth from chattering and her body from trembling. The man who had her in his clutches was stark-raving mad. Anything could set him off.

His eyes seemed to snap back into focus. "You're Jo O'Malley. But you look like Denise. You're playing her role in the wedding. You'll do fine as her stand-in. Only this time, things are going to come out differently.

Her control cracked. "You can't get away with this. The police will catch you."

"No they won't. The police can't trace the phone calls. And they don't know who I am." He giggled and reached up to his full head of blond hair. "You thought you were so clever with your costumes. Mine are better." With a deft motion, he tugged at the covering. It was a wig, and it came away in his hand to reveal stringy brown hair.

Jo couldn't stifle a tiny exclamation. He grinned at her as he tossed the wig into the trash can. "The punk hairdo was another one of my disguises," he boasted. Crossing to the mirror he pulled a layer of rubber makeup away from one cheek and then from the other. More rubber came off his nose. "Good stuff," he commented. "I should have used it that day in Dundalk. But I didn't think you were going to claw my face."

Jo watched the skinlike appliances follow the wig into the trash. She hadn't spotted the camouflage.

"No more Art Thorp," he said airily. "After this, I'll have to build up another persona. Get a job at another catering company."

"Art Thorp?"

"That's who they think I am." He giggled again. "They don't know anything about the real me. Art Nugent." He was still speaking into the mirror, suddenly he turned and faced Jo again. "I've been waiting for weeks to tell you all this," he crowed.

"You know so much. Like the stuff you told me on the phone. About Cam."

"I just pointed you toward the files."

"That wasn't a lucky guess. You have inside information."

"Yes!"

The way he said the word brought a choking feeling to Jo's chest. But she kept up the game.

"I was impressed."

He took a step forward, and she thought again about all the sexual references he'd made in those tapes. She backed up on the narrow bed and found her shoulders pressed against the wall.

He smiled. But only with his lips, not his eyes. "You

don't like me any more than Denise did. She was just pretending to be nice. Until the wedding was over.''

''That's not true. I do like you.''

''I know what you're trying to do with your clever little conversation. You're trying to feed my ego—and get information. It won't make any difference what you do. I have you, and Cameron Randolph doesn't. I keep wondering, was it chance or fate that paired you with Randolph that night of the Franklin party?''

''Why do you care so much about Cam?''

''Your boyfriend is that inventor bastard who thinks he's the king of Randolph Enterprises. The man who wouldn't let me into the design department, even after Collin recommended me. His majesty Cameron Randolph still thought I wasn't good enough. Well, I was. And I paid him back.'' He couldn't repress one of the giggles that had made her skin crawl when he'd talked to her on the phone. Only now they were in the same room. ''Too bad Skip O'Malley isn't around to sweat out where you are. I beat him once, but I can't touch him now. I can only make sure Randolph pays.''

At that moment, Jo was too stunned to reply. Later she thought about good and bad luck—and what it meant to her that Art Nugent chose that moment to turn and bolt from the room.

GOOD AND BAD LUCK. Was this all going to hinge on good and bad luck, Cam wondered as he sat before his computer, which was swiftly running through number and letter combinations.

As the digits flashed on the screen, he took off his glasses and rubbed the bridge of his nose. He looked like a man who had gone ten rounds with Mike Tyson. Then he shook his head and roused himself from the dark mood.

You're going to make it, Jo. We'll find you. It's going to be all right, he prayed. He had to believe that. Because if they didn't, there was no more meaning to his life.

The door opened behind him, and he looked around expectantly. It was Abby. Silently she shook her head, and he turned quickly back to the screen so that she wouldn't see the raw disappointment on his face.

He, Laura, Abby, Steve and Noel had established a command post at his town house. Most of them were still out checking various leads and looking for clues they might have missed at Jo's house or office. He was manning the computer link to the police department and doing his own checking of data bases.

"You and Steve should be off on your honeymoon," he said in a low voice.

"You don't really think we could leave now, do you?"

"I wasn't suggesting that you go. I'm just trying to tell you I feel guilty."

"Don't."

"If I'd been straight with her, this wouldn't have happened."

"The man who grabbed her had every detail planned. He would have gotten to her anyway."

Cam had been over all the arguments with himself. Why punish Abby by continuing the discussion with her? He glanced at the screen. The program didn't need any help from him at this point, so that his mind was free to rehash the events of the past few hours.

There had been no problem convincing Hamill or the Baltimore County police that Jo's life was in jeopardy. Cam had been amazed at the way the detective had cut through red tape that would have tied another man's hands for days. Because the Social Security Administration was in Baltimore, Hamill had worked personally with a number of executives in the government agency. One of them agreed to go down to the office and check out Art Thorp, even though it was Saturday afternoon. He called back with the news that an area man named Art Thorp had applied for a social security number three years ago. Regular deposits had been made into his account since then by employers.

The recent vintage of the account almost certainly meant the kidnapper was using an assumed name. And the address on file was a town house in Camden occupied by a young couple who knew nothing about a man named Art Thorp.

The information from the Social Security Administration led nowhere. Also, Thorp's personnel file had disappeared from the catering office, and his phone number had been pulled from the office Rolodex. On the other hand, a number of the employees at the catering service remembered Art Thorp's gray van—which had been parked near the entrance through which Jo had been hustled out of the building. Thorp had been very secretive about what was inside. When another waiter had recently asked him for a ride to the bus stop because his car was in the shop, Thorp had made what sounded like a flimsy excuse not to grant the small favor.

The incident in itself wouldn't have been significant, except that the waiter remembered looking at the license plate on the van. Although he didn't recall the whole number-letter combination, he was sure that the last two digits were 64—because that was the year he'd been born.

Hamill had arranged for the Randolph Enterprise computer system to access the records at the Motor Vehicles Administration. Cam was now laboriously searching the data base, looking for vehicles with that particular combination in the last two positions. There were thousands. Which meant they needed to eliminate most of the tags from the list.

Abby came up behind Cam again and stood watching the numbers moving across the screen. "You must be tired."

"I'm all right."

"Want some dinner? I brought some food back from the reception. I figured we might as well eat it."

"Maybe later."

Abby reached out and began to knead the tense muscles of his shoulders.

Cam sighed. "That feels good. But what would your fiancé think if he came in right now?"

"Her husband, buddy. He's her husband." Steve regarded them from the doorway. He'd come in quietly and chosen to wait for the right moment to make his presence known.

"Luckily he knows you're just good friends," Steve continued. "Otherwise, he'd break a few important bones in your body. Besides, you've got a girl of your own. As soon as we get her back, she can take over the R and R duties."

JO SAT STARING at the closed door, feeling Art's presence on the other side. Her ears detected tiny clicks as he set the security alarm.

She raised her hand and looked at the metal chain and cuff. Medieval technology. But the security system was state-of-the-art. Her captor was covering all the bases. At least she hadn't given him another advantage by blurting the first thing that had sprung to her tongue when he'd mentioned Cam and Skip.

But how did you act with a lunatic? How did you keep from setting him off? His grip on reality was so fragile. Sometimes he didn't even know who she was.

Denise. Margaret. Jo.

The depth of Nugent's insanity brought a wave of cold sweat sweeping across her body. Then, by brute force, she pulled her mind back from the brink of its own destruction. Maybe his previous victims had simply given up. She wasn't going to do that.

She had too much to live for. *Cam. Oh, Cam,* she thought. *I'm coming back to you.*

For precious moments she let her lids flutter closed and allowed herself to think about him. How it had been in his arms. How it would be again. Warm. Loved. Cherished. Everything she'd secretly longed for but hadn't dared seek.

At first in the fantasy, he simply held her and told her over and over that everything was going to be all right. But as she clung to him, he began to talk to her in a low, urgent voice.

"Use what he said to you. He's given you some clues. Some important information."

"Yes!"

Deliberately she focused on Art Nugent's mad babblings. He'd worked for Randolph Electronics, gotten angry and paid Cam back for not letting him into the design department. He talked as if he hated Cam. Could she use that? How? She had to think of a plan.

Jo glanced at the closed door again. How long did she have before he came back? And what could she accomplish in his absence?

Methodically, as if she were going over a crime scene for clues, Jo began to inspect her surroundings. The first thing she determined was that the security system covered the window as well as the door.

Next she began to inspect the bed. It was made of iron and bolted to the floor. The ring that attached her chain to the wall seemed solidly mounted. Perhaps she could find some tool to pry it loose.

The length of the chain was also of considerable interest. It allowed her to move a few feet away from the bed. She could reach the dresser. Hopefully there was something in one of the drawers that would be useful.

She had gotten up when a noise in the hall stopped her in her tracks. The realization that her captor was coming back was like a blast of frigid air against her skin, and she wrapped her arms around her shoulders. What was his timetable? How fast did he plan to move? What she needed was to buy herself some time.

Buy some time! The phrase triggered an idea—the plan she'd been searching for began to jell.

Do it right, she warned herself. *Don't let him catch on to what you're trying to pull.*

THERE WAS STILL no way to narrow down the thousands of license numbers flagged by Cam's computer program. The police didn't have a clue about the real identity of the man holding Jo. And Cam felt as if the seconds of her life were ticking by.

Abby had gone off to interview some of the other women from the phone company list.

Laura still hadn't come back from Jo's office.

Cam wandered into the den, sat down on the sofa and began to fiddle with the stereo system. The last time Jo had been here, they'd listened to Kenny Rogers.

He found the compact disc and began to play it again, unable to hold back the wave of longing for Jo that would have knocked him off his feet if he'd been standing up.

You'll be here with me again, he promised silently. *Safe and sound. Then I'll tell you all the things I was going to say when Cahill burst into the kitchen.*

He'd thought the music would make him feel closer to her. It only made things worse.

Getting up again, he went back to his home office. Hamill had dropped off the tapes from Jo's answering machine. Maybe if he played them, he'd get some clue.

There was nothing useful, but because he'd just been listening to music, the faint tune in the background caught his attention. The police had told them the notes were too distorted to recapture. But his equipment was probably better than theirs. If he ran the recording through his computer, he could bring the tune into sharper focus. Picking up the tapes, he started for his electronics workshop.

It took several hours of fiddling, but Cam finally got an acceptable rendition of the music. It sounded like a college football song, but sports had never been one of his big interests.

Had Art Thorp, or whatever his name was, been watching the game of the week when he'd made the call? That seemed unlikely.

People had come in and out of the house while he'd been working but no one had disturbed him. But when Laura wandered back to see what he was doing, the music made her linger in the doorway.

"Why are you playing that?" she asked.

He turned bloodshot eyes toward her. "You don't recognize it, do you?"

"Of course I recognize it. It's 'Stand up Towson.'"

"What?"

She sang a few bars. "'Stand up Towson, Stand up Towson, Strike that note of fame.' It's my old high-school song. Why are you playing it?"

"You never heard the tapes?"

"Tapes?" She looked puzzled for a moment. "You mean the ones Jo got."

There was a note of excitement in his voice. "Yes. The song was in the background, but until I enhanced it, it was too faint to identify." He rewound the cassette and played it again. At one point the music stopped, backed up several bars, and started again. Later the drum was definitely out of synch with the rest of the instruments.

"It sounds like the band practicing," Laura mused.

"Which means that the place he was calling from must be within hailing range of the high-school football field."

Cam pointed to the computer terminal, which was networked to the one in his office. "I've been racking my brain trying to figure out a way to narrow down the set of license numbers from the DMV. And you've just handed it to me. Where is Towson High School?"

"Off York Road. Near the Towson State University."

Cam brought up a gridded map of Baltimore County on the screen and zoomed in on the area around the school. "Right here." He pointed at the screen. "The bastard was right around here when he made two of those calls. Let's hope he still is."

As THE DOORKNOB turned, Jo schooled her features to match the role she needed to play.

Art was carrying a tray. The pinched look on his face, the spacey expression in his eyes told her that his hold on reality was slipping.

"Macaroni and cheese," he announced in a cheery voice that didn't sound as if it were coming from his lips. He set the tray down on the stand beside the bed. "One of your favorites."

Jo peered at the goopy, overcooked mess and pictured it sticking to the roof of her mouth. But she dutifully sat down on the edge of the bed and picked up the fork in her unbound hand. *Better follow directions. Better act as if you're eager to do what he says.*

A glass of Coke and a brownie completed the menu. As soon as she got home, she'd have to start eating better, Jo told herself. And she would get home, she added.

"So how long have you lived here?" she asked in a conversational tone.

"I grew up here. I kept the house after my parents died."

"Oh."

"Don't you like your dinner?" He sat down in the over-stuffed chair across from the bed.

"Oh, yes, it's very good. I just can't eat very fast," she murmured.

"You need to keep your strength up. We're going to have a very special time together, Denise. It's going to be the way it should have been all along." He was looking at her again in that strange, unfocused way. The tone of his voice was suddenly leaden with grief. "I killed a man, you know. He was my best friend."

"What?"

"It was an accident. Please. You have to believe me. I didn't mean for it to happen."

"I believe you."

"He just got caught in—in—the investigation. And he didn't know what else to do." Art buried his head in his hands for long seconds.

Jo hardly dared breath, wondering what this erratic madman would do next.

When he looked back up at her, his eyes were bright. "I was a lost soul. Damned to hell for everything I'd done. Then I met you. That day when I saw you standing there in church, I thought you were my salvation. You were an angel come to save me, Denise. Angel face, I called you. You were going to change my destiny. Make everything different. Make me pure and whole again."

"I will make you whole again. Just tell me what to do," she whispered.

"You had your chance. Now it's too late for you to do it on your own. I'm the one in charge."

Oh, God. He was so mixed up. Angels. Salvation. Destiny. Could she get him to remember who she really was—to think about her and Cam, again.

"You're such a good engineer," she said softly. "Cameron Randolph should have let you work in the design department."

"Yes!" His face reformed into a mask of anger.

"And now you're going to get even with him," Jo continued. "You're going to use me to get money out of Cam, aren't you?" she asked in a small, trembly voice.

The room grew very still. Jo didn't dare glance up. Instead she pushed a clump of macaroni and cheese around the plate.

"Yeah, that's right," Art finally said. "Your boyfriend is worth millions, and I'm going to get some of that undeserved cash away from him."

Jo was positive he hadn't thought of the idea until now. He'd been too focused on Denise being his salvation and how she'd betrayed him. "You're going to trade me for the money," Jo stated as if the assumption were fact.

He looked at her consideringly. "That depends on how you treat me, angel face. Maybe I'm going to get the money and keep you."

"The money is the important thing."

"No. The important thing is our relationship."

Jo held her breath.

"Denise wouldn't marry me. She wouldn't save me. Denise—" He stopped abruptly and stared at her face. "But you will."

The words and the way he was looking at her made a tide of nausea rise in her throat. What did she have to do to save him? She wanted to scream out her denial. It was all a mistake. He had the wrong woman. She was mixed up in his madness—and some fantasy he'd conjured up about salvation for his sins.

She hadn't really expected him to jump at the idea of letting her go. But collecting a ransom took time.

He got slowly out of the chair, and she stopped breathing.

"I'm going out for a while. When I come back, you can practice being nice to me," he said in a chatty voice as though the whole previous conversation had never existed.

Jo felt a mixture of elation and revulsion.

Time. He'd just given her some time. But then what?

Chapter Fourteen

Cam looked at the salmon pâté from the reception and thought that if he tried to swallow a bite, it would stick to the roof of his mouth. None of the food on the kitchen table held much appeal—to him or anyone else. Even Hamill had given up his smokehouse almonds.

Everyone except the detective from Baltimore County who'd recently joined the task force looked dead tired. But no one seemed inclined to go to bed—except Laura who'd excused herself an hour ago.

When the phone rang, Cam listlessly crossed the room and picked up the receiver.

"Hello?"

"I have your girlfriend." It was the same electronically distorted voice he'd come to know so well.

Fatigue rolled off him like water after a rainstorm. He stood up straighter. He'd never handled a call like this, but he'd better get it right. "Who's calling? Where's Jo? Is she all right?"

The voice on the other end of the line ignored all but the middle question. "It's going to cost you a million bucks to find out."

"That's a lot of money."

Cam glanced toward the table. Everybody was watching him, their tension mirroring his own.

"Don't you think little Ms. O'Malley's worth it?" the caller prodded. "She sure is hot in bed."

"You bastard."

"Now now. You have to learn to share. I expect to have the money in small bills tomorrow."

"Nobody can raise a million dollars that fast."

"You'd better try."

"You'd better prove to me that Jo is alive before I pay out anything. I want to talk to her."

"That's impossible."

"I'll pay the money, but only if I can be sure of what I'm getting."

"I'll think about it," the voice rasped.

The line went dead.

"I'll tell you where the call was made in a minute," Hamill said.

"Oh God, he said he raped her."

Abby got up and put her arm around Cam's shoulder. "He could be lying to get a rise out of you."

He tried to comfort himself with that.

"I wasn't sure what to say. I didn't expect him to contact me."

"The most important thing is that he's changed his pattern. He's never asked for a ransom before—which means it was probably Jo's idea."

"She's manipulating him?"

"Yes."

"Then she must be...okay."

"Yes."

He felt the two-ton weight pressing against his chest ease up an inch or two.

Hamill joined the conversation again. "Another phone booth. In a shopping center north of the city."

"Not far from Towson?"

"Right. I've got every patrol car in the area looking for a van with those last two numbers on the license plate."

"We'll catch him," Abby cut in.

Cam didn't answer. Instead he reached for the phone again.

"Who are you calling?" Steve asked.

"My bank. I'll have to cash in some securities."

"You can't call the bank. It's closed."

Cam blinked. He hadn't been thinking about the time or the day of the week. All he'd been thinking about was Jo.

"He's not going to exchange Ms. O'Malley for the money," Hamill said in a quiet voice.

"I'm going to have to operate under the assumption that he will."

ART HAD BEEN GONE for over an hour. Jo hadn't wasted a moment of the reprieve. As soon as he'd closed the door and set the security lock, she'd pushed away the food and taken a good look at the arrangement that held her chain to the wall. A round metal ring similar to the type used to cover a plumbing pipe hid the attachment. Jo couldn't remove it with her hands so she went looking for a tool. It wasn't too difficult to pry off a metal corner brace from the bottom of the bed. With it she carefully pulled up the ring. Underneath she could see that a bolt had been cemented into the wall.

Experimentally she began to work at the cement with the corner brace. It yielded to her efforts, but it was going to be slow work. What if her captor discovered what she was doing? The speculation made her go momentarily numb. What would he do if she didn't get away?

Slipping the ring back against the wall, she saw that it would hide her handiwork as effectively as it had hidden the connection. If Art didn't lift up the covering, she'd be all right. Except that chipping away at cement was going to create dust and other debris. A dead giveaway. She'd have to contain the mess.

In the middle dresser drawer, she found one of her T-shirts. Spreading it out along the edge of the bed, she began to chisel at the cement. It was slow going. She forced herself to get up periodically, empty the dust into the bottom dresser drawer, and cover the evidence with the remaining pieces of clothing.

While she worked, she imagined Cam there beside her. Encouraging her. Telling her that she could get away.

Conjuring up his image again helped more than she would have believed possible.

She kept her ears tuned for outside sounds. But in her mind, as her hands worked, she was continuing the silent dialogue she'd started with Cam.

"In the van, he said I reminded him of a boy. But that he couldn't—"

"That makes it sound like he's gay."

"Yes!" Her heart began to thump. "All those sexual threats—he just wants to talk about sex with women. He won't actually follow through." She prayed it was true.

Her hand chipped away at the cement. Her mind kept up the internal dialogue.

"He said he worked at Randolph Enterprises and you wouldn't let him in the design department. He said he killed his best friend—but it was an accident."

"Collin?"

"Maybe Collin tried to get him the job because the two of them were involved. Maybe that's how he got the designs, too. It fits what we know. Your brother killed himself after he found out someone he trusted was responsible for the industrial espionage.

"Cam, I'm scared. He's so crazy." Jo had been fighting to keep her thoughts on a logical, rational level. Now she stopped chipping at the cement and let out the little whimper she'd been holding in.

"Honey, I know you're afraid. But we're going to get through this," Cam whispered reassuringly in her mind. Jo swallowed and went on with the silent speculation. "Probably he was pretty unstable—but he managed to hide it. Collin's suicide tipped the balance. It drove him insane because he couldn't cope with what he'd done."

"Yes. Suppose he's one of those gay men who never came to terms with his sexual identity? Maybe he'd sworn to himself that he was going to turn over a new leaf after his lover died. He told me Denise looked like an angel come to save him. In his crazed mind, he pinned all his hopes on her. Then she rejected him."

"I'll bet she was afraid of the madness in him as much as anything else. Maybe he was already so far gone that he started babbling to her about angels and lost souls and damnation."

"Maybe."

"The important thing is that when she turned him away, she confirmed his worst feelings about himself."

"He punished her for that. And he's kept on punishing her—through women who looked like her and who were playing the same role."

It all made a kind of terrible sense. Jo went over it again, refining the theory and thinking about how to use what she'd figured out as she worked on freeing herself. What if she could convince Art she was really his savior? Would he let his guard down? Unchain her? Or was he too far gone for that?

When she heard the back door to the house open, every muscle in her body tensed. Fearfully she looked down at the pile of cement dust. Not much!

With rapid, jerky motions, Jo pushed the ring back into

place, folded the mess into the T-shirt, and shoved it under the edge of the mattress. Her improvised tool followed.

As she looked wildly around, she saw that a few flakes of cement remained. She was just sweeping them away as heavy footsteps came down the hall. The security alarm gave her a few extra seconds.

Heart pounding, Jo smoothed out the quilt, flopped back against the wall, and struck an attitude with head bowed as if she'd been sitting in defeat the whole time Art had been gone. Silently she prayed that he wouldn't figure out what she'd been doing.

He opened the door and stood studying her for several moments.

"Your boyfriend isn't sure he wants to pay to get you back," he finally said, his voice rising on a taunting note.

She kept her expression blank.

"I told him you were great in bed."

She couldn't hold back a choked little sound.

Her captor stared at her for endless seconds, his tongue sweeping across his lips. "Maybe we'll find out about that later. Right now Randolph wants me to prove that you're still breathing before he coughs up the cash. How did you meet him, Denise?" He looked puzzled.

"I—uh—"

His expression brightened. "At that party. It was my lucky day when you met at the party."

"Yes. Please, let me talk to him," she begged.

"Not a chance. You might give something away."

"You could make a recording and play it."

She could see he was considering the idea.

"I'll write the message and you can read it over before I make the tape. It will be a lot more persuasive if it's in my own words like the interview in the paper. Remember, you read it?"

He nodded slowly.

"We're going to get married so I can be your savior. But we need to start off with a nest egg," she tossed out casually. She sat as still as a nun in prayer while he considered the proposal.

"All right," he finally agreed.

Did he believe her? Or was he playing his own game?

"If you try any tricks, I'll slit your throat. And I won't wait for the ceremony."

Jo tried to swallow. Her throat felt scorched. "No tricks," she managed.

"I'll get you a pencil and paper."

For once, she was glad that her captor came back so quickly.

"Here." He handed her the writing materials.

"Thank you," she whispered, almost overwhelmed by the chance to communicate with Cam. But she couldn't let Nugent realize how much it meant to her.

Oh, Cam, she thought, blinking back the moisture that filmed her eyes. *When I'm alone, I can pretend you're here. But there's so much I want to say—need to say—to you in person. He's letting me send you a short message, but it won't really be personal. I want to tell you I love you. I can't do that. What I say has to be just the right words. It has to say what Nugent wants—and give you a clue to help you find me.*

"I'M SORRY to bother you. Phil Mercer says he wants to talk to you," Abby interrupted Cam's reveries. He'd been sitting at the computer pretending he was having a conversation with Jo.

Without turning, Cam snapped out an answer. "I told him he was in complete charge at Randolph for the time being. I don't want to be bothered with any details."

"He says it's important."

Sighing, the inventor got up, stretched cramped muscles, and reached for the phone.

"He's not calling. He's in the living room."

Cam didn't bother to mask his surprise as he started for the door.

The Randolph CEO stood by the window. The thinning hair on his round head was mussed, as if he'd run his fingers through it repeatedly. His normally ruddy complexion was tinged with gray. A manila folder that hadn't been there before lay in the middle of the coffee table.

"What brings you out here?" Cam asked.

"The two of us haven't always seen eye to eye on policy at Randolph."

Cam acknowledged the observation with a slight inclination of his head.

"I've tried to keep things running smoothly. Then this terrible business with Ms. O'Malley made me—" He stopped and started again. "Remember a couple of weeks ago when someone used that EMP generator against her, and you had me checking our records?"

Cam nodded.

"When Collin and your father died, you were pretty upset. I decided you wouldn't want to rake all that up again—"

"For God sakes, man, stop stuttering and spit it out."

"Your brother Collin requested copies of the EMP files. He had them for several weeks before they went into inactive storage."

"Collin?"

"It was his signature on the request." Mercer gestured toward the folder on the table.

Cam snatched it up and flipped through the contents. "This request form?" he asked, shoving a piece of paper toward Mercer.

"Yes."

"I know my brother's signature," Cam said in a deceptively quiet voice. "This isn't it."

"But—"

"Someone forged his name."

"Cam, are you sure?" Abby interjected from where she stood in the doorway.

He whipped around to face her. "You think I'm still not able to deal with it, don't you?"

"I just want you to admit the possibility your brother was involved."

He snapped the folder closed and stalked past Abby out of the room with the papers clutched in stiff fingers.

"Cam—wait."

"I'm not going off to sulk," he said in a strained voice. "I'm going off to think."

It wasn't exactly the truth. But it was as close as he could come at the moment.

Like a man walking some grim last mile, Cam climbed the stairs to the attic. With the same solemn determination, he brought down the boxes of Collin's papers that he hadn't looked at in three years.

He hadn't been capable of sorting through them after his brother's death. Now he knew he had to face the truths he wanted to deny.

Was the man who had kidnapped Jo linked to the stolen designs, the EMP generator, Collin's secret relationships? Cam was afraid he already knew the answer. But he'd been too stubborn to listen when Jo had waved the evidence in his face.

With his lips pressed together in a tight line, he tackled the contents of the boxes. The first one contained greeting cards Collin had saved over the years. As he looked through them, he remembered some of their good times—birthdays and Easters and Valentine's Days.

Another box held old school papers. He didn't bother with those.

The next was full of work Collin had brought from Randolph Enterprises to his home office from time to time. It was all pretty predictable, until he got to a sealed manila envelope buried underneath a stack of interoffice memos.

Inside were photocopies of requests for various project specs—including a duplicate of the EMP request Mercer had showed him. Why would Collin have that? Or applications for other designs that had turned up in rival product lines? If he'd been stealing from his own company, wouldn't he have wanted to destroy the evidence?

For long moments Cam sat like a man in a trance. Then he flipped to the back of the first request. It bore the same forged signature that he had seen downstairs.

But Collin had known about it. He'd gone to the trouble of collecting the requests. Had someone else and Collin been in on the industrial espionage plot together? Was Collin protecting himself with proof of the forged signatures? Or had his brother finally realized his secret relationships had made him vulnerable?

Cam raised his eyes and stared off into the distance, trying to imagine his brother's sick panic after his conversation with Skip O'Malley. Maybe it had triggered his own investigation. He wanted to believe that. He wasn't sure he could.

Cam's breath was shallow as he sat sifting through the evidence of what had happened at Randolph Enterprises. He hadn't believed Skip. He hadn't listened to what Jo was trying to tell him about his brother because he still hadn't wanted to know the truth.

The guilt was terrible. If he hadn't tried to block out what Jo was saying, maybe she wouldn't be in the clutches of some madman now. With a curse, he flung the papers across the room and buried his head in his hands.

After a long while he stood up and wiped his eyes. Then

he gathered up the scattered papers and went down to do everything in his power to repair the damage. He didn't allow himself to wonder if it might be too late. That possibility was too great a threat to his sanity.

He needed hard copy data from the personnel office. He was halfway out the front door when he remembered he couldn't leave the house. He had to stay here in case the kidnapper called.

Jogging back to the living room, he was surprised to see Phil Mercer still there talking in a low voice to Abby. Maybe the man wasn't as emotionless as he'd thought. "Phil, I want you to go to the office and bring me the Randolph personnel files. Everybody who was working for us three years ago."

"You're talking about a lot of files."

"I expect to see a batch of them on my desk in an hour. Then you can go back for more."

TIME HAD BLURRED into a strange distortion of reality. It was the middle of the night. Jo's nerves were raw as she watched Art read the message she had composed for Cam.

> I guess you're wondering what's happened to me. Unfortunately, I'm not free to tell you what's going on. Give the man the money. Everything will be all right. Not to worry, Superman. Trust me.

When her captor's eyes narrowed, her heart leaped into her throat. Had he figured out what she was doing? Please, God, don't let him get it, she prayed.

"Why does it say not to worry, Superman?" he demanded.

It's the only personal thing I could say. "That's what I call him. That way he'll know it's really me. It's important for him to believe he's hearing my own words."

She held her breath as Art mulled over her logic.

"Yeah. All right. It's just like that bozo to think of himself as Superman."

Jo bit back any comment.

"What about the last sentence?" Art continued. "Superman's supposed to trust me—not you."

"We can make it trust *him*. You're the one with the power."

"Yeah. Right. That's a lot better."

Jo watched him pull a small recorder out of the canvas bag he'd brought with him. He was in a hurry. Would that make him careless?

Was he going to kill her as soon as he'd proved to Cam that she was alive? Was he going to stop her if she made a small but critical change in the first sentence?

She gripped the edge of the bed with numb fingers as she waited for him to press the button.

Holding the recorder in his lap, he reached into the canvas bag again and pulled out something that looked like a portable microphone. The wire was attached to some device still hidden by the bag.

First he turned on the recorder. Then he lifted the microphone to his lips and spoke.

"Your girlfriend made you a tape."

The words had the familiar high-pitched electronic distortion. Jo gasped and literally jumped several inches off the bed. Over the past few weeks he'd sensitized her to that unnatural voice like a lover stroking her skin. Again, she felt a cloud of mechanical insects skittering over her body. Frantically her hands tried to brush them away.

When Art saw her reaction, he laughed into the microphone. It was all she could do to keep from screaming.

She had to get a grip on herself. Wrapping her arms around her shoulders, she hugged herself tightly and rocked back and forth.

He thrust the microphone toward her. Your turn, he mouthed.

"Now—now—I guess you're wondering what's happened to me..."

Her voice was unsteady when she began to talk. It gained strength as she read the message she'd composed for Cam.

IT WAS FIVE in the morning. Cam's compulsively neat work area was littered with hundreds of haphazardly scattered personnel files. He was looking through the record of every engineer who had worked for the company eight to three years ago—looking for some link to Collin.

We'll find him, Jo, he muttered under his breath. *We'll find him. Just hang on until we find him.*

So far he'd turned up nothing.

Laura Roswell burst into the room. Her eyes were bright with excitement. Cam's gaze fixed on the photograph she was waving in her hand.

"Look at this. Look at this," she shouted, shoving the picture at him.

He held it under the light. It showed a man with stringy hair and an intense face bent over a trash can.

"What the hell—"

"It's him. The guy who has Jo. Don't you see, it's got to be him. He's been following her around—learning about her. He must have gone back some time in the last couple of weeks and looked through Jo's trash." The words tumbled out one after the other. "I didn't want to get your hopes up, so I didn't say anything when I left. A couple of hours ago, I remembered the camera Jo set up to get a picture of those dogs."

Cam studied the face in the photograph. It didn't look familiar. Not even much like the waiter who had abducted Jo. But maybe—

Quickly he began to shuffle files together.

"You take that stack," he directed Laura. "I'll take this one. They've each got a photograph. One of them may be the guy."

Forty-five minutes later, he acknowledged that none of the men looked like the creep at the trash can. He cursed under his breath.

Another desperate lead that hadn't panned out. Like the van. It wasn't registered in the Towson area.

Cam was sitting with his palms pressed against his burning eyelids when the phone rang.

"Your girlfriend made you a tape."

There was no need to explain who was calling. His hand jerked as he activated the ultrasensitive recorder that he'd hooked up to the phone.

There was a pause of several seconds. Then Jo's voice came on the line. It quavered and he pictured her alone with this madman and terrified.

"Now—now—I guess you're wondering what's happened to me."

Her voice grew in strength and confidence. *That's it, Jo,* he silently encouraged.

"Unfortunately, I'm not free to tell you what's going on. Give the man the money. Everything will be all right. Not to worry, Superman. Trust him."

The sound of her voice sent little prickles of electricity along his nerve endings.

"Jo!"

"Just a recording, stupid."

"How do I know—"

"You don't. But if you want to see her again, you'll put the money in your car and drive to the big boulders near the science building at Goucher College. Monday evening at five. You'll find further instructions there. If the police are following you, your girlfriend is dead."

Cam tried to imagine the further instructions. They probably included disabling his car phone.

"Wait. What if I can't get the money together that fast?"

"Too bad for Ms. O'Malley."

JO WORKED STEADILY—chipping and gouging and hiding the cement dust. Every few minutes she gave a harsh tug on the chain. It didn't budge. The bolt was deeper in the wall than she'd imagined. There wasn't a chance that she could dig it out in time. But she had to try.

Again she tried to keep her spirits up by thinking of Cam. Of getting back to him. Of how happy they'd both be when he held her in his arms again. Now it was hard to make the fantasy work, and she realized she was losing hope.

Denise. Margaret. Jo.

No, she wasn't going to end up like the other two.

When she heard the outside door open, her hand froze, and she looked down at the pile of cement dust and chips on the T-shirt. More cement dust clung to the front of her ruined dress. She'd forgotten to keep things cleaned up.

Eager footsteps hurried down the hall.

Jo swiped her hand across the front of the dress. Then, as the doorknob turned, she swept the metal brace, T-shirt and cement under the covers.

Arthur Nugent's eyes were bright as he opened the door and stood looking at her with strange possessiveness.

"It's time for the wedding ceremony, Denise."

She didn't bother to tell him she was Jo. What difference would that make now?

"We haven't had our rehearsal dinner yet," she murmured instead.

"Dinner! It's almost morning."

"Please. I'm hungry now. Fix me something special."

He considered the request and then grinned as if pleased

with one more opportunity to show his knowledge of her habits. "Biscuits. You like biscuits for breakfast."

"Yes."

"All right. I guess that's fair. It will have to be the kind from the refrigerator."

"That's fine."

"I'll be back in a few minutes. Then Denise and I—I mean you and..." He let the sentence trail off, his eyes looking at her meaningfully.

The second the door closed, Jo pulled out the piece of metal and turned back to the wall. Desperately she began to gouge away at the cement around the bolt. She didn't try to work neatly now. This was her last chance. Either she got it loose, or he came to take her away for the ceremony.

THEY HAD ALL GATHERED around the tape recorder. Cam played the message for the fifth time while he stared at the transcription he'd made.

She'd called him Superman so there was a good chance the message was in her own words. Had she used the recording to send him some information?

Cam tried to focus on the message. He'd always been good at word games—at seeing patterns. Now when Jo's life depended on him, his brain was almost too numb to function.

Doggedly he repeated the words.

"Now I guess you're wondering..." That was a strange way to start off, and not at all like Jo's usual speech patterns. "Unfortunately... Give the man... Everything..."

He looked around the room and knew that everybody else was engaged in the same life or death struggle. Steve was hunched forward with his fists clenched. Laura's eyes were shut in concentration. His friends. Jo's friends. And he'd been riding them unmercifully. When this was over...

He realized his mind was wandering and forced it back to the word puzzle.

For endless minutes there was complete silence.

"Nuget," Abby murmured.

Cam's head swiveled toward her. "What?"

"No. *N-U-G-E-N-T*. If you look at the first letter of each sentence's first word, they spell out "nugent." I thought it was "nuget"—that maybe it meant something."

"Nugent." Cam's mind was racing. He'd seen that word. It was a name. A familiar name. Because—because he'd just read it on one of the Randolph Enterprises personnel files.

Leaping up, he began to scramble through the stacks of folders.

"Nugent. It's a name. There's a guy named Nugent here somewhere," he practically shouted.

The others joined him in the hunt. Steve was the one who pulled out the file.

The guy's picture looked as if it had come from a high-school yearbook. He appeared twenty years younger than the man who'd been caught by the trash can. Which was why Cam had passed right over him without reading the contents of the file. Now he could see a resemblance.

COLD SWEAT broke out on Jo's forehead as she hewed away at the cement. When she stopped to tug at the chain, it moved. It moved! With renewed will, she doubled her efforts.

She could wiggle it back and forth now. If she just had a few more minutes—

She'd been so intent on her task that she hadn't heard the door open.

"You bitch! You lied to me again."

With every ounce of strength she possessed, Jo yanked on the chain. The superhuman effort paid off. The bolt came free of the wall. But she hadn't really expected it to give way. In the next second, she tumbled backward onto the hard wooden floor.

Art tossed away the tray he was holding. As biscuits, jelly and hot coffee crashed against the wall, he was sprinting toward Jo.

He was on her in seconds. With more instinct than finesse, she flailed at him with the chain still attached to her left wrist. He grunted as the end careened into his shoulder.

She didn't have time to draw her arm back for another whack. Cursing, face contorted with rage, he went crazy. His hands came up around her neck, shaking and choking. In blind panic, she struggled and gasped for breath. But her air supply was completely blocked. Blackness rose up to meet her.

ARTHUR NUGENT. Skimming his performance appraisals, Cam understood why he didn't remember the man. As an engineer he'd been mediocre. Yet buried in the middle of the material were several recommendations from Collin. He'd hired Nugent above the objections of a senior manager. Later he'd tried to get him transferred to the design department.

Nugent had quit the company three years ago. Just before Collin had died.

Cam felt a mixture of old sadness and new excitement constrict his chest. He'd been looking for someone like this. Someone with a personal connection to his brother. And Jo had sent him the name.

He flipped to the back for the personal data.

"Six years ago he lived in a town house in Randallstown. He listed his father as the person he wanted notified in case of emergency. His father lives in Towson," he told the circle of waiting faces.

"What's the address?" Abby demanded.

Cam read it aloud.

"That's right in back of Towson High School," Laura confirmed.

JO WAS CONSCIOUS of several sensations. Her neck hurt. Drawing in a breath was like sucking in fire. Firm hands grasped her ankles. The handcuff was gone. She was no longer dressed in the ruined maid of honor dress. Cold stone scraped against her hips.

Cautiously she looked down at her body. She was wearing a white dress now. A thin white dress that would have been more appropriate for June than December. The flimsy fabric had ridden up around her waist as Arthur Nugent dragged her across a stone floor.

She held back the scream of black terror that bubbled in her chest. Instead she willed her body to remain limp and peered at the maniac through a screen of lashes. Let him think she was still unconscious. Above her was a vaulted church ceiling. He'd dragged her to a church? How was that possible?

The ceiling looked like granite. No, it was painted plywood. On either side were stained-glass windows made from heavy panes of plastic. Spotlights behind them made the colors glow.

Around her, recorded organ music floated. The wedding march. She could hear Art muttering the words of the ceremony, his voice high and cracking now, weirdly distorted without the need of the electronic device.

"We have gathered here to give thanks for the gift of marriage and to witness the joining together of Arthur and Denise."

He'd brought Denise here. And Margaret, too.

The scream hovered in her throat now. She refused to give it life.

The chapel was tiny—only two rows of pews and then

the altar flanked by white flowers. On a low table covered
with white linen, a long knife had been laid out. Behind it
loomed the brass bed. The one from the home movie. Jo
lost the battle to remain limp. Her body jerked, and a scream
tore from her lips.

Arthur turned and cuffed the side of her head, momentarily stunning her again. "Shut up! You're spoiling everything. You tried to trick me," he shrieked. "Now we don't
have time to do things right."

As he spoke, he hoisted her onto the bed and dragged her
arm toward one of the handcuffs that dangled from the
headboard.

When she began to struggle, he climbed on top of her,
straddling her writhing body with his legs, pressing her
down with his weight. She fought him with every remaining
ounce of strength. It wasn't enough. Closer, closer. Her right
hand drew inexorably closer to the cuff. If he chained her
to the bed, the game was over.

Instead of concentrating on Arthur, she switched her attention to the band of metal. Her fingers scrabbled and slid
against the smooth surface. Then, miraculously, she had the
thing in her hand. With a little gasp of triumph, she
squeezed. The cuff snapped shut around empty air. Her
hand was still free.

Arthur howled with rage.

Another cuff dangled from the other side of the headboard. He grasped her left hand and folded the fingers
closed in a painful grip. Then he began to repeat the process
that had just failed.

Somewhere above the music she thought she heard a
shout and then an alarm bell clanging. The security alarm.
No. It was probably a fantasy. A last desperate rescue fantasy. Her mind had finally provided her with the only escape
route possible.

In the next second she was slammed back to reality. Her

world had narrowed to the man on top of her dragging her fist toward the handcuff. This time she couldn't close the metal band. This time he had her.

Just as the metal touched her flesh, the door burst open.

"Hold it right there, Nugent," a deep voice barked.

She saw the dazed look on her captor's features. He whirled as if to face the police officers spilling into the room. Then he was lunging for the knife.

It was swinging down toward her chest when shots rang out and he fell backward onto the stone floor.

Chapter Fifteen

Hamill had tried to keep him from joining the rescue operation. But Cam hadn't taken no for an answer. The detective had given in, but when they'd arrived at the house, Cam had been held back behind the police vans while a special unit armed with automatic weapons had surrounded the house and broken in.

It was the longest fifteen minutes of his life. Each hammer beat of his heart was an accusation. The more he thought about it, the more he felt his own culpability. *If you'd had the guts to face up to your brother's role in the industrial espionage, this wouldn't have happened to Jo.*

Now he was finally in the house. But he wore his guilt like a coat of nails with the points gouging into his skin. Jo had to be all right. She had to be! Determinedly he pushed his way through the dozen armed men who separated him from the woman he loved.

He could see her now, huddled on the bed in a torn white dress. She was alive. Thank God she was alive! But she was crying quietly.

Everything else faded into the background. The wedding march that was still playing at full volume. The pews that must have been salvaged from an old church, the garish windows, the cloying smell of the gardenias flanking the altar.

He had to step around a pool of blood on the floor where Nugent's body had lain moments earlier. For an instant he was struck with a strange sense of déjà vu. Another killer. Another threat to Jo's life had ended in a very similar fashion. Only this time the man was dead.

He knelt beside the figure huddled on the bed. She looked so young and defenseless. Against the white sheets, her skin was as pale as marble.

"Jo, honey. It's all over."

Even after the torture of the EMP and the television set, she'd held on to some shreds of self-control. Now somehow his words brought a fresh torrent of tears. What had that bastard done to her?

Or was she crying because she didn't want to face him?

"Oh, God, Jo, are you all right?" *Please be all right.*

He reached out and pulled her into his arms. She hid her face against his chest and clutched his arms as she continued to sob into his shirt.

His fingers soothed over her back and shoulders. It was so damn good just to hold her again. "Oh, Jo, Jo. You're safe. Thank God you're safe."

He could sense her struggling for control. "You got here...I'm sorry...I just..." But she couldn't finish the sentence.

"Jo, forgive me."

She didn't answer. Maybe he didn't deserve her forgiveness.

He felt the sobs ebb. She was still trembling. "Cam—please—"

"Anything, honey. Anything."

"Where is he?"

"Dead. He won't hurt you anymore."

He heard her sigh, felt her relax against him. As she began to speak, he knew she'd gotten back some measure of control. "He was so crazy. I never knew what he was going to do. I couldn't be sure he remembered who I was, even.''

It was hard to imagine the horror of it.

"Cam, you saved me."

"We got your message."

"Not just the message. I would have cracked up without you. Well—maybe I did. I kept imagining you there with me, encouraging me, telling me I was going to make it."

"Oh, Jo, honey. I kept thinking those things. Maybe you read my mind."

But as he held her and stroked her and talked softly to her, they both silently admitted that they hadn't been sure they would see each other again.

"I'd like to examine her," a police doctor broke into their reunion.

Cam reluctantly relinquished the contact and moved aside.

"How is she?" he asked anxiously.

"She needs rest. I'm going to give her a sedative. And I want to keep her in the hospital for observation."

After the man had administered the drug, Jo stretched out her hand to Cam. "Don't leave me."

"I won't."

He was still holding her fingers tightly as he felt them relax and saw her eyelids flutter.

"I'm riding in the ambulance with her," he told the doctor.

"She won't know you're there."

"I think she will."

JO AWOKE to ribbons of sunlight filtering through half-closed venetian blinds. She didn't know where she was. For one terrible moment of confusion, the fear was back.

Dig the bolt out of the wall. Get away. Before he takes

you to the chapel. She struggled to push herself up. A hand pressed against her shoulder, and she gasped.

"Jo. It's all over. The nightmare is over."

"Cam."

Safety. Freedom. She looked up at him in wonder, still not quite able to believe that they were here together.

"You've been sitting there beside my bed," she said softly.

"Yes."

Eons passed as they stared at each other—taking in details that only lovers see. Transmitting silent messages that only lovers hear.

She was still so pale.

A two-day growth of beard darkened his jaw.

Her eyes were so large and blue.

A lock of dark hair had fallen across his forehead. She reached up to push it back.

"Jo, I've been sitting here, wondering how you were going to feel about me when you woke up."

"Why?"

His voice was raw. "Because if I'd only believed what you were trying to tell me about Collin, none of this would have happened."

"Oh, Cam, that's not true."

He swallowed. "My brother and Art Nugent, the man who kidnapped you, had a—a—relationship. Art was the one who stole the designs from Randolph Electronics."

"I figured that out—from things he said, hints he dropped."

"Did you figure out why he picked you for his next victim? He wanted to get back at me—for not giving him a job in the design department at Randolph."

She found his hand and squeezed it. "No, Cam. Getting back at you was just a dividend. An accident, really. He told me it was a piece of luck for him."

She saw some of the tension go out of Cam's expression and continued, "He kidnapped me because I was the maid of honor in a wedding—like Denise. He was doing the same thing over and over again—repeating his experience with her."

"Denise?"

"He talked a lot about her—about what she meant to him. It's all pretty crazy. But it made some kind of twisted sense to him. It goes back to Collin. I think he really cared for your brother, and he cracked up after he died. He blamed himself for the suicide. It made him want to change his life—to go straight. Right after that, he saw Denise in church and in his disturbed mind, she reminded him of an angel. He thought she could save him—turn his life around. He tried to convince himself he was attracted to her. But she rejected him, and he killed her."

"Oh, my God. He told you all that?"

"Some of it. In bits and pieces. Some I figured out. After that, he kept repeating the experience because he hated her so much and blamed her for his failures."

Cam's voice struggled for even timbre. "Jo, the tapes. The things he said he was going to do to you—"

"Just threats. To make it sound like he wanted a woman. I don't think he could function with a female."

"Jo—I—"

"Cam, stop punishing yourself. It's over. Just hold me, please."

There was no way he could refuse that request. But there were still things he had to say. "Jo, I need you so damn much. I didn't realize how much pain was locked up inside me until I started loving you. But I was still afraid to trust my feelings. It was as if I had to choose either you or Collin. Then when I started to suspect what he'd done to his own company, to my father, I really couldn't handle it."

Jo tightened her arms around him, knowing that it would

take time for him to get over the sorrow. But she would be there to help him. "What Collin did doesn't wipe out all the good years when you were growing up. I know it's hard for you now, but you'll see that eventually."

"But he—"

"Probably he was being used—not doing the actual stealing. I think he realized that and couldn't find a way out."

"Yes."

"It's hard to let go of the past—to let yourself see things differently."

"Yes."

"I'm not just talking about you. I'm talking about myself, too." She raised her head so she could meet his eyes. "I was attracted to you the moment we met."

"Attracted to a nutty inventor?"

"Not nutty. Intense. But I was afraid to trust my feelings, too. Abby helped me understand what I was doing. I kept telling myself no one could replace Skip. I was really afraid to take another chance on happiness."

"Jo, I swear I'll make you happy."

"I know you will."

They smiled at each other. Then his lips found hers again for a long, deep kiss, rich with promise for the future.

It was incredible to be held by him again. She felt sheltered. Cherished. Everything she'd been terrified to let herself want.

It was incredible to hold her again. His joy soared. She wanted him. She wasn't blaming him for all the things he'd failed to see and all the things he'd failed to do. Instead she was clinging to him with the same desperation he felt.

"Jo, I love you."

"Oh, Cam, I love you, too. I wanted to tell you that when I made the recording. I knew he wouldn't let me."

"Hearing your voice—knowing he had you..." He

couldn't say the rest of it. But he didn't have to. She understood.

All the forces of nature couldn't have separated them as they clung together.

After long moments, she looked up into his eyes, her own twinkling. "I guess this means you've gotten over your aversion to detectives."

"You do have a smart remark for every occasion."

"Yup."

"How would you feel about my putting a certain sassy redheaded private eye on a lifetime retainer?"

For once, Jo O'Malley was speechless.

"Does that mean she'll take the job?"

"You've got a deal."

THE COLTONS

invite you to a thrilling holiday wedding in

A Colton Family Christmas

Meet the Oklahoma Coltons—a proud, passionate clan who will risk everything for love and honor. As the two Colton dynasties reunite this Christmas, new romances are sparked by a near-tragic event!

This 3-in-1 holiday collection includes:
"The Diplomat's Daughter" by Judy Christenberry
"Take No Prisoners" by Linda Turner
"Juliet of the Night" by Carolyn Zane

And be sure to watch for **SKY FULL OF PROMISE** by Teresa Southwick this November from Silhouette Romance (#1624), the next installment in the Colton family saga.